THREE FROM THE 87th

THREE FROM THE 87th

HAIL, HAIL, THE GANG'S ALL HERE!

JIGSAW • FUZZ

ED McBAIN

NELSON DOUBLEDAY, INC.

Garden City, New York

HAIL, HAIL,
THE GANG'S ALL HERE!

This modest volume is dedicated to the Mystery Writers of America, who, if they do not award it the Edgar for the best *ten* mystery novels of the year, should have their collective mysterious heads examined.

(COERCION: *A person who with a view to compel another person to do or to abstain from doing an act which such other person has a legal right to do or to abstain from doing wrongfully and unlawfully, is guilty of a misdemeanor. Section 530, New York State Penal Law.*)

The city in these pages is imaginary.
The people, the places are all fictitious.
Only the police routine is based on
established investigatory techniques.

1

NIGHTSHADE

THE MORNING HOURS of the night come imperceptibly here.

It is a minute before midnight on the peeling face of the hanging wall clock, and then it is midnight, and then the minute hand moves visibly and with a lurch into the new day. The morning hours have begun, but scarcely anyone has noticed. The stale coffee in soggy cardboard containers tastes the same as it did thirty seconds ago, the spastic rhythm of the clacking typewriters continues unabated, a drunk across the room shouts that the world is full of brutality, and cigarette smoke drifts up toward the face of the clock, where, unnoticed and unmourned, the old day has already been dead for two minutes. The telephone rings.

The men in this room are part of a tired routine, somewhat shabby about the edges, as faded and as gloomy as the room itself, with its cigarette-scarred desks and its smudged green walls. This could be the office of a failing insurance company were it not for the evidence of the holstered pistols hanging from belts on the backs of wooden chairs painted a darker green than the walls. The furniture is ancient, the typewriters are ancient, the building itself is ancient—which is perhaps only fitting since these men are involved in what is an ancient pursuit, a pursuit once considered honorable. They are law enforcers. They are, in the words of the drunk still hurling epithets from the grilled detention cage across the room, rotten prick cop bastards.

The telephone continues to ring.

The little girl lying in the alley behind the theater was wearing a belted white trench coat wet with blood. There was blood on the floor of the alley, and blood on the metal fire door behind her, and blood on her face and matted in her blond hair, blood on her miniskirt and on the lavender tights she wore. A neon sign across the street stained the girl's ebbing life juices green and then orange, while from the open knife wound in her chest, the blood sprouted like some ghastly night flower, dark and rich, red, orange, green, pulsing in time to the neon flicker, a grotesque psychedelic light show, and then losing the rhythm, welling up with less force and power. She opened her mouth, she tried to speak, and the scream of an ambulance approaching the theater seemed to come instead from her mouth on a fresh bubble of blood. The blood stopped, her life ended, the girl's eyes rolled back into her head. Detective Steve Carella turned away as the ambulance attendants rushed a stretcher into the alley. He told them the girl was already dead.

"We got here in seven minutes," one of the attendants said.

"Nobody's blaming you," Carella answered.

"This is Saturday night," the attendant complained. "Streets are full of traffic. Even *with* the damn siren."

Carella walked to the unmarked sedan parked at the curb. Detective Cotton Hawes, sitting behind the wheel, rolled down his frost-rimed window and said, "How is she?"

"We've got a homicide," Carella answered.

The boy was eighteen years old, and he had been picked up not ten minutes ago for breaking off car aerials. He had broken off twelve on the same street, strewing them behind him like a Johnny Appleseed planting radios; a cruising squad car had spotted him as he tried to twist off the aerial of a 1966 Cadillac. He was drunk or stoned or both, and when Sergeant Murchison at the muster desk asked him to read the Miranda-Escobedo warning signs on the wall, printed in both English and Spanish, he could read neither. The arresting patrolman took the boy to the squadroom upstairs, where Detective Bert Kling was talking to Hawes on the telephone. He signaled for the patrolman to wait with his prisoner on the bench outside the slatted wooden rail divider, and then buzzed Murchison at the desk downstairs.

"Dave," he said, "we've got a homicide in the alley of the Eleventh Street Theater. You want to get it rolling?"

"Right," Murchison said, and hung up.

Homicides are a common occurrence in this city, and each one is treated identically, the grisly horror of violent death reduced to routine by a police force that would otherwise be overwhelmed by statistics. At the muster desk switchboard downstairs, while upstairs Kling waved the patrolman and his prisoner into the squadroom, Sergeant Murchison first reported the murder to Captain Frick, who commanded the 87th Precinct, and then to Lieutenant Byrnes, who commanded the 87th Detective Squad. He then phoned Homicide, who in turn set into motion an escalating process of notification that spread cancerously to include the Police Laboratory, the Telegraph, Telephone and Teletype Bureau at Headquarters, the Medical Examiner, the District Attorney, the District Commander of the Detective Division, the Chief of Detectives, and finally the Police Commissioner himself. Someone had thoughtlessly robbed a young woman of her life, and now a lot of sleepy-eyed men were being shaken out of their beds on a cold October night.

Upstairs, the clock on the squadroom wall read 12:30 A.M. The boy who had broken off twelve car aerials sat in a chair alongside Bert Kling's desk. Kling took one look at him and yelled to Miscolo in the Clerical Office to bring in a pot of strong coffee. Across the room, the drunk in the detention cage wanted to know where he was. In a little while, they would release him with a warning to try to stay sober till morning.

But the night was young.

They arrived alone or in pairs, blowing on their hands, shoulders hunched against the bitter cold, breaths pluming whitely from their lips. They marked the dead girl's position in the alleyway, they took her picture, they made drawings of the scene, they searched for the murder weapon and found none, and then they stood around speculating on sudden death. In this alleyway alongside a theater, the policemen were the stars and the celebrities, and a curious crowd thronged the sidewalk where a barricade had already been set up, anxious for a glimpse of these men with their shields pinned to their overcoats—the identifying *Playbills* of law enforcement, without which you could not tell the civilians from the plainclothes cops.

Monoghan and Monroe had arrived from Homicide, and they watched dispassionately now as the Assistant Medical Examiner fluttered around the dead girl. They were both wearing black overcoats, black mufflers, and black fedoras, both heavier men than Carella, who stood between them with the lean look of an overtrained athlete, a pained expression on his face.

"He done some job on her," Monroe said.

"Son of a bitch," Monoghan added.

"You identified her yet?"

"I'm waiting for the M.E. to get through," Carella answered.

"Might help to know what she was doing here in the alley. What's that door there?" Monroe asked.

"Stage entrance."

"Think she was in the show?"

"I don't know," Carella said.

"Well, what the hell," Monoghan said, "they're finished with her pocketbook there, ain't they? Why don't you look through it? You finished with that pocketbook there?" he yelled to one of the lab technicians.

"Yeah, anytime you want it," the technician shouted back.

"Go on, Carella, take a look."

The technician wiped the blood off the dead girl's bag, and handed it to Carella. Monoghan and Monroe crowded in on him as he twisted open the clasp.

"Bring it over to the light," Monroe said.

The light, with a metal shade, hung over the stage door. So violently had the girl been stabbed that flecks of blood had even dotted the enameled white underside of the shade. In her bag they found a driver's license identifying her as Mercy Howell of 1113 Rutherford Avenue, Age 24, Height 5'3", Eyes Blue. They found an Actors Equity card in her name, as well as credit cards for two of the city's largest department stores. They found an unopened package of Virginia Slims, and a book of matches advertising an art course. They found a rat-tailed comb. They found seventeen dollars and forty-three cents in cash. They found a package of Kleenex, and an appointment book. They found a ball-point pen with shreds of tobacco clinging to its tip, an eyelash curler, two subway tokens, and an advertisement for a see-through blouse, clipped from one of the local newspapers.

In the pocket of her trench coat, when the M.E. had finished with her and pronounced her dead from multiple stab wounds in the chest and throat, they found an unfired Browning .25 caliber automatic. They tagged the gun and the handbag, and they moved the girl out of the alleyway and into the waiting ambulance for removal to the morgue. There was now nothing left of Mercy Howell but a chalked outline of her body and a pool of her blood on the alley floor.

"You sober enough to understand me?" Kling asked the boy.

"I was never drunk to begin with," the boy answered.

"Okay then, here we go," Kling said. "In keeping with the Supreme Court decision in *Miranda* v. *Arizona,* we are not permitted to ask you any questions until you are warned of your right to counsel and your privilege against self-incrimination."

"What does that mean?" the boy asked. "Self-incrimination?"

"I'm about to explain that to you now," Kling said.

"This coffee stinks."

"First, you have the right to remain silent if you so choose," Kling said. "Do you understand that?"

"I understand it."

"Second, you do not have to answer any police questions if you don't want to. Do you understand that?"

"What the hell are you asking me if I understand for? Do I look like a moron or something?"

"The law requires that I ask whether or not you understand these specific warnings. *Did* you understand what I just said about not having to answer . . . ?"

"Yeah, yeah, I understood."

"All right. Third, if you *do* decide to answer any questions, the answers may be used as evidence against you, do you . . . ?"

"What the hell did I do, break off a couple of car aerials? Jesus!"

"Did you understand that?"

"I understood it."

"You also have the right to consult with an attorney before or during police questioning. If you do not have the money to hire a lawyer, a lawyer will be appointed to consult with you."

Kling gave this warning straight-faced even though he knew that under the Criminal Procedure Code of the city for which he worked, a public defender could not be appointed by the courts until the preliminary hearing. There was no legal provision for the courts *or* the police to appoint counsel during questioning, and there were certainly no police funds set aside for the appointment of attorneys. In theory, a call to the Legal Aid Society should have brought a lawyer up there to the old squadroom within minutes, ready and eager to offer counsel to any indigent person desiring it. But in practice, if this boy sitting beside Kling told him in the next three seconds that he was unable to pay for his own attorney and would like one provided, Kling would not have known just what the hell to do—other than call off the questioning.

"I understand," the boy said.

"You've signified that you understand all the warnings," Kling said, "and now I ask you whether you are willing to answer my questions without an attorney here to counsel you."

"Go shit in your hat," the boy said. "I don't want to answer nothing."

So that was that.

They booked him for Criminal Mischief, a Class-A Misdemeanor defined as intentional or reckless damage to the property of another person, and they took him downstairs to a holding cell, to await transportation to the Criminal Courts Building for arraignment. The phone was ringing again, and a woman was waiting on the bench just outside the squadroom.

The watchman's booth was just inside the metal stage door. An electric clock on the wall behind the watchman's stool read 1:10 A.M. The watchman was a man in his late seventies who did not at all mind being questioned by the police. He came on duty, he told them, at seven-thirty each night. The company call was for eight, and he was there at the stage door waiting to greet everybody as they arrived to get made up and in costume. Curtain went down at eleven-twenty, and usually most of the kids was out of the theater by quarter to twelve or, latest, midnight. He stayed on till nine the next morning, when the theater box office opened.

"Ain't much to do during the night except hang around and make sure nobody runs off with the scenery," he said, and chuckled.

"Did you happen to notice what time Mercy Howell left the theater?" Carella asked.

"She the one got killed?" the old man asked.

"Yes," Hawes said. "Mercy Howell. About this high, blond hair, blue eyes."

"They're *all* about that high, with blond hair and blue eyes," the old man said, and chuckled again. "I don't know hardly none of them by name. Shows come and go, you know. Be a hell of a chore to have to remember all the kids who go in and out that door."

"Do you sit here by the door all night?" Carella asked.

"Well, no, not all night. What I do, is I lock the door after everybody's out and then I check the lights, make sure just the work light's on. I won't touch the switchboard, not allowed to, but I can turn out lights in the lobby, for example, if somebody left them on, or down in the toilets, sometimes they leave lights on down in the toilets. Then I come back here to the booth, and read or listen to the radio. Along about two o'clock, I check the theater again, make sure we ain't got no fires or nothing, and then I come back here and make the rounds again at four o'clock, and six o'clock, and again about eight. That's what I do."

"You say you lock this door . . ."

"That's right."

"Would you remember what time you locked it tonight?"

"Oh, must've been about ten minutes to twelve. Soon as I knew everybody was out."

"How do you know when they're out?"

"I give a yell up the stairs there. You see those stairs there? They go up to the dressing rooms. Dressing rooms are all upstairs in this house. So I go to the steps, and I yell, 'Locking up! Anybody here?' And if somebody yells back, I know somebody's here, and I say, 'Let's shake it, honey,' if it's a girl, and if it's a boy, I say, 'Let's hurry it up, sonny.' " The old man chuckled again. "With *this* show, it's sometimes hard to tell which's the girls and which's the boys. I manage, though," he said, and again chuckled.

"So you locked that door at ten minutes to twelve?"

"Right."

"And everybody had left the theater by that time."

" 'Cept me, of course."

"Did you look out into the alley before you locked the door?"

"Nope. Why should I do that?"

"Did you hear anything outside while you were locking the door?"

"Nope."

"Or at anytime *before* you locked it?"

"Well, there's always noise outside when they're leaving, you know. They got friends waiting for them, or else they go home together, you know, there's always a lot of chatter when they go out."

"But it was quiet when you locked the door."

"Dead quiet," the old man said.

The woman who took the chair beside Detective Meyer Meyer's desk was perhaps thirty-two years old, with long straight black hair trailing down her back, and wide brown eyes that were terrified. It was still October, and the color of her tailored coat seemed suited to the season, a subtle tangerine with a small brown fur collar that echoed an outdoors trembling with the colors of autumn.

"I feel sort of silly about this," she said, "but my husband insisted that I come."

"I see," Meyer said.

"There are ghosts," the woman said.

Across the room, Kling unlocked the door to the detention cage and said, "Okay, pal, on your way. Try to stay sober till morning, huh?"

"It ain't one-thirty yet," the man said, "the night is young." He stepped out of the cage, tipped his hat to Kling, and hurriedly left the squadroom.

Meyer looked at the woman sitting beside him, studying her with new interest because, to tell the truth, she had not seemed like a nut when she first walked into the squadroom. He had been a detective for more years than he chose to count, and in his time had met far too many nuts of every stripe and persuasion. But he had never met one as pretty as Adele Gorman with her well-tailored, fur-collared coat, and her Vassar voice and her skillfully applied eye makeup, lips bare of color in her pale white face, pert and reasonably young and seemingly intelligent—but apparently a nut besides.

"In the house," she said. "Ghosts."

"Where do you live, Mrs. Gorman?" he asked. He had written her name on the pad in front of him, and now he watched her with his pencil poised and recalled the lady who had come into the squadroom only last month to report a gorilla peering into her bedroom from the fire escape outside. They had sent a patrolman over to make a routine check, and had even called the zoo and the circus (which was coincidentally in town, and which lent at least *some* measure of possibility to her claim) but there had been no ape on the fire escape, nor had any simians recently escaped from their cages. The lady came back the next day to report that her visiting gorilla had put in another appearance the night before, this time wearing a top hat and carrying a black cane with an ivory head. Meyer had assured her that he would have a platoon of cops watching her building that night, which seemed to calm her at least somewhat. He had then led her personally out of the squadroom and down the iron-runged steps, and through the high-ceilinged muster room, and past the hanging green globes on the front stoop, and onto the sidewalk outside the station house. Sergeant Murchison, at the muster desk, shook his head after the lady was gone, and muttered, "More of them outside than in."

Meyer watched Adele Gorman now, remembered what Murchison had said, and thought *Gorillas in September, ghosts in October*.

"We live in Smoke Rise," she said. "Actually, it's my father's house, but my husband and I are living there with him."

"And the address?"

"374 MacArthur Lane. You take the first access road into Smoke Rise, about a mile and a half east of Silvermine Oval. The name on the mailbox is Van Houten. That's my father's name. Willem Van

Houten." She paused and studied him, as though expecting some reaction.

"Okay," Meyer said, and ran a hand over his bald pate, and looked up, and said, "Now, you were saying, Mrs. Gorman . . ."

"That we have ghosts."

"Um-huh. What kind of ghosts?"

"Ghosts. Poltergeists. Shades. I don't know," she said, and shrugged. "What kinds of ghosts *are* there?"

"Well, they're *your* ghosts, so suppose you tell me," Meyer said.

The telephone on Kling's desk rang. He lifted the receiver and said, "Eighty-seventh Squad, Detective Kling."

"There are two of them," Adele said.

"Male or female?"

"One of each."

"Yeah," Kling said into the telephone, "go ahead."

"How old would you say they were?"

"Centuries, I would guess."

"No, I mean . . ."

"Oh, how old do they *look?* Well, the man . . ."

"You've *seen* them?"

"Oh, yes, many times."

"Um-huh," Meyer said.

"I'll be right over," Kling said into the telephone. "You stay there." He slammed down the receiver, opened his desk drawer, pulled out a holstered revolver, and hurriedly clipped it to his belt. "Somebody threw a bomb into a storefront church. 7133 Culver Avenue. I'm heading over."

"Right," Meyer said. "Get back to me."

"We'll need a couple of meat wagons. The minister and two other people were killed, and it sounds as if there're a lot of injured."

"Will you tell Dave?"

"On the way out," Kling said, and was gone.

"Mrs. Gorman," Meyer said, "as you can see, we're pretty busy here just now. I wonder if your ghosts can wait till morning."

"No, they can't," Adele said.

"Why not?"

"Because they appear precisely at two forty-five A.M., and I want someone to see them."

"Why don't you and your husband look at them?" Meyer said.

"You think I'm a nut, don't you?" Adele said.

"No, no, Mrs. Gorman, not at all."

"Oh, yes you do," Adele said. "I didn't believe in ghosts, either, until I saw these two."

"Well, this is all very interesting, I assure you, Mrs. Gorman, but really we do have our hands full right now, and I don't know what we can do about these ghosts of yours, even if we did come over to take a look at them."

"They've been stealing things from us," Adele said, and Meyer thought *Oh, we have got ourselves a prime lunatic this time.*

"What sort of things?"

"A diamond brooch that used to belong to my mother when she was alive. They stole that from my father's safe."

"What else?"

"A pair of emerald earrings. They were in the safe, too."

"When did these thefts occur?"

"Last month."

"Isn't it possible the jewelry was mislaid someplace?"

"You don't mislay a diamond brooch and a pair of emerald earrings that are locked inside a wall safe."

"Did you report any of these thefts?"

"No."

"Why not?"

"Because I knew you'd think I was crazy. Which is just what you're thinking right this minute."

"No, Mrs. Gorman, but I'm sure you can appreciate the fact that we, uh, can't go around arresting ghosts," Meyer said, and tried to smile.

Adele Gorman did not smile back. "Forget the ghosts," she said. "I was foolish to mention them, I should have known better." She took a deep breath, looked him squarely in the eye, and said, "I'm here to report the theft of a diamond brooch valued at six thousand dollars, and a pair of earrings worth thirty-five hundred dollars. Will you send a man to investigate tonight, or should I ask my father to contact your superior officer?"

"Your father? What's he got to . . . ?"

"My father is a retired Surrogate's Court judge," Adele said.

"I see."

"Yes, I hope you do."

"What time did you say these ghosts arrive?" Meyer asked, and sighed heavily.

Between midnight and two o'clock, the city does not change very much. The theaters have all let out, and the average Saturday

night revelers, good citizens from Bethtown or Calm's Point, Riverhead or Majesta, have come into the Isola streets again in search of
a snack or a giggle before heading home to their separate beds. The
city is an ants' nest of after-theater eateries ranging from chic
French cafés to pizzerias to luncheonettes to coffee shops to hot
dog stands to delicatessens, all of them packed to the ceilings because Saturday night is not only the loneliest night of the week, it
is also the night to howl. And howl they do, these good burghers
who have put in five long hard days of labor and who are anxious
now to relax and enjoy themselves before Sunday arrives, bringing
with it the attendant boredom of too damn much leisure time,
anathema for the American male. The crowds shove and jostle
their way along The Stem, moving in and out of bowling alleys,
shooting galleries, penny arcades, strip joints, night clubs, jazz emporiums, souvenir shops, lining the sidewalks outside plate glass
windows in which go-go girls gyrate, or watching with fascination
as a roast beef slowly turns on a spit. Saturday night is a time for
pleasure, and even the singles can find satisfaction, briefly courted
by the sidewalk whores standing outside the shabby hotels in the
side streets off The Stem, searching out homosexuals in gay bars on
the city's notorious North Side or down in The Quarter, thumbing
through dirty books in the myriad "back magazine" shops, or
slipping into darkened screening rooms to watch 16mm films of
girls taking off their clothes, good people all or most, with nothing
more on their minds than a little fun, a little enjoyment of the
short respite between Friday night at five and Monday morning at
nine.

But along around 2 A.M., the city begins to change.

The citizens have waited to get their cars out of parking garages
(more damn garages than there are barbershops) or have staggered
their way sleepily into subways to make the long trip back to the
outlying sections, the furry toy dog won in the Pokerino palace
clutched limply in arms that may or may not later succumb to less
than ardent embrace, the laughter a bit thin, the voice a bit
croaked, a college song being sung on a rattling subway car, but
without much force or spirit, Saturday night has ended, it is really
Sunday morning already, the morning hours are truly upon the city
now, and the denizens appear.

The hookers brazenly approach any straying male, never mind
the "Want to have a good time, sweetheart?", never mind the
euphemisms now. Now it's "Want to fuck, honey?", yes or no, a
quick sidewalk transaction and the attendant danger of later getting

mugged and rolled or maybe killed by a pimp in a hotel room stinking of Lysol while your pants are draped over a wooden chair. The junkies are out in force, too, looking for cars foolishly left unlocked and parked on the streets, or—lacking such fortuitous circumstance—experienced enough to force the side vent with a screwdriver, hook the lock button with a wire hanger, and open the door that way. There are pushers peddling their dream stuff, from pot to hoss to speed, a nickel bag or a twenty-dollar deck; fences hawking their stolen goodies, anything from a transistor radio to a refrigerator, the biggest bargain basement in town; burglars jimmying windows or forcing doors with a Celluloid strip, this being an excellent hour to break into apartments, when the occupants are asleep and the street sounds are hushed. But worse than any of these people (for they are, after all, only citizens engaged in commerce of a sort) are the predators who roam the night in search of trouble. In cruising wedges of three or four, sometimes high but more often not, they took for victims—a taxicab driver coming out of a cafeteria, an old woman poking around garbage cans for hidden treasures, a teenage couple necking in a parked automobile, it doesn't matter. You can get killed in this city at any time of the day or night, but your chances for extinction are best after 2 A.M. because, paradoxically, the night people take over in the morning. There are neighborhoods that terrify even cops in this lunar landscape, and certain places they will not enter unless they have first checked to see that there are two doors, one to get in by, and the other to get out through, fast, should someone decide to block the exit from behind.

The Painted Parasol was just such an establishment.

They had found in Mercy Howell's appointment book a notation that read Harry, 2 A.M., The Painted Parasol, and since they knew this particular joint for exactly the kind of hole it was, and since they wondered what connection the slain girl might have had with the various unappetizing types who frequented the place from dusk till dawn, they decided to hit it and find out. The front entrance opened on a long flight of stairs that led down to the main room of what was not a restaurant, and not a club, though it combined features of both. It did not possess a liquor license, and so it served only coffee and sandwiches, but occasionally a rock singer would plug in his amplifier and guitar and whack out a few numbers for the patrons. The back door of the—hangout?—opened onto a side-street alley. Hawes checked it out, reported back to Carella, and they both made a mental floor plan in case they needed it later.

Carella went down the long flight of steps first, Hawes immediately behind him. At the bottom of the stairway, they moved through a beaded curtain and found themselves in a large room overhung with an old Air Force parachute painted in a wild psychedelic pattern. A counter upon which rested a coffee urn and trays of sandwiches in Saran Wrap was just opposite the hanging beaded curtain. To the left and right of the counter were perhaps two dozen tables, all of them occupied. A waitress in a black leotard and black high-heeled patent leather pumps was swiveling among and around the tables, taking orders. There was a buzz of conversation in the room, hovering, captured in the folds of the brightly painted parachute. Behind the counter, a man in a white apron was drawing a cup of coffee from the huge silver urn. Carella and Hawes walked over to him. Carella was almost six feet tall, and he weighed a hundred and eighty pounds, with wide shoulders and a narrow waist and the hands of a street brawler. Hawes was six feet two inches tall, and he weighed a hundred and ninety-five pounds bone-dry, and his hair was a fiery red with a white streak over the left temple, where he had once been knifed while investigating a burglary. Both men looked like exactly what they were: fuzz.

"What's the trouble?" the man behind the counter asked immediately.

"No trouble," Carella said. "This your place?"

"Yeah. My name is Georgie Bright, and I already been visited, thanks. Twice."

"Oh? Who visited you?"

"First time a cop named O'Brien, second time a cop named Parker. I already cleared up that whole thing that was going on downstairs."

"What whole thing going on downstairs?"

"In the men's room. Some kids were selling pot down there, it got to be a regular neighborhood supermarket. So I done what O'Brien suggested, I put a man down there outside the toilet door, and the rule now is only one person goes in there at a time. Parker came around to make sure I was keeping my part of the bargain. I don't want no narcotics trouble here. Go down and take a look if you like. You'll see I got a man watching the toilet."

"Who's watching the man watching the toilet?" Carella asked.

"That ain't funny," Georgie Bright said, looking offended.

"Know anybody named Harry?" Hawes asked.

"Harry who? I know a lot of Harrys."

"Any of them here tonight?"

"Maybe."

"Where?"

"There's one over there near the bandstand. The big guy with the blond hair."

"Harry what?"

"Donatello."

"Make the name?" Carella asked Hawes.

"No," Hawes said.

"Neither do I."

"Let's talk to him."

"You want a cup of coffee or something?" Georgie Bright asked.

"Yeah, why don't you send some over to the table?" Hawes said, and followed Carella across the room to where Harry Donatello was sitting with another man. Donatello was wearing gray slacks, black shoes and socks, a white shirt open at the throat, and a double-breasted blue blazer. His long blond hair was combed straight back from the forehead, revealing a sharply defined widow's peak. He was easily as big as Hawes, and he sat with his hands folded on the table in front of him, talking to the man who sat opposite him. He did not look up as the detectives approached.

"Is your name Harry Donatello?" Carella asked.

"Who wants to know?"

"Police officers," Carella said, and flashed his shield.

"I'm Harry Donatello, what's the matter?"

"Mind if we sit down?" Hawes asked, and before Donatello could answer, both men sat, their backs to the empty bandstand and the exit door.

"Do you know a girl named Mercy Howell?" Carella asked.

"What about her?"

"Do you know her?"

"I know her. What's the beef? She underage or something?"

"When did you see her last?"

The man with Donatello, who up to now had been silent, suddenly piped, "You don't have to answer no questions without a lawyer, Harry. Tell them you want a lawyer."

The detectives looked him over. He was small and thin, with black hair combed sideways to conceal a receding hairline. He was badly in need of a shave. He was wearing blue trousers and a striped shirt.

"This is a field investigation," Hawes said drily, "and we can ask anything we damn please."

"Town's getting full of lawyers," Carella said. "What's *your* name, counselor?"

"Jerry Riggs. You going to drag *me* in this, whatever it is?"

"It's a few friendly questions in the middle of the night," Hawes said. "Anybody got any objections to that?"

"Getting so two guys can't even sit and talk together without getting shook down," Riggs said.

"You've got a rough life, all right," Hawes said, and the girl in the black leotard brought their coffee to the table, and then hurried off to take another order. Donatello watched her jiggling behind as she swiveled across the room.

"So when's the last time you saw the Howell girl?" Carella asked again.

"Wednesday night," Donatello said.

"Did you see her tonight?"

"No."

"Were you *supposed* to see her tonight?"

"Where'd you get that idea?"

"We're full of ideas," Hawes said.

"Yeah, I was supposed to meet her here ten minutes ago. Dumb broad is late, as usual."

"What do you do for a living, Donatello?"

"I'm an importer. You want to see my business card?"

"What do you import?"

"Souvenir ashtrays."

"How'd you get to know Mercy Howell?"

"I met her at a party in The Quarter. She got a little high, and she done her thing."

"What thing?"

"The thing she does in that show she's in."

"Which is what?"

"She done this dance where she takes off all her clothes."

"How long have you been seeing her?"

"I met her a couple of months ago. I see her on and off, maybe once a week, something like that. This town is full of broads, you know, a guy don't have to get himself involved in no relationship with no specific broad."

"What was your relationship with *this* specific broad?"

"We have a few laughs together, that's all. She's a swinger, little Mercy," Donatello said, and grinned at Riggs.

"Want to tell us where you were tonight between eleven and twelve?"

"Is this still a *field* investigation?" Riggs asked sarcastically.

"Nobody's in custody yet," Hawes said, "so let's cut the legal crap, okay? Tell us where you were, Donatello."

"Right here," Donatello said. "From ten o'clock till now."

"I suppose somebody saw you here during that time."

"A *hundred* people saw me."

A crowd of angry black men and women were standing outside the shattered window of the storefront church. Two fire engines and an ambulance were parked at the curb. Kling pulled in behind the second engine, some ten feet away from the hydrant. It was almost 2:30 A.M. on a bitterly cold October night, but the crowd looked and sounded like a mob at an afternoon street-corner rally in the middle of August. Restless, noisy, abrasive, anticipative, they ignored the penetrating cold and concentrated instead on the burning issue of the hour, the fact that a person or persons unknown had thrown a bomb through the plate glass window of the church. The beat patrolman, a newly appointed cop who felt vaguely uneasy in this neighborhood even during his daytime shift, greeted Kling effusively, his pale white face bracketed by earmuffs, his gloved hands clinging desperately to his nightstick. The crowd parted to let Kling through. It did not help that he was the youngest man on the squad, with the callow look of a country bumpkin on his unlined face, it did not help that he was blond and hatless, it did not help that he walked into the church with the confident youthful stride of a champion come to set things right. The crowd knew he was fuzz, and they knew he was Whitey, and they knew, too, that if this bombing had taken place on Hall Avenue crosstown and downtown, the Police Commissioner himself would have arrived behind a herald of official trumpets. This, however, was Culver Avenue, where a boiling mixture of Puerto Ricans and Negroes shared a disintegrating ghetto, and so the car that pulled to the curb was not marked with the Commissioner's distinctive blue-and-gold seal, but was instead a green Chevy convertible that belonged to Kling himself, and the man who stepped out of it looked young and inexperienced and inept despite the confident stride he affected as he walked into the church, his shield pinned to his overcoat.

The bomb had caused little fire damage, and the firemen already had the flames under control, their hoses snaking through and around the overturned folding chairs scattered about the small room. Ambulance attendants picked their way over the hoses and around the debris, carrying out the injured—the dead could wait.

"Have you called the Bomb Squad?" Kling asked the patrolman.

"No," the patrolman answered, shaken by the sudden possibility that he had been derelict in his duty.

"Why don't you do that now?" Kling suggested.

"Yes, *sir,*" the patrolman answered, and rushed out. The ambulance attendants went by with a moaning woman on a stretcher. She was still wearing her eyeglasses, but one lens had been shattered and blood was running in a steady rivulet down the side of her nose. The place stank of gunpowder and smoke and charred wood. The most serious damage had been done at the rear of the small store, furthest away from the entrance door. Whoever had thrown the bomb must have possessed a damn good pitching arm to have hurled it so accurately through the window and across the fifteen feet to the makeshift altar. The minister lay across his own altar, dead, one arm blown off in the explosion. Two women who had been sitting on folding chairs closest to the altar lay upon each other on the floor now, tangled in death, their clothes still smoldering. The sounds of the injured filled the room, and then were suffocated by the overriding siren-shriek of the arriving second ambulance. Kling went outside to the crowd.

"Anybody here witness this?" he asked.

A young man, black, wearing a beard and a natural hair style, turned away from a group of other youths, and walked directly to Kling.

"Is the minister dead?" he asked.

"Yes, he is," Kling answered.

"Who else?"

"Two women."

"Who?"

"I don't know yet. We'll identify them as soon as the men are through in there." He turned again to the crowd. "Did anybody see what happened?" he asked.

"I saw it," the young man said.

"What's your name, son?"

"Andrew Jordan."

Kling took out his pad. "All right, let's have it."

"What good's this going to do?" Jordan asked. "Writing all this shit in your book?"

"You said you saw what . . ."

"I saw it, all right. I was walking by, heading for the poolroom up the street, and the ladies were inside singing, and this car pulled up, and a guy got out, threw the bomb, and ran back to the car."

"What kind of a car was it?"

"A red VW."

"What year?"

"Who can tell with those VWs?"

"How many people in it?"

"Two. The driver and the guy who threw the bomb."

"Notice the license plate?"

"No. They drove off too fast."

"Can you describe the man who threw the bomb?"

"Yeah. He was white."

"What else?" Kling asked.

"That's all," Jordan replied. "He was *white*."

There were perhaps three dozen estates in all of Smoke Rise, a hundred or so people living in luxurious near seclusion on acres of valuable land through which ran four winding, interconnected, private roadways. Meyer Meyer drove between the wide stone pillars marking Smoke Rise's western access road, entering a city within a city, bounded on the north by the River Harb, shielded from the River Highway by stands of poplars and evergreens on the south— exclusive Smoke Rise, known familiarly and derisively to the rest of the city's inhabitants as "The Club."

374 MacArthur Lane was at the end of the road that curved past the Hamilton Bridge. The house was a huge gray stone structure with a slate roof and scores of gables and chimneys jostling the sky, perched high in gloomy shadow above the Harb. As he stepped from the car, Meyer could hear the sounds of river traffic, the hooting of tugs, the blowing of whistles, the eruption of a squawk box on a destroyer midstream. He looked out over the water. Reflected lights glistened in shimmering liquid beauty, the hanging globes on the bridge's suspension cables, the dazzling reds and greens of signal lights on the opposite shore, single illuminated window slashes in apartment buildings throwing their mirror images onto the black surface of the river, the blinking wing lights of an airplane overhead moving in watery reflection like a submarine. The air was cold, a fine piercing drizzle had begun several minutes ago. Meyer shuddered, pulled the collar of his coat higher on his neck, and walked toward the old gray house, his shoes crunching on the driveway gravel, the sound echoing away into the high surrounding bushes.

The stones of the old house oozed wetness. Thick vines covered the walls, climbing to the gabled, turreted roof. He found a doorbell set over a brass escutcheon in the thick oaken doorjamb, and pressed it. Chimes sounded somewhere deep inside the house. He waited.

The door opened suddenly.

The man looking out at him was perhaps seventy years old, with piercing blue eyes, bald except for white thatches of hair that sprang wildly from behind each ear. He wore a red smoking jacket and black trousers, a black ascot around his neck, red velvet slippers.

"What do you want?" he asked immediately.

"I'm Detective Meyer of the Eighty-seventh . . ."

"Who sent for you?"

"A woman named Adele Gorman came to the . . ."

"My daughter's a fool," the man said. "We don't need the police here," and slammed the door in his face.

Meyer stood on the doorstep feeling somewhat like a horse's ass. A tugboat hooted on the river. A light snapped on upstairs, casting an amber rectangle into the dark driveway. He looked at the luminous dial of his watch. It was 2:35 A.M. The drizzle was cold and penetrating. He took out his handkerchief, blew his nose, and wondered what he should do next. He did not like ghosts, and he did not like lunatics, and he did not like nasty old men who did not comb their hair and who slammed doors in a person's face. He was about to head back for his car when the door opened again.

"Detective Meyer?" Adele Gorman said. "Do come in."

"Thank you," he said, and stepped into the entrance foyer.

"You're right on time."

"Well, a little early actually," Meyer said. He still felt foolish. What the hell was he doing in Smoke Rise investigating ghosts in the middle of the night?

"This way," Adele said, and he followed her through a somberly paneled foyer into a vast, dimly lighted living room. Heavy oaken beams ran overhead, velvet draperies hung at the window, the room was cluttered with ponderous old furniture. He could believe there were ghosts in this house, he could suddenly believe it. A young man wearing dark glasses rose like a specter from the sofa near the fireplace. His face, illuminated by the single standing floor lamp, looked wan and drawn. Wearing a black cardigan sweater over a white shirt and dark slacks, he approached Meyer unsmilingly with his hand extended—but he did not accept Meyer's hand when it was offered in return.

Meyer suddenly realized that the man was blind.

"I'm Ralph Gorman," he said, his hand still extended. "Adele's husband."

"How do you do, Mr. Gorman," Meyer said, and took his hand. The palm was moist and cold.

"It was good of you to come," Gorman said. "These apparitions have been driving us crazy."

"What time is it?" Adele asked suddenly, and looked at her watch. "We've got five minutes," she said. There was a tremor in her voice. She seemed suddenly very frightened.

"Won't your father be here?" Meyer asked.

"No, he's gone up to bed," Adele said. "I'm afraid he's bored with the whole affair, and terribly angry that we notified the police."

Meyer made no comment. Had he known that Willem Van Houten, former Surrogate's Court judge, had *not* wanted the police to be notified, Meyer would not have been here in the first place. He debated leaving now, but Adele Gorman had begun talking again, and it was impolite to depart in the middle of another person's sentence.

". . . is in her early thirties, I would guess. The other ghost, the male, is about your age—forty or forty-five, something like that."

"I'm thirty-seven," Meyer said.

"Oh."

"The bald head fools a lot of people."

"Yes."

"I was bald at a very early age."

"Anyway," Adele said, "their names are Elisabeth and Johann, and they've probably been . . ."

"Oh, they have names, do they?"

"Yes. They're ancestors, you know. My father is Dutch, and there actually *were* an Elisabeth and Johann Van Houten in the family centuries ago, when Smoke Rise was still a Dutch settlement."

"They're Dutch, um-huh, I see," Meyer said.

"Yes. They always appear wearing Dutch costumes. And they also speak Dutch."

"Have *you* heard them, Mr. Gorman?"

"Yes," Gorman said. "I'm blind, you know . . ." he added, and hesitated, as though expecting some comment from Meyer. When none came, he said, "But I *have* heard them."

"Do you speak Dutch?"

"No. My father-in-law speaks it fluently, though, and he identified the language for us, and told us what they were saying."

"What *did* they say?"

"Well, for one thing, they said they were going to steal Adele's jewelry, and they damn well did."

"Your *wife's* jewelry? But I thought . . ."

"It was willed to her by her mother. My father-in-law keeps it in his safe."

"Kept, you mean."

"No, keeps. There are several pieces in addition to the ones that were stolen. Two rings and also a necklace."

"And the value?"

"Altogether? I would say about forty thousand dollars."

"Your ghosts have expensive taste."

The floor lamp in the room suddenly began to flicker. Meyer glanced at it and felt the hackles rising at the back of his neck.

"The lights are going out, Ralph," Adele whispered.

"Is it two forty-five?"

"Yes."

"They're here," Gorman whispered.

Mercy Howell's roommate had been asleep for close to four hours when they knocked on her door. But she was a wily young lady, hip to the ways of the big city, and very much awake as she conducted her own little investigation without so much as opening the door a crack. First she asked them to spell their names slowly. Then she asked them their shield numbers. Then she asked them to hold their shields and their I.D. cards close to the door's peephole, where she could see them. Still unconvinced, she said through the locked door, "You just wait there a minute." They waited for closer to five minutes before they heard her approaching the door again. The heavy steel bar of a Fox lock was pushed noisily to the side, a safety chain rattled on its track, the tumblers of one lock clicked open, and then another, and finally the girl opened the door.

"Come in," she said. "I'm sorry I kept you waiting. I called the station house and they said you were okay."

"You're a very careful girl," Hawes said.

"At this hour of the morning? Are you kidding?" she said.

She was perhaps twenty-five, with her red hair up in curlers, her face cold-creamed clean of makeup. She was wearing a pink quilted robe over flannel pajamas, and although she was probably a very pretty girl at 9 A.M., she now looked about as attractive as a Buffalo nickel.

"What's your name, miss?" Carella asked.

"Lois Kaplan. What's this all about? Has there been another burglary in the building?"

"No, Miss Kaplan. We want to ask you some questions about Mercy Howell? Did she live here with you?"

"Yes," Lois said, and suddenly looked at them shrewdly. "What do you mean *did*? She still *does*."

They were standing in the small foyer of the apartment, and the foyer went so still that all the night sounds of the building were clearly audible all at once, as though they had not been there before but had only been summoned up now to fill the void of silence. A toilet flushed somewhere, a hot water pipe rattled, a baby whimpered, a dog barked, someone dropped a shoe. In the foyer now filled with noise, they stared at each other wordlessly, and finally Carella drew a deep breath and said, "Your roommate is dead. She was stabbed tonight as she was leaving the theater."

"No," Lois said, simply and flatly and unequivocally. "No, she isn't."

"Miss Kaplan . . ."

"I don't give a damn what you say, Mercy isn't dead."

"Miss Kaplan, she's dead."

"Oh Jesus," Lois said, and burst into tears, "oh Jesus, oh damn damn, oh Jesus."

The two men stood by feeling stupid and big and awkward and helpless. Lois Kaplan covered her face with her hands and sobbed into them, her shoulders heaving, saying over and over again, "I'm sorry, oh Jesus, please, I'm sorry, please, oh poor Mercy, oh my God," while the detectives tried not to watch. At last the crying stopped and she looked up at them with eyes that had been knifed, and said softly, "Come in. Please," and led them into the living room. She kept staring at the floor as she talked. It was as if she could not look them in the face, not these men who had brought her the news.

"Do you know who did it?" she asked.

"No. Not yet."

"We wouldn't have waked you in the middle of the night . . ."

"That's all right."

"But very often, if we get moving on a case fast enough, before the trail gets cold . . ."

"Yes, I understand."

"We can often . . ."

"Yes, before the trail gets cold," Lois said.

"Yes."

The apartment went silent again.

"Would you know if Miss Howell had any enemies?" Carella asked.

"She was the sweetest girl in the world," Lois said.

"Did she argue with anyone recently, were there . . . ?"

"No."

". . . any threatening telephone calls or letters?"

Lois Kaplan looked up at them.

"Yes," she said. "A letter."

"A *threatening* letter?"

"We couldn't tell. It frightened Mercy, though. That's why she bought the gun."

"What kind of gun?"

"I don't know. A small one."

"Would it have been a .25 caliber Browning?"

"I don't know guns."

"Was this letter mailed to her, or delivered personally?"

"It was mailed to her. At the theater."

"When?"

"A week ago."

"Did she report it to the police?"

"No."

"Why not?"

"Haven't you seen *Rattlesnake?*" Lois said.

"What do you mean?" Carella said.

"*Rattlesnake*. The musical. Mercy's show. The show she was in."

"No, I haven't."

"But you've *heard* of it."

"No."

"Where do you live, for God's sake? On the moon?"

"I'm sorry, I just haven't . . ."

"Forgive me," Lois said immediately. "I'm not usually . . . I'm trying very hard to . . . I'm sorry. Forgive me."

"That's all right," Carella said.

"Anyway, it's . . . it's a big hit now but . . . there was trouble in the beginning, you see . . . are you *sure* you don't know about this? It was in all the newspapers."

"Well, I guess I missed it," Carella said. "What was the trouble about?"

"Don't *you* know about this either?" she asked Hawes.

"No, I'm sorry."

"About Mercy's dance?"

"No."

"Well, in one scene, Mercy danced the title song without any clothes on. Because the idea was to express . . . the *hell* with what the idea was. The point is that the dance wasn't at all prurient, it wasn't even sexy! But the police *missed* the point, and closed the show down two days after it opened. The producers had to go to court for a writ to get the show opened again."

"Yes, I remember it now," Carella said.

"What I'm trying to say is that nobody involved with *Rattlesnake* would report *anything* to the police. Not even a threatening letter."

"If she bought a pistol," Hawes said, "she would have *had* to go to the police. For a permit."

"She didn't have a permit."

"Then how'd she get the pistol? You can't buy a handgun without first . . ."

"A friend of hers sold it to her."

"What's the friend's name?"

"Harry Donatello."

"An importer," Carella said drily.

"Of souvenir ashtrays," Hawes said.

"I don't know what he does for a living," Lois said. "But he got the gun for her."

"When was this?"

"A few days after she received the letter."

"What did the letter say?" Carella asked.

"I'll get it for you," Lois said, and went into the bedroom. They heard a dresser drawer opening, the rustle of clothes, what might have been a tin candy box being opened. Lois came back into the room. "Here it is," she said.

There didn't seem much point in trying to preserve latent prints on a letter that had already been handled by Mercy Howell, Lois Kaplan, and God knew how many others. But Carella nonetheless accepted the letter on a handkerchief spread over the palm of his hand, and then looked at the face of the envelope. "She should have brought this to us immediately," he said. "It's written on hotel stationery, we've got an address without lifting a finger."

The letter had indeed been written on stationery from The Addison Hotel, one of the city's lesser-known fleabags, some two blocks north of the Eleventh Street Theater, where Mercy Howell had worked. There was a single sheet of paper in the envelope. Carella unfolded it. Lettered in pencil were the words:

PUT ON YOUR
CLOSE, MISS!
The Avenging Angel

The lamp went out, the room was black.

At first there was no sound but the sharp intake of Adele Gorman's breath. And then, indistinctly, as faintly as though carried on a swirling mist that blew in wetly from some desolated shore, there came the sound of garbled voices, and the room grew suddenly cold. The voices were those of a crowd in endless debate, rising and falling in cacophonous cadence, a mixture of tongues that rattled and rasped. There was the sound, too, of a rising wind, as though a door to some forbidden landscape had been sharply and suddenly blown open (How cold the room was!) to reveal a host of corpses incessantly pacing, involved in formless dialogue. The voices rose in volume now, carried on that same chill penetrating wind, louder, closer, until they seemed to overwhelm the room, clamoring to be released from whatever unearthly vault contained them. And then, as if two and only two of those disembodied voices had succeeded in breaking away from the mass of unseen dead, bringing with them a rush of bone-chilling air from some world unknown, there came a whisper at first, the whisper of a man's voice, saying the single word "Ralph!" sharp-edged and with a distinctive foreign inflection, "Ralph!" and then a woman's voice joining it, "Adele!" pronounced strangely and in the same cutting whisper, "Adele!" and then "Ralph!" again, the voices overlapping, unmistakably foreign, urgent, rising in volume until the whispers commingled to become an agonizing groan and the names were lost in the shrilling echo of the wind.

Meyer's eyes played tricks in the darkness. Apparitions that surely were not there seemed to float on the crescendo of sound that saturated the room. Barely perceived pieces of furniture assumed amorphous shapes as the male voice snarled and the female voice moaned above it in contralto counterpoint. And then the babel of other voices intruded again, as though calling these two back to whatever grim mossy crypt they had momentarily escaped. The sound of the wind became more fierce, and the voices of those numberless pacing dead receded, and echoed, and were gone.

The lamp sputtered back into dim illumination. The room seemed perceptibly warmer, but Meyer Meyer was covered with a cold clammy sweat.

"Now do you believe?" Adele Gorman asked.

Detective Bob O'Brien was coming out of the men's room down the hall when he saw the woman sitting on the bench just outside the squadroom. He almost went back into the toilet, but he was an instant too late; she had seen him, there was no escape.

"Hello, Mr. O'Brien," she said, and performed an awkward little half-rising motion, as though uncertain whether she should stand to greet him or accept the deference due a lady. The clock on the squadroom wall read 3:02 A.M., but the lady was dressed as though for a brisk afternoon's hike in the park, brown slacks and low-heeled walking shoes, brief beige car coat, a scarf around her head. She was perhaps fifty-five or thereabouts, with a face that once must have been pretty, save for the overlong nose. Green-eyed, with prominent cheekbones and a generous mouth, she executed her abortive rise, and then fell into step beside O'Brien as he walked into the squad-room.

"Little late in the night to be out, isn't it, Mrs. Blair?" O'Brien asked. He was not an insensitive cop, but his manner now was brusque and dismissive. Faced with Mrs. Blair for perhaps the seventeenth time in a month, he tried not to empathize with her loss because, truthfully, he was unable to assist her, and his inability to do so was frustrating.

"Have you seen her?" Mrs. Blair asked.

"No," O'Brien said. "I'm sorry, Mrs. Blair, but I haven't."

"I have a new picture, perhaps that will help."

"Yes, perhaps it will," he said.

The telephone was ringing. He lifted the receiver and said, "Eighty-seventh Squad, O'Brien here."

"Bob, this's Bert Kling over on Culver, the church bombing."

"Yeah, Bert."

"Seems I remember seeing a red Volkswagen on that hot car bulletin we got yesterday. You want to dig it out and let me know where it was snatched?"

"Yeah, just a second," O'Brien said, and began scanning the sheet on his desk.

"Here's the new picture," Mrs. Blair said, "I know you're very good with runaways, Mr. O'Brien, the kids all like you and give you information. If you see Penelope, all I want you to do is tell her I love her and am sorry for the misunderstanding."

"Yeah, I will," O'Brien said. Into the phone, he said, "I've got *two* red VWs, Bert, a '64 and a '66. You want them both?"

"Shoot," Kling said.

"The '64 was stolen from a guy named Art Hauser. It was parked outside 861 West Meridian."

"And the '66?"

"Owner is a woman named Alice Cleary. Car was stolen from a parking lot on Fourteenth."

"North or South?"

"South. 303 South."

"Right. Thanks, Bob," Kling said, and hung up.

"And ask her to come home to me," Mrs. Blair said.

"Yes, I will," O'Brien said. "If I see her, I certainly will."

"That's a nice picture of Penny, don't you think?" Mrs. Blair asked. "It was taken last Easter. It's the most recent picture I have. I thought it would be most helpful to you."

O'Brien looked at the girl in the picture, and then looked up into Mrs. Blair's green eyes, misted now with tears, and suddenly wanted to reach across the desk and pat her hand reassuringly, the one thing he could *not* do with any honesty. Because whereas it was true that he was the squad's runaway expert, with perhaps fifty snapshots of teenage boys and girls crammed into his bulging notebook, and whereas his record of finds was more impressive than any other cop's in the city, uniformed or plainclothes, there wasn't a damn thing he could do for the mother of Penelope Blair, who had run away from home last June.

"You understand . . ." he started to say.

"Let's not go into *that* again, Mr. O'Brien," she said, and rose.

"Mrs. Blair . . ."

"I don't want to hear it," Mrs. Blair said, walking quickly out of the squadroom. "Tell her to come home. Tell her I love her," she said, and was gone down the iron-runged steps.

O'Brien sighed and stuffed the new picture of Penelope into his notebook. What Mrs. Blair did not choose to hear again was the fact that her runaway daughter Penny was twenty-four years old, and there was not a single agency on God's green earth, police or otherwise, that could force her to go home again if she did not choose to.

Fats Donner was a stool pigeon with a penchant for Turkish baths. A mountainous white Buddha of a man, he could usually be found at one or another of the city's steam emporiums at any given hour of the day, draped in a towel and reveling in the heat that saturated his flabby body. Bert Kling found him in an all-night place called Steam-Fit. He sent the masseur into the steam room to tell Donner he was there, and Donner sent word out that he would be through in five minutes, unless Kling wished to join him. Kling did not wish to join him. He waited in the locker room, and in seven minutes' time, Donner came out, draped in his customary towel, a ludicrous sight at *any* time, but particularly at close to 3:30 A.M.

"Hey!" Donner said. "How you doing?"

"Fine," Kling said. "How about yourself?"

"Comme ci, comme ça," Donner said, and made a see-sawing motion with one fleshy hand.

"I'm looking for some stolen heaps," Kling said, getting directly to the point.

"What kind?" Donner said.

"Volkswagens. A '64 and a '66."

"What color are they?"

"Red."

"Both of them?"

"Yes."

"Where were they heisted?"

"One from in front of 861 West Meridian. The other from a parking lot on South Fourteenth."

"When was this?"

"Both last week sometime. I don't have the exact dates."

"What do you want to know?"

"Who stole them."

"You think it's the same guy on both?"

"I doubt it."

"What's so important about these heaps?"

"One of them may have been used in a bombing tonight."

"You mean the church over on Culver?"

"That's right."

"Count me out," Donner said.

"What do you mean?"

"There's a lot of guys in this town who're in *sympathy* with what happened over there tonight. I don't want to get involved in none of this black-white shit."

"Who's going to know whether you're involved or not?" Kling asked.

"The same way *you* get information, *they* get information."

"I need your help, Donner."

"Yeah, well, I'm sorry on this one," Donner said, and shook his head.

"In that case, I'd better hurry downtown to High Street."

"Why? You got another source down there?"

"No, that's where the D.A.'s office is."

Both men stared at each other, Donner in a white towel draped around his belly, sweat still pouring from his face and his chest even though he was no longer in the steam room, Kling looking like a slightly tired advertising executive rather than a cop threatening a man with revelation of past deeds not entirely legal. They stared at each other with total understanding, caught in the curious symbiosis of law breaker and law enforcer, an empathy created by neither man, but essential to the existence of both. It was Donner who broke the silence.

"I don't like being coerced," he said.

"I don't like being refused," Kling answered.

"When do you need this?"

"I want to get going on it before morning."

"You expect miracles, don't you?"

"Doesn't everybody?"

"Miracles cost."

"How much?"

"Twenty-five if I turn up one heap, fifty if I turn up both."

"Turn them up first. We'll talk later."

"And if somebody breaks my head later?"

"You should have thought of that before you entered the profession," Kling said. "Come on, Donner, cut it out. This is a routine bombing by a couple of punks. You've got nothing to be afraid of."

"No?" Donner asked. And then, in a very professorial voice, he uttered perhaps the biggest understatement of the decade. "Racial tensions are running very high in this city right now."

"Have you got my number at the squadroom?"

"Yeah, I've got it," Donner said glumly.

"I'm going back there now. Let me hear from you soon."

"You mind if I get dressed first?" Donner asked.

The night clerk at The Addison Hotel was alone in the lobby when Carella and Hawes walked in. Immersed in an open book on the desk in front of him, he did not look up as they approached. The lobby was furnished in faded Gothic: a threadbare oriental rug, heavy curlicued mahogany tables, ponderous stuffed chairs with sagging bottoms and soiled antimacassars, two spittoons resting alongside each of two mahogany-paneled supporting columns. A real Tiffany lampshade hung over the registration desk, one leaded glass panel gone, another badly cracked. In the old days, The Addison had been a luxury hotel. It now wore its past splendor with all the style of a two-dollar hooker in a moth-eaten mink she'd picked up in a thrift shop.

The clerk, in contrast to his ancient surroundings, was a young man in his mid-twenties, wearing a neatly pressed brown tweed suit, a tan shirt, a gold-and-brown silk rep tie, and eyeglasses with tortoiseshell rims. He glanced up at the detectives belatedly, squinting after the intense concentration of peering at print, and then he got to his feet.

"Yes, gentlemen," he said. "May I help you?"

"Police officers," Carella said. He took his wallet from his pocket, and opened it to where his detective's shield was pinned to a leather flap.

"Yes, sir."

"I'm Detective Carella, this is my partner Detective Hawes."

"How do you do? I'm the night clerk, my name is Ronnie Sanford."

"We're looking for someone who may have been registered here two weeks ago," Hawes said.

"Well, if he was registered here two weeks ago," Sanford said, "chances are he's still registered. Most of our guests are residents."

"Do you keep stationery in the lobby here?" Carella asked.

"Sir?"

"Stationery. Is there any place here in the lobby where someone could walk in off the street and pick up a piece of stationery?"

"No, sir. There's a writing desk there in the corner, near the staircase, but we don't stock it with stationery, no, sir."

"Is there stationery in the rooms?"

"Yes, sir."

"How about here at the desk?"

"Yes, of course, sir."

"Is there someone at this desk twenty-four hours a day?"

"Twenty-four hours a day, yes, sir. We have three shifts. Eight to four in the afternoon. Four to midnight. And midnight to eight A.M."

"You came on at midnight, did you?"

"Yes, sir."

"Any guests come in after you started your shift?"

"A few, yes, sir."

"Notice anybody with blood on his clothes?"

"Blood? Oh, no, sir."

"Would you have noticed?"

"What do you mean?"

"Are you generally pretty aware of what's going on around here?"

"I try to be, sir. At least, for most of the night. I catch a little nap when I'm not studying, but usually . . ."

"What do you study?"

"Accounting."

"Where?"

"At Ramsey U."

"Mind if we take a look at your register?"

"Not at all, sir."

He walked to the mail rack and took the hotel register from the counter there. Returning to the desk, he opened it, and said, "All of our present guests are residents, with the exception of Mr. Lambert in 204, and Mrs. Grant in 701."

"When did they check in?"

"Mr. Lambert checked in . . . last night, I think it was. And Mrs. Grant has been here for four days. She's leaving on Tuesday."

"Are these the actual signatures of your guests?"

"Yes, sir. All guests are asked to sign the register, as required by state law."

"Have you got that note, Cotton?" Carella asked, and then turned again to Sanford. "Would you mind if we took this over to the couch there?"

"Well, we're not supposed . . ."

"We can give you a receipt for it, if you like."

"No, I guess it'll be all right."

They carried the register to a couch upholstered in faded red velvet. With the book supported on Carella's lap, they unfolded the note Mercy Howell had received, and began comparing the signatures of the guests with the only part of the note that was not written in block letters, the words "The Avenging Angel."

There were fifty-two guests in the hotel. Carella and Hawes went through the register once, and then started through it a second time.

"Hey," Hawes said suddenly.

"What?"

"Look at this one."

He took the note and placed it on the page so that it was directly above one of the signatures:

PUT ON YOUR
CLOSE, MISS!
The Avenging Angel

_____

Timothy Allen Ames

"What you think?" he asked.

"Different handwriting," Carella said.

"Same initials," Hawes said.

Detective Meyer Meyer was still shaken. He did not like ghosts. He did not like this house. He wanted to go home. He wanted to be in bed with his wife Sarah. He wanted her to stroke his hand and tell him that such things did not exist, there was nothing to be afraid of, a grown man? How could he believe in poltergeists, shades, Dutch spirits? Ridiculous.

But he had heard them, and he had felt their chilling presence, and had almost thought he'd seen them, if only for an instant. He turned fresh shock now toward the hall staircase and the sound of descending footsteps. Eyes wide, he waited for whatever new manifestation might present itself. He was tempted to draw his revolver, but he was afraid such an act would appear foolish to the Gormans. He had come here a skeptic, and he was now at least *willing* to believe, and he waited in dread for whatever was coming down those steps with such ponderous footfalls—some ghoul trailing winding sheets and rattling chains? some specter with a bleached skull for a head and long bony clutching fingers dripping the blood of babies?

Willem Van Houten, wearing his red velvet slippers and his red smoking jacket, his hair still jutting wildly from behind each ear, his blue eyes fierce and snapping, came into the living room and walked directly to where his daughter and son-in-law were sitting.

"Well?" he asked. "Did they come again?"

"Yes, Daddy," Adele said.

"What did they want this time?"

"I don't know. They spoke Dutch again."

"Bastards," Van Houten said, and then turned to Meyer. "Did you see them?" he asked.

"No, sir, I did not," Meyer said.

"But they were *here*," Gorman protested, and turned his blank face to his wife, "I heard them."

"Yes, darling," Adele assured him. "We *all* heard them. But it was like that other time, don't you remember? When we could hear them even though they couldn't quite break through."

"Yes, that's right," Gorman said, and nodded. "This happened once before, Detective Meyer." He was facing Meyer now, his head tilted quizzically, the sightless eyes covered with their black reflecting glasses. When he spoke, his voice was like that of a child seeking reassurance. "But you *did* hear them, didn't you, Detective Meyer?"

"Yes," Meyer said. "I heard them, Mr. Gorman."

"And the wind?"

"Yes, the wind, too."

"And felt them? It . . . it gets so cold when they appear. You *did* feel their presence, didn't you?"

"I felt something," Meyer said.

Van Houten suddenly asked, "Are you satisfied?"

"About what?" Meyer said.

"That there are ghosts in this house? That's why you're here, isn't it? To ascertain . . ."

"He's here because I asked Adele to contact the police," Gorman said.

"Why did you do that?"

"Because of the stolen jewelry," Gorman said. "And because . . ." He paused. "Because I . . . I've lost my sight, yes, but I wanted to . . . to make sure I wasn't losing my mind as well."

"You're quite sane, Ralph," Van Houten said.

"About the jewelry . . ." Meyer said.

"They took it," Van Houten said.

"Who?"

"Johann and Elisabeth. Our friendly neighborhood ghosts, the bastards."

"That's impossible, Mr. Van Houten."

"Why is it impossible?"

"Because ghosts . . ." Meyer started, and hesitated.

"Yes?"

"Ghosts, well, ghosts don't go around stealing jewelry. I mean, what use would they have for it?" he said lamely, and looked at the Gormans for corroboration. Neither of them seemed to be in a supportive mood. They sat on the sofa near the fireplace, looking glum and defeated.

"They want us out of this house," Van Houten said. "It's as simple as that."

"How do you know?"

"Because they said so."

"When?"

"Before they stole the necklace and the earrings."

"They told this to you?"

"To me and to my children. All three of us were here."

"But I understand the ghosts speak only Dutch."

"Yes, I translated for Ralph and Adele."

"And then what happened?"

"What do you mean?"

"When did you discover the jewelry was missing?"

"The very instant they were gone."

"You mean you went to the safe . . ."

"Yes, and opened it, and the jewelry was gone."

"We had put it in the safe not ten minutes before that," Adele said. "We'd been to a party, Ralph and I, and we got home very late, and Daddy was still awake, reading, sitting in that chair you're in this very minute. I asked him to open the safe, and he did, and he put the jewelry in, and closed the safe and . . . and then *they* came and . . . and made their threats."

"What time was this?"

"The usual time. The time they always come. Two forty-five in the morning."

"And you say the jewelry was put into the safe at what time?"

"About two-thirty," Gorman said.

"And when was the safe opened again?"

"Immediately after they left. They only stay a few moments. This time they told my father-in-law they were taking the necklace and the earrings with them. He rushed to the safe as soon as the lights came on again . . ."

"Do the lights always go off?"

"Always," Adele said. "It's always the same. The lights go off, and the room gets very cold, and we hear these . . . strange voices arguing." She paused. "And then Johann and Elisabeth come."

"Except that *this* time they didn't come," Meyer said.

"And one other time," Adele said quickly.

"They want us out of this house," Van Houten said, "that's all there is to it. Maybe we *ought* to leave. Before they take *everything* from us."

"Everything? What do you mean?"

"The rest of my daughter's jewelry. Some stock certificates. Everything that's in the safe."

"Where *is* the safe?" Meyer asked.

"Here. Behind this painting." Van Houten walked to the wall opposite the fireplace. An oil painting of a pastoral landscape hung there in an ornate gilt frame. The frame was hinged to the wall. Van Houten swung the painting out as though opening a door, and revealed the small, round, black safe behind it. "Here," he said.

"How many people know the combination?" Meyer asked.

"Just me," Van Houten said.

"Do you keep the number written down anywhere?"

"Yes."

"Where?"

"Hidden."

"Where?"

"I hardly think that's any of your business, Detective Meyer."

"I'm only trying to find out whether some other person could have got hold of the combination somehow."

"Yes, I suppose that's possible," Van Houten said. "But highly un-likely."

"Well," Meyer said, and shrugged. "I don't really know what to say. I'd like to measure the room, if you don't mind, get the di-mensions, placement of doors and windows, things like that. For my report." He shrugged again.

"It's rather late, isn't it?" Van Houten said.

"Well, I *got* here rather late," Meyer said, and smiled.

"Come, Daddy, I'll make us all some tea in the kitchen," Adele said. "Will you be long, Detective Meyer?"

"I don't know. It may take a while."

"Shall I bring you some tea?"

"Thank you, that would be nice."

She rose from the couch and then guided her husband's hand to her arm. Walking slowly beside him, she led him past her father and out of the room. Van Houten looked at Meyer once again, nodded briefly, and followed them out. Meyer closed the door behind them and immediately walked to the standing floor lamp.

The woman was sixty years old, and she looked like anybody's grandmother, except that she had just murdered her husband and three children. They had explained her rights to her, and she had told them she had nothing to hide and would answer any questions they chose to ask. She sat in a straight-backed squadroom chair, wearing a black cloth coat over bloodstained pajamas and robe, her handcuffed hands in her lap, her hands unmoving on her black leather pocketbook. O'Brien and Kling looked at the police stenographer, who glanced up at the wall clock, noted the time of the interroga-tion's start as 3:55 A.M., and then signaled that he was ready whenever they were.

"What is your name?" O'Brien asked.

"Isabel Martin."

"How old are you, Mrs. Martin?"

"Sixty."

"Where do you live?"

"On Ainsley Avenue."

"Where on Ainsley?"

"657 Ainsley."

"With whom do you live there?"

"With my husband Roger, and my son Peter, and my daughters Annie and Abigail."

"Would you like to tell us what happened tonight, Mrs. Martin?" Kling asked.

"I killed them all," she said. She had white hair, a fine aquiline nose, brown eyes behind rimless spectacles. She stared straight ahead of her as she spoke, looking neither to her right nor to her left, ignoring her questioners completely, seemingly alone with the memory of what she had done not a half-hour before.

"Can you give us some of the details, Mrs. Martin?"

"I killed *him* first, the son of a bitch."

"Who do you mean, Mrs. Martin?"

"My husband."

"When was this?"

"When he came home."

"What time was that, do you remember?"

"A little while ago."

"It's almost four o'clock now," Kling said. "Would you say this was at, what, three-thirty or thereabouts?"

"I didn't look at the clock," she said. "I heard his key in the latch, and I went in the kitchen, and there he was."

"Yes?"

"There's a meat cleaver I keep on the sink. I hit him with it."

"Why did you do that, Mrs. Martin?"

"Because I wanted to."

"Were you arguing with him, is that it?"

"No. He was locking the door, and I just went over to the sink and picked up the cleaver, and then I hit him with it."

"Where did you hit him, Mrs. Martin?"

"On his head and on his neck and I think on his shoulder."

"You hit him three times with the cleaver?"

"I hit him a lot of times, I don't know how many times."

"Were you aware that you were hitting him?"

"Yes, I was aware."

"You knew you were striking him with a cleaver."

"Yes, I knew."

"Did you intend to kill him with the cleaver?"

"I intended to kill him with the cleaver."

"And afterwards, did you know you had killed him?"

"I knew he was dead, yes, the son of a bitch."

"What did you do then?"

"My oldest child came into the kitchen. Peter. My son. He yelled at me, he wanted to know what I'd done, he kept yelling at me. I hit him, too, to get him to shut up. I hit him only once, across the throat."

"Did you know what you were doing at the time?"

"I knew what I was doing. He was *another* one, that Peter. Little bastard."

"What happened next, Mrs. Martin?"

"I went in the back bedroom where the two girls sleep, and I hit Annie with the cleaver first, and then I hit Abigail."

"Where did you hit them, Mrs. Martin?"

"On the face. Their faces."

"How many times?"

"I think I hit Annie twice, and Abigail only once."

"Why did you do that, Mrs. Martin?"

"Who would take care of them after I was gone?" Mrs. Martin asked of no one.

"Is there anything else you want to tell us?" Kling asked.

"There's nothing more to tell. I done the right thing."

The detectives walked away from the desk. They were both pale. "Man," O'Brien whispered.

"Yeah," Kling said. "We'd better call the night D.A. right away, get him to take a full confession from her."

"Killed four of them without batting an eyelash," O'Brien said, and shook his head, and went back to where the stenographer was typing up Mrs. Martin's statement.

The telephone was ringing. Kling walked to the nearest desk and lifted the receiver. "Eighty-seventh Squad, Detective Kling," he said.

"This is Donner."

"Yeah, Fats."

"I think I got a lead on one of those heaps."

"Shoot."

"This would be the one heisted on Fourteenth Street. According to the dope I've got, it happened yesterday morning. Does that check out?"

"I'll have to look at the bulletin again. Go ahead, Fats."

"It's already been ditched," Donner said. "If you're looking for it, try outside the electric company on the River Road."

"Thanks, I'll make a note of that. Who stole it, Fats?"

"This is strictly *entre nous*," Donner said. "I don't want *no* tie-in with it *never*. The guy who done it is a mean little bastard, rip out his mother's heart for a dime. He hates niggers, killed two of them in a street rumble four years ago, and managed to beat the rap. I think maybe some officer was on the take, huh, Kling?"

"You can't square homicide in this city, and you know it, Fats."

"Yeah? I'm surprised. You can square damn near anything else for a couple of bills."

"What's his name?"

"Danny Ryder. 3541 Grover Avenue, near the park. You won't find him there now, though."

"Where *will* I find him now?"

"Ten minutes ago, he was in an all-night bar on Mason, place called Felicia's. You going in after him?"

"I am."

"Take your gun," Donner said.

There were seven people in Felicia's when Kling got there at a quarter to five. He cased the bar through the plate glass window fronting the place, unbuttoned the third button of his overcoat, reached in to clutch the butt of his revolver, worked it out of the holster once and then back again, and went in through the front door.

There was the immediate smell of stale cigarette smoke and beer and sweat and cheap perfume. A Puerto Rican girl was in whispered consultation with a sailor in one of the leatherette booths. Another sailor was hunched over the jukebox, thoughtfully considering his next selection, his face tinted orange and red and green from the colored tubing. A tired, fat, fifty-year-old blonde sat at the far end of the bar, watching the sailor as though the next button he pushed might destroy the entire world. The bartender was polishing glasses. He looked up when King walked in and immediately smelled the law.

Two men were seated at the opposite end of the bar.

One of them was wearing a blue turtleneck sweater, gray slacks, and desert boots. His brown hair was cut close to his scalp in a military cut. The other man was wearing a bright orange team jacket, almost luminous, with the words *Orioles, S.A.C.* lettered across its back in Old English script. The one with the crew cut said something softly, and the other one chuckled. Behind the bar, a glass clinked as the bartender replaced it on the shelf. The jukebox erupted in sound, Jimi Hendrix rendering "All Along the Watchtower."

Kling walked over to the two men.

"Which one of you is Danny Ryder?" he asked.

The one with the short hair said, "Who wants to know?"

"Police officer," Kling said, and the one in the orange jacket whirled with a pistol in his hand, and Kling's eyes opened wide in surprise, and the gun went off.

There was no time to think, there was hardly any time to breathe. The explosion of the gun was shockingly close, the acrid stink of cordite rushed into his nostrils. The knowledge that he was still alive, the sweet rushing clean awareness that the bullet had somehow missed him was only a fleeting click of intelligence accompanying what was essentially a reflexive act. The .38 came free of its holster, his finger was inside the trigger guard and around the trigger, he squeezed off his shot almost before the gun had cleared the flap of his overcoat, fired into the orange jacket and threw his shoulder simultaneously against the chest of the man with the short hair, knocking him backward off his stool. The man in the orange jacket, his face twisted in pain, was leveling the gun for another shot. Kling fired again, squeezing the trigger without thought or rancor, and then whirling on the man with the short hair, who was crouched on the floor against the bar.

"Get up!" he yelled.

"Don't shoot."

"Get up, you son of a bitch!"

He yanked the man to his feet, hurled him against the bar, thrust the muzzle of his pistol at the blue turtleneck sweater, ran his hands under the armpits and between the legs while the man kept saying over and over again, "Don't shoot, please don't shoot."

He backed away from him and leaned over the one in the orange jacket.

"Is this Ryder?" he asked.

"Yes."

"Who're you?"

"Frank . . . Frank Pasquale. Look, I . . ."

"Shut up, Frank," Kling said. "Put your hands behind your back! Move!"

He had already taken his handcuffs from his belt. He snapped them onto Pasquale's wrist now, and only then became aware that Jimi Hendrix was still singing, the sailors were watching with pale white faces, the Puerto Rican girl was screaming, the fat faded blonde had her mouth open, the bartender was frozen in mid-motion, the tip of his bar towel inside a glass.

"All right," Kling said. He was breathing harshly. "All right," he said again, and wiped his forehead.

Timothy Allen Ames was a pot-bellied man of forty, with a thick black mustache, a mane of long black hair, and brown eyes sharply alert at five minutes past five in the morning. He answered the door as though he'd been already awake, asked for identification, and then asked the detectives to wait a moment, and closed the door, and came back shortly afterwards, wearing a robe over his striped pajamas.

"Is your name Timothy Ames?" Carella asked.

"That's me," Ames said. "Little late to be paying a visit, ain't it?"

"Or early, depending how you look at it," Hawes said.

"One thing I can do without at five A.M. is humorous cops," Ames said. "How'd you get up here, anyway? Is that little jerk asleep at the desk again?"

"Who do you mean?" Carella asked.

"Lonnie Sanford, whatever the hell his name is."

"Ronnie Sanford."

"Yeah, him. Little bastard's always giving me trouble."

"What kind of trouble?"

"About broads," Ames said. "Acts like he's running a nunnery here, can't stand to see a guy come in with a girl. I notice he ain't got no compunctions about letting *cops* upstairs, though, no matter *what* time it is."

"Never mind Sanford, let's talk about you," Carella said.

"Sure, what would you like to know?"

"Where were you between eleven-twenty and twelve o'clock to-night?"

"Right here."

"Can you prove it?"

"Sure. I got back here about eleven o'clock, and I been here since. Ask Sanford downstairs . . . no, never mind, he wasn't on yet. He don't come on till midnight."

"Who *else* can we ask, Ames?"

"Listen, you going to make trouble for me?"

"Only if you're *in* trouble."

"I got a broad here. She's over eighteen, don't worry. But, like, she's a junkie, you know? She ain't holding or nothing, but I know you guys, and if you want to make trouble . . ."

"Where is she?"

"In the john."

"Get her out here."

"Look, do me a favor, will you? Don't bust the kid. She's trying to kick the habit, she really is. I been helping her along."

"How?"

"By keeping her busy," Ames said, and winked.

"Call her."

"Bea, come out here!" Ames shouted.

There was a moment's hesitation, and then the bathroom door opened. The girl was a tall, plain brunette wearing a short terry cloth robe. She sidled into the room cautiously, as though expecting to be struck in the face at any moment. Her brown eyes were wide with expectancy. She knew fuzz, and she knew what it was like to be busted on a narcotics charge, and she had listened to the conversation from behind the closed bathroom door, and now she waited for whatever was coming, expecting the worst.

"What's your name, miss?" Hawes asked.

"Beatrice Norden."

"What time did you get here tonight, Beatrice?"

"About eleven."

"Was this man with you?"

"Yes."

"Did he leave here at any time tonight?"

"No."

"Are you sure?"

"I'm positive. He picked me up about nine o'clock . . ."

"Where do you live, Beatrice?"

"Well, that's the thing, you see," the girl said. "I been put out of my room."

"So where'd he pick you up?"

"At my girl friend's house. You can ask her, she was there when he came. Her name is Rosalie Dewes. Anyway, Timmy picked me up at nine, and we went to eat Chink's, and we came up here around eleven."

"I hope you're telling us the truth, Miss Norden," Carella said.

"I swear to God, we been here all night," Beatrice answered.

"All right, Ames," Hawes said, "we'd like a sample of your handwriting."

"My *what?*"

"Your handwriting."

"What for?"

"We collect autographs," Carella said.

"Gee, these guys really break me up," Ames said to the girl. "Regular night-club comics we get in the middle of the night."

Carella handed him a pen and then tore a sheet from his pad. "You want to write this for me?" he said. "The first part's in block lettering."

"What the hell is block lettering?" Ames asked.

"He means *print* it," Hawes said.

"Then why didn't he say so?"

"Put on your clothes, miss," Carella said.

"What for?" Beatrice said. "I mean, the thing is, I was in bed when you guys . . ."

"That's what I want him to write," Carella explained.

"Oh."

"Put on your clothes, miss," Ames repeated, and lettered it onto the sheet of paper. "What else?" he asked, looking up.

"Now sign it in your own handwriting with the following words: The Avenging Angel."

"What the hell is this supposed to be?" Ames asked.

"You want to write it, please?"

Ames wrote the words, and then handed the slip of paper to Carella. He and Hawes compared it with the note that had been mailed to Mercy Howell:

PUT ON YOUR
CLOSE, MISS!

The Avenging Angel

PUT ON YOUR CLOTHES,
MISS.

The Avenging Angel

"So?" Ames asked.

"So you're clean," Hawes said.

"Imagine if I was dirty," Ames answered.

At the desk downstairs, Ronnie Sanford was still immersed in his accounting textbook. He got to his feet again as the detectives came out of the elevator, adjusted his glasses on his nose, and then said, "Any luck?"

"Afraid not," Carella answered. "We're going to need this register for a while, if that's okay."

"Well . . ."

"Give him a receipt for it, Cotton," Carella said. It was late, and he didn't want a debate in the lobby of a run-down hotel. Hawes quickly made out a receipt in duplicate, signed both copies and handed one to Sanford.

"What about this torn cover?" Hawes asked belatedly.

"Yeah," Carella said. There was a small rip on the leather binding of the book, and he fingered it briefly now, and then said, "Better note that on the receipt, Cotton." Hawes took back the receipt and, on both copies, jotted the words "Small rip on front cover." He handed the receipts back to Sanford.

"Want to just sign these, Mr. Sanford?" he said.

"What for?" Sanford asked.

"To indicate we received the register in this condition."

"Oh, sure," Sanford said. He picked up a ball-point pen from its desk holder, and asked. "What do you want me to write?"

"Your name and your title, that's all."

"My title?"

"Night Clerk, The Addison Hotel."

"Oh, sure," Sanford said, and signed both receipts, "This okay?" he asked. The detectives looked at what he had written.

"You like girls?" Carella asked suddenly.

"What?" Sanford asked.

"Girls," Hawes said.

"Sure. Sure, I like girls."

"Dressed or naked?"

"What?"

"With clothes or without?"

"I . . . I don't know what you mean, sir."

"Where were you tonight between eleven-twenty and midnight?" Hawes asked.

"Getting . . . getting ready to come to . . . to work," Sanford
said.

"You sure you weren't in the alley of the Eleventh Street Theater
stabbing a girl named Mercy Howell?"

"What? No . . . no, of course . . . of course not. I was . . . I was
. . . I was home . . . getting . . . getting dressed . . . to . . .
to . . ." Sanford took a deep breath and decided to get indignant.
"Listen, what's this all about?" he said. "Would you mind telling
me?"

"It's all about *this*," Carella said, and turned one of the receipts
so that Sanford could read the signature:

Ronald Sanford
Night Clerk
The Addison Hotel

"Get your hat," Hawes said. "Study hall's over."

It was twenty-five minutes past five when Adele Gorman came
into the room with Meyer's cup of tea. He was crouched near the
air-conditioning unit recessed into the wall to the left of the drapes,
and he glanced over his shoulder when he heard her, and then rose.

"I didn't know what you took," she said, "so I brought everything."

"Thank you," he said. "Just a little milk and sugar is fine."

"Have you measured the room?" she asked, and put the tray
down on the table in front of the sofa.

"Yes, I think I have everything I need now," Meyer said. He
put a spoonful of sugar into the tea, stirred it, added a drop of
milk, stirred it again, and then lifted the cup to his mouth. "Hot,"
he said.

Adele Gorman was watching him silently. She said nothing. He
kept sipping his tea. The ornate clock on the mantelpiece ticked in a
swift whispering tempo.

"Do you always keep this room so dim?" Meyer asked.

"Well, my husband is blind, you know," Adele said. "There's
really no need for brighter light."

"Mmm. But your father reads in this room, doesn't he?"

"I beg your pardon?"

"The night you came home from that party. He was sitting in the chair over there near the floor lamp. Reading. Remember?"

"Oh. Yes, he was."

"Bad light to read by."

"Yes, I suppose it is."

"I think maybe those bulbs are defective," Meyer said.

"Do you think so?"

"Mmm. I happened to look at the lamp, and there are three hundred-watt bulbs in it, all of them burning. You should be getting a lot more illumination with that kind of wattage."

"Well, I really don't know too much about . . ."

"Unless the lamp is on a rheostat, of course."

"I'm afraid I don't know what a rheostat is."

"It's an adjustable resistor. You can dim your lights or make them brighter with it. I thought maybe the lamp was on a rheostat, but I couldn't find a control knob anywhere in the room." Meyer paused. "You wouldn't know if there's a rheostat control someplace in the house, would you?"

"I'm sure there isn't," Adele said.

"Must be defective bulbs then," Meyer said, and smiled. "Also, I think your air conditioner is broken."

"No, I'm sure it isn't."

"Well, I was just looking at it, and all the switches are turned to the 'On' position, but it isn't working. So I guess it's broken. That's a shame, too, because it's such a nice unit. Sixteen thousand BTUs. That's a lot of cooling power for a room this size. We've got one of those big old price-fixed apartments on Concord, my wife and I, with a large bedroom, and we get adequate cooling from a half-ton unit. It's a shame this one is broken."

"Yes. Detective Meyer, I don't wish to appear rude, but it *is* late . . ."

"Sure," Meyer said. "Unless, of course, the air conditioner's on a remote switch, too. So that all you have to do is turn a knob in another part of the house and it comes on." He paused. "*Is* there such a switch someplace, Mrs. Gorman?"

"I have no idea."

"I'll just finish my tea and run along," Meyer said. He lifted the cup to his lips sipped at the tea, glanced at her over the rim, took the cup away from his mouth, and said, "But I'll be back."

"I hardly think there's any need for that," Adele said.

"Well, some jewelry's been stolen . . ."

"The ghosts . . ."

"Come off it, Mrs. Gorman."

The room went silent.

"Where are the loudspeakers, Mrs. Gorman?" Meyer asked. "In the false beams up there? They're hollow, I checked them out."

"I think perhaps you'd better leave," Adele said slowly.

"Sure," Meyer said. He put the teacup down, sighed, and got to his feet.

"I'll show you out," Adele said.

They walked to the front door and out into the driveway. The night was still. The drizzle had stopped, and a thin layer of frost covered the grass rolling away toward the river below. Their footsteps crunched on the gravel as they walked slowly toward the automobile.

"My husband was blinded four years ago," Adele said abruptly. "He's a chemical engineer, there was an explosion at the plant, he could have been killed. Instead, he was only blinded." She hesitated an instant, and then said again, "Only blinded," and there was such a sudden cry of despair in those two words that Meyer wanted to put his arm around her, console her the way he might his daughter, tell her that everything would be all right come morning, the night was almost done, and morning was on the horizon. He leaned on the fender of his car, and she stood beside him looking down at the driveway gravel, her eyes not meeting his. They could have been conspirators exchanging secrets in the night, but they were only two people who had been thrown together on a premise as flimsy as the ghosts that inhabited this house.

"He gets a disability pension from the company," Adele said, "they've really been quite kind to us. And, of course, I work. I teach school, Detective Meyer. Kindergarten. I love children." She paused. She would not raise her eyes to meet his. "But . . . it's sometimes very difficult. My father, you see . . ."

Meyer waited. He longed suddenly for dawn, but he waited patiently, and heard her catch her breath as though committed to go ahead now, however painful the revelation might be, compelled to throw herself upon the mercy of the night before the morning sun broke through.

"My father's been retired for fifteen years." She took a deep breath, and then said, "He gambles, Detective Meyer. He's a horse player. He loses large sums of money."

"Is that why he stole your jewels?" Meyer asked.

"You know, don't you?" Adele said simply, and raised her eyes to his. "Of course you know. It's quite transparent, his ruse, a shoddy little show really, a performance that would fool no one but . . . no one but a blind man." She brushed at her cheek; he could not tell whether the cold air had caused her sudden tears. "I . . . I really don't care about the theft, the jewels were left to me by my mother, and after all it was my father who bought them for her, so it's . . . it's really like returning a legacy, I really don't care about that part of it. I . . . I'd have *given* the jewelry to him if only he'd asked, but he's so proud, such a proud man. A proud man who . . . who steals from me and pretends that ghosts are committing the crime. And my husband, in his dark universe, listens to the sounds my father puts on tape and visualizes things he cannot quite believe and so he asks me to contact the police because he needs an impartial observer to contradict the suspicion that someone is stealing pennies from his blind man's cup. That's why I came to you, Detective Meyer. So that you would arrive here tonight and perhaps be fooled as I was fooled at first, and perhaps say to my husband, 'Yes, Mr. Gorman, there *are* ghosts in your house.'" She suddenly placed her hand on his sleeve. The tears were streaming down her face, she had difficulty catching her breath. "Because you see, Detective Meyer, there *are* ghosts in this house, there really and truly are. The ghost of a proud man who was once a brilliant judge and lawyer and who is now a gambler and a thief; and the ghost of a man who once could see, and who now trips and falls in . . . in the darkness."

On the river, a tugboat hooted. Adele Gorman fell silent. Meyer opened the door of his car and got in behind the wheel.

"I'll call your husband tomorrow," he said abruptly and gruffly. "Tell him I'm convinced something supernatural is happening here."

"And will you be back, Detective Meyer?"

"No," he said. "I won't be back, Mrs. Gorman."

In the squadroom, they were wrapping up the night. Their day had begun at 7:45 P.M. yesterday, and they had been officially relieved at 5:45 A.M., but they had not left the office yet because there were still questions to be asked, reports to be typed, odds and ends to put in place before they could go home. And since the relieving detectives were busy getting *their* approaching workday organized, the squadroom at 6 A.M. was busier than it might have been on any given afternoon, with two teams of cops getting in each other's way.

In the Interrogation Room, Carella and Hawes were questioning young Ronald Sanford in the presence of the assistant district attorney who had come over earlier to take Mrs. Martin's confession, and who now found himself listening to another one when all he wanted to do was go home to sleep. Sanford seemed terribly shocked that they had been able to notice the identical handwriting in "The Addison Hotel" and "The Avenging Angel," he couldn't get over it. He thought he had been very clever in misspelling the word "clothes," because then if they ever *had* traced the note, they would think some illiterate had written it, and not someone who was studying to be an accountant. He could not explain why he had killed Mercy Howell. He got all mixed up when he tried to explain that. It had something to do with the moral climate of America, and people exposing themselves in public, people like that shouldn't be allowed to pollute others, to foist their filth upon others, to intrude upon the privacy of others who only wanted to make a place for themselves in the world, who were trying so very hard to make something of themselves, studying accounting by day and working in a hotel by night, what right had these other people to ruin it for everybody else?

Frank Pasquale's tune, sung in the Clerical Office to Kling and O'Brien, was not quite so hysterical, but similar to Sanford's nonetheless. He had got the idea together with Danny Ryder. They had decided between them that the niggers in America were getting too damn pushy, shoving their way in where they didn't belong, taking jobs away from decent hard-working people who only wanted to be left alone, what right did they have to force themselves on everybody else? So they had decided to bomb the church, just to show the goddamn boogies that you couldn't get away with shit like that, not in America. He didn't seem too terribly concerned over the fact that his partner was lying stone cold dead on a slab at the morgue, or that their little Culver Avenue expedition had cost three people their lives, and had severely injured a half-dozen others. All he wanted to know, repeatedly, was whether his picture would be in the newspaper.

At his desk, Meyer Meyer started to type up a report on the Gorman ghosts, and then decided the hell with it. If the lieutenant asked him where he'd been half the night, he would say he had been out cruising, looking for trouble in the streets. Christ knew there was enough of *that* around. He pulled the report forms and their separating sheets of carbon paper from the ancient typewriter, and noticed that Detective Hal Willis was pacing the room anxiously, waiting to get at the desk the moment he vacated it.

"Okay, Hal," he said, "it's all yours."

"Finalmente!" Willis, who was not Italian, said.

The telephone rang.

The sun was up when they came out of the building and walked past the hanging green "87" globes and down the low flat steps to the sidewalk. The park across the street shimmered with early morning autumn brilliance, the sky above it clear and blue. It was going to be a beautiful day. They walked toward the diner on the next block, Meyer and O'Brien ahead of the others, Carella, Hawes, and Kling bringing up the rear. They were tired, and exhaustion showed in their eyes and in the set of their mouths, and in the pace they kept. They talked without animation, mostly about their work, their breaths feathery and white on the cold morning air. When they reached the diner, they took off their overcoats and ordered hot coffee and cheese Danish and toasted English muffins. Meyer said he thought he was coming down with a cold. Carella told him about some cough medicine his wife had given one of the children. O'Brien, munching on a muffin, glanced across the diner and saw a young girl in one of the booths. She was wearing blue jeans and a brightly colored Mexican serape, and she was talking to a boy wearing a Navy pea jacket.

"I think I see somebody," he said, and he moved out of the booth past Kling and Hawes, who were talking about the new goddamn regulation on search and seizure.

The girl looked up when he approached the booth.

"Miss Blair?" he said. "Penelope Blair?"

"Yes," the girl answered. "Who are you?"

"Detective O'Brien," he said, "the Eighty-seventh Squad. Your mother was in last night, Penny. She asked me to tell you . . ."

"Flake off, cop," Penelope Blair said. "Go stop a riot some-place."

O'Brien looked at her silently for a moment. He nodded then, and turned away, and went back to the table.

"Anything?" Kling asked.

"You can't win 'em all," O'Brien said.

2

DAYWATCH

THE BOY who lay naked on the concrete in the backyard of the tenement was perhaps eighteen years old. He wore his hair quite long, and he had recently begun growing a beard. His hair and his beard were black. His body was very white, and the blood that oozed onto the concrete pavement beneath him was very red.

The superintendent of the building discovered him at two minutes before 6 A.M., when he went to put his garbage in one of the cans out back. The boy was lying face down in his own blood, and the super did not recognize him. He was shocked, of course. He did not ordinarily discover naked dead men in the backyard when he went to put out his garbage. But considering his shock, and considering his advanced age (he was approaching eighty), he managed to notify the police with considerable dispatch, something not every good citizen of the city managed to do quite so well or so speedily.

Hal Willis arrived on the scene at fifteen minutes past six, accompanied by Richard Genero, who was the newest man on the squad, having been recently promoted from patrolman to Detective 3rd/Grade. Forbes and Phelps, the two men from Homicide, were already there. It was Willis' contention that any pair of Homicide cops was the same as any other pair of Homicide cops. He had never, for example, seen Forbes and Phelps in the same room with Monoghan and Monroe. Was this not undeniable proof that they were one and the same couple? Moreover, it seemed to Willis that all Homicide cops exchanged clothing regularly, and that Forbes and Phelps could on any given day of the week be found wearing suits and overcoats belonging to Monoghan and Monroe.

"Good morning," Willis said.

"Morning," Phelps said.

Forbes grunted.

"Nice way to start a goddamn Sunday, right?" Phelps asked.

"You fellows got here pretty fast," Genero said.

Forbes looked at him. "Who're you?"

"Dick Genero."

"Never heard of you," Forbes said.

"I never heard of you, neither," Genero answered, and glanced to Willis for approval.

"Who's the dead man?" Willis asked drily. "Anybody ever hear of *him?*"

"He sure as hell ain't carrying any identification," Phelps said, and cackled hoarsely.

"Not unless he's got it shoved up his ass someplace," Forbes said, and began laughing along with his partner.

"Who found the body?" Willis asked.

"Building superintendent."

"Want to get him, Dick?"

"Right," Genero said, and walked off.

"I hate to start my day like this," Phelps said.

"Grisly," Forbes said.

"All I had this morning was a cup of coffee," Phelps said. "And now *this*. Disgusting."

"Nauseating," Forbes said.

"Least have the decency to put on some goddamn clothes before he jumps off the roof," Phelps said.

"How do you know he jumped off the roof?" Willis asked.

"I don't. I'm only saying."

"What do you *think* he was doing?" Forbes asked. "Walking around the backyard naked?"

"I don't know," Willis said, and shrugged.

"Looks like a jumper to me," Phelps said. He glanced up at the rear wall of the building. "Isn't that a broken window up there?"

"Where?"

"Fourth floor there. Isn't that window broken there?"

"Looks like it," Forbes said.

"Sure looks like it to me," Phelps said.

"Hal, here's the super," Genero said, approaching with the old man. "Name's Mr. Dennison, been working here for close to thirty years."

"How do you do, Mr. Dennison? I'm Detective Willis."

Dennison nodded and said nothing.

"I understand you found the body."

"That's right."

"When was that?"

"Just before I called the cops."

"What time was that, Mr. Dennison?"

"Little after six, I guess."

"Know who it is?"

"Can't see his face," Dennison said.

"We'll roll him over for you as soon as the M.E. gets here," Genero said.

"Don't do me no favors," Dennison answered.

Unlike patrolmen, detectives—with the final approval of the Chief downtown—decide upon their own work schedules. As a result, the shifts will vary according to the whims of the men on the squad. For the past three months, and based on the dubious assumption that the night shift was more arduous than the day, the detectives of the 87th Squad had broken their working hours into two shifts, the first beginning at six in the morning and ending at eight in the evening, the second beginning then and ending at six the next day. The daywatch was fourteen hours long, the nightwatch only ten. But there were more men on duty during the day, and presumably this equalized the load. That some of those men were testifying in court or out on special assignments some of the time seemed not to bother any of the detectives, who considered the schedule equitable. At least for the time being. In another month or so, someone would come up with suggestions for a revised schedule, and they'd hold a meeting in the Interrogation Office and agree that they ought to try something new. A change was as good as a rest, provided the Chief approved.

As with any schedule, though, there were ways of beating it if you tried hard enough. Relieving the departing team at fifteen minutes before the hour was a mandatory courtesy, and one way of avoiding a 5:45 A.M. arrival at the squadroom was to plant yourself in a grocery store that did not open its doors until six-thirty. Detective Andy Parker found himself just such a grocery store on this bright October morning. The fact that the store had been robbed three times in broad daylight during the past month was only incidental. The point was that *some* detective had to cover the joint, and Andy Parker fortuitously happened to *be* that detective. The first thing he did to ingratiate himself with the owner was to swipe an apple from the fruit stand outside the store. The owner, one Silvio Corradini, who was sharp of eye for all his seventy-two years, noticed the petty larceny the moment it was committed. He was about to run out on the sidewalk to apprehend the brigand, when the man began walking directly into the store, eating the apple as he came. It was then that Silvio realized the man could be nothing but a cop.

"Good morning," Parker said.

"Good morning," Silvio replied. "You enjoy the fruit?"

"Yeah, very good apple," Parker said. "Thanks a lot." He grinned amiably. "I'm Detective Parker," he said, "I've been assigned to these holdups."

"What happened to the other detective?"

"Di Maeo? He's on vacation."

"In October?"

"We can't all get the summertime, huh?" Parker said, and grinned again. He was a huge man wearing rumpled brown corduroy trousers and a soiled tan windbreaker. He had shaved this morning before eating breakfast, but he managed to look unshaven nonetheless. He bit into the apple ferociously, juice spilling onto his chin. Silvio, watching him, thought he resembled a hired gun for the Mafia.

"Lei è italiano?" he asked.

"What?"

"Are you Italian?"

"No, are you?" Parker said, and grinned.

"Yes," Silvio answered. He drew back his shoulders. "Yes, I'm Italian."

"Well, good, good," Parker said. "You always open the store on Sunday?"

"What?"

"I said : . ."

"I only stay open till twelve o'clock, that's all," Silvio said, and shrugged. "I get the people coming home from church."

"That's against the law in this state, you know that?"

"Nobody ever said anything."

"Well, just because somebody's willing to look the other way every now and then, that doesn't make it legal," Parker said. He stared deep into Silvio's eyes. "We'll talk about it later, huh? Meantime, fill me in on these holdups, okay?"

Silvio hesitated. He knew that talking about it later would cost him money. He was beginning to be sorry he'd ever told the police about the holdups. He sighed now and said, "It is three times in the past month."

"Same guy each time?"

"Two of them. I don't know if it's the same. They are wearing— *come si dice? Maschere."*

"Masks?"

"Si, masks."

"Same masks each time?"

"No. Once it was stockings, another time black ones, the third time handkerchiefs."

Parker bit into the apple again. "Are they armed?" he asked.

"If they did not have guns, I would break their heads and throw them out on the sidewalk."

"Handguns?" Parker asked.

"What?"

"Pistols?"

"Yes, yes, pistols."

"Both of them armed, or just one?"

"Both."

"What time do they usually come in?"

"Different times. The first time was early in the morning, when I just opened the store. The next time was at night, maybe six, six-thirty. The last time was around lunch, the store was very quiet."

"Did they take anything but cash?"

"Only cash."

"Well," Parker said, and shrugged. "Maybe they'll come back, who knows? If you don't mind, I'll just hang around, okay? You got a back room or something?"

"Behind the curtain," Silvio said. "But if they come back again, I am ready for them myself."

"What do you mean?"

"I got a gun now."

He walked behind the counter to the cash register, opened it, and removed from the drawer a .32 Smith & Wesson.

"You need a permit for that, you know," Parker said.

"I got one. A man gets held up three times, nobody argues about giving him a permit."

"Carry or premises?"

"Premises."

"You know how to use that thing?" Parker asked.

"I know how, yes."

"I've got some advice for you," Parker said. "If those hoods come back, leave your gun in the drawer. Let *me* take care of any shooting needs to be done."

A woman was coming into the store. Without answering, Silvio turned away from Parker, smiled, and said to her, *"Buon giorno, signora."*

Parker sighed, threw the curtain back, and went into the other room.

"What do you think?" Willis asked the assistant medical examiner.

"Fell or was pushed from someplace up there," the M.E. said. "Split his skull wide open when he hit the ground. Probably dead on impact."

"Anything else?"

"What more do you want? You're lucky we haven't got an omelette here." He snapped his bag shut, rose from where he was crouched beside the body, and said, "I'm finished, you can do what you like with him."

"Thanks, Al," Willis said.

"Yeah," the M.E. answered, and walked off.

The body was now lying on its back. Genero looked down at the open skull and turned away. Dennison, the building superintendent, walked over with his hands in the pockets of his bib overalls. He looked down at the boy's bloody face and nodded.

"That's the kid in 4C," he said.

"What's his name?"

"Scott."

"That the first name or the last?"

"The last. I got his first name written down someplace inside. I got all the tenants' names written down. You want me to look it up for you?"

"Would you please?"

"Sure," Dennison said.

"Would that be 4C up there?" Willis asked. "The apartment with the broken window?"

"That's it, all right," Dennison said.

The telephone on Arthur Brown's desk was ringing. He lifted the receiver, tucked it between his shoulder and his ear, said, "Eighty-seventh Squad, Detective Brown," and then glanced toward the slatted rail divider, where a patrolman was leading a handcuffed prisoner into the squadroom.

"Is this a detective?" the woman on the telephone asked.

"Yes, ma'am, Detective Brown."

"I want to report a missing person," the woman said.

"Yes, ma'am, just one second, please."

Brown opened his desk drawer, took out a block of wood to which was attached the key to the detention cage across the room, and flipped it to the patrolman, who missed the catch. The prisoner laughed. The patrolman picked up the key, led the prisoner to the cage, opened the grillwork door, and shoved him inside.

"Take it easy, man," the prisoner warned.

The patrolman locked the cage door without answering him. Then he walked to Brown's desk and sat on the edge of it, tilting his peaked cap back on his forehead and lighting a cigarette. On the telephone, Brown was saying, "Now, what's your name, please, ma'am?"

"Mary Ellingham. Mrs. Donald Ellingham."

"Would you spell that for me, please?"

"E-L-L . . ."

"Yep . . ."

". . . I-N-G, H-A-M."

"And your address, Mrs. Ellingham?"

"742 North Trinity."

"All right, who's missing, Mrs. Ellingham?"

"My husband."

"That his full name? Donald Ellingham?"

"Yes. Well, no. Donald *E*. Ellingham. For Edward."

"Yes, ma'am. How long has he been gone?"

"He was gone a week this past Friday."

"Has this ever happened before, Mrs. Ellingham?"

"No. Never."

"He's never been gone before? Never any unexplained absences?"

"Never."

"And you say he's been missing since, let's see, that'd be Friday the ninth?"

"Yes."

"Did he go to work on Monday morning? The twelfth?"

"No."

"You called his office?"

"Yes, I did."

"And he wasn't there."

"He hasn't been there all week."

"Why'd you wait till today to report this, Mrs. Ellingham?"

"I wanted to give him a chance to come back. I kept extending the deadline, you see. I thought I'd give him a few days, and then it turned into a week, and then I thought I'd give him just another day, and then Saturday went by, and . . . well, I decided to call today."

"Does your husband drink, Mrs. Ellingham?"

"No. That is, he drinks, but not excessively. He's not an alcoholic, if that's what you mean."

"Has there ever been any problem with . . . well . . . other women?"

"No."

"What I'm trying to say, Mrs. Ellingham . . ."

"Yes, I understand. I don't think he's run off with another woman, no."

"What *do* you think has happened, Mrs. Ellingham?"

"I'm afraid he's been in an accident."

"Have you contacted the various hospitals in the city?"

"Yes. He's not at any of them."

"But you still think he may have been in an accident."

"I think he may be dead someplace," Mrs. Ellingham said, and began weeping.

Brown was silent. He looked up at the patrolman.

"Mrs. Ellingham?"

"Yes."

"I'll try to get over there later today if I can, to get the information I'll need for the Missing Persons Bureau. Will you be home?"

"Yes."

"Shall I call first?"

"No, I'll be here all day."

"Fine, I'll see you later then. If you should hear anything mean-while . . ."

"Yes, I'll call you."

"Good-by, Mrs. Ellingham," Brown said, and hung up. "Lady's husband disappeared," he said to the patrolman.

"Went down for a loaf of bread a year ago, right?" the patrolman said.

"Right. Hasn't been heard from since." Brown gestured toward the detention cage. "Who's the prize across the room?"

"Caught him cold in the middle of a burglary on Fifth and Friedlander. On a third-floor fire escape. Jimmied open the window, and was just entering."

"Any tools on him?"

"Yep. I left them on the bench outside."

"Want to get them for me?"

The patrolman went out into the corridor. Brown walked over to the detention cage. The prisoner looked at him.

"What's your name?" Brown asked.

"What's yours?"

"Detective Arthur Brown."

"That's appropriate," the prisoner said.

"I find it so," Brown said coolly. "Now what's yours?"

"Frederick Spaeth."

The patrolman came back into the room carrying a leather bag containing a hand drill and bits of various sizes, a jimmy, a complete set of picklocks, several punches and skeleton keys, a pair of nippers, a hacksaw, a pair of brown cotton gloves, and a crowbar designed so that it could be taken apart and carried in three sections. Brown looked over the tools and said nothing.

"I'm a carpenter," Spaeth said in explanation.

Brown turned to the patrolman. "Anybody in the apartment, Simms?"

"Empty," Simms replied.

"Spaeth," Brown said, "we're charging you with burglary in the third degree, which is a felony. And we're also charging you with Possession of Burglar's Instruments, which is a Class-A Misdemeanor. Take him down, Simms."

"I want a lawyer," Spaeth said.

"You're entitled to one," Brown said.

"I want him *now*. *Before* you book me."

Because policemen are sometimes as confused by Miranda-Escobedo as are laymen, Brown might have followed the course pursued by his colleague Kling, who, the night before, had advised a prisoner of his rights even though cruising radio patrolmen had arrested him in the act. Instead, Brown said, "What for, Spaeth? You were apprehended entering an apartment illegally. Nobody's asking you any questions, we caught you cold. You'll be allowed three telephone calls after you're booked, to your lawyer, your mother, your bail bondsman, your best friend, whoever the hell you like. Take him down, Simms."

Simms unlocked the cage and prodded Spaeth out of it with his nightstick. "That is illegal!" Spaeth shouted.

"So's breaking and entry," Brown answered.

The woman in the apartment across the hall from 4C was taller than both Willis and Genero, which was understandable. Hal Willis was the shortest man on the squad, having cleared the minimum five-feet-eight-inch height requirement by a scant quarter of an inch. Built like a soft shoe dancer, brown-haired and brown-eyed, he stood alongside Genero, who towered over him at five feet nine inches. Hal Willis knew he was short. Richard Genero thought he was very tall. From his father, he had inherited beautiful curly black hair and a strong Neapolitan nose, a sensuous mouth and soulful brown eyes. From his mother, he had inherited the tall Milanese carriage of all his male cousins and uncles—except Uncle Dominick, who was only five feet six. But this lady who opened the door to apartment 4B was a very big lady indeed. Both Willis and Genero looked up at her simultaneously, and then glanced at each other in something like stupefied awe. The lady was wearing a pink slip and nothing else. Barefooted, big-breasted, redheaded, green-eyed, she put her hands on her nylon-sheathed hips and said, "Yeah?"

"Police officers," Willis said, and showed her his shield.

The woman scrutinized it, and then said, "Yeah?"

"We'd like to ask you a few questions," Genero said.

"What about?"

"About the young man across the hall. Lewis Scott."

"What about him?"

"Do you know him?"

"Slightly."

"Only slightly?" Genero said. "You live directly across the hall from him . . ."

"So what? This is the city."

"Even so . . ."

"I'm forty-six years old, he's a kid of what? Eighteen? Nineteen? How do you *expect* me to know him? Intimately?"

"Well, no, ma'am but . . ."

"So that's how I know him. Slightly. Anyway, what about him?"

"Did you see him at any time last night?" Willis asked.

"No. Why? Something happen to him?"

"Did you hear anything unusual in his apartment anytime last night?"

"Unusual like what?"

"Like glass breaking?"

"I wasn't home last night. I went out to supper with a friend."

"What time was that?"

"Eight o'clock."

"And what time did you get back?"

"I didn't. I slept over."

"With your friend?"

"Yes."

"What's her name?" Genero asked.

"Her name is Morris Strauss, *that's* her name."

"Oh," Genero said. He glanced at Willis sheepishly.

"When *did* you get home, ma'am?" Willis asked.

"About five o'clock this morning. Morris is a milkman. He gets up very early. We had breakfast together, and then I came back here. Why? What's the matter? Did Lew do something?"

"Did you happen to see him at *any* time yesterday?"

"Yeah. When I was going to the store. He was just coming in the building."

"What time was that, would you remember?"

"About four-thirty. I was going out for some coffee. I ran out of coffee. I drink maybe six hundred cups of coffee a day. I'm always running out. I was going up the street to the A&P to get some more. That's when I saw him."

"Was he alone?"

"No."

"Who was with him?"

"Another kid."

"Boy or girl?"

"A boy."

"Would you know who?" Genero asked.

"I don't hang around with teenagers, how would I . . . ?"

"Well, you might have seen him around the neighborhood . . ."

"No."

"How old would you say he was?" Willis asked.

"About Lew's age. Eighteen, nineteen, I don't know. A big kid."

"Can you describe him?"

"Long blond hair, a sort of handlebar mustache. He was wearing a crazy jacket."

"What do you mean, crazy?"

"It was like an animal skin, with the fur inside and the, you know, what do you call it, the pelt. Is that what you call it?"

"Go ahead."

"The raw side, you know what I mean? The skin part. That was the outside of the jacket, and the fur was the inside. White fur. And there was a big orange sun painted on the back of the jacket."

"Anything else?"

"Ain't that enough?"

"Maybe it is," Willis said. "Thank you very much, ma'am."

"You're welcome," she answered. "You want some coffee? I got some on the stove."

"No, thanks, we want to take a look at the apartment here," Genero said. "Thanks a lot, though. You've been very kind."

The woman smiled so suddenly and so radiantly that it almost knocked Genero clear across the hallway to the opposite wall.

"Not at all," she said in a tiny little voice, and gently eased the door shut. Genero raised his eyebrows. He was trying to remember exactly what he had said, and in what tone of voice. He was still new at this business of questioning people, and any trick he could learn might prove helpful. The trouble was, he couldn't remember his exact words.

"What did I say?" he asked Willis.

"I don't remember," Willis answered.

"No, come on, Hal, what did I say? What made her smile that way, and all of a sudden get so nice?"

"I think you asked her if she'd like to go to bed with you," Willis said.

"No," Genero said seriously, and shook his head. "No, I don't think so."

With the passkey the superintendent had provided, Willis opened the door to 4C, and stepped into the apartment. Behind him, Genero was still pondering the subtleties of police interrogation.

There were two windows facing the entrance door. The lower pane of the window on the left was almost completely shattered, with here and there an isolated shard jutting from the window frame. Sunlight streamed through both windows, dust motes rising silently.

The apartment was sparsely furnished, a mattress on the floor against one wall, a bookcase on the opposite wall, a stereo record player and a stack of LP albums beside it, a bridge table and two chairs in the kitchen alcove, where another window opened onto the fire escape. A black camp trunk studded with brass rivets served as a coffee table in the center of the room, near the record player. Brightly colored cushions lined the wall on either side of the bookcase. Two black-and-white anti-war posters decorated the walls. The windows were curtainless. In the kitchen alcove, the shelves over the stove carried only two boxes of breakfast cereal and a bowl of sugar. A bottle of milk and three containers of yogurt were in the refrigerator. In the vegetable tray, Willis found a plastic bag of what looked like oregano. He showed it to Genero.

"Grass?" Genero said.

Willis shrugged. He opened the bag and sniffed the greenish-brown, crushed leaves. "Maybe," he said. He pulled an evidence tag from his pad, filled it out, and tied it to the plastic bag.

They went through the apartment methodically. There were three coffee mugs on the camp trunk. Each of them smelled of wine, and there was a red lipstick stain on the rim of one cup. They opened the camp trunk and found it stuffed with dungarees, flannel shirts, undershorts, several sweaters, a harmonica, an army blanket, and a small metal cash box. The cash box was unlocked. It contained three dollars in change, and a high school G.O. card encased in plastic. In the kitchen, they found two empty wine bottles in the garbage pail. A sprung mousetrap, the bait gone, was under the kitchen sink. On top of the closed toilet seat in the bathroom, they found a pair of dungarees with a black belt through the trouser loops, an orange Charlie Brown sweatshirt with the sleeves cut off raggedly at the elbows, a pair of white sweat socks, a pair of loafers and a woman's black silk blouse.

The blouse had a label in it.

They came into the grocery store at twenty minutes past seven, each of them wearing a Halloween mask, even though this was only the middle of the month and Halloween was yet two weeks away. They were both holding drawn guns, both dressed in black trench coats and black trousers. They walked rapidly from the front door to the counter, with the familiarity of visitors who had been there before. One of them was wearing a Wolf Man mask and the other was wearing a Snow White mask. The masks completely covered their faces and lent a terrifying nightmare aspect to their headlong rush for the counter.

Silvio's back was turned when they entered the store. He heard the bell over the door, and whirled quickly, but they were almost to the counter by then, and he had time to shout only the single word *"Ancora!"* before he punched the NO SALE key on the register and reached into the drawer for his gun. The man wearing the Snow White mask was the first to realize that Silvio was going for a gun. He did not say a word to his partner. Instead, he fired directly into Silvio's face at close range. The slug almost tore off Silvio's head and sent him spinning backward against the shelves. Canned goods clattered to the floor. The curtain leading to the back room was suddenly thrown open and Parker stood in the doorway with a .38 Police Special in his fist. The man with the Wolf Man mask had his hand in the cash drawer and was scooping up a pile of bills.

"Hold it!" Parker shouted, and the man with the Snow White mask fired again. His slug caught Parker in the right shoulder. Parker bent low and pulled off a wild shot just as the man at the cash register opened fire, aiming for Parker's belly, catching him in the leg instead. Parker grabbed for the curtain behind him, clutching for support, tearing it loose as he fell to the floor screaming in pain.

The two men in their Halloween masks ran out of the store and into the Sunday morning sunshine.

There were 186 patrolmen assigned to the 87th Precinct and on any given day of the week, their work schedule was outlined by a duty chart that required a PhD in Arabic literature to be properly understood. In essence, six of these patrolmen worked from 8 A.M. to 4 P.M., Monday through Friday, two of them serving as the Captain's clerical force, one as a highway safety patrolman, and the last two as community relations patrolman and roll call man respectively. The remaining 180 patrolmen were divided into twenty squads with nine men on each squad. Their duty chart looked like this:

SCHEDULE OF DUTY FOR PATROLMEN §

1969

JAN.	FEB.	MAR.	APR	MAY	JUNE	JULY	AUG.	SEPT.	OCT.	NOV.	DEC.
3-23	12	4-24	(13)	(3)-23	12	2-22	11-(31)	(20)	10-30	19	9-29
(4)-24	13	5-25	14	(4)-24	13	3-23	12	1-(21)	(11)-31	20	10-30
(5)-(25)	14	6-26	15	5-(25)	(14)	4-24	13	2-22	(12)	(1)-(21)	11-31
6-(26)	(15)	7-27	16	6-26	(15)	(5)-25	14	3-23	13	(2)-(22)	12
7-27	(16)	(8)-28	17	7-27	16	(6)-(26)	15	4-24	14	3-(23)	(13)
8-28	17	(9)-(29)	(18)	8-28	17	7-(27)	(16)	5-25	15	4-24	(14)
9-29	(18)	10-(30)	(19)	9-29	18	8-28	(17)	6-26	16	5-25	15
10-30	19	11-31	(20)	10-30	19	9-29	18	(7)-(27)	17	6-26	16
(11)-31	20	12	1-21	(11)-31	20	10-30	19	(8)-(28)	(18)	7-27	17
12	(1)-21	13	2-22	12	(1)-(21)	11-31	20	9-(29)	(19)	(8)-28	18
13	(2)-(22)	14	3-23	13	(2)-(22)	(12)	1-21	10-30	20	(9)-(29)	19
14	(3)-(23)	(15)	4-24	14	3-23	(13)	(2)-22	11	1-21	10-(30)	20
15	4-24	(16)	(5)-25	15	4-24	14	(3)-23	12	2-22	11	1-21
16	5-25	17	(6)-(26)	16	5-25	15	4-24	(13)	3-23	12	2-22
17	6-26	18	7-27	(17)	6-26	16	5-25	(14)	4-24	13	3-23
(18)	(7)-27	19	8-28	(18)	(7)-27	17	6-26	15	(5)-25	14	4-24
(19)	(8)-28	20	9-29	19	(8)-(28)	18	7-27	16	6-(26)	(15)	5-25
20	(9)	(1)-21	10-30	20	(9)-(29)	(19)	8-28	17	7-27	(16)	(6)-26
1-21	10	(2)-(22)	11	1-21	10-30	(20)	(9)-29	18	8-28	17	(7)-27
2-22	11	3-(23)	(12)	2-22	11	1-21	(10)-(30)	19	9-29	18	8-28

TOURS OF DUTY

DAY ON CHART	4 P.M. TO 12 MID. SQUAD	8 A.M. TO 4 P.M. SQUAD	12 MID. TO 8 A.M. SQUAD
1	15-16-17-18-19	8-9-10-11-12	(1)2-3-4-5
2	16-17-18-19-20	9-10-11-12-13	(2)3-4-5-6
3	17-18-19-20-1	10-11-12-13-14	(3)4-5-6-7
4	18-19-20-1-2	11-12-13-14-15	(4)5-6-7-8
5	19-20-1-2-3	12-13-14-15-16	(5)6-7-8-9
6	20-1-2-3-4	13-14-15-16-17	(6)7-8-9-10
7	1-2-3-4-5	14-15-16-17-18	(7)8-9-10-11
8	2-3-4-5-6	15-16-17-18-19	(8)9-10-11-12
9	3-4-5-6-7	16-17-18-19-20	(9)10-11-12-13
10	4-5-6-7-8	17-18-19-20-1	(10)11-12-13-14
11	5-6-7-8-9	18-19-20-1-2	(11)12-13-14-15
12	6-7-8-9-10	19-20-1-2-3	(12)13-14-15-16
13	7-8-9-10-11	20-1-2-3-4	(13)14-15-16-17
14	8-9-10-11-12	1-2-3-4-5	(14)15-16-17-18
15	9-10-11-12-13	2-3-4-5-6	(15)16-17-18-19
16	10-11-12-13-14	3-4-5-6-7	(16)17-18-19-20
17	11-12-13-14-15	4-5-6-7-8	(17)18-19-20-1
18	12-13-14-15-16	5-6-7-8-9	(18)19-20-1-2
19	13-14-15-16-17	6-7-8-9-10	(19)20-1-2-3
20	14-15-16-17-18	7-8-9-10-11	(20)1-2-3-4

O AROUND SQUAD NUMBER INDICATES EXCUSAL EXCEPT WHEN IT CORRESPONDS WITH O AROUND DATE

O INDICATES SATURDAYS & SUNDAYS

§ TO BE USED BY: PATROL PRECINCTS, EMERGENCY SERVICE, ACCIDENT INVESTIGATION SQUAD, SGTS & PTL. OF HARBOR PCT.

EFF. 1-1-66

All of which meant that patrolmen worked five tours for a forty-hour week, and then were off for fifty-six hours except when they were working the midnight to 8 A.M. shift, in which case they then worked only *four* tours and were off for eighty hours. Unless, of course, the *fifth* midnight tour happened to fall on a Friday or Saturday night, in which case they were required to work. All clear?

Patrolmen were supposed to be relieved on post as soon as possible after the hour by the squad that had just answered roll call in the precinct muster room. But most patrolmen began to drift back toward the station house shortly before the hour, so that seconds after the new shift trotted down the precinct steps, the old one entered the building and headed for the locker room to change into street clothes. There were a lot of cops in and around a police station when the shift was changing, and Sunday morning was no exception. If anything, the precinct was busier on Sunday because Saturday night brought thieves out like cockroaches and their resultant handiwork spilled over onto the day of rest.

This particular Sunday morning was more chaotic than usual because a cop had been shot, and nothing can galvanize a police department like the knowledge that one of their own has been gunned down. Lieutenant Peter Byrnes, who was in command of the sixteen detectives on the 87th Squad, saw fit to call in three men who were on vacation, perhaps on the theory that one wounded cop is worth at least three who were ambulatory. Not content to leave it at that, he then put in a call to Steve Carella at his home in Riverhead, ostensibly to inform him of the shooting.

Sitting behind his desk in the corner room upstairs, looking down at the front steps of the building, where the patrolmen filed out in pairs, the green globes flanking the steps and burning with sunshine as though fired from within, Byrnes must have known that Carella had worked the night shift and that the man did not now need a call from his superior officer. But he dialed the number nonetheless, and waited while the phone rang repeatedly on the other end. When at last Carella answered, Byrnes said, "Steve? Were you asleep?"

"No, I was just getting into my pajamas."

"Sorry to bother you this way."

"No, no, what is it, Pete?"

"Parker just got shot in a grocery store on Ainsley."

"No kidding?"

"Yeah."

"Jesus," Carella said.

"Two hoods killed the proprietor, wounded Parker in the shoulder and leg. He's been taken to Buenavista Hospital. It looks pretty serious."

"Jesus," Carella said again.

"I've already called in Di Maeo, Levine, and Meriwether. They're on vacation, Steve, but I had to do it, I don't like it when cops get shot."

"No, neither do I."

"I just thought I'd tell you."

"Yeah, I'm glad you did, Pete."

The line went silent.

"Pete?"

"Yeah, Steve?"

"What is it? Do you want *me* to come in, too?"

"Well, you had a long night, Steve."

The line was silent again.

"Well . . . what do you want me to do, Pete?"

"Why don't you see how you feel?" Byrnes said. "Go to bed, get some rest, maybe you'll feel like coming in a little later, okay?" Byrnes paused. "I can use you, Steve. It's up to you."

"What time is it, anyway?" Carella asked.

Byrnes looked up at the wall clock. "Little after eight. Get some rest, okay?"

"Yeah, okay," Carella said.

"I'll talk to you later," Byrnes said, and hung up. He rose from behind his desk, hooked his thumbs into his belt just above both hip pockets and walked to the window overlooking the park. He was a compact man with gray hair and flinty blue eyes, and he stood looking silently at the sun-washed foliage across the street, his face expressionless, and then turned suddenly and walked to the frosted glass door of his office, yanked it open, and went out into the squad-room.

A marine corporal was sitting with Detective Carl Kapek at the desk closest to the lieutenant's office. A swollen discolored lump the size of a baseball sat just over the marine's left eye. His uniform was rumpled and soiled, and he looked extremely embarrassed, his hands clasped in his lap rather like a schoolboy's. He spoke in a very low voice, almost a whisper, to Kapek as the lieutenant walked past them to where Brown was on the telephone at his own desk.

"Right, I'll tell him," Brown said, and replaced the phone on its cradle.

"That about Parker?" Byrnes asked.

"No, that was Delgado over on South Sixth. Guy was on his way to church, four other guys grabbed him as he came out of his building, damn near killed him. Delgado's on it now."

"Right. The hospital call back on Parker?"

"Not yet."

"Who's that in the holding cell downstairs?"

"A burglar Simms picked up on Fifth and Friedlander."

"You'd better get over to that grocery store, Artie."

"That'll leave Kapek all alone here."

"I've got some men coming in. They should be here anytime now."

"Okay then."

"I want some meat on this, Artie. I don't like my squad getting shot up."

Brown nodded, opened the top drawer of his desk, and took from it a holstered .38 Detective's Special. He fastened the holster to his belt just slightly forward of his right hip pocket, put on his jacket, and then went to the locker room to get his coat and hat. On his way out of the squadroom, he stopped at Kapek's desk and said, "I'll be at that grocery store, you need me."

"Okay," Kapek said, and turned back to the marine. "I still don't understand exactly how you got beat up," he said. "You mind going over it one more time?"

The marine looked even more embarrassed now. He was short and slender, dwarfed by Kapek, who sat beside him in his shirt sleeves with his tie pulled down, collar open, straight blond hair falling onto his forehead, wearing a shoulder holster from which protruded the walnut butt of a .38.

"Well, you know, I got jumped, is all," the marine said.

"How?"

"I was walking along, and I got jumped, is all."

"Where was this, Corporal Miles?"

"On The Stem."

"What time?"

"Must've been about three in the morning."

"What were you doing?"

"Just walking."

"Going any place in particular?"

"I'd just left this bar, you see? I'd been drinking in this bar on Seventeenth Street, I think it was."

"Anything happen in the bar?"

"Well, like what?"

"Any trouble? Any words?"

"No, no, it was a real nice bar."

"And you left there about three o'clock and started walking up The Stem."

"That's right."

"Where were you going?"

"Oh, just for a little walk, that's all. Before heading back to the ship. I'm on this battleship over to the Navy Yard. It's in dry dock there."

"Um-huh," Kapek said. "So you were walking along and this man jumped you."

"Mmm."

"Just one man?"

"Yeah. One."

"What'd he hit you with?"

"I don't know."

"And you came to just a little while ago, is that it?"

"Yeah. And found out the bastards had taken my wallet and watch."

Kapek was silent for several seconds. Then he said, "I thought there was only one of them."

"That's right. Just one."

"You said 'bastards.'"

"Huh?"

"Plural."

"Huh?"

"How many were there actually, Corporal?"

"Who hit me, you mean? Like I said. Just one."

"Never mind who hit you or who didn't. How many were there altogether?"

"Well . . . two."

"All right, let's get this straight now. It was *two* men who jumped you, not . . ."

"Well, no. Not exactly."

"Look, Corporal," Kapek said, "you want to tell me about this, or you want to forget it? We're pretty busy around here right now, and I don't have time for this kind of thing, I mean it. You want us to try to recover your stuff, then give us a little help, okay? Otherwise, so long, it was nice meeting you, I hope you get back to your ship all right."

Miles was silent for several moments. Then he sighed deeply and said, "I feel like a goddamn jackass, is all."

"Why? What happened?"

"There was this girl in the bar . . ."

"I figured," Kapek said, and nodded.

"In a red dress. She kept wiggling her ass at me all night long, you know? So I finally started a conversation with her, and she was real friendly and all, I mean she didn't seem to be *after* nothing, I think I maybe bought her only two drinks the whole night long."

"Yeah, go ahead."

"So a little before three, she tells me she's awful tired and wants to go home to bed, and she says good night to everybody, and then goes to the door and winks at me and gives me a kind of a little come-on move with her head, you know? Like this, you know? Like just this little movement of her head, you know? To tell me I should follow her. So I paid the check, and hurried on outside, and there she was on the corner, and she starts walking the minute she sees me, looking back over her shoulder, and giving me that same come-on again, trotting her little ass right up the avenue, and then turning off into one of the side streets. So I turned the corner after her and there's this guy standing there, and wham, he clobbers me. Next thing I know, I wake up with *this* fucking thing over my eye, and my money gone, and my watch, too. Little bitch."

"Was she black or white?"

"Black."

"And the man?"

"White."

"Would you recognize her if you saw her again?"

"I'll never forget her long as I live."

"What about the man?"

"I only got a quick look at him. He hit me the minute I come around that corner. Man, I saw stars. They musta moved me after I went out because I woke up in this hallway, you see. I mean, I was laying on the sidewalk when . . ." Miles stopped and looked down at his hands.

"Yes, Corporal?"

"What gets me is, I mean, she *kicked* me, the little bitch. When I was down on the sidewalk, she kicked me with this goddamn pointed shoe of hers. I mean, man, *that's* what put me out, not the guy hitting me. It was her kicking me with that pointed shoe of hers." Corporal Miles looked up plaintively. "Why'd she do *that,* huh? I was nice to her. I mean it. I was only nice."

The ambulance had come and gone, carrying away the man who had been attacked as he was leaving his home to go to church. It was now nine o'clock and there was still blood on the front stoop of the building. Detective 3rd/Grade Alexiandre Delgado stood on the steps with the victim's wife and two children, and tried to believe they were unaware of the blood drying in the early morning sunshine. Mrs. Huerta was a black-haired woman with brown eyes filled now with tears. Her two daughters, dressed to go to church, wearing identical green wool coats and black patent leather shoes and white ankle socks, resembled their mother except for the tears. Their brown eyes were opened wide in curiosity and fright and incomprehension. But neither of the two was crying. A crowd of bystanders kept nudging toward the stoop, despite the efforts of the beat patrolman to disperse them.

"Can you tell me exactly what happened, Mrs. Huerta?" Delgado asked. Like the woman he was questioning, he was Puerto Rican. And like her, he had been raised in a ghetto. Not this one, but a similar one (when you've seen *one* slum, you've seen them all, according to certain observers) in the shadow of the Calm's Point Bridge downtown. He could have spoken to her in fluent Spanish, but he was still slightly embarrassed by his accent when he was speaking English, and as a result he tried to speak it *all* the time. Mrs. Huerta, on the other hand, was not so sure she wanted to conduct the conversation in English. Her young daughters understood and spoke English, whereas their Spanish was spotty at best. At the same time, many of Mrs. Huerta's neighbors (who were eagerly crowding the front stoop now) spoke *only* Spanish, and she recognized that talking to this detective in English might enable her to keep at least *some* of her business to herself. She silently debated the matter only a moment longer, and then decided to answer in English.

"We were going down to church," she said, "the eight o'clock mass. The church is right up the street, it takes five minutes. We came out of the building. José and me and the two girls, and these men came at him."

"How many men?"

"Four."

"Did you recognize any of them?"

"No," Mrs. Huerta said.

"What happened?"

"They hit him."

"With what?"

"Broom handles. Short. You know, they take the broom and saw it off."

"Did they say anything to your husband?"

"Nada. Nothing."

"Did he say anything to them?"

"No."

"And you didn't recognize any of them? They weren't men from the *barrio,* the neighborhood?"

"I never saw them before."

One of the little girls looked up at her mother and then turned quickly away.

"Sí, qué hay?" Delgado asked immediately.

"Nothing," the little girl answered.

"What's your name?" Delgado said.

"Paquita Huerta."

"Did you see the men who attacked your father, Paquita?"

"Yes," Paquita said, and nodded.

"Did you know any of those men?"

The little girl hesitated.

"Puede usted decirme?"

"No," Paquita said. "I did not know any of them."

"And you?" Delgado said, turning to the other girl.

"No. None of them."

Delgado searched their eyes. The little girls watched him un-blinkingly. He turned to Mrs. Huerta again. "Your husband's full name is José Huerta?" he asked.

"José Vicente Huerta."

"How old is he, *señora?"*

"Forty-seven."

"What does he do for a living?"

"He is a real estate agent."

"Where is his place of business, Mrs. Huerta?"

"In Riverhead. 1345 Harrison Avenue. It is called J-R Realty."

"Does he own the business?"

"Yes."

"No partners?"

"Yes, he has a partner."

"What's his partner's name?"

"Ramon Castañeda. That's how they got the J-R. From José and Ramon."

"And where does Mr. Castañeda live?"

"Two blocks from here. On Fourth Street."

"The address?"

"112 South Fourth."

"All right, thank you," Delgado said. "I'll let you know if we come up with anything."

"Por favor," Mrs. Huerta said, and took both her daughters by their hands and led them into the building.

The black blouse found in Lewis Scott's bathroom had come from a clothing store called The Monkey Wrench, on Culver Avenue. Since this was a Sunday, the store was closed. The patrolman on the beat spotted Willis and Genero peering through the plate glass window and casually ambled over to them.

"Help you fellows?" he asked.

Both Genero and Willis looked at him. Neither of them recognized him. "You new on the beat, kid?" Genero said. The patrolman was perhaps three or four years *older* than Genero, but since his rank was lower, Genero felt perfectly free to address him in this manner. The patrolman could not decide whether he was dealing with hoods or fellow law enforcers; the distinction was sometimes difficult to make. He debated whether he should answer smart-ass or subservient. While he was deciding, Willis said, "I'm Detective Willis. This is my partner, Detective Genero."

"Oh," the patrolman said, managing to make the single word sound eloquent.

"How long you been on the beat, kid?" Genero asked.

"Just this past week. They flew me in from Majesta."

"Special assignment?"

"Yeah. This is a glass post, you know, there's been lots of breakage and looting lately. They almost doubled the force here, from what I understand."

"Where's the regular beat man?"

"He's catching a cup of coffee at the diner up the street. Anything I can help you with?"

"What's his name?"

"Haskins. You know him?"

"Yeah," Willis said. "Diner on the corner there?"

"Right."

"See you later, kid," Genero said, and both detectives walked off toward the diner. Behind them, the patrolman shrugged in a manner clearly indicating that he thought all detectives were no-good rotten bastards who were always pulling rank.

The diner at fifteen minutes before ten was empty save for Patrolman Haskins and a man behind the counter. Haskins was hunched over a cup of coffee. He looked as though he had not had much sleep the night before. Genero and Willis walked to the counter and took stools on either side of him.

"Hello, Bill," Willis said.

Haskins looked up from his coffee. "Hey, hi," he said.

"Two coffees," Genero said to the counterman.

"You looking for me," Haskins asked, "or you just happen in?"

"We're looking for you."

"What's up?"

"How you want those coffees?" the counterman asked.

"Regular," Willis said.

"One regular, one black," Genero said.

"Two regulars, one black," the counterman said.

"One regular, *one* black," Genero said.

"He wants a regular," the counterman insisted, "and *you* want a regular and a black."

"What are you, a comedian?" Genero said.

"It's all on the arm anyway, ain't it?" the counterman answered.

"Who says?"

"The day a cop pays for a cup of coffee in here, that's the day they give me a parade up Hall Avenue."

None of the policemen answered him. They were not, as a matter of fact, in the habit of paying for coffee in local eateries. Neither did they enjoy being reminded of it.

"Bill, we're looking for a kid about eighteen, nineteen," Willis said. "Long blond hair, handlebar mustache. See anybody around like that?"

"I seen a hundred of them," Haskins said. "Are you kidding?"

"This one was wearing a jacket with the fur side inside, the skin side out."

Haskins shrugged.

"Big sun painted on the back of it," Willis said.

"Yeah, that rings a bell. I think I seen that jacket around."

"Remember the kid wearing it?"

"Where the hell did I see that jacket?" Haskins asked aloud.

"He might have been with another kid his age, black beard, black hair."

"No," Haskins said, and shook his head. "An orange sun, right? Like an orange sun with rays coming out of it, right?"

"That's right, orange."

"Yeah, I seen that jacket," Haskins said. "Just the other day. Where the hell did I see it?"

"Two coffees, one regular, one black," the counterman said, and put them down.

"Jerry, you ever see a kid in here wearing a fur jacket with a sun painted on the back of it?" Haskins asked.

"No," the counterman said flatly, and walked back into the kitchen.

"White fur, right?" Haskins said to Willis. "On the inside, right? Like white fur?"

"That's right."

"Sure, I seen that goddamn jacket. Just give me a minute, okay?"

"Sure, take your time," Willis said.

Haskins turned to Genero and conversationally said, "I see you got the gold tin. Who's your rabbi?"

"I was promoted a long time ago," Genero said, somewhat offended. "Where the hell have you been?"

"I guess I don't keep up with what's happening around the station house," Haskins said, and grinned.

"You *know* I was promoted."

"Yeah, I guess it just slipped my mind," Haskins said. "How you like the good life, Genero?"

"Beats laying bricks all to hell," Genero answered.

"What *doesn't?*" Haskins said.

"About that jacket . . ." Willis interrupted.

"Yeah, yeah, just give me a minute, it'll come to me," Haskins said, and lifted his coffee cup in both hands, and sipped at it and said, "That new kid covering out there?"

"He's doing fine, don't worry about him."

"The Monkey Wrench!" Haskins said, snapping his fingers. *"That's* where I seen the damn thing. In the window of The Monkey Wrench. Right up the street."

"Good," Willis said, and nodded. "Got any idea who runs that shop?"

"Yeah, these two dykes who live over on Eighth. Just around the corner from the store."

"What're their names?"

"Flora Schneider and Frieda something, I don't know what. Flora and Frieda, everybody calls them."

"What's the address on Eighth?"

"327 North. The brownstone right around the corner."

"Thanks," Willis said.

"Thanks for the coffee," Genero yelled to the kitchen.

The counterman did not answer.

Detective Arthur Brown was a black man with a very dark complexion, kinky hair, large nostrils, and thick lips. He was impressively good-looking, though unfortunately not cast in the Negro mold acceptable to most white people, including liberals. In short, he did not resemble Harry Belafonte, Sidney Poitier, or Adam Clayton Powell. He resembled only himself, which was quite a lot since he was six feet four inches tall and weighed two hundred and twenty pounds. Arthur Brown was the sort of black man who caused white men to cross the street when he approached, on the theory that this mean-looking son of a bitch (mean-looking only because he was big and black) would undoubtedly mug them or knife them or do something possibly worse, God knew what. Even after Brown identified himself as a police detective, there were many white people who still harbored the suspicion that he was really some kind of desperate criminal impersonating an officer.

It was therefore a pleasant surprise for Brown to come across a witness to the grocery store shootings who did not seem at all intimidated by either his size or his color. The person was a little old lady who carried a bright blue umbrella on her arm, despite the fact that the day was clear, with that sharp penetrating bite in the air that comes only with October. The umbrella matched the lady's eyes, which were as clear and as sharp as the day itself. She wore a little flowered hat on her head. If she had been a younger woman, the black coat she was wearing might have been called a maxi. She leaped to her feet as Brown came through the front door of the grocery, and said to him in a brisk resonant voice, "Ah, at last!"

"Ma'am?" Brown said.

"You're the detective, aren't you?"

"I am," Brown admitted.

"My name is Mrs. Farraday, how do you do?"

"Detective Brown," he said, and nodded, and would have let it go at that, but Mrs. Farraday was holding out her hand. Brown clasped it, shook it, and smiled pleasantly. Mrs. Farraday returned the smile and released his hand.

"They told me to wait in here, said a detective would be along any minute. I've been waiting half the morning. It's past ten-thirty now."

"Well, Mrs. Farraday, I've been talking to people in the neighborhood since a little after eight o'clock. Takes a little while to get around to all of them."

"Oh, I can well imagine," she said.

"Patrolman outside says you've got some information for me, though. Is that right?"

"That's right. I saw the two men who held up the store."

"Where'd you see them?"

"Running around the corner. I was on my way home from church, I always go to six o'clock mass, and I'm generally out by seven, and then I stop at the bakery for buns, my husband likes buns with his breakfast on Sundays, or coffee cake."

"Um-huh."

"Never goes to church himself," she said, "damn heathen."

"Um-huh."

"I was coming out of the bakery—this must have been, oh, close to seven-thirty—when I saw the two of them come running around the corner. I thought at first . . ."

"What were they wearing, Mrs. Farraday?"

"Black coats. And masks. One of them was a girl's face—the mask, I mean. And the other was a monster mask, I don't know which monster. They had guns. Both of them. But none of that's important, Detective Brown."

"What *is* important?"

"They took the masks *off*. As soon as they turned the corner, they took the masks off, and I got a very good look at both of them."

"Can you describe them to me now?"

"I certainly can."

"Good." Brown took out his pad and flipped it open. He reached into his pocket for his pen—he was one of the few cops on the squad who still used a fountain pen rather than a ball-point—took off the cap, and said, "Were they white or black, Mrs. Farraday?"

"White," Mrs. Farraday said.

"How old would you say they were?"

"Young."

"How young? Twenty? Thirty?"

"Oh, no. In their forties, I would say. They were young, but they were definitely not *kids*, Detective Brown."

"How tall were they?"

"One was about your height, a very big man. How tall are you?"

"Six four," Brown said.

"My, that *is* big," Mrs. Farraday said.

"And the other one?"

"Much shorter. Five eight or nine, I would guess."

"Notice the hair color?"

"The short one was blond. The tall one had dark hair."

"I don't suppose you saw the color of their eyes."

"They passed close enough, but I just didn't see. They went by very quickly."

"Any scars? Tattoos? Birthmarks?"

"Not that I could see."

"Both clean-shaven?"

"Do you mean did they have beards or mustaches?"

"Yes, ma'am."

"No, both clean-shaven."

"You say they took the masks off as they came around the corner, is that right?"

"Yes. They just ripped them off. It must be difficult to see through those things, wouldn't you imagine?"

"Was there a car waiting for them?"

"No, I don't think they had a car, Detective Brown. They were running too fast for that. It's my guess they were trying to make their escape on foot. Wouldn't that be your guess as well?"

"I really couldn't say yet, Mrs. Farraday. I wonder if you could show me where that bakery store is."

"Certainly. It's right around the corner."

They walked out of the grocery, and the patrolman outside said to Brown, "You know anything about when I'm supposed to be relieved here?"

"What do you mean?" Brown asked.

"I think there's some kind of foul-up. I mean, this ain't even my post."

"Where *is* your post?"

"On Grover Avenue. Near the park."

"So what're you doing here?"

"That's just it. I collared this guy around quarter to seven, must've been, and took him back to the station house to book him—he was trying to bust into a Mercedes parked on South Second. By the time I got finished there, it was like seven-fifteen, and Nealy and O'Hara are going by in a patrol car, so I hail them and ask for a lift back to my post. We're on the way when all of a sudden they catch the radio squeal about the shooting here at the grocery store. So we all rush over here, and there's a big hullabaloo, you know,

Parker caught some stuff, you know, and Nealy and O'Hara take off on a Ten-Thirteen, and the sergeant tells me to stay here outside the door. So I been here all morning. I was supposed to be relieved on post at eight o'clock, but how's my relief supposed to know where I am so he can relieve me? You going back to the station house?"

"Not right away."

"Listen, I hate to leave here, because the sarge might get sore, you know? He told me to stay right here."

"I'll call in from the nearest box," Brown said.

"Would you do that? I certainly would appreciate it."

"Right away," Brown said.

He and Mrs. Farraday walked around the corner to the bakery shop. "This is where I was standing when they ran by," Mrs. Farraday said. "They were taking off the masks as they came around the corner, and they had them off by the time they passed me. Then they went racing up the street there and . . . oh, my goodness!" she said, and stopped.

"What is it, Mrs. Farraday?"

"I just remembered what they did with those masks, Detective Brown. They threw them down the sewer there. They stopped at the sewer grating and just threw them away, and then they started running again."

"Thank you, Mrs. Farraday," Brown said, "you've been most helpful."

"Oh, well," she said, and smiled.

Flora and Frieda did not get back to their apartment on North Eighth until seven minutes past eleven. They were both pretty women in their late twenties, both wearing pants suits and short car coats. Flora was a blonde, Frieda a redhead. Flora wore big gold hoop earrings. Frieda had a tiny black beauty spot near the corner of her mouth. They explained to the detectives that they always walked in the park on Sunday mornings, rain or shine. Flora offered them tea, and when they accepted, Frieda went upstairs to the kitchen, to put the kettle on.

Their apartment was in a brownstone that had run the gamut from luxury dwelling fifty years back, to crumbling tenement for as many years, to reconverted town house in a block of similar buildings trying desperately to raise their heads above the slime of the neighborhood. The women owned the entire building, and Flora explained now that the bedrooms were on the top floor, the kitchen, dining room and spare room on the middle floor, and the living room on the ground floor. The detectives were sitting with her in that room now, sunlight streaming through the damask-hung windows. A cat lay before the tiled fireplace, dozing. The living room ran the entire length of the ground floor, and was warmly and beautifully furnished. There was a false sense here of being someplace other than the city—some English country home in Dorset perhaps, or some Welsh manor, quiet and secluded, with gently rolling grassy hills just outside the door. But it was one thing to convert a slum building into a beautiful town house, and quite another to ignore the whirlpool surrounding it. Neither Flora nor Frieda were fools; there were iron gates over the windows facing the backyard, and a Fox lock on the front door.

"The store hasn't been burglarized, has it?" Flora asked. Her voice was somewhat throaty. She sounded very much like a torch singer holding the mike too close to her lips.

"No, no," Willis assured her. "We merely want to ask about some articles of clothing that may have been purchased there."

"Thank heavens," Flora said. Frieda had come down from the kitchen and stood now behind Flora's wingback chair, her hand delicately resting on the lace antimacassar just behind her partner's head.

"We've been burglarized four times since we opened the store," Frieda said.

"Each time they've taken, oh, less than a hundred dollars worth of merchandise. It's ridiculous. It costs us more to replace the broken glass each time. If they'd just come in the store and *ask* for the damn stuff, we'd give it to them outright."

"We've had the locks changed four times, too. That all costs money," Frieda said.

"We operate on a very low profit margin," Flora said.

"It's junkies who do it," Frieda said. "Don't you think so, Flora?"

"Oh, no question," Flora said. "Hasn't that been your experience?" she asked the detectives.

"Well, sometimes," Willis said. "But not all burglars are junkies."

"Are all junkies burglars?" Frieda asked.

"Some of them."

"Most of them?"

"A lot of them. Takes quite a bit of money to support a habit, you know."

"The city ought to do something about it," Flora said.

The cat near the fireplace stirred, stretched, blinked at the detectives, and then stalked out of the room.

"Pussy's getting hungry," Flora said.

"We'll feed her soon," Frieda answered.

"What clothes did you want to ask about?" Flora said.

"Well, primarily a jacket you had in the window last week. A fur jacket with . . ."

"The llama, yes, what about it?"

"With an orange sun painted on the back?" Genero said.

"Yes, that's it."

"Would you remember who you sold it to?" Willis asked.

"I didn't sell it," Flora said. She glanced up at her partner. "Frieda?"

"Yes, I sold it," Frieda said.

"Would you remember who bought it?"

"A boy. Long blond hair and a mustache. A young boy. I explained to him that it was really a woman's coat, but he said that didn't matter, he thought it was groovy and wanted it. It has no buttons, you realize, so that wasn't any problem. A woman's garment buttons differently . . ."

"Yes, I know that."

"This particular coat is held closed with a belt. I remember him trying it *with* the belt and then *without* the belt."

"Excuse me," Genero said, "but is that a coat or a jacket?"

"Well, it's a short coat, actually. Mid-thigh. It's really designed for a woman, to go with a miniskirt. It's about that length."

"I see."

"I guess a man could wear it, though," Frieda said dubiously.

"Do you know who the boy was?"

"I'm sorry, I don't. I'd never seen him before."

"How much did the coat cost?"

"A hundred and ten dollars."

"Did he pay for it in cash?"

"No, by . . . oh, of course."

"Yes?" Willis said.

"He gave me a check. His name would be on the check, wouldn't it?" She turned to Flora. "Where are the checks we're holding for deposit tomorrow?" she asked.

"Upstairs," Flora said. "In the locked drawer." She smiled at the detectives and said, "One drawer in the dresser locks. Not that it would do any good if someone decided to break in here."

"Shall I get it for you?" Frieda asked.

"If you would," Willis said.

"Certainly. The tea must be ready, too."

She went out of the room. Her tread sounded softly on the carpeted steps leading upstairs.

"There was one other item," Willis said. "Dick, have you got that blouse?"

Genero handed him a manila envelope. Willis unclasped it, and removed from it the black silk blouse they had found on Scott's bathroom floor, the police evidence tag dangling from one of its buttons. Flora took the blouse and turned it over in her hands.

"Yes, that's ours," she said.

"Would you know who bought it from you?"

Flora shook her head. "I really couldn't say. We sell dozens of blouses every week." She looked at the label. "This is a thirty-four, a very popular size." She shook her head again. "No, I'm sorry."

"Okay," Willis said. He put the blouse back into the envelope. Frieda was coming into the room with a tray upon which was a teapot covered with a cozy, four cups and saucers, a milk pitcher, a sugar bowl, and several sliced lemons in a low dish. A check was under the sugar bowl. Frieda put down the tray, lifted the sugar bowl and handed the check to Willis.

A name and an address were printed across the top of the check:

ROBERT HAMLING
3541 Carrier Avenue
Isola

The check was made out to the order of The Monkey Wrench for one hundred thirty-five dollars and sixty-eight cents; it was signed by Hamling in a broad, sprawling hand. Willis looked up. "I thought the coat cost a hundred and ten dollars. This check . . ."

"Yes, he bought a blouse as well. The blouse cost eighteen dollars. The rest is tax."

"A black silk blouse?" Genero asked.

"Yes," Frieda said.

"This one?" Genero asked, and pulled the blouse from its envelope like a magician pulling a rabbit from a hat.

"Yes, that's the blouse," Frieda said.

Genero nodded in satisfaction. Willis turned the check over. On the back of it were the penned words: "Drivers Lic" and the numbers "21546 68916 506607–52."

"Did you write this?" Willis asked.

"Yes," Frieda answered.

"He showed you identification, I take it."

"Oh yes, his driver's license. We never accept checks without proper identification."

"Can I see that?" Genero asked. Willis handed him the check. "Carrier Avenue," Genero said. "Where's that?"

"Downtown," Willis answered. "In The Quarter."

"What do you take in your tea, gentlemen?" Flora asked.

They sat sipping tea in the living room streaming with sunlight. Once, during a lull in the small talk over their steaming cups, Genero asked, "Why'd you name your store The Monkey Wrench?"

"Why not?" Frieda answered.

It was clearly time to go.

The curious thing about fishing in the sewer for those Halloween masks was that it filled Brown with a sense of exhilaration he had not known since he was a boy. He could remember a hundred past occasions when he and his childhood friends had removed an iron sewer grating and climbed down into the muck to retrieve a rubber ball hit by a stickball bat, or an immie carelessly aimed, or even now and then a dime or a quarter that had slipped from a clenched fist and rolled down into the curbside drain. He was too large now to squeeze through the narrow opening of the sewer, but he could see at least one of the masks some five feet below him, resting on the pipe elbow in a brownish paper-littered slime. He stretched out flat on the pavement, head twisted away from the curb and tried to reach the mask. His arm, as long as it was, was not long enough. His fingertips wiggled below, touching nothing but stagnant air. He got to his feet, brushed off the knees of his trousers and the elbows of his coat, and then looked up the block. Not a kid in sight. Never a kid around when you needed one. He began searching in his pockets. He found a paper clip holding a business card to one of the pages in his pad. He removed the clip, put the card into his wallet, and then took a sheaf of evidence tags from his inside jacket pocket. Each of the tags had a short length of string tied through a hole at one end. He unfastened the strings from ten tags, knotted them all together and came up with a five-foot-long piece of string. He opened the paper clip so that it resembled a fish hook, and then tied it to one end of the string. Weighting the line with the duplicate key to his station house locker, he grinned and began fishing in the sewer. On the twentieth try, he hooked the narrow piece of elastic clipped to the mask. Slowly, carefully, patiently, he reeled in his line.

He was looking at a somewhat soiled Snow White, but this was the seventies, and nobody expected to find virgins in sewers anymore.

Still grinning, Brown replaced the grating, brushed himself off again, and headed back for the squadroom.

In the city for which Brown worked, the Identification Section and the Police Laboratory operated on weekends with only a skeleton force, which was often only slightly better than operating with no force at all. Most cases got put over till Monday, unless they were terribly urgent. The shooting of a police detective was considered terribly urgent, and so the Snow White mask Brown dispatched to the lab downtown on High Street was given top priority. Detective-Lieutenant Sam Grossman, who ran the lab, was of course not working on a Sunday. The task of examining the mask for latent fingerprints (or indeed *any* clue as to its wearer's identity) fell to Detective 3rd/Grade Marshall Davies, who, like Genero, was a comparatively new detective and therefore prone to catching weekend duty at the lab. He promised Brown he would get back to him as soon as possible, mindful of the fact that a detective had been shot and that there might be all kinds of pressure from upstairs, and then set to work.

In the squadroom, Brown replaced the telephone on its cradle and looked up as a patrolman approached the slatted rail divider with a prisoner in tow. At his desk, Carl Kapek was eating an early lunch, preparatory to heading for the bar in which the marine had encountered the girl with the bewitching behind, bars in this city being closed on Sundays until twelve, at which time it was presumably acceptable for churchgoers to begin getting drunk. The clock on the squadroom wall read fifteen minutes to noon. The squadroom was somewhat more crowded than it might have been at this hour on a Sunday because Levine, Di Maeo and Meriwether, the three detectives who had been called in when they were supposed to be on vacation, were sitting at one of the desks waiting to see the lieutenant, who at the moment was talking to Captain Frick, commander of the precinct, about the grocery store

shooting and the necessity to get some more men on it. The three
detectives were naturally grumbling. Di Maeo said that next time
he was going to Puerto Rico on his vacation because then the
lieutenant could shove it up his ass if he wanted him to come back.
Cooperman was on vacation, too, wasn't he? But he was in the Virgin
Islands, and the loot sure as hell didn't call *him* down there and drag
him in, did he? Besides, Levine pointed out, Andy Parker was a
lousy cop and who the hell cared if he got shot or even killed? Meriwether, who was a mild-mannered hair-bag in his early sixties, and
a detective/first to boot, said, "Now, now, fellows, it's all part of the
game, all part of the game," and Di Maeo belched.

The patrolman walked over to Brown's desk, told his prisoner to
sit down, took Brown aside, and whispered something to him. Brown
nodded and came back to the desk. The prisoner was handcuffed,
sitting with his hands in his lap. He was a pudgy little man with
green eyes and a pencil-line mustache. Brown estimated his age at
forty or thereabout. He was wearing a brown overcoat, a brown suit
and shoes, white shirt with a button-down collar, gold-and-brown
striped silk tie. Brown asked the patrolman to advise the man of his
rights, a job the patrolman accepted with some trepidation, while
he called the hospital to ask about Parker's condition. They told
him that Parker was doing fine. Brown accepted the report without
noticeable enthusiasm. He hung up the phone, heard the prisoner
tell the patrolman he had nothing to hide and would answer any
questions they wanted to ask, swiveled his chair around to face
the man, and said, "What's your name?"

The man would not look Brown in the eye. Instead, he kept
staring past his left ear to the grilled windows and the sky outside.

"Perry Lyons," he said. His voice was very low. Brown could
barely hear him.

"What were you doing in the park just now, Lyons?" Brown
said.

"Nothing," Lyons answered.

"Speak up!" Brown snapped. There was a noticeable edge to his
voice. The patrolman, too, was staring down at Lyons in what
could only be described as an extremely hostile way, his brow
twisted into a frown, his eyes hard and mean, his lips tightly com-
pressed, his arms folded across his chest.

"I wasn't doing nothing," Lyons answered.

"Patrolman Brogan here seems to think otherwise."

Lyons shrugged.

"What about it, Lyons?"

"There's no law against talking to somebody."

"Who were you talking to, Lyons?"

"A kid."

"What'd you say to him?"

"Just it was a nice day, that's all."

"That's not what the kid told Patrolman Brogan."

"Well, kids, you know kids," Lyons said.

"How old was the kid, Joe?" Brown asked.

"About nine," Brogan answered.

"You always talk to nine-year-old kids in the park?" Brown asked.

"Sometimes."

"How often?"

"There's no law against talking to kids. I like kids."

"I'll bet you do," Brown said. "Tell him what the boy told you, Brogan."

Brogan hesitated a moment and then said, "The boy said you asked him to blow you, Lyons."

"No," Lyons said. "No, I never said anything like that. You're mistaken."

"I'm not mistaken," Brogan said.

"Well then, the kid's mistaken. He never heard anything like that from me, nossir."

"You ever been arrested before?" Brown asked.

Lyons did not answer.

"Come on," Brown said impatiently, "we can check it in a minute."

"Well, yes," Lyons said. "I have been arrested before."

"How many times?"

"Twice."

"What for?"

"Well . . ." Lyons said, and shrugged.

"What *for,* Lyons?"

"Well, it was, uh, I got in trouble with somebody a while back."

"What kind of trouble?"

"With some kid."

"What was the charge, Lyons?"

Lyons hesitated again.

"What was the charge?" Brown repeated.

"Carnal Abuse."

"You're a child molester, huh, Lyons?"

"No, no, it was a bum rap."

"Were you convicted?"

"Yes, but that don't mean a thing, you guys know that. The kid was lying. He wanted to get even with me, he wanted to get me in trouble, so he told all kinds of lies about me. Hell, what would I want to fool around with a kid like that for? I had a girl friend and everything, this waitress, you know? A real pretty girl, what would I want to fool around with a little kid for?"

"You tell me."

"It was a bum rap, that's all. These things happen, that's all. You guys know that."

"And the second arrest?"

"Well, that . . ."

"Yeah?"

"Well, you see what happened, after I got paroled, you know, I went back to live in this motel I used to live in before I got put away, you know?"

"Where'd you serve your time?"

"Castleview."

"Go ahead."

"So I had this same room, you know? That I had before they locked me up. And it turned out the kid who got me in trouble before, he was living there with his mother."

"Just by coincidence, huh?"

"Well, no, not by coincidence. I mean, I can't claim it was coincidence. His mother ran the place, you see. I mean, she and her father owned it together. So it wasn't coincidence, you know. But I didn't think the kid was going to cause me no more trouble, you see what I mean? I done my time, he already got even with me, so I didn't expect no more trouble from him. Only thing is he come around to my cabin one day, and he made me do things to him. He said he'd tell his mother I was bothering him again if I didn't do these things to him. I mean, I was on parole, you know what I mean? If the kid had went to his mother, they'd have packed me off again in a minute."

"So what *did* you do, Lyons?"

"Argh, the fuckin' little bastard started yelling. They . . . they busted me again."

"Same charge?"

"Well, not the same 'cause the kid was older now. You know, like there's Carnal Abuse with a kid ten years old or younger, and then there's Carnal Abuse with a kid over ten and less than sixteen. He was eight years old the first time and eleven the next time. It was a bum rap both times. Who the hell needs that kind of stuff, you think I need it? Anyway, this was a long time ago. I already served *both* sentences. You think I'd be crazy enough to risk a third fall?"

"You could've been put away for life the *second* time," Brown said.

"Don't you think I know it? So why would I take another chance?" He looked up at Brogan. "That kid must've heard me wrong, Officer. I didn't say nothing like that to him. Honest. I really didn't."

"We're booking you for Endangering the Morals of a Child, as defined in Section 483-a of the Penal Law," Brown said. "You're allowed three telephone . . ."

"Hey, hey, look," Lyons said, "give me a break, will you? I didn't mean no harm to the kid, I swear it. We were just sitting there talking, I swear to God. I *never* said nothing like that to him, would I say something like that to a little kid? Jesus, what do you take me for? Hey, come on, give me a break, will you? Come on, Officer, give me a break."

"I'd advise you to get a lawyer," Brown said. "You want to take him down, Brogan?"

"Hey, come on," Lyons said.

Brown watched as the patrolman led Lyons out of the squad-room. He stared at the retreating figure, and thought *The guy's sick, why the hell are we sending him away again, instead of helping him,* and then he thought *I have a seven-year-old daughter—* and then he stopped thinking because everything seemed suddenly too complex, and the telephone on his desk was ringing.

He lifted the receiver.

It was Steve Carella reporting that he was on his way to the squadroom.

José Vicente Huerta was in a bad way. Both of his legs had been broken by the four assailants who'd attacked him, and his face was swathed in bandages that covered the multiple wounds that had spilled his blood all over the front stoop of the building. He resembled a not so invisible Invisible Man, his brown eyes burning fiercely through the holes left in the bandages.

His mouth, pink against the white, showed through another hole below the eye holes, and looked like a gaping wound itself. He was conscious now, but the doctors advised Delgado that their patient was heavily sedated and might drift in and out of sleep as he talked. Delgado figured he would take his chances.

He sat in a chair by the side of Huerta's bed. Huerta, both legs in traction, his hands lying on the covers, palms up, his head turned into the pillow in Delgado's direction, the brown eyes burning fiercely, the wound of the mouth open and pathetically vulnerable, listened as Delgado identified himself, and then nodded when asked if he felt able to answer some questions.

"First," Delgado said, "do you know who the men were?"

"No," Huerta answered.

"You didn't recognize any of them?"

"No."

"Were they young men?"

"I don't know."

"You saw them as they attacked you, didn't you?"

"Yes."

"Well, how old would you say they were?"

"I don't know."

"Were they neighborhood men?"

"I don't know."

"Mr. Huerta, any information you can give us . . ."

"I don't know who they were," Huerta said.

"They hurt you very badly. Surely . . ."

The bandaged head turned away from Delgado, into the pillow.

"Mr. Huerta?"

Huerta did not answer.

"Mr. Huerta?"

Again, he did not answer. As had been promised by the doctors, he seemed to have drifted off into sleep. Delgado sighed and stood up. Since he was at Buenavista Hospital, anyway, and just so his visit shouldn't be a total loss, he decided to stop in on Andy Parker to see how he was doing. Parker was doing about as well as Huerta. He, too, was asleep. The interne on the floor informed Delgado that Parker was out of danger.

Delgado seemed as thrilled by the information as Brown had earlier been.

The trouble with being a detective in any given neighborhood is that almost everybody in the neighborhood knows you're a detective.

Since detection is supposed to be undercover secret stuff at least some of the time, snooping around becomes a little difficult when 90 per cent of the people you encounter know you're a snoop. The bartender at Bar Seventeen (which was the name of the bar in which the marine had first encountered the girl who later kicked him in the head, such bar being thus imaginatively named since it was located on Seventeenth Street) knew that Carl Kapek was a bull, and Kapek knew that the bartender knew, and since they *both* knew, neither of them made any pretense of playing at cops and robbers. The bartender set up beers for Kapek, who was not supposed to drink on duty, and Kapek accepted them without offering payment, and everybody had a nice little understanding going. Kapek did not even attempt to ask the bartender about the kicking girl and her boyfriend. Nor did the bartender try to find out why Kapek was there. If he was there, he was there for a reason, and the bartender knew it, and Kapek knew he knew it, and so the two men kept a respectful distance, coming into contact only when the bartender refilled Kapek's glass from time to time. It was a cool symbiosis. The bartender merely hoped that Kapek was not there investigating some minor violation that would inevitably cost him money. He was already paying off two guys from the Fire Department, not to mention the police sergeant on the beat; one more guy with his hand out, and it would be cheaper to take care of the goddamn violations instead. Kapek, for his part, merely hoped that the bartender would not indicate to too many of his early afternoon patrons that the big blond guy sitting at the bar was a police detective. It was difficult enough these days to earn a living.

The way he decided to earn his living on this particular bright October Sunday—bright *outside,* dim and cheerless inside—was to engage a drunk in conversation. Kapek had been in the bar for close to an hour now, studying the patrons, trying to decide which of them were regulars, which of them came here infrequently, which of them recognized him from around the streets, which of them had not the faintest inkling that he was fuzz. He did all of this in what he hoped was a surreptitious manner, going to the phone booth once to pretend he was making a call, going to the men's room once, going to the jukebox three or four times, casing everyone in the place on his various excursions, and then settling down on a stool within listening distance of the bartender and a man in a dark blue suit. Kapek opened the Sunday tabloid he had carried with him into the bar, and turned to the sports section. He pretended to be pondering yesterday's racing results, working figures with a pencil in the margin of the newspaper, while simultaneously listening intently to everything the man in the blue suit said. When the bartender walked off to serve someone at the other end of the bar, Kapek made his move.

"Damn horse never delivers when he's supposed to," he said.

"I beg your pardon?" the man in the blue suit said, turning on his stool. He was already very intoxicated, having presumably begun his serious drinking at home before the bar could legally open its doors. He looked at Kapek now with the benign expression of someone anxious to be friendly with anyone at all, even if he happened to be a cop. He did not seem to know that Kapek was a cop, nor was Kapek anxious to let him in on the secret.

"You follow the ponies?" Kapek asked.

"I permit myself a tiny wager every so often," the man in the blue suit said. He had bleary blue eyes and a veined nose. His white shirt looked unironed, his solid blue tie was haphazardly knotted, his suit rumpled. He kept his right hand firmly clutched around a water tumbler full of whiskey on the bar top in front of him.

"This nag's the goddamn favorite nine times out of ten," Kapek said, "but he never wins when he's supposed to. I think the jocks got it all fixed between them."

The bartender was ambling back. Kapek shot him a warning glance: *Stay out of this, pal. You work your side of the street, I'll work mine.* The bartender hesitated in mid-stride, then turned on his heel and walked over to his other customer.

"My name's Carl Kapek," Kapek said, and closed his newspaper, encouraging further conversation. "I've been playing the horses for twelve years now, I made only one decent killing in all that time."

"How much?" the man in the blue suit asked.

"Four hundred dollars on a long shot. Had two dollars on his nose. It was beautiful, beautiful," Kapek said, and grinned and shook his head remembering the beauty of this event that had never taken place. The most he had ever won in his life was a chemistry set at a church bazaar.

"How long ago was that?" the man in the blue suit asked.

"Six years ago," Kapek said, and laughed.

"That's a long time between drinks," the man said, and laughed with him.

"I don't think I got your name," Kapek said, and extended his hand.

"Leonard Sutherland," the man said. "My friends all call me Lennie."

"How do you do, Lennie?" Kapek said, and they shook hands.

"What do *your* friends all call *you?*" Lennie asked.

"Carl."

"Nice meeting you, Carl," Lennie said.

"A pleasure," Kapek answered.

"My game's poker," Lennie said. "Playing the horses, you'll pardon me, is for suckers. Poker's a game of skill."

"No question," Kapek agreed.

"Do you actually *prefer* beer?" Lennie asked suddenly.

"What?"

"I notice you have been drinking beer exclusively. If you would permit me, Carl, I'd consider it an honor to buy you something stronger."

"Little early in the day for me," Kapek said, and smiled apologetically.

"Never too early for a little rammer," Lennie said, and smiled.

"Well, I was out drinking late last night," Kapek said, and shrugged.

"I am out drinking late *every* night," Lennie said, "but it's still never too early for a little rammer." To emphasize his theory, he lifted the water glass and swallowed half the whiskey in it. "Mmm, boy," he said, and coughed.

"You usually do your drinking here?" Kapek asked.

"Hm?" Lennie asked. His eyes were watering. He took a handkerchief from his back pocket and dabbed at them. He coughed again.

"In this place?"

"Oh, I drift around, drift around," Lennie said, and made a fluttering little motion with the fingers of one hand.

"Reason I ask," Kapek said, "is I was in here last night, and I didn't happen to see you."

"Oh, I was here all right," Lennie said, which Kapek already knew because this was what he had overheard in the conversation between Lennie and the bartender, a passing reference to a minor event that had taken place in Bar Seventeen the night before, the bartender having had to throw out a twenty-year-old who was noisily expressing his views on lowering the age to vote.

"Were you here when they threw out that young kid?" Kapek asked.

"Oh, indeed," Lennie said.

"Didn't see you," Kapek said.

"Oh yes, here indeed," Lennie said.

"There was a marine . . ." Kapek said tentatively.

"Hm?" Lennie asked with a polite smile, and then lifted his glass and threw down the rest of the whiskey. He said, "Mmm, boy," coughed again, dabbed at his watering eyes, and then said, "Yes, yes, but he came in later."

"After they threw that kid out, you mean?"

"Oh yes, much later. Were you here when the marine came in?"

"Oh, sure," Kapek said.

"Funny we didn't notice each other," Lennie said, and shrugged and signaled to the bartender. The bartender slouched toward them, shooting Kapek his own warning glance: *This guy's a good steady customer. If I lose him 'cause you're pumping him for information here, I'm gonna get sore as hell.*

"Yeah, Lennie?" the bartender said.

"I'll have another double, please," Lennie answered. "And please see what my friend here is having, won't you?"

The bartender shot the warning glance at Kapek again. Kapek stared back at him implacably and said, "I'll just have another beer." The bartender nodded and walked off.

"There was this girl in here about then," Kapek said to Lennie. "You remember her?"

"Which girl?"

"Colored girl in a red dress," Kapek said.

Lennie was watching the bartender as he poured whiskey into the tumbler. "Hm?" he said.

"Colored girl in a red dress," Kapek repeated.

"Oh yes, Belinda," Lennie answered.

"Belinda what?"

"Don't know," Lennie said.

His eyes brightened as the bartender came back with his whiskey and Kapek's beer. Lennie lifted the tumbler immediately and drank. "Mmm, boy," he said, and coughed. The bartender hovered near them. Kapek met his eyes, decided if he wanted so badly to get in on the act, he'd let him.

"Would *you* happen to know?" Kapek said.

"Know what?"

"There was a girl named Belinda in here last night. Wearing a red dress. Would you know her last name?"

"Me," the bartender said, "I'm deaf, dumb, and blind." He paused. "This guy's a cop, Lennie, did you know that?"

"Oh yes, certainly," Lennie said, and fell off his stool and passed out cold.

Kapek got up, bent, seized Lennie under the arms and dragged him over to one of the booths. He loosened his tie and then looked up at the bartender, who had come over and was standing with his hands on his hips.

"You always serve booze to guys who've had too much?" he asked.

"You always ask them questions?" the bartender said.

"Let's ask *you* a couple instead, okay?" Kapek said. "Who's Belinda?"

"Never heard of her."

"Okay. Just make sure *she* never hears of *me.*"

"Huh?"

"You were pretty anxious just now to let our friend here know I was a cop. I'm telling you something straight, pal. I'm looking for Belinda, who*ever* the hell she is. If she finds out about it, from whatever source, I'm going to assume you're the one who tipped her. And that might just make you an accessory, pal."

"Who you trying to snow?" the bartender said. "I run a clean joint here. I don't know nobody named Belinda, and whatever she done or didn't do, I'm out of it completely. So what's this 'accessory' crap?"

"Try to forget I was in here looking for her," Kapek said. "Otherwise you're liable to find out *just* what this 'accessory' crap is. Okay?"

"You scare me to death," the bartender said.

"You know where Lennie lives?" Kapek asked.

"Yeah."

"He married?"

"Yeah."

"Call his wife. Tell her to come down here and get him."

"She'll kill him," the bartender said. He looked down at Lennie and shook his head. "I'll sober him up and get him home, don't worry about it."

He was already talking gently and kindly to the unconscious Lennie as Kapek went out of the bar.

Ramon Castañeda was in his undershirt when he opened the door for Delgado.

"Sí, qué quiere usted?" he asked.

"I'm Detective Delgado, Eighty-seventh Squad," Delgado said, and flipped his wallet open to show his shield. Castañeda looked at it closely.

"What's the trouble?" he asked.

"May I come in, please?" Delgado said.

"Who is it, Ray?" a woman called from somewhere in the apartment.

"Policeman," Castañeda said over his shoulder. "Come in," he said to Delgado.

Delgado went into the apartment. There was a kitchen on his right, a living room dead ahead, two bedrooms beyond that. The woman who came out of the closest bedroom was wearing a brightly flowered nylon robe and carrying a hairbrush in her right hand. She was quite beautiful, with long black hair and a pale complexion, gray-green eyes, a full bosom, ripely curving hips. She was barefoot, and she moved soundlessly into the living room, and stood with her legs slightly apart, the hairbrush held just above her hip, somewhat like a hatchet she had just unsheathed.

"Sorry to bother you this way," Delgado said.

"What is it?" the woman said.

"This is my wife," Castañeda said. "Rita, this is Detective . . . what's your name again?"

"Delgado."

"You Spanish?"

"Yes."

"Good," Castañeda said.

"What is it?" Rita said again.

"Your partner José Huerta . . ."

"What's the matter with him?" Castañeda asked immediately. "Is something the matter with him?"

"Yes. He was attacked by four men this morning . . ."

"Oh, my God!" Rita said, and brought the hand holding the hairbrush to her mouth, pressing the back of it to her lips as though stifling a scream.

"Who?" Castañeda said. "Who did it?"

"We don't know. He's at Buenavista Hospital now." Delgado paused. "Both his legs were broken."

"Oh, my God!" Rita said again.

"We'll go to him at once," Castañeda said, and turned away,

ready to leave the room, seemingly anxious to dress and leave for the hospital immediately.

"If I may . . ." Delgado said, and Castañeda remembered he was there, and paused, still on the verge of departure, and impatiently said to his wife, "Get dressed, Rita," and then said to Delgado, "Yes, what is it? We want to see Joe as soon as possible."

"I'd like to ask some questions before you go," Delgado said.

"Yes, certainly."

"How long have you and Mr. Huerta been partners?"

The woman had not left the room. She stood standing slightly apart from the two men, the hairbrush bristles cradled on the palm of one hand, the other hand clutched tightly around the handle, her eyes wide as she listened.

"I told you to get dressed," Castañeda said to her.

She seemed about to answer him. Then she gave a brief complying nod, wheeled, and went into the bedroom, closing the door only partially behind her.

"We have been partners for two years," Castañeda said.

"Get along with each other?"

"Of course. Why?" Castañeda put his hands on his hips. He was a small man, perhaps five feet seven inches tall, and not particularly good-looking, with a pockmarked face and a longish nose and a mustache that sat just beneath it and somehow emphasized its length. He leaned toward Delgado belligerently now, defying him to explain that last question, his brown eyes burning as fiercely as had his partner's through the hospital bandages.

"A man has been assaulted, Mr. Castañeda. It's routine to question his relatives and associates. I meant no . . ."

"It sounded like you meant plenty," Castañeda said. His hands were still on his hips. He looked like a fighting rooster Delgado had once seen in a cock fight in the town of Vega Baja, when he had gone back to the island to visit his dying grandmother.

"Let's not get excited," Delgado said. There was a note of warning in his voice. The note informed Castañeda that whereas both men were Puerto Ricans, one of them was a cop entitled to ask questions about a third Puerto Rican who had been badly beaten up. The note further informed Castañeda that however mild Delgado's manner might appear, he wasn't about to take any crap, and Castañeda had better understand that right from go. Castañeda took his hands from his hips. Delgado stared at him a moment longer.

"Would you happen to know whether or not your partner had

any enemies?" he asked. His voice was flat. Through the partially open door of the bedroom, he saw Rita Castañeda move toward the dresser, and then away from it, out of sight.

"No enemies that I know of," Castañeda replied.

"Would you know if he'd ever received any threatening letters or phone calls?"

"Never."

The flowered robe flashed into view again. Delgado's eyes flicked momentarily toward the open door. Castañeda frowned.

"Would you have had any business deals recently that caused any hard feelings with anyone?"

"None," Castañeda said. He moved toward the open bedroom door, took the knob in his hand, and pulled the door firmly shut. "We're real estate agents for apartment buildings. We rent apartments. It's as simple as that."

"No trouble with any of the tenants?"

"We hardly ever come into contact with them. Once in a while we have trouble collecting rents. But that's normal in this business, and nobody bears a grudge."

"Would you say your partner is well liked?"

Castañeda shrugged.

"What does that mean, Mr. Castañeda?"

"Well-liked, who knows? He's a man like any other man. He is liked by some and disliked by others."

"Who *dislikes* him?" Delgado asked immediately.

"No one dislikes him enough to have him beaten up," Castañeda said.

"I see," Delgado answered. He smiled pleasantly. "Well," he said, "thank you for your information. I won't keep you any longer."

"Fine, fine," Castañeda said. He went to the front door and opened it. "Let me know if you find the men who did it," he said.

"I will," Delgado answered, and found himself in the hallway. The door closed behind him. In the apartment, he heard Castañeda shout, "Rita, *esta lista?*"

He put his ear to the door.

He could hear Castañeda and his wife talking very quietly inside the apartment, their voices rumbling distantly, but he could not tell what they were saying. Only once, when Rita raised her voice, did Delgado catch a word.

The word was *hermano,* which in Spanish meant "brother."

It was close to 2 P.M., and things were pretty quiet in the squadroom.

Kapek was looking through the Known Muggers file, trying to get a lead on the black girl known only as Belinda. Carella had arrived in time to have lunch with Brown, and both men sat at a long table near one of the windows, one end of it burdened with fingerprinting equipment, eating tuna fish sandwiches and drinking coffee in cardboard containers. As they ate, Brown filled him in on what he had so far. Marshall Davies at the lab, true to his word, had gone to work on the Snow White mask the moment he received it, and had reported back not a half-hour later. He had been able to recover only one good print, that being a thumbprint on the inside surface, presumably left there when the wearer was adjusting the mask to his face. He had sent this immediately to the Identification Section, where the men on Sunday duty had searched their Single-Fingerprint file, tracking through a maze of arches, loops, whorls, scars, and accidentals to come up with a positive identification for a man named Bernard Goldenthal.

His yellow sheet was now on Brown's desk, and both detectives studied it carefully:

| PRISONER'S CRIMINAL RECORD | | | POLICE DEPARTMENT | | IDENTIFICATION SECTION |

NAME ___BERNARD GOLDENTHAL___

ALIAS ___"Bernie Gold," "Goldie," "Goldfinger."___

DATE OF BIRTH ___February 12, 1931___

FINGERPRINT CLASSIFICATION ___27 L 1 T r 20___
___L 1 U___

B # 47-61042

I.S. # G-21-3479

F.B.I. # 74-01-22
89234

This certifies that the finger impressions of the above-named person have been compared and the following is a true copy of the records of this section.

Date of Arrest	Location	Charge	Arresting Officer	Date, Disposition, Judge and Court
5-7-47	Isola	Burg. Juv. Del.	D of C	Jewish Home for Boys
2-9-48	Calm's Point	Burg. Fin. Chg. Unlaw	Werner 75 Pct.	Judge McCarthy County Court

Date	Location	Charge	Officer	Disposition
6-5-49	Isola	Robbery	Janus 19 Sqd.	6-30-49 Dismissed Judge Evans Sup. Court
8-17-49	Isola	Robbery Gun	Cowper 19 Sqd.	11-28-49 Discharged Judge Mastro Gen.Sess.
1-21-51	Riverhead	Gr. Larc 1st Burg. 3rd	Franklin	3-11-51 5 to 10 Yrs. on Gr. Larc. 5 to 10 Yrs. on Burg. 3rd. Judge Lefkin, County Court.
12-19-59	Isola	Theft from Interstate Shipment	F.B.I.	3 yrs to serve followed by 10 yrs probation Judge O'Hare U.S. So. Dist. Court.
12-23-69	Isola	974 PL	Magruder 2 Div	1-28-70 $50 or 10 days Judge Fields Spec. Sess.
1-9-70	Isola	974 PL	Donovan 2 Div	1-28-70 $100/30 days Judge Fields Spec. Sess.
9-19-70	Isola	974a PL	Donato CIU	11-25-70 Gen.Sess. Unl. Poss. Policy Slips $150 or 60 days. Ashworth.

X represent notations unsupported by fingerprints in Identification Section files.

"This record is furnished solely for the official use of law enforcement agencies. Unauthorized use of this information is in violation of Sections 554 and 2050, Penal Law."

A man's yellow sheet (so called because the record actually *was* duplicated on a yellow sheet of paper; bar owners were not the *only* imaginative people in this city) was perhaps not as entertaining, say, as a good novel, but it did have a shorthand narrative power all its own. Goldenthal's record had the added interest of a rising dramatic line, a climax of sorts, and then a slackening of tension just before the denouement—which was presumably yet to come.

His first arrest had been at the age of sixteen, for Burglary and Juvenile Delinquency, and he had been remanded to the Jewish Home for Boys, a correctional institution. Less than a year later, apparently back on the streets again, he had been arrested again for Burglary, with the charge reduced to Unlawful Entry and (the record was incomplete here) the courts had apparently shown leniency in consideration of his age—he was barely seventeen at the time—and let him off scot-free. Progressing to bigger and better things during the next year, he was arrested first on a Robbery charge and then on a Robbery with a Gun charge, and again the courts showed mercy and let him go. Thus emboldened and encouraged, he moved on to Grand Larceny First and Burglary Third, was again busted and this time was sent to prison. He had probably served both terms concurrently, and was released on parole sometime before 1959, when apparently he decided to knock over a truck crossing state lines, thereby inviting the Federal Bureau of Investigation to step in. Carella and Brown figured the "3 yrs to serve" were the three years remaining from his prior conviction; the courts were again being lenient.

And perhaps this leniency was finally paying off. The violations he'd been convicted of since his second release from prison were not too terribly serious, especially when compared to Grand Larceny or Interstate Theft. Section 974 of the Penal Law was defined as "keeping a place for or transferring money in the game of policy," and was a misdemeanor. Section 974a was a bit heavier—"Operating a policy business"—and was a felony punishable by imprisonment for a term not exceeding five years. In either case, Goldenthal seemed to have moved into a more respectable line of work, employing himself in the "policy" or "numbers game," which many hard-working citizens felt was a perfectly harmless recreation and hardly anything for the Law to get all excited about. The Law had not, in fact, got too terribly excited about Goldenthal's most recent offenses. He could have got five years on his last little adventure, when in fact all he had drawn was a fine of a hundred and fifty dollars or sixty days, on a reduced charge of Unlawful Possession of Policy Slips, Section 975 of the Penal Law.

Goldenthal had begun his criminal career at the age of sixteen. He was now almost forty years old, and had spent something better than ten years of his adult life in prison. If they found him, and busted him again, and convicted him of the grocery store holdup and murder, he would be sent away forever.

There were several other pieces of information in the packet the I.S. had sent uptown—a copy of Goldenthal's fingerprint card, with a complete description of him on the reverse side; a final report from his probation officer back in '69; a copy of the Detective Division report on his most recent arrest—but the item of chief interest to Carella and Brown was Goldenthal's last known address. He had apparently been living in uptown Isola with his mother, a Mrs. Minnie Goldenthal, until the time of her death three months ago. He had then moved to an apartment downtown, and was presumably still living there.

They decided to hit it together.

They were no fools.

Goldenthal had once been arrested on a gun charge, and either he or his partner had put three bullets into two men not seven hours before.

The show began ten minutes after Carella and Brown left the squadroom. It had a cast of four and was titled *Hookers' Parade*. It starred two young streetwalkers who billed themselves as Rebecca and Sally Good.

"Those are not your real names," Kapek insisted.

"Those are our real names," Sally answered, "and you can all go to hell."

The other two performers in the show were the patrolman who had answered the complaint and made the arrest, and a portly gentleman in a pinstriped suit who looked mortally offended though not at all embarrassed, rather like a person who had wet his pajamas in a hospital bed, where illness is expected and annoying but certainly nothing to be ashamed of.

"All right, what's the story, Phil?" Kapek asked the patrolman.

"Well, what happened . . ."

"If you don't mind," the portly gentleman said, *"I* am the injured party here."

"Who the hell injured you, would you mind telling me?" Rebecca said.

"All right, let's calm down here," Kapek said. He had finished with the Known Muggers file and was anxious to get to the Modus Operandi file, and he found all this tumult distracting. The girls, one black and one white, were both wearing tan sweaters, suede miniskirts, and brown boots. Sally, the white one, had long blond hair. Rebecca, the black one, had her hair done in an Afro cut and bleached blond. They were both in their early twenties, both quite attractive, long and leggy and busty and brazen and cheap as a bottle of ninety-cent wine. The portly gentleman sat some distance away from them, on the opposite side of Kapek's desk, as though afraid of contracting some dread disease. His face was screwed into an offended frown, his eyes sparked with indignation.

"I wish these young ladies arrested," he said. "I am the man who made the complaint, the injured party, and I am willing to press charges, and I wish them arrested at once."

"Fine, Mr. . . ." Kapek consulted his pad. "Mr. Searle," he said. "Do you want to tell me what happened?"

"I am from Independence, Missouri," Searle said. "The home of Harry S. Truman."

"Yes, sir," Kapek said.

"Big deal," Sally said.

"I am here in the city on business," Searle said. "I usually stay midtown, but I have several appointments in this area tomorrow morning, and I thought it would be more convenient to find lodgings in the neighborhood." He paused and cleared his throat. "There is a rather nice hotel overlooking the park. The Grover."

"Yes, sir," Kapek said.

"Or at least *I thought* it was a rather nice hotel."

"It's a fleabag," Rebecca said.

"How about knocking it off?" Kapek said.

"What the hell for? This hick blows the whistle for no reason at all, and we're supposed . . ."

"Let's hear what the man has to say, okay?" Kapek said sharply.

"Okay," Rebecca said.

"Whatever he has to say," Sally said, "he's full of crap."

"Listen, sister," Kapek warned.

"Okay, okay," Sally said, and tossed her long blond hair. Rebecca crossed her legs, and lighted a cigarette. She blew the stream of smoke in Searle's direction, and he waved it away with his hands.

"Mr. Searle?" Kapek prompted.

"I was sitting in my room reading the *Times*," Searle said, "when a knock sounded on the door."

"When was this, Mr. Searle?"

"An hour ago? I'm not sure."

"What time did you catch the squeal, Phil?"

"One-twenty."

"Just *about* an hour ago," Kapek said.

"Then it must have been a little earlier than that," Searle said. "They must have arrived at about one-ten or thereabouts."

"Who's that, Mr. Searle?"

"These young ladies," he answered, without looking at them.

"They knocked on your door?"

"They did."

"And then what?"

"I opened the door. They were standing there in the corridor. Both of them. They said . . ." Searle shook his head. "This is entirely inconceivable to me."

"What did they say?"

"They said the elevator operator told them I wanted some action, and they were there to supply it. I didn't know what they meant at first. I asked them what they meant. They told me exactly what they meant."

"What did they tell you, Mr. Searle?"

"Do we have to go into this?"

"If you're going to press charges, why, yes, I guess we do. I'm not sure yet what these girls did or said to . . ."

"They offered to sleep with me," Searle said, and looked away.

"Who the hell would want to sleep with *you?*" Sally muttered.

"Got to be out of your mind," Rebecca said, and blew another stream of smoke at him.

"They told me they would *both* like to sleep with me," Searle said. "Together."

"Uh-huh," Kapek said, and glanced at Rebecca. "Is that right?" he asked.

"Nope," Rebecca answered.

"So, okay, what happened next?" Kapek asked.

"I told them to come back in five minutes."

"Why'd you tell them that?"

"Because I wanted to inform the police."

"And did you?"

"I did."

"And did the girls come back?"

"In seven minutes. I clocked them."

"And then what?"

"They came into the room and said it would be fifty dollars for each of them. I told them that was very expensive. They both took off their sweaters to show me what I would be getting for the money. Neither of them was wearing a brassiere."

"Is that right?" Kapek asked.

"Nobody wears bras today," Sally said.

"Nobody," Rebecca said.

"That don't make us hookers," Sally said.

"Ask the officer here in what condition he found them when he entered the room."

"Phil?"

"Naked from the waist up," the patrolman said.

"I wish them arrested," Searle said. "For prostitution."

"You got some case, Fatty," Rebecca said.

"You know what privates are, Fatty," Sally asked.

"Must I be submitted to this kind of talk?" Searle said. "Surely . . ."

"Knock it off," Kapek said to the girls. "What they're trying to tell you, Mr. Searle, is that it's extremely difficult in this city to make a charge of prostitution stick unless the woman has exposed her privates, do you see what I mean? Her genitals," Kapek said. "That's been our experience. That's what it is," he concluded, and shrugged. Rebecca and Sally were smiling.

"They did expose themselves to me," Searle said.

"Yes, but not the privates, you see. They have to expose the privates. That's the yardstick, you see. For arrest. To make a conviction stick. That's been the, you see, experience of the police department in such matters. Now, of course, we can always book them for disorderly conduct . . ."

"Yes, do that," Searle said.

"That's Section 722," Kapek said, "Subdivision 9, but then you'd have to testify in court that the girls were soliciting, you know, were hanging around a public place for the purpose of committing a crime against nature or any other lewdness. That's the way it's worded, that subdivision. So you'd have to explain in court what happened. I mean, what they said to you and all. You know what I mean, Mr. Searle?"

"I think so, yes."

"We could also get them on Section 887, Subdivision 4 of the

Code of Criminal Procedure. That's, you know, inducing, enticing or procuring another to commit lewdness, fornication . . ."

"Yes, yes, I quite understand," Searle said, and waved his hand as though clearing away smoke, though Rebecca had not blown any in his direction.

". . . unlawful sexual intercourse or any other indecent act," Kapek concluded. "But there, too, you'd have to testify in court."

"Wouldn't the patrolman's word be enough? He saw them all exposed that way."

"Well, we got half a dozen plays running in this town where the girls are naked from the waist up, and also down, and that doesn't mean they're offering to commit prostitution." Kapek turned to the patrolman. "Phil, you hear them *say* anything about prostitution?"

"Nope," the patrolman answered, and grinned. He was obviously enjoying himself.

"*I* heard them," Searle said.

"Sure. And like I said, if you're willing to testify in court . . ."

"They're *obvious* prostitutes," Searle said.

"Probably got records, too, no question," Kapek said. "But . . ."

"I've never been busted," Sally said.

"How about you, Rebecca?" Kapek asked.

"If you're going to start asking me questions, I want a lawyer. *That's* how about me."

"Well, what do you say, Mr. Searle? You want to go ahead with this, or not?" Kapek asked.

"When would I have to go to court?"

"Prostitution cases usually get immediate hearings. Dozens of them each day. I guess it would be tomorrow sometime."

"I have business to take care of tomorrow. That's why I'm here to begin with."

"Well," Kapek said, and shrugged.

"I hate to let them get away with this," Searle said.

"Why?" Sally asked. "Who did you any harm?"

"You offended me gravely, young lady."

"How?" Rebecca asked.

"Would you ask them to go, please?" Searle said.

"You've decided not to press charges?"

"That is my decision."

"Beat it," Kapek said to the girls. "Keep your asses out of that hotel. Next time, you may not be so lucky."

Neither of the girls said a word. Sally waited while Rebecca ground out her cigarette in the ashtray. Then they both swiveled out of the squadroom. Searle looked somewhat dazed. He sat staring ahead of him. Then he shook his head and said, "When they think *that,* when they think a man needs *two* women, they're really thinking he can't even handle *one.*" He shook his head again, rose, put his homburg onto his head, and walked out of the squadroom. The patrolman tilted his nightstick at Kapek, and ambled out after him.

Kapek sighed and went to the Modus Operandi file.

The last known address for Bernard Goldenthal was on the North Side, all the way downtown in a warehouse district adjacent to the River Harb. The tenement in which he reportedly lived was shouldered between two huge edifices that threatened to squash it flat. The street was deserted. This was Sunday, and there was no traffic. Even the tugboats on the river, not two blocks away, seemed motionless. Carella and Brown went into the building, checked the mailboxes—there was a name in only one of them, and it was not Goldenthal's—and then went up to the third floor, where Goldenthal was supposed to be living in Apartment 3A. They listened outside the door, and heard nothing. Carella nodded to Brown, and Brown knocked.

"Who is it?" a man's voice asked from behind the door.

"Mr. Goldenthal?" Brown asked.

"No," the man answered. "Who is it?"

Brown looked at Carella. Carella nodded.

"Police officers," Brown said. "Want to open up, please?"

There was a slight hesitation from behind the door. Carella unbuttoned his coat and put his hand on the butt of his revolver. The door opened. The man standing there was in his forties, perhaps as tall as Carella, heavier, with black hair that sprang from his scalp like weeds in a small garden, brown eyes opened wide in inquiry, thick black brows arched over them. Whoever he was, he did not by any stretch of the imagination fit the description on Goldenthal's fingerprint card.

"Yes?" he said. "What is it?"

"We're looking for Bernard Goldenthal," Brown said. "Does he live here?"

"No, I'm sorry," the man said. "He doesn't." He spoke quite softly, the way a very big man will sometimes speak to a child or an old person, as though compensating for his hugeness by lowering the volume of his voice.

"Our information says he lives here," Carella said.

"Well, I'm sorry," the man said, "but he doesn't. He may have at one time, but he doesn't now."

"What's *your* name?" Carella asked. His coat was still open, and his hand was resting lightly on his hip, close to his holster.

"Herbert Gross."

"Mind if we come in, Mr. Gross?"

"Why would you want to?" Gross asked.

"To see if Mr. Goldenthal is here."

"I just told you he wasn't," Gross said.

"Mind if we check it for ourselves?" Brown said.

"I really don't see why I should let you," Gross said.

"Goldenthal's a known criminal," Carella said, "and we're looking for him in connection with a recent crime. The last address we have for him is 911 Forrester, Apartment 3A. This is 911 Forrester, Apartment 3A, and we'd like to come in and check on whether or not our information is correct."

"Your information is wrong," Gross insisted. "It must be very old information."

"No, it's recent information."

"How recent?"

"Less than three months old."

"Well, I've been living here for two months now, so he must have moved before that."

"Are you going to let us in, Mr. Gross?"

"No, I don't think so," Gross said.

"Why not?"

"I don't think I like the idea of policemen crashing in here on a Sunday afternoon, that's all."

"Anybody in there with you?"

"I don't think that's any of your business," Gross said.

"Look, Mr. Gross," Brown said, "we can come back here with a warrant, if that's what you'd like. Why not make it easy for us?"

"Why should I?"

"Why shouldn't you?" Carella said. "Have you got anything to hide?"

"Nothing at all."

"Then how about it?"

"Sorry," Gross said, and closed the door and locked it.

The two detectives stood in the hallway and silently weighed their next move. There were two possibilities open to them, and both of them presented considerable risks. The first possibility was that Goldenthal was indeed in the apartment and armed, in which event he was now warned and if they kicked in the door he would open fire immediately. The second possibility was that the I.S. information *was* dated, and that Goldenthal had indeed moved from the apartment more than two months ago, in which event Gross would have a dandy case against the city if they kicked in the door and conducted an illegal search. Brown gestured with his head, and both men moved toward the stairwell, away from the door.

"What do you think?" Brown whispered.

"There were two of them on the grocery store job," Carella said. "Gross might just be the other man."

"He fits the description I got from the old lady," Brown said. "Shall we kick it in?"

"I'd rather wait downstairs. He expects us to come back. If he's in this with Goldenthal, he's going to run, sure as hell."

"Right," Brown said. "Let's split."

They had parked Brown's sedan just outside the building. Knowing that Gross's apartment overlooked the street, and hoping that he was now watching them from his window, they got into the car and drove north toward the river. Brown turned right under the River Highway, and headed uptown. He turned right again at the next corner, and then drove back to Scovil Avenue and Forrester Street, where he pulled the car to the curb. Both men got out.

"Think he's still watching?" Brown asked.

"I doubt it, but why take chances?" Carella said. "The street's deserted. If we plant ourselves in one of the doorways on this end of the block, we can see anybody going in or out of his building."

The first doorway they found had obviously been used as a nest by any number of vagrants. Empty pint bottles of whiskey in brown paper bags littered the floor, together with empty crumpled cigarette packages, and empty half-gallon wine bottles, and empty candy bar wrappers. The stench of urine was overpowering.

"No job's worth *this,*" Brown said.

"Don't care if he killed the goddamn *governor,*" Carella said.

They walked swiftly into the clean brisk October air. Brown looked up the street toward Gross's building. Together, he and Carella ducked into the next doorway. It was better, but only a trifle so.

"Let's hope he makes his move fast," Brown said.

"Let's hope so," Carella agreed.

They did not have long to wait.

In five minutes flat, Gross came down the front steps of his building and began walking south, toward the building where they waited. They moved back against the wall. He walked past swiftly, without even glancing into the hallway. They gave him a good lead, and then took off after him, one on each side of the street, so that they formed an isosceles triangle with Gross at the point and Brown and Carella at either end of the base.

They lost him on Payne Avenue, when he boarded an uptown bus that left them running up behind it to choke in a cloud of carbon monoxide. They decided then to go back to the apartment and kick the door in, which is maybe what they should have done in the goddamn first place.

There is an old Spanish proverb which, when translated into city slang, goes something like this: *When nobody knows nothing, everybody knows everything.*

Nobody seemed to know nothing about the José Vicente Huerta assault. He had been attacked in broad daylight on a clear day by four men carrying sawed-off broom handles, and they had beaten him severely enough to have broken both his legs and opened a dozen or more wounds on his face, but nobody seemed to have had a good look at them, even though the beating had lasted a good five minutes or more.

Delgado was not a natural cynic, but he certainly had his doubts about this one. He went through Huerta's building talking to the tenants on each floor, and then he went to the candy store across the street, from which the front stoop of the building was clearly visible, and talked to the proprietor there, but nobody knew nothing. He decided to try another tack.

There was a junkie hooker in the *barrio,* a nineteen-year-old girl who had only one arm. Her handicap, rather than repelling any prospective customers, seemed instead to excite them wildly. From far and wide, the panting Johns came uptown seeking the One-Armed Bandit, as she was notoriously known. She was more familiarly known as Blanca Diaz to those neighborhood men who were among her regular customers, she having a habit as long as the River Harb, and they knowing a good lay when they stumbled across it, one-armed or not, especially since the habit caused her to charge bargain rates most of the time. Conversely, many of the neighborhood men were familiarly known to Blanca, and it was for this reason alone that Delgado sought her out.

Blanca was not too terribly interested in passing the time of day with a cop, Puerto Rican or otherwise. But she knew that most of the precinct detectives, unlike Vice Squad cops, were inclined to look the other way where she was concerned, perhaps because of her infirmity. Moreover, she had just had her 3 P.M. fix and was feeling no pain when Delgado approached her. She was, in fact, enjoying the October sunshine, sitting on a bench on one of the grassy ovals running up the center of The Stem. She spotted Delgado from the corner of her eye, debated moving, thought *Oh, the hell with it,* and sat where she was, basking.

"Hello, Blanca," Delgado said.

"Hullo," she answered.

"You okay?"

"I'm fine. I'm not holding, if that's what you mean."

"That's not what I mean."

"I mean, if you're looking for a cheap dope bust . . ."

"I'm not."

"Okay," Blanca said, and nodded. She was not an unattractive girl. Her complexion was dark, her hair was black, her eyes a light shade of brown; her lips were perhaps a trifle too full, and there was a small unsightly scar on her jawline, where she had been stabbed by a pimp when she was just sixteen and already shooting heroin three times a day.

"You want to help me?" Delgado asked.

"Doing what?"

"I need some information."

"I'm no stoolie," Blanca said.

"If I ask you anything you don't want to answer, you don't have to."

"Thanks for nothing."

"Querida," Delgado said, "we're very nice to you. Be nice back, huh?"

She looked him full in the face, sighed, and said, "What do you want to know?"

"Everything you know about Joe Huerta."

"Nothing."

"He ever come to visit you?"

"Never."

"What about his partner?"

"Who's his partner?"

"Ray Castañeda."

"I don't know him," Blanca said. "Is he related to Pepe Castañeda?"

"Maybe. Tell me about Pepe."

Blanca shrugged. "A punk," she said.

"How old is he?"

"Thirty? Something like that."

"What's he do?"

"Who knows? Maybe numbers, I'm not sure. He used to be a junkie years ago, he's one of the few guys I know who kicked it. He was with this street gang, they called themselves The Spanish Nobles or some shit like that, this was when he was still a kid, you know. I was only five or six myself, you know, but he was a very big man in the neighborhood, rumbling all the time with this wop gang from the other side of the park, I forget the name of the gang, it was a very big one. Then, you know, everybody started doing dope, the guys all lost interest in gang-busting. Pepe was a very big junkie, but he kicked it. I think he went down to Lexington, I'm not sure. Or maybe he just got busted and sent away and kicked it cold turkey, I'm not sure. But he's off it now, I know that." She shrugged. "He's still a punk, though."

"Have you seen him lately?"

"Yeah, he's around all the time. You always see him on the stoop someplace. Always with a bunch of kids around him, you know, listening to his crap. Big man. The reformed whore," Blanca said, and snorted.

"Have you seen him today?"

"No. I just come down a little while ago. I had a trick with me all night."

"Where can I find him, would you know?"

"Pepe or the trick?" Blanca asked, and smiled.

"Pepe," Delgado said, and did not smile back.

"There's a pool hall on Ainsley," Blanca said. "He hangs around there a lot."

"Let's get back to Huerta for a minute, okay?"

"Why?" Blanca asked, and turned to look at a bus that was rumbling up the avenue.

"Because we got away from him too fast," Delgado said.

"I hardly know him," Blanca said. She was still watching the bus. Its blue-gray exhaust fumes seemed to fascinate her.

"You mind looking at me?" Delgado said.

She turned back toward him sharply. "I told you I'm not a stoolie," Blanca said. "I don't want to answer no questions about Joe Huerta."

"Why not? What's he into?"

"No comment."

"Dope?"

"No comment."

"Yes or no, Blanca? We know where you live, we can have the

Vice Squad banging on your door every ten minutes. Tell me about Huerta."

"Okay, he's dealing, okay?"

"I thought he had a real estate business."

"Sure. He's got an acre of land in Mexico, and he grows pot on it."

"Is he pushing the hard stuff, too?"

"No. Only grass."

"Does his partner know this?"

"I don't know what his partner knows or don't know. I'm not his partner. Go ask his partner."

"Maybe I will," Delgado said. "After I talk to his partner's brother."

"You going to look for Pepe now?"

"Yes."

"Tell him he still owes me five bucks."

"What for?"

"What do you think for?" Blanca asked.

Genero was waiting on the sidewalk when Willis came out of the phone booth.

"What'd they say?" he asked.

"Nothing yet. They've got a lot of stuff ahead of what we sent them."

"So how we supposed to know if it's grass or oregano?" Genero said.

"I guess we wait. They told me to call back in a half-hour or so."

"Those guys at the lab give me a pain in the ass," Genero said.

"Yeah, well, what're you gonna do?" Willis said. "We all have our crosses to bear." The truth was that Genero gave *him* a pain in the ass. They had arranged for pickup and delivery to the lab of the plastic bag full of oregano/marijuana and had asked for a speedy report on it. But the lab was swamped with such requests every day of the week, the average investigating officer never being terribly certain about a suspect drug until it was checked out downtown. Willis had been willing to wait for the report; Genero had insisted that he call the lab and find out what was happening. Now, at twenty minutes to four, they knew what was happening: nothing. So now Genero was beginning to sulk, and Willis was beginning to wish he would go home and explain to his mother how tough it was to be a working detective in this city.

They were in an area of The Quarter that was not as chic

as the section further south, lacking its distinctive Left Bank flair, but boasting of the same high rentals nonetheless, this presumably because of its proximity to all the shops and theaters and coffee houses. 3541 Carrier Avenue was a brownstone in a row of identical brownstones worn shoddy by the passage of time. They found a nameplate for Robert Hamling in one of the mailboxes in the entrance hallway downstairs. Willis rang the bell for apartment 22. An answering buzz on the inner door sounded almost immediately. Genero opened the door and both moved into a dim ground-floor landing. A flight of steps was directly ahead of them. The building smelled of Lysol. They went up to the second floor, searched for Apartment 22, listened outside the door, heard nothing, and knocked.

"Bobby?" a girl's voice said.

"Police officers," Willis said.

"What do you want?" the girl asked.

"Open the door," Genero said.

There was silence inside the apartment. They kept listening. They knew that Robert Hamling wasn't in there with the girl, because the first word out of her mouth had been "Bobby?" But nobody knows better than cops that the female is the deadlier of the species, and so they waited apprehensively for her to unlock the door, their coats open, their guns within ready drawing distance. When the door finally opened, they were looking at a teenage girl wearing dungarees and a tie-dyed T-shirt. Her face was round, her eyes were blue, her brown hair was long and matted.

"Yes, what do you want?" she said. She seemed very frightened and very nervous. She kept one hand on the doorknob. The other fluttered at the throat of the T-shirt.

"We're looking for Robert Hamling," Willis said. "Does he live here?"

"Yes?" she said, tentatively.

"Is he home?"

"No."

"When do you expect him?"

"I don't know."

"What's your name, miss?" Genero asked.

"Sonia."

"Sonia what?"

"Sonia Sobolev."

"How old are you, Sonia?"

"Seventeen."

"Do you live here?"

"No."

"Where *do* you live?"

"In Riverhead."

"What are you doing here?"

"Waiting for Bobby. He's a friend of mine."

"When did he go out?"

"I don't know."

"How'd you get in here?"

"I have a key."

"Mind if we come in and wait with you?"

"I don't care," she said, and shrugged. "If you want to come in, come in." She stood aside. She was still very frightened. As they entered, she looked past them into the hallway, as if anxious for Hamling to appear and wishing it would be damn soon. Willis caught this, though Genero did not. She closed the door behind them, and together they went into a room furnished with several battered easy chairs, a foam rubber sofa, and a low, slatted coffee table. "Well, sit down," she said.

The detectives sat on the sofa. Sonia took one of the chairs opposite them.

"How well do you know Robert Hamling?" Willis asked.

"Pretty well."

"When did you see him last?"

"Oh . . ." she said, and shrugged, and seemed to be thinking it over.

"Yes?"

"Well, what difference does it make?"

"It might make a difference."

"Last week sometime, I guess."

"When last week?"

"Well, why don't you ask Bobby when he gets here?"

"We will," Genero said. "Meantime, we're asking you. When did you see him last?"

"I don't remember," Sonia said.

"Do you know anybody named Lewis Scott?" Willis asked.

"No."

"Ever hear of a clothing store called The Monkey Wrench?"

"Yes, I think so."

"Ever buy any clothes there?"

"I don't remember."

"Ever buy a black silk blouse there?" Genero asked.

"I don't remember."

"Show her the blouse, Dick," Willis said.

Genero produced the manila envelope again. He took the blouse from it and handed it to the girl. "This yours?" he asked.

"I don't know."

"Yes or no?" Genero said.

"It could be, I can't tell for sure. I have a lot of clothes."

"Do you have a lot of black silk blouses bought at a store called The Monkey Wrench?"

"Well, no, but a person could get confused about her clothes. I mean, it's a black silk blouse, it could be *any* black silk blouse. How do I know it's mine?"

"What size blouse do you take?"

"Thirty-four."

"This is a thirty-four," Willis said.

"That still doesn't make it mine, does it?" Sonia asked.

"Were you here in Isola last night?" Willis asked.

"Well, yes."

"Where?"

"Oh, banking around."

"Where?"

"Here and there."

"Here and there *where?*"

"You don't have to answer him, Sonia," a voice from the doorway said, and both detectives turned simultaneously. The boy standing there was about eighteen, with long blond hair and a handlebar mustache. He had on blue jeans and a blue corduroy shirt, over which he wore an open coat with white fur showing on the inside.

"Mr. Hamling, I presume," Willis said.

"That's me," Hamling said. He turned to close the entrance door. A bright orange, radiating sun was painted on the back of the coat.

"We've been looking for you," Willis said.

"So now you found me," Hamling said. "This is about Lew, isn't it?"

"You tell *us,*" Genero said.

"Sure, it's about Lew," Hamling said. "I figured you'd get to me sooner or later."

"What about him?"

"He jumped out the window last night."

"Were you there when he jumped?"

"We were *both* there," Hamling said, and glanced at the girl. The girl nodded.

"Want to tell us what happened?"

"He was on a bum trip," Hamling said. "He thought he could fly. I tried to hold him down, but he ran for the window and jumped out. End of story."

"Why didn't you report this to the police?"

"What for? I've got long hair."

Willis sighed. "Well," he said, "we're here now, so why don't you just tell us everything that happened, and we'll file the damn report and close out the case."

Genero looked at him. Willis was taking out his pad. "Want to tell me what time you went over there?"

"It must've been about four-thirty or so. Look," Hamling said, "am I gonna get in any trouble on this?"

"Why should you? If Scott jumped out the window, that's suicide, plain and simple."

"Yeah, well he did."

"Okay, so help us close it out, will you? This is a headache for us, too," Willis said, and again Genero looked at him. "What happened when you got there?"

"Why do *I* have to be in it, that's all I want to know?" Hamling said.

"Well, you *were* in it, weren't you?"

"Yeah, but . . ."

"So what are we supposed to do? Make believe you *weren't* there? Come on, give us a break. Nobody's trying to get you in trouble. You know how many acid freaks jump out the window every day of the week?"

"I just don't want it to get in the papers or anything," Hamling said. "That's why I didn't call you in the first place."

"We realize that," Willis said. "We'll do everything we can to protect you. Just give us the information we need to get a report typed up, that's all."

"Well, okay," Hamling said reluctantly.

"So what happened? Did all three of you go up there together, or what?" Willis said.

"No, I ran into him on the street," Hamling said. "I was alone at the time. I called Sonia up later, and she came over."

Willis was writing on the pad. Genero was still watching him. Genero had the strangest feeling that something was going on, but he didn't know quite what. He also had the feeling that he was about to learn something. He was both confused and somewhat exhilarated. He kept his mouth shut and simply watched and listened. "All right," Willis said, "you ran into this friend of yours and . . ."

"No, no, he wasn't a friend of mine," Hamling said.

"You didn't know him?"

"No, I just ran into him in this coffee joint, and we began talking, you know? So he asked me if I wanted to come up to his place and hear some records, you know, and . . . listen, can I get in trouble if I *really* level with you guys?"

"I'd appreciate it if you would," Willis said.

"Well, he said he had some good stuff and maybe we could have a smoke. That's all I thought it was at the time. Just a smoke, you see. I mean, if I'd known the guy had acid in his apartment . . ."

"You didn't know that at the time?"

"No, hell, no. I usually try to stay away from these plastic hippies, anyway, they're usually a lot of trouble."

"How do you mean, trouble?"

"Oh, you know, they're trying to show off all the time, trying to be something they really aren't. Weekend hippies, plastic hippies, same damn thing. None of them are *really* making the scene, they're only *pretending* to make it."

"How about you?"

"I consider myself genuine," Hamling said with dignity.

"How about Sonia?"

"Well, she's sort of a weekend hippie," Hamling said, "but she's also a very groovy chick, so I put up with her." He smiled broadly. Sonia did not smile back. She was still frightened. Her hands were clasped in her lap, and she kept shifting her eyes from Willis to Hamling as though knowing that a dangerous game was being played, and wanting desperately to be elsewhere. Genero sensed this, and also sensed in his inexperienced, newly promoted way that the girl was Willis' real prey and that it would only be a matter of time before he sprang for her jugular. The girl knew this, too. Hamling seemed to be the only person in the room who did *not* know it. Supremely confident of himself, he plunged on.

"Anyway, we went up there and smoked a few joints and drank some wine, and it was then I suggested I give Sonia a ring and have her come over, join in the celebration."

"What were you celebrating?" Willis asked.

Hamling hesitated. He thought the question over for several moments, and then grinned and said, "Life. Living. Being alive."

"Okay," Willis said.

Genero was still watching very closely, learning as he went along. He knew, for example, that Hamling had just told a lie. Whatever they'd been celebrating, it had not been life or living or being alive.

He could not have told *how* he knew Hamling had lied, but he knew it. And Willis knew it. And the girl knew it. And Genero knew that before long Willis would come back to the reason for the celebration, in an attempt to expose Hamling's lie. Genero felt great. He felt as though he were watching a cops-and-robbers movie on television. He didn't want it to end, ever. It never once occurred to him, as he watched and listened to Willis, that he himself was a detective. All he knew was that he was having a great time. He almost asked the girl how she was enjoying herself. He wished he had a bag of popcorn.

"So I went down to the street," Hamling said. "He didn't have a phone in the apartment. I went to a pay phone to call Sonia. She . . ."

"Where was Sonia?"

"Here. I was supposed to meet her here at seven o'clock, and this was now maybe close to eight. She has a key, so I knew she'd let herself in."

"Was she here?"

"Oh, yeah. So I asked her to meet me uptown. She said she wasn't too familiar with that part of the city, so I told her what train to take, and I met her at the subway stop."

"What time was that?"

"She must've got there about eight-thirty. Wouldn't you say it was eight-thirty, Sonia?"

The girl nodded.

"Did you go back to the apartment then?"

"Yes," Hamling said. "That was the *first* mistake."

"Why?"

"He was naked when he opened the door. I thought at first . . . hell, I didn't know *what* to think. Then I realized he was high. And then I realized he was on an acid trip. A bummer. I tried to find out what he'd dropped, there's all kinds of stuff, you know, good and bad. Like there's a whole lot of difference between white owsley and green flats; you get shit with strychnine and arsenic mixed into it, man, that's bad news. But he wasn't making any sense at all, didn't know what he'd dropped, didn't know where he was, kept running around the room bare-assed and screaming and yelling he could fly. Scared Sonia half out of her mind, right, honey?"

The girl nodded.

"When did he jump out the window?" Willis asked.

"I don't know, we must've been there maybe twenty minutes. I was trying to talk him down, you know, telling him to cool it, calm it, like that, when all of a sudden he jumps up and makes a break for the window. I tried to grab him, but I was too late. The window was closed, you dig? He went through it head first, man oh man. I looked down in the yard, and there he was laying there like . . ." Hamling shook his head.

"So what'd you do?"

"I grabbed Sonia, and we split. I didn't want to get mixed up in it. You got long hair, you're dead."

"Well, looks open and shut to me," Willis said, and closed his pad. "What do you think, Dick?"

Genero nodded. "Yeah, looks open and shut to me, too," he said. He was beginning to think he'd been mistaken about Willis. Was it possible his more experienced partner had *really* only been after the details of a suicide? He felt vaguely disappointed.

"Just one more question, I guess," Willis said, "and then we can leave you alone. Can't thank you enough for your cooperation. People just don't realize how much trouble they cause when they decide to kill themselves."

"Oh, I can imagine," Hamling said.

"We have to treat suicides just like homicides, you know. Same people to notify, same reports to fill out, it's a big job."

"Oh, sure," Hamling said.

"Well, thanks again," Willis said, and started for the door. "Coming, Dick?"

"Yep," Genero said, and nodded. "Thanks a lot," he said to Hamling.

"Glad to be of help," Hamling said. "If I'd known you guys were going to be so decent, I wouldn't have split, I mean it."

"Oh, that last question," Willis said, as though remembering something that had momentarily slipped his mind. "Miss Sobolev . . ."

Hamling's eyes darted to the girl.

"Miss Sobolev, did you take off your blouse before or after Scott jumped out the window?"

"I don't remember," she said.

"I guess it was before," Willis said. "Because you both left immediately after he jumped."

"Yes, I suppose it was before," Sonia said.

"Miss Sobolev . . . *why* did you take off your blouse?"

"Well . . . I don't know why, really. I mean, I guess I just felt like taking it off."

"I guess she took it off because . . ."

"Well, let's let *her* answer it, okay? So we can clear this up, and leave you alone, okay? Why'd you take it off, Miss Sobolev?"

"I guess it was . . . I guess it was warm in the apartment."

"So you took off your blouse?"

"Yes."

"You'd never met Scott before, but you took off your blouse . . ."

"Well, it was warm."

"He was on a bum trip running around the place and screaming, and you decided to take off your blouse."

"Yes."

"Mmm," Willis said. "Do you want to know how *I* read this, Mr. Hamling?"

"How?" Hamling said, and looked at the girl. Genero looked at both of them, and then looked at Willis. He didn't know *what* was going on. He was so excited, he almost wet his pants.

"I think you're protecting the girl," Willis said.

"Yeah?" Hamling said, puzzled.

"Yeah. It's my guess they were balling in that apartment, and something happened, and the girl here shoved Scott out the window, that's my guess." The girl's mouth had fallen open. Willis turned to her and nodded. "We're going to have to take you with us, Miss Sobolev."

"What do you . . . *mean?*" she said.

"Uptown," Willis answered. "Mr. Hamling, we won't be needing you for now, but the District Attorney may want to ask some more questions after we've booked Miss Sobolev. Please don't leave the city without informing us of your . . ."

"Hey, *wait* a minute," the girl said.

"You want to get your coat, please?" Willis said.

"Listen, *I* didn't push anybody out that damn window!" she said, standing suddenly and putting her hands on her hips.

"Scott was naked, you had your blouse off, what do you expect . . . ?"

"That was *his* idea!" Sonia shouted, hurling the words at Hamling.

"Cool it, Sonia," Hamling warned.

"It was *his* idea to get undressed, he wanted to find the damn . . ."

"The damn *what?*" Willis snapped.

"The damn money belt!"

Hamling was breaking for the front door. Genero watched in fascinated immobility. Willis was directly in Hamling's path, between him and the door. Hamling was a head taller than Willis and a foot wider, and Genero was certain the boy would now knock his partner flat on his ass. He almost wished he would, because then it would be terribly exciting to see what happened next. Hamling was charging for that front door like an express train, and Genero fully expected him to bowl Willis over and continue running into the corridor, down the steps, into the street, and all the way to China. If he was in Willis' place, he would have got out of the way very quickly, because a man can get hurt by a speeding locomotive. But instead of getting out of the way, Willis started running *toward* Hamling, and suddenly dropped to his right knee. Hamling's right foot was ahead of his left at that moment, with all the weight on it, and as he rushed forward, Willis grabbed his left ankle, and began pulling Hamling forward and pushing him upward at the same time, his right hand against Hamling's chest as he rose. The result was somewhat similar to a football quarterback being hit high and low at the same instant from two opposite directions. Hamling flew over backward, his ankle still clutched in Willis' hand, his head banging back hard against the floor.

Genero blinked.

Willis was stooping over the fallen Hamling now, a gun in his right hand, his handcuffs open in the other hand. He slapped one onto Hamling's wrist, squeezed it closed. The sawtooth edges clicked shut into the retaining metal of the receiver. Willis pulled hard on the cuffs and yanked Hamling to his feet. He whirled him around, pulled his other arm behind his back, and snapped the second cuff shut.

Genero was out of breath.

Danny Gimp was a stool pigeon who told everybody he was a burglar. This was understandable. In a profession where access to underworld gossip was absolutely essential, it was a decided advantage to be considered one of the boys.

Actually, Danny was not a burglar, even though he had been arrested and convicted for burglary in the city of Los Angeles, California, back in the year nineteen hundred and thirty-eight. He had always been a sickly person, and had gone out West to cure himself of a persistent cold. He had met a drinking companion in a bar on La Brea, and the guy had asked Danny to stop by his house while he picked up some more money so that they could continue their all-night revel. They had driven up the Strip past La Cienega and had both entered the guy's house through the back door. The guy had gone into the bedroom and come back a little while later to where Danny was waiting for him in the kitchen. He had picked up several hundred dollars in cash, not to mention a diamond and ruby necklace valued at forty-seven thousand five hundred dollars. But it seemed that Danny was not the only person waiting for his drinking companion to come out of the bedroom. The Los Angeles police were also waiting. In fact, the way Danny found out about the value of the necklace was that the police happened to tell him. Danny tried to explain all this to the judge. He also mentioned to the judge that he had suffered polio as a child, and was a virtual cripple, and that jail would not be very good for his health or his disposition. The judge had kindly considered everything Danny had to say and then had sentenced Danny and his drinking companion to a minimum of five and a maximum of ten. Danny never spoke to his drinking companion again after that night, even though the men were in the same cell block. The guy was killed by a black homosexual prisoner a year later, stabbed in the throat with a table knife honed to razor sharpness in the sheet metal shop. The black homosexual stood trial for murder, was convicted, and was executed. Danny served his time thinking about the vagaries of justice, and left prison with the single qualification he would need to pursue a profitable career as a snitch. He was an ex-con. If you can't trust an ex-con, who *can* you trust? Such was the underworld belief, and it accounted for the regularity with which Danny Gimp received choice bits of information, which he then passed on to the police at a price. It was a living, and not a bad one.

Carl Kapek had put in a call to Danny that afternoon. The two men met in Grover Park at seven minutes before five. The afternoon was beginning to wane. They sat together on a park bench and watched governesses wheeling their charges home in baby buggies, watched touch football games beginning to break up, watched a little girl walking slowly by on the winding path, trailing a skip rope behind her and studying the ground the way only little girls can, with an intense concentration that indicated she was pondering all the female secrets of the universe.

"Belinda, huh?" Danny said.

"Yeah. Belinda."

Danny sniffed. He always seemed to have a cold lately, Kapek noticed. Maybe he was getting old.

"And you don't know Belinda *what,* huh?" Danny said.

"That's why I called you," Kapek said.

"She's a spade, huh?"

"Yeah."

"I don't read her right off," Danny said. He sniffed again. "It's getting to be winter already, you realize that?"

"It's not so bad," Kapek said.

"It stinks," Danny answered. "Why do you want this broad?"

"She mugged a marine."

"You're putting me on," Danny said, and laughed.

"She didn't do it alone."

"A guy was in it with her?"

"Yeah. She played up to the marine in a bar on Seventeenth, indicated she wanted him to follow her. When he did, she led him to her partner, and they put him out of action."

"Is the guy a spade, too?"

"No, he's white."

"Belinda," Danny said. "That's a pretty name. I knew a girl named Belinda once. Only girl I ever knew who didn't mind the leg. This was in Chicago one time. I was in Chicago one time. I got people in Chicago. Belinda Kolaczkowska. A Pole. Pretty as a picture, blond hair, blue eyes, big tits." Danny demonstrated with his hands, and then immediately put them back in his pockets. "I asked her one time how come she was going out with a guy like me. I was talking about the limp, you know? She said, 'What do you mean, a guy like you?' So I looked her in the eye, and I said, 'You know what I mean, Belinda.' And she said, 'No, I don't know what you mean, Danny.' So I said, 'Belinda, the fact is that I limp.' So she smiled and said, 'You *do?*' I'll never forget that smile. I swear to God, if I live to be a hundred and ten, I'll never forget the way Belinda smiled at me that day in Chicago. I felt I could run a mile that day. I felt I could win the goddamn Olympics." He shook his head, and then sniffed again. A flock of pigeons suddenly took wing not six feet from where the men were sitting, filling the air with the sound of their flight. They soared up against the sky, wheeled, and alighted again near a bench further on, where an old man in a threadbare brown coat was throwing bread crumbs into the air.

"Anyway, that ain't the Belinda you're looking for," Danny said. He thought a moment longer, and then seemed to suppress the memory completely, pulling his head into his overcoat, thrusting his hands deeper into his pockets. "Can you give me a description of her?" he asked.

"All I know is she's black, and well built, and she was wearing a red dress."

"That could mean two thousand girls in this city," Danny said. "What about the guy?"

"Nothing."

"Great."

"What do you think?"

"I think you're very good for a chuckle on a Sunday when winter's coming, that's what I think."

"Can you help or not?"

"Let me listen a little, who knows? Will you be around?"

"I'll be around."

"I'll get back."

There are times in the city when night refuses to come.

The afternoon lingers, the light changes only slowly and imperceptibly, there is a sense of sweet suspension.

This was just such a day.

There was a briskness to the air, you could never confuse this with a spring day. And yet the afternoon possessed that same luminous quality, the sky so intensely blue that it seemed to vibrate indignantly against encroachment, flatly resisting passage through the color spectrum to darkness. When the street lights came on at five-thirty, they did so in vain. There was nothing to illuminate, the day was still bright. The sun hung stubbornly over the buildings to the west in downtown Majesta and Calm's Point, defying the earth's rotation, balking at extinction behind roof copings and chimney pots. The citizens of the city lingered in the streets bemused, reluctant to go indoors, as though witnessing some vast astronomical disorder, some realized Nostradamus prediction—it would be daytime forever, the night would never come; there would be dancing in the streets.

The sky to the west yielded at last.

In Herbert Gross's apartment, the light was beginning to fade.

Carella and Brown had been in there for close to three hours now, and whereas they had searched the place from floor to ceiling, wall to wall, timber to toilet tank, they had not found a single clue that told them where Gross had been heading when he hopped that uptown bus.

The clue was everywhere around them. They just hadn't found it yet.

The apartment was a contradiction in itself. It was small and cramped, a cubicle in a crumbling tenement surrounded by warehouses. But it was crowded with furniture that surely had been purchased in the early thirties, when solidity was a virtue and inlaid mahogany was the decorative rule. In the living room, a huge overstuffed sofa was upholstered in maroon mohair, its claw feet clutching the faded Persian rug that covered the floor. The sofa alone would have been quite enough to overwhelm the dimensions of the small room, but there were two equally overstuffed easy chairs, and a credenza that seemed to have wandered in from an ornate dining room someplace, and a standing floor lamp with a pink, fringed shade, and an ornately framed painting of snow-clad mountain peaks towering over a placid lake, and a Stromberg-Carlson floor model radio complete with push buttons and a jukebox look, and mahogany end tables on either side of the sofa, each with a tiny drawer, each carrying a huge porcelain lamp with a shade covered in plastic.

The first bedroom had a huge double bed with mahogany head-board and footboard and an unmade mattress. A heavy mahogany dresser of the type that used to be called a "bureau" when Busby Berkeley was all the rage, complete with its own mahogany-framed mirror, was on the wall opposite the bed. A taller version of it—the male counterpart, so to speak—with longer hanging space for trousers and suits and a row of drawers one atop the other for the storing of handkerchiefs, cuff links, and sundries (Jimmy Walker would have called it a "chiffonier"), was on the window wall.

The second bedroom was furnished in more modern terms, with two narrow beds covered with simple throws, a Mexican rug hanging on the wall over them. A bookcase was on the wall opposite, along-side a closet without a door. With the exception of the kitchen and the bathroom, there was one other room in the apartment, and this room seemed to have escaped from Arthur Miller's play *The Price*. It was literally packed from floor to ceiling with furniture and china and glassware and marked and unmarked cartons (among those marked was one lettered with the words "WORLD'S FAIR 1939") and piles of books tied with twine, and cooking utensils, and even old articles of clothing draped over chairs or cartons, a veritable child's dream of an attic hideout, equipped with anything needed to serve whatever imaginary excursion suited the fancy.

"I don't get this place," Carella said.

"Neither do I," Brown said. He turned on the floor lamp in the living room, and they sat opposite each other, tired and dusty, Carella on the monstrous sofa, Brown in one of the big easy chairs. The room was washed with the glow of the pink, fringed lampshade. Carella almost felt as if he were sitting down to do his homework to the accompaniment of "Omar the Mystic" flooding from the old Stromberg-Carlson.

"Everything's wrong but that one bedroom," he said. "The rest of it doesn't fit."

"Or maybe vice versa," Brown said.

"I mean, who the hell has furniture like that nowadays?"

"My mother has furniture like that," Brown said.

Both men were silent. It was Carella who broke the silence at last.

"When did Goldenthal's mother die?" he asked.

"Three months ago, I think the report said. He was living with her until then."

"You think all this crap might have been hers?"

"Maybe. Maybe he moved it all here when he left the other apartment."

"You remember her first name?"

"Minnie."

"How many Goldenthals do you suppose there are in the telephone book?"

They did not even consider looking in the directories for Bethtown, Majesta, or Calm's Point, because Gross had been heading *uptown,* and access to all those other sections of the city would have required going *downtown.* They did not consider looking in the Riverhead directory, either, because Gross had taken a bus, and bus transportation all the way to Riverhead was a hell of a slow way to go, when there were express trains running all day long. So they limited their search to the Isola directory alone. (There was one other reason they consulted just this one phone book; it happened to be the *only* one Gross had in the apartment.)

There were eight Goldenthals listed in the Isola directory.

But only one of them was Minnie Goldenthal—now deceased, poor lady, her name surviving in print only until next year's directory would be published by the telephone company.

Sic transit gloria mundi.

The building in which Minnie Goldenthal had lived was a twelve-story yellow brick structure bristling with television antennae. It was fronted by a small cement courtyard flanked by two yellow brick pillars, atop which sat two stone urns that were probably planted with flowers in the spring, but that now contained only withered stalks. Enclosing this courtyard were the two wings of the building, and a row of apartments connecting both wings, so that the result was an architectural upside-down U facing the low flat entrance steps to the courtyard. The mailboxes for each wing were in the entryway to the right and left. Carella checked one entry, Brown the other. There was no listing for Goldenthal, Minnie or otherwise.

"What do you think?" Carella asked.

"Let's check the super," Brown suggested.

The superintendent lived on the ground floor, in an apartment behind the staircase. He came to the door in his undershirt. A television set was going somewhere in his apartment, but apparently the show had not completely captured his attention, because he was carrying the Sunday comics in his right hand. The detectives identified themselves. The super looked at Carella's shield. He looked at Carella's I.D. card. Then he said, "Yes?"

"Was there a Minnie Goldenthal living here recently?" Carella asked.

The super listened attentively to his every word, as though he were being asked a question which, if answered correctly, would cause him to win a hundred-thousand-dollar jackpot.

Then he said, "Yes."

"Which apartment?"

"Nine-D."

"Anyone living in that apartment now?"

"Son's still living in it."

"Bernie Goldenthal?"

"That's right. Don't know *why* he's living in it, mind you. Moved all the furniture out a little while after Minnie died. Still pays the rent, though." The super shrugged. "Tell you the truth, the owners wish he'd get out. That apartment's price-fixed. Nice big old apartment. If he gets out, they can put a new tenant in and legally raise the rent."

"Anybody up there now?" Carella asked.

"Don't know," the super said. "Don't keep tabs on the comings and goings of the people who live here. Their business is their business, and mine is mine."

"Law requires you to have a key to all the apartments in the dwelling," Carella said. "Have you got one for Nine-D?"

"Yep."

"All right if we use it?"

"What for?"

"To enter the apartment."

"That's illegal, ain't it?"

"We won't tell anybody if you won't," Brown said.

"Well," the super said, and shrugged. "Okay," he said, and shrugged again. "I guess."

Carella and Brown took the elevator up to the ninth floor and stepped into the corridor. Neither man said a word to the other, but both simultaneously drew their revolvers. 9D was at the far end of the hall. They listened outside the door and heard nothing. Cautiously, Carella inserted the passkey into the lock. He nodded to Brown, and twisted the key. There was only a small click as the lock turned, but it must have sounded like a warning shot inside that apartment. Carella and Brown burst into a long narrow entrance foyer. At the far end of the foyer, they saw Herbert Gross and a blond man they assumed to be Bernard Goldenthal, both of them armed.

"Hold it right there!" Carella shouted, but neither of the two men were holding anything right there or right anywhere. They opened fire just as Carella and Brown threw themselves flat on the linoleum-covered floor. Goldenthal made a break for a doorway to the right of the long foyer. Brown shouted a warning and fired almost before the words left his lips. The slug caught Goldenthal in the leg, knocked him off his feet and sent him flailing against the corridor wall, where he slid to the floor. Gross held his ground, firing down the long length of the foyer, pulling off shot after shot until his pistol clicked empty. He was reaching into his jacket pocket, presumably for fresh cartridges, when Carella shouted, "Move and you're dead!"

Gross's hand stopped in mid-motion. He squinted down the corridor, silhouetted in the light that spilled from the room Goldenthal had tried to reach.

"Drop the gun," Carella said.

Gross did not move.

"*Drop* it!" Carella shouted. "Now!"

"You, too, Goldie!" Brown shouted.

Goldenthal and Gross—one crouched against the wall clutching his bleeding leg, the other with his hand still hanging motionless over his jacket pocket—exchanged quick glances. Without saying a word to each other, they dropped their guns to the floor. Gross kicked them away as if they were contaminated. The guns came spinning down the length of the corridor one after the other, sliding along the waxed linoleum.

Carella got to his feet, and started toward the two men. Behind him, Brown was crouched on one knee, his gun resting on his forearm and pointing directly at the far end of the foyer. Carella threw Gross against the wall, quickly frisked him, and then bent over Goldenthal.

"Okay," he called to Brown, and then glanced into the room on the right of the foyer. It, too, was loaded with household goods. But unlike the stuff in the apartment downtown, this had not come from a dead woman's home, this was not the accumulation of a lifetime. This was, instead, the result of God knew how many recent burglaries and robberies, a veritable storehouse of television sets, radios, typewriters, tape recorders, broilers, mixers, luggage, you name it, right down to a complete set of the Encyclopaedia Britannica—a criminal bargain basement, awaiting only the services of a good fence.

"Nice little place you've got here," Carella said, and then handcuffed Gross to Goldenthal and Goldenthal to the radiator. From a telephone on the kitchen wall, the late Minnie's last shopping list still tacked up beside it, he called the station house and asked for a meat wagon. It arrived at exactly 6 P.M., not seven minutes after Carella requested it. By that time, Goldenthal had spilled a goodly amount of blood all over his mother's linoleum.

"I'm bleeding to death here," he complained to one of the hospital orderlies who was lifting him onto the stretcher.

"That's the least of your worries," the orderly answered.

Delgado had not found Pepe Castañeda in the pool hall, nor had he found him in any one of a dozen bars he tried in the neighborhood. It was now a quarter past six, and he was about ready to give up the search. On the dubious assumption, however, that a pool shooter might also be a bowler, he decided to hit the Ponce Bowling Lanes on Culver Avenue before heading back to the squadroom.

The place was on the second floor of an old brick building. Delgado went up the narrow flight of steps and came into a fluorescent-lighted room with a counter just opposite the entrance doorway. A bald-headed man was sitting on a stool behind the counter, reading a newspaper. He looked up as Delgado came in, went back to the newspaper, finished the story he was reading, and then put both hands flat on the countertop. "All the alleys are full," he said. "You got maybe a half-hour wait."

"I don't want an alley," Delgado said.

The man behind the counter looked at him more carefully, decided he was a cop, gave a brief knowledgeable nod, but said nothing.

"I'm looking for a man named Pepe Castañeda. Is he here?"

"What do you want him for?" the man said.

"I'm a police officer," Delgado said, and flashed the tin. "I want to ask him some questions."

"I don't want no trouble here," the man said.

"Why should there be trouble? Is Castañeda trouble?"

"*He's* not the trouble," the man said, and looked at Delgado meaningfully.

"Neither am I," Delgado said. "Where is he?"

"Lane number five," the man said.

"Thanks."

Delgado went through the doorway adjacent to the counter and found himself in a larger room than the small reception area had promised. There were twelve alleys in all, each of them occupied with bowlers. A bar was at the far end of the place, with tables and chairs set up around it. A jukebox was playing a rock-and-roll song. The record ended as Delgado moved past the racks of bowling balls against the low wall that separated the lanes from the area behind them. A Spanish-language song erupted from the loud-speakers. Everywhere, there was the reverberating clamor of falling pins, multiplied and echoing in the high-ceilinged room, joined by voices raised in jubilant exclamation or disgruntled invective.

There were four men bowling in lane number five. Three of them were seated on the leatherette banquette that formed a semi-circle around the score pad. The fourth man stood waiting for his ball to return. It came rolling down the tracks from the far end of the alley, hit the stop mechanism, eased its way toward his waiting hand. He picked up the ball, stepped back some five feet from the foul line, crouched, started his forward run, right arm coming back, left arm out for balance, stopped dead, and released the ball. It curved down the alley and arced in true between the one and three pins. The bowler hung frozen in motion, his right arm still ex-tended, left arm back, crouched and waiting for the explosion of pins. They flew into the air like gleeful cheerleaders, there was the sound of their leap as the ball sent them helter-skelter, the additional sound of their pell-mell return to the polished alley floor. The bowler shouted, "Made it!" and turned to the three men on the banquette.

"Which one of you is Pepe Castañeda?" Delgado asked.

The bowler, who was walking back toward the score pad to supervise the correct marking of the strike, stopped in his tracks and looked up at Delgado. He was a short man with straight black hair and a pockmarked face, thin, with the light step of a dancer, a step that seemed even airier in the red, rubber-soled bowling shoes.

"I'm Castañeda," he said. "Who're you?"

"Detective Delgado, Eighty-seventh Squad," Delgado said. "Mind if I ask you a few questions?"

"What about?"

"Is Ramon Castañeda your brother?"

"That's right."

"Why don't we walk over there and talk a little?"

"Over where?"

"The tables there."

"I'm in the middle of a game."

"The game can wait."

Castañeda shrugged. One of the men on the banquette said, "Go ahead, Pepe. We'll order a round of beer meanwhile."

"How many frames we got to go?"

"Just three," the other man said.

"This gonna take long?" Castañeda asked.

"I don't think so," Delgado said.

"Well, okay. We're ahead here, I don't want to cool off."

They walked together to the bar at the far end of the room. Two young girls in tight slacks were standing near the jukebox, pondering their next selection. Castañeda looked them over, and then pulled out a chair at one of the tables. The men sat opposite each other. The jukebox erupted again with sound. The intermittent rumble of exploding pins was a steady counterpoint.

"What do you want to know?" Castañeda asked.

"Your brother's got a partner named José Huerta," Delgado said.

"That's right."

"Do you know him?"

"Yeah, I know Joe."

"Do you know he was beaten up this morning?"

"He was? No, I didn't know that. You got a cigarette? I left mine on the table back there."

"I don't smoke," Delgado said.

"I didn't used to smoke, either," Castañeda said. "But, you know . . ." He shrugged. "You break one habit, you pick up another, huh?" He grinned. The grin was wide and infectious. He was perhaps three or four years younger than Delgado, but he suddenly looked like a teenager. "I used to be a junkie, you know. Did you know that?"

"Yes, I've heard it."

"I kicked it."

"I've heard that, too."

"Ain't you impressed?"

"I'm impressed," Delgado said.

"So am I," Castañeda said, and grinned again. Delgado grinned

with him. "So, I still don't know what you want from me," Castañeda said.

"He got beat up pretty badly," Delgado said. "Broke both his legs,
chopped his face up like hamburger."

"Gee, that's too bad," Castañeda said. "Who done it?"

"Four men."

"Boy," Castañeda said, and shook his head.

"They got him on the front stoop of his building. He was on his
way to church."

"Yeah? Where does he live?"

"On South Sixth."

"Oh yeah, that's right," Castañeda said. "Across the street from
the candy store, right?"

"Yes. The reason I wanted to talk to you," Delgado said, "is that
your brother seemed to think the four men who beat up Huerta were
asked to beat him up."

"I don't follow you," Castañeda said.

"When I asked your brother who disliked Huerta, he said, 'No one
dislikes him enough to have him beaten up.' "

"So? What does that mean?"

"It means . . ."

"It don't mean nothing," Castañeda said, and shrugged.

"It means your brother thinks the men who beat up Huerta were
doing it for somebody else, not themselves."

"I don't see where you get that," Castañeda said. "That was just a
way of speaking, that's all. My brother didn't mean nothing by it."

"Let's say he did. Let's say for the moment that somebody *wanted*
Huerta beaten up. And let's say he asked four men to do the favor
for him."

"Okay, let's say that."

"Would you happen to know who those four men might be?"

"Nope," Castañeda said. "I really could use a cigarette, you know?
You mind if I go back to the table for them?"

"The cigarette can wait, Pepe. There's a man in the hospital with
two broken legs and a busted face."

"Gee, that's too bad," Castañeda said, "but maybe the man
should've been more careful, you know? Then maybe nobody
would've *wanted* him beaten up, and nobody would've talked to anybody *about* beating him up."

"Who wanted him hurt, Pepe?"

"You interested in some guesses?"

"I'm interested."

"Joe's a pusher, did you know that?"

"I know that."

"Grass. For now. But I never yet met a guy selling grass who didn't later figure there was more profit in the hard stuff. It's just a matter of time, that's all."

"So?"

"So maybe somebody didn't like the idea of him poisoning the neighborhood, you dig? I'm only saying. But it's something to consider, right?"

"Yes, it's something to consider."

"And maybe Joe was chasing after somebody's wife, too. Maybe somebody's got a real pretty wife, and maybe Joe's been making it with her, you dig? That's another thing to consider. So maybe somebody decided to break both his legs so he couldn't run around no more balling somebody else's wife and selling poison to the kids in the *barrio*. And maybe they decided to mess up his face for good measure, you dig? So he wouldn't look so pretty to other guys' wives, and so maybe when he come up to a kid in the neighborhood and tried to get him hooked, the kid might not want to deal with somebody who had a face looked like it hit a meat grinder." Castañeda paused. "Those are all things to consider, right?"

"Yes, they're all things to consider," Delgado said.

"I don't think you're ever gonna find those guys who beat him up," Castañeda said. "But what difference does it make?"

"What do you mean?"

"He got what he deserved. That's justice, ain't it? That's what you guys are interested in, ain't it? Justice?"

"Yes, we're interested in justice."

"So this was justice," Castañeda said.

Delgado looked at him.

"Wasn't it?" Castañeda asked.

"Yes, I think it was," Delgado said. He nodded, rose from the table suddenly, pushed his chair back under it, and said, "Nice talking to you. See you around."

"Buy you a drink or something?" Castañeda asked.

"Thanks, I've still got an hour before I'm off duty," Delgado answered, and walked away from the table.

Behind him, Castañeda raised his hand in farewell.

It was 7 P.M. by the time Brown finally got around to Mary Ellingham, the lady who had called in twelve hours before to report that her husband was missing. Full darkness was upon the city now, but it was not yet nighttime; it was still that time of day called "evening," a poetic word that always stirred something deep inside Brown, perhaps because he had never heard the word as a child and only admitted it to his vocabulary after he met Connie, his wife-to-be, when things stopped being merely night and day, or black and white; Connie had brought shadings to his life, and for that he would love her forever.

North Trinity was a two-block-long street off Silvermine Oval, adjacent to fancy Silvermine Road, which bordered on the River Harb and formed the northern frontier of the precinct. From where Brown had parked the car, he could see the waters of the river, and uptown the scattered lights of the estates in Smoke Rise, the brighter illumination on the Hamilton Bridge. The lights were on along Trinity, too, beckoning warmly from windows in the rows of brown-stones that faced the secluded street. Brown knew that behind most of those windows, the occupants were enjoying their cocktail hour. One could always determine the socio-economic standing of anybody in this city by asking him what time he ate his dinner. In a slum like Diamondback, the dinner hour had already come and gone. On Trinity Street, the residents were having their before-dinner drinks. Further uptown in Smoke Rise, the dinner hour would not start until nine or nine-thirty—although the cocktail hour may have started at noon.

Brown was hungry.

There were no lights burning at 742 North Trinity. Brown looked at his watch, shrugged, and rang the front doorbell. He waited, rang the doorbell a second time, and then stepped down off the front stoop to look up at the second story of the building, where a light had suddenly come on. He went back up the steps and waited. He heard someone approaching the door. A peephole flap was thrown back.

"Yes?" a woman's voice asked.

"Mrs. Ellingham?"

"Yes?"

"Detective Brown, Eighty-seventh Squad."

"Oh," Mrs. Ellingham said. "Oh, just a minute, please." The peephole flap fell back into place. He heard the door being unlocked.

Mary Ellingham was about forty years old. She was wearing a man's flannel robe. Her hair was disarrayed. Her face was flushed.

"I'm sorry I got here so late," Brown said. "We had a sort of busy day."

"Oh," Mrs. Ellingham said. "Yes."

"I won't keep you long," Brown said, reaching into his pocket for his pad and pen. "If you'll just give me a description of your husband . . ."

"Oh," Mrs. Ellingham said.

"His name is Donald Ellingham, is that correct?"

"Yes, but . . ."

"How old is he?"

"Well, you see . . ."

Brown looked up from his pad. Mrs. Ellingham seemed terribly embarrassed all at once. Before she uttered another word, Brown realized what he had walked in on, and he too was suddenly embarrassed.

"You see," Mrs. Ellingham said, "he's back. My husband. He got back just a little while ago."

"Oh," Brown said.

"Yes," she said.

"Oh."

"Yes. I'm sorry. I suppose I should have called . . ."

"No, no, that's all right," Brown said. He put his pad and his pen back into his pocket, and reached behind him for the doorknob. "Glad he's back, glad everything worked out all right."

"Yes," Mrs. Ellingham said.

"Good night," Brown said.

"Good night," she said.

She closed the door gently behind him as he went down the steps. Just before he got into his automobile, he glanced back at the building. The upstairs light had already gone out again.

Back at the squadroom, the three detectives who had been called in off vacation were bitching about the speed with which Carella and Brown had cracked the grocery store case. It was one thing to interrupt a man's vacation if there was a goddamn *need* for it; it was another to call him in and trot him around all day asking questions and gathering data while two other guys were out following a hot lead that resulted in an arrest.

"You know what I coulda been doing today?" Di Maeo asked.

"What?" Levine said.

"I coulda been watching the ball game on television, and I coulda had a big dinner with the family. My sister is in from Scranton, she come all the way in from Scranton 'cause she knows I'm on vacation. So instead I'm talking to a bunch of people who couldn't care less whether a grocer got shot, and who couldn't care at *all* whether a cop caught one."

Meriwether the hairbag said, "Now, now, fellows, it's all part of the game, all part of the game."

In two separate locked rooms down the corridor, Willis was interrogating Sonia Sobolev, and Genero was interrogating Robert Hamling. Neither of the suspects had exercised their right to an attorney. Hamling, who claimed he had nothing to hide, seemed pleased in fact that he could get his story on the record. He repeated essentially what he had told them in the apartment: Lewis Scott had been on a bum acid trip and had thrown himself out the window while Hamling had done all he could to prevent the suicide. The stenographer listened to every word, his fingers moving silently over his machine.

Sonia Sobolev apparently felt no need for an attorney because she did not consider herself mixed up in the death of Lewis Scott. Her version of the story differed greatly from Hamling's. According to Sonia, Hamling had met the bearded Scott that afternoon and the two had banked around the city for a while, enjoying each other's company. Scott was indeed celebrating something—the arrival from home of a two-hundred-dollar money order, which he had cashed and which, in the form of ten-dollar bills, was now nestling in a money belt under his shirt. Hamling had gone back to Scott's apartment with him, and tried to get him drunk. When that failed, he asked Scott if he didn't think they needed a little female company, and when Scott agreed that might not be a bad idea, Hamling had gone downstairs to call Sonia.

"What did he tell you when he met you later?" Willis asked.

"Well, I got off the train," Sonia said, "and Bobby was waiting there for me. He said he had this dumb plastic hippie in an apartment nearby, and the guy had a money belt with two hundred dollars in it, and Bobby *wanted* that money. He said the only way to get it was to convince the guy to take off his clothes. And the only way to do that was for me to do it first." Sonia shrugged. "So we went up there."

"Yes, what happened then?"

"Well, I went in the john and combed my hair and then I took off my blouse. And I went out to the other room without any blouse on. To see if I could, well, get him excited, you know. So he would take off his clothes. We were all drinking a lot of wine."

"Were you smoking?"

"Pot, you mean? No."

"So what happened?"

"Well, he finally went in the john, too, and got undressed. He was wearing blue jeans and a Charlie Brown sweat shirt. And he *did* have a money belt. He was wearing a money belt."

"Did he take that off, too?"

"Yes."

"And then what?"

"Well, he came back to the mattress, and we started fooling around a little, you know, just touching each other. Actually, I was sort of keeping him busy while Bobby went through the money belt. Trouble is, he *saw* Bobby. And he jumped up and ran to where Bobby was standing with the money belt in his hands, and they started fighting, and that . . . that was when Bobby pushed him out the window. We split right away. I just threw on my jacket, and Bobby put on his coat, and we split. I didn't even remember the blouse until much later."

"Where's the money belt now?" Willis asked.

"In Bobby's apartment. Under his mattress."

In the other room, Hamling kept insisting that Lewis Scott was an acid freak who had thrown himself out the window to the pavement below. Di Maeo knocked on the door, poked his head inside, and said, "Dick, you send some suspect dope to the lab?"

"Yeah," Genero said.

"They just phoned. Said it was oregano."

"Thanks," Genero said. He turned again to Hamling. "The stuff in Lewis Scott's refrigerator was oregano," he said.

"So what?" Hamling said.

"So tell me one more time about this big acid freak you got involved with."

In the squadroom outside, Carella sat at his desk typing a report on Goldenthal and Gross. Goldenthal had been taken to Buenavista, the same hospital that was caring for Andy Parker, whom he had shot. Gross had refused to say a word to anyone. He had been booked for Armed Robbery and Murder One, and was being held in one of the detention cells downstairs. Carella looked extremely tired. When the telephone on his desk rang, he stared at it for several moments before answering it.

"Eighty-seventh Squad," he said, "Carella."

"Steve, this is Artie Brown."

"Hello, Artie," Carella said.

"I just wrapped up this squeal on North Trinity. Guy came home, and they're happily in the sack."

"Good for them," Carella said. "I wish *I* was happily in the sack."

"You want me to come back there, or what?"

"What time is it?"

"Seven-thirty."

"Go home, Artie."

"You sure? What about the report?"

"I'm typing it now."

"Okay then, I'll see you," Brown said.

"Right," Carella said, and put the receiver back onto its cradle, and looked up at the wall clock, and sighed. The telephone on Carl Kapek's desk was ringing.

"Eighty-seventh," he said, "Kapek speaking."

"This is Danny Gimp," the voice on the other end said.

"Hello, Danny, what've you got for me?"

"Nothing," Danny said.

Di Maeo, Meriwether, and Levine were packing it in, hoping to resume their vacations without further interruption. Levine seemed certain that Brown and Carella would get promotions out of this one; there were always promotions when you cracked a case involving somebody doing something to a cop. Di Maeo agreed with him, and commented that some guys had all the luck. They went down the iron-runged steps and past the muster desk, and through the old building's entrance doors. Meriwether stopped on the front steps to tie his shoelace. Alex Delgado was just getting back to the station house. He chatted for only a moment, said good night to all of them, and went inside. It was almost seven forty-five, and some of the relieving shift was already in the squadroom.

In a little while, the daywatch could go home.

Kapek had been cruising from bar to bar along The Stem since 8 P.M. It was now twenty minutes past eleven, and his heart skipped a beat when the black girl in the red dress came through the doors of Romeo's on Twelfth Street. The girl sashayed past the men sitting on stools along the length of the bar, took a seat at the far end near the telephones, and crossed her legs. Kapek gave her ten minutes to eye every guy in the joint, and then walked past her to the telephones. He dialed the squadroom, and got Finch, the catcher on the relieving team.

"What are you doing?" Finch wanted to know.

"Oh, cruising around," Kapek said.

"I thought you went home hours ago."

"No rest for the weary," Kapek said. "I'm about to make a bust. If I'm lucky."

"Need some help?"

"Nope," Kapek said.

"Then why the hell did you call?"

"Just to make some small talk," Kapek said.

"I've got a knifing on Ainsley," Finch answered. "Go make small talk someplace else."

Kapek took his advice. He hung up, felt in the coin return chute for his dime, shrugged, and went out to sit next to the girl at the bar.

"I'll bet your name is Suzie," he said.

"Wrong," the girl said, and grinned. "It's Belinda."

"Belinda, you are one beautiful piece," Kapek said.

"You think so, huh?"

"I do most sincerely think so," Kapek said. "May I offer to buy you a drink?"

"I'd be flattered," Belinda said.

They chatted for close to twenty minutes. Belinda indicated that she found Kapek highly attractive; it was rare that a girl could just wander into a neighborhood bar and find someone of Kapek's intelligence and sensitivity, she told him. She indicated, too, that she would like to spend some time with Kapek a little later on, but that her husband was a very jealous man and that she couldn't risk leaving the bar with Kapek because word might get back to her husband and then there would be all kinds of hell to pay. Kapek told her he certainly understood her position. Still, Belinda said, I sure would love to spend some time with you, honey. Kapek nodded.

"What do you suppose we can do?" he asked.

"You can meet me outside, can't you?"

"Sure," he said. "Where?"

"Let's drink up. Then I'll leave, and you can follow me out in a few minutes. How does that sound?"

Kapek looked up at the clock behind the bar. It was ten minutes to twelve. "That sounds fine to me," he said.

Belinda lifted her whiskey sour and drained it. She winked at him and swiveled away from the bar. At the door, she turned, winked again, and then went out. Kapek gave her five minutes. He finished his scotch and soda, paid for the drinks, and went out after her. Belinda was waiting on the next corner. She signaled to him, and began walking rapidly up The Stem. Kapek nodded and followed her. She walked two blocks east, looked back at him once again, and turned abruptly left on Fifteenth Street. Kapek reached the corner and drew his pistol. He hesitated, cleared his throat to let them know he was coming, and then rounded the corner.

A white man was standing there with his fist cocked. Kapek

thrust the gun into his face and said, "Everybody stand still." Belinda started to break. He grabbed her wrist, flung her against the brick wall of the building, said, "You, too, honey," and took his handcuffs from his belt.

He looked at his watch.

It was a minute to midnight.

Another day was about to start.

JIGSAW

This is for
Helen and Gene Federico

1

DETECTIVE Arthur Brown did not like being called black.

This might have had something to do with his name, which was Brown. Or his color, which was also brown. Or it might have had something to do with the fact that when he was but a mere strip of a boy coming along in this fair city, the word "black" was usually linked alliteratively with the word "bastard." He was now thirty-four years old and somewhat old-fashioned, he supposed, but he still considered the word derogatory, no matter how many civil rights leaders endorsed it. Brown didn't need to seek identity in his color or in his soul. He searched for it in himself as a man, and usually found it there with ease.

He was six feet four inches tall, and he weighed two hundred and twenty pounds in his undershorts. He had the huge frame and powerful muscles of a heavyweight fighter, a square clean look emphasized by the way he wore his hair, clipped close, clinging to his skull like a soft black cap, a style he had favored even before it became fashionable to look "natural." His eyes were brown, his nostrils were large, he had thick lips and thicker hands, and he wore a .38 Smith & Wesson in a shoulder holster under his jacket.

The two men lying on the floor at his feet were white. And dead.

One of them was wearing black shoes, blue socks, dark blue trousers, a pale blue shirt open at the throat, a tan poplin zippered jacket, a gold Star-of-David on a slender gold chain around his neck, and two bullet holes in his chest. The other one was dressed more elegantly—brown shoes, socks and trousers, white shirt, green tie, houndstooth-check sports jacket. The broken blade of a switch knife was barely visible in his throat, just below the Adam's apple. A Luger was on the floor near his open right hand.

The apartment was a shambles.

It was not a great apartment to begin with; Brown had certainly seen better apartments, even in the ghetto where he had spent the first twenty-two years of his life. This one was on the third floor of a Culver Avenue tenement, two rooms and a bathroom, rear exposure, meaning that it faced on a back yard with clotheslines flapping Wednesday's wash. It was now close to 10 P.M., six minutes after the building's landlady had stopped the cop on the beat to say she had heard shots upstairs, four minutes after the patrolman had forced the door, found the stiffs, and called the station house. Brown, who had been catching, took the squeal.

The Homicide cops had not yet arrived, which was just as well. Brown could never understand the department regulation that made it mandatory for Homicide to check in on every damn murder committed in this city, even though the case was invariably assigned to the precinct answering the call. He found most Homicide cops grisly and humorless. His wife, Caroline, was fond of telling him that he himself was not exactly a very comical fellow, but Brown assumed that was merely a case of the prophet going unappreciated in his native land. In fact, *he* thought he was hilarious at times. As now, for example, when he turned to the police photographer and said, "I wonder who did the interior decorating here." The police photographer apparently shared Caroline Brown's opinion. Without cracking a smile, he did his little dance around the two corpses, snapping, twisting for another angle, snapping again, shifting now to this side of the dead men, now to the other, while Brown waited for his laugh.

"I said . . ." Brown said.

"I heard you, Artie," the photographer said, and clicked his camera again.

"This is certainly not the Taj Mahal," Brown said.

"Hardly anything is," the photographer answered.

"What are you so grumpy about?" Brown asked.

"Me? Grumpy? Who's grumpy?"

"Nobody," Brown said. He glanced at the corpses again, and then walked to the far side of the room, where two windows overlooked the back yard. One of the windows was wide open. Brown checked the latch on it, and saw immediately that it had been forced. Okay, he thought, that's how one of them got in. I wonder which one. And I also wonder *why*. What did he expect to steal in this dump?

Brown leaned over the window sill. There was nothing but an empty milk carton, a crumpled wad of waxed paper, and a flower pot on the fire escape outside. The flower pot had a dead plant in it. Brown looked down into the yard below. A woman was dumping her garbage into one of the cans adjacent to the alley wall. She accidentally dropped the lid of the can, clearly and resoundingly said, "Oh, shit!" and stooped to retrieve it. Brown turned away from the window.

Monoghan and Monroe, the detectives from Homicide, were just coming through the doorway. They were dressed almost identically, both wearing blue serge confirmation suits, brown shoes, and gray fedoras. Monroe was wearing a maroon knit tie. Monoghan wore a yellow silk tie. Their shields were pinned to the breast pockets of their suit jackets. Monroe had recently begun growing a mustache, and the sparse collection of hairs over the lip seemed to embarrass him. He kept blowing his nose into his handkerchief, even though he didn't have a cold, as though trying to hide his unsightly brush behind the white cotton square. Monoghan seemed even more embarrassed by the mustache than Monroe did. It seemed to him that after fifteen years of working together with a man, the man should not suddenly start growing a mustache one morning without first consulting his partner. Monoghan hated Monroe's mustache. He considered it unesthetic. It embarrassed him. It offended his eye. And because it offended his eye, he constantly stared at it. And the more often he stared at it, the more often Monroe took out his handkerchief and blew his nose, hiding his mustache.

"Well, well, what have we got here?" Monroe said, blowing his nose. "Hello, Brown."

"Hello, Brown," Monoghan said.

"Now this is what I call a thorough job," Monroe said, pocketing his handkerchief. "Whoever went through this place was an expert."

"A professional," Monoghan said.

"It almost looks like the *police* shook it down."

"Or the firemen," Monoghan said, and looked at his partner's mustache. Monroe took out his handkerchief again.

"Must have wanted something pretty bad," he said, and blew his nose.

"What could anybody want in *this* joint?" Monoghan asked. "You know what you find in a joint like this?"

"What?" Brown asked.

"Cockroaches," Monoghan said.

"Bedbugs," Monroe added.

"Cockroaches and bedbugs," Monoghan summarized.

Monroe put away his handkerchief.

"Look at this joint," Monoghan said, and shook his head.

Brown looked at the joint. The bed had been stripped, the

mattress slashed on both sides, cotton batting strewn all over the floor. The same thorough job had been done on the bed pillows and on the seat cushion, arms and back of the single easy chair in the room. Fademarks on the walls showed where several framed prints had been hanging, but the pictures had been yanked down, their backs probably examined, and then thrown carelessly onto the floor. The contents of all the dresser drawers were similarly tossed all over the room, and the drawers themselves had been pulled out of the dresser and then flung aside. The one floor lamp in the room, overturned, had had its shade removed and discarded. Through the bathroom doorway, Brown could see the open medicine cabinet, its contents thrown into the sink. The top of the toilet tank had been taken off. Even the toilet paper had been removed from its roller. In the kitchen, the refrigerator door was open, and food had been hurled haphazardly onto the floor. The one drawer in the kitchen table had been emptied onto the white enamel tabletop, utensils scattered everywhere. As Monroe had wisely commented, someone must have wanted something pretty bad.

"You know who the stiffs are?" Monoghan asked Brown.

"Not yet."

"You figure it for an interrupted burglary?"

"Right."

"How'd he get in?"

"Through the fire escape window. Tool marks on the frame."

"Other guy came home unexpectedly, and *bingo!*"

"Think he got what he came after?"

"Haven't checked him out," Brown said.

"What're you waiting for?"

"Lou's still taking pictures. And the M.E. isn't here yet."

"Who reported the crime?" Monroe asked.

"The landlady. She heard shots, stopped Kiely on the beat."

"Get her up here," Monoghan said.

"Right," Brown answered. He went to the door, told the patrolman there to go get the landlady, and then saw Marshall Davies hurrying down the hallway toward the apartment.

"I'm sorry I'm late, Artie," he said. "I had a goddamn flat."

"There was a call for you," Brown said.

"Who from?"

"Lieutenant Grossman."

"What'd he want?"

"Said you should go right back to the lab."

"The lab? What for? Who's going to handle *this* if I go back to the lab?"

"Don't know," Brown said.

"You know what he's probably got waiting for me downtown? Some nice little surprise, that's what. Some nice hit-and-run victim. Some guy who got run over by a trailer truck. I'll be down there picking headlight splinters out of his ass all night. Boy oh boy, what a day."

"It's hardly started," Brown said.

"It started for me at seven o'clock this morning," Davies said. He sighed heavily. "Okay, I'm heading back. If he should call again, tell him I'm on my way. I don't know who's going to handle this for you, Artie. The M.E. been here yet?"

"No, not yet."

"Situation normal," Davies said, and walked out.

The patrolman came upstairs with the landlady not five minutes later. By that time, the Assistant Medical Examiner had arrived and was checking out the corpses. Brown and the two Homicide detectives took the landlady into the kitchen, where they could talk to her without the fascinating distraction of two bodies lying on the floor. She was a woman in her late forties, not unattractive, her blond hair pulled into a bun at the back of her head. She had wide Irish eyes, as green as County Cork, and she spoke with the faintest hint of a brogue. Her name was Mrs. Walter Byrnes.

"No kidding?" Monoghan said. "You any relation to the lieutenant?"

"What lieutenant?"

"Runs the Eight-seven," Monroe said.

"The Eighty-seventh squad," Monoghan said.

"He's a cop," Monroe said.

"I'm not related to any cops," Mrs. Byrnes said.

"He's a very good cop," Monoghan said.

"I'm not related to him," Mrs. Byrnes said, firmly.

"You want to tell us what happened, Mrs. Byrnes?" Monroe said.

"I heard shots. I went right outside and yelled for the police."

"Did you come up here?"

"Nope."

"Why not?"

"Would *you?*"

"Mrs. Byrnes," Brown said, "when you came in just now, did you happen to notice the bodies in the other room?"

"I'd have to be deaf, dumb, and blind not to, wouldn't I?" she said.

"Do you know either of those two men?"

"One of them, yes."

"Which one?"

"The one wearing the sports jacket," she said. Unflinchingly, she added, "The one with the knife blade sticking out of his throat."

"And who is he, Mrs. Byrnes?"

"His name is Donald Renninger. He's been living here in the building for more than two years."

"And the other man? The one wearing the Jewish star?"

"Never saw him before in my life."

"He's the one who broke in, I guess," Monroe said.

"We've had a *lot* of burglaries around here," Mrs. Byrnes said, and looked at the detectives reproachfully.

"Well, we try to do our best," Monoghan said dryly.

"Sure you do," Mrs. Byrnes said, even more dryly.

"Any idea what Mr. Renninger did for a living?" Brown asked.

"He worked at a filling station."

"Would you know where?"

"In Riverhead someplace. I don't know exactly where."

"Is he married?"

"No."

"He was a bachelor, right?" Monroe asked.

"If he wasn't married, why yes, I guess he was a bachelor," Mrs. Byrnes said sarcastically, and then looked at Monroe's mustache.

Monroe took out his handkerchief. Apologetically, he blew his nose and said, "He *could* have been divorced."

"That's true," Monoghan said.

Monroe smiled at him, and put away his handkerchief.

"But you never saw the other man?" Brown said.

"Never."

"Not here in the building . . ."

"No."

". . . or in the neighborhood either?"

"No place," she said.

"Thank you, Mrs. Byrnes."

The landlady went to the door. She turned before she went out, and said, "What's his first name?"

"Whose?"

"The lieutenant's?"

"Peter."

"We don't have a Peter Byrnes in our family," she said, and went out, satisfied.

The M.E. was finished with the bodies. As he passed the detectives, he said, "We'll give you written reports soon as the autopsies are made. You want some guesses for now?"

"Sure," Brown said.

"Looks like the first bullet hit the guy in the poplin jacket a little low, probably got deflected off a rib. Anyway, it didn't stop him right away. Left fist is clenched, he probably threw a punch and still had time to stick his knife in the other guy's throat, probably just as the gun went off a second time. *That* shot went clear through the heart, I'd guess. The guy in the poplin jacket started to drop, and the knife blade broke off as he fell. The other guy went down, too, probably died within minutes. Looks to me as if the knife caught his jugular, awful lot of blood in there. Okay?"

"Okay, thanks," Brown said.

"You handling this, Artie?"

"Looks like I'm stuck with it."

"Well, it's open and shut. I'll get the reports up to you tomorrow morning, that soon enough?"

"Nobody's going any place," Brown said.

"Toodle-oo," the M.E. said, and waggled his fingers and went out.

"So what'd the burglar *want* here?" Monoghan asked.

"Maybe *this,*" Monroe said. He was crouched near the corpse in the poplin jacket. He pried open the dead man's clenched left hand to reveal what appeared to be a portion of a glossy photograph clutched into the palm. He lifted the photo scrap and handed it to Brown. "Take a look at it," he said.

2

"WHAT IS IT?" Detective Steve Carella asked.

"Piece of a snapshot," Brown said.

They were in a corner of the squadroom, Brown sitting behind his desk, Carella perched on one end of it. Early morning June sunshine streamed into the office. A mild breeze filtered through the wire grilles covering the open windows. Carella, sitting on the edge of the desk, sniffed of the late spring air, and wished he were sleeping in the park someplace. A tall, wiry man with wide shoulders and narrow hips, he gave the impression of being an athlete in training, even though the last time he'd engaged in any sportlike activity was the snorkeling he'd done in Puerto Rico on his last vacation. Unless one wished to count the various footraces he had run with criminals of every stripe and persuasion. Carella did not like to count those. A man could get winded just counting those. He brushed a strand of longish brown hair off his forehead now, squinted his brown eyes at the photo scrap, and wondered if he needed glasses.

"What does it look like to you?" he asked.

"A dancing girl in a leotard," Brown answered.

"Looks more like a bottle of Haig & Haig Pinch to me." Carella said. "What do you suppose this furry stuff is?"

"What furry stuff?"

"This textured stuff, whatever-the-hell-it-is."

"Mud, I would guess."

"Or part of a wall. A stucco wall." Carella shrugged, and dropped the scrap onto the desktop. "You really think this is why . . . *what's* his name?"

"According to the identification in his wallet, his name was Eugene Edward Ehrbach."

"Ehrbach. Anything on him?"

"I'm running a check with the I.B. right now. On *both* of them."

"You think Ehrbach really broke into the apartment to get *this?*" Carella asked, and tapped the photograph segment with a pencil.

"Well, why else would it be in his hand, Steve? I can't see him going up there with a piece of a snapshot in his hand, can you?"

"I guess not."

"Anyway, I'll tell you the truth, I don't see as it makes a hell of a lot of difference. The M.E. said it's open and shut, and I'm inclined to agree with him. Ehrbach broke into the apartment, Renninger suddenly came home and surprised him, and we get a neat double homicide."

"And the photograph?"

"Well, let's say Ehrbach *was* after it. So what? He could just as easily have been after Renninger's wrist watch. Either way, they're both dead. The snapshot doesn't change the disposition of the case either way."

"No, it doesn't."

"Soon as we get those autopsy reports, I'm going to type this up as closed. You see any other way?"

"No, it looks pretty clear."

"M.E. promised them for this morning." Brown looked at his watch. "Well, it's still a little early."

"I wonder what kind of customers we're dealing with here," Carella said.

"How do you mean?"

"Two nice ordinary citizens, one of them carrying a Luger, and the other one carrying a switch knife with an eight-inch blade."

"Whatever Ehrbach was, he wasn't a nice ordinary citizen. He opened that window like a pro."

"And Renninger?"

"Landlady says he worked at a filling station."

"I wish the I.B. would get off its dead ass," Carella said.

"Why?"

"I'm curious."

"Les's say they *have* got records," Brown said. "It still wouldn't change anything, would it?"

"You sound anxious to close this out," Carella said.

"I got a caseload up to my eyeballs, but that's not why I want to close it. There's just no reason to keep it *open,*" Brown said.

"Unless there was a third party in that apartment," Carella said.

"There's no indication of that, Steve."

"Or unless . . ."

"Unless what?"

"I don't know. But why would anyone risk a burglary rap just to get a piece of a snapshot?"

"Excuse me," a voice called from across the squadroom. Both detectives turned simultaneously toward the slatted wooden railing at the far end of the office. A tall hatless man in a gray nailhead suit stood just outside the gate. He was perhaps thirty-five years old, with a thatch of black hair and a thick black handle-bar mustache that would have caused serious pangs of envy in someone like Monroe. His eyebrows were thick and black as well, raised now in polite inquiry over startlingly blue eyes that glinted in the squadroom sunshine. His speech stamped him immediately as a native of the city, with not a little trace of Calm's Pointese in it. "The desk sergeant said I should come right up," he said. "I'm looking for Detective Brown."

"That's me," Brown said.

"Okay to come in?"

"Come ahead."

The man searched briefly for the latch on the inside of the gate, found it, and strode into the office. He was a big man with big hands, the left one clutched around the handle of a dispatch case. He held the case very tightly. Brown had the feeling it should have been chained to his wrist. Smiling pleasantly, he extended his right hand and said, "Irving Krutch. Nice to meet you." His teeth were dazzling, the smile framed by a pair of dimples, one on either side of his mouth. He had high cheekbones, and a straight unbroken nose, and he looked like the lead in an Italian Western. The only thing he needed to attain instant stardom on the silver screen, Brown thought, was a change of name. Irving Krutch did nothing for his image. Steve Stunning, Hal Handsome, Geoff Gorgeous, any of those might have suited him better.

"How do you do?" Brown said, and took his hand briefly. He did not bother introducing Carella; cops rarely observed such formalities during business hours.

"Okay to sit down?" Krutch said.

"Please," Brown said, and indicated a chair to the right of his desk. Krutch sat. Carefully preserving the knife-crease in his trousers, he crossed his legs, and unleashed the dazzling smile again.

"So," he said, "looks like you've got yourselves a little murder, huh?"

Neither of the cops answered him. They *always* had themselves a little murder, and they weren't in the habit of discussing homicides, little or otherwise, with strange, handsome, mustached, well-dressed smiling civilians who barged into the squadroom.

"The two guys over on Culver Avenue," Krutch said. "I read about them in the paper this morning."

"What about them?" Brown asked.

"I guess I should tell you I'm an insurance investigator," Krutch said. "Trans-American Insurance."

"Mm-huh," Brown said.

"Do you know the company?"

"The name sounds familiar."

"I've been with them for twelve years now, started there when I got out of college." He paused, then added, "Princeton." He waited for some response, saw that mention of his illustrious alma mater was not generating too much excitement, and then said, "I've worked with this squad before. Detective named Meyer Meyer. He still with you?"

"He's still with us," Brown said.

Carella, who had been silent until now, said, "What were you working on?"

"The National Savings & Loan Association holdup," Krutch said. "Six years ago."

"In what capacity?"

"I told you. I'm an insurance investigator. They're one of our clients." He smiled again. "Took us for a bundle on that one."

The men were silent again.

"So?" Brown said at last.

"So," Krutch said, "I read about your two corpses in the paper this morning, and I thought I'd better get up here right away."

"Why?"

"Lend you a hand," Krutch said, smiling. "Or maybe vice versa."

"You know something about those killings?" Brown asked.

"Yep."

"What do you know?"

"The newspaper said you found a piece of a photograph in Ehrbach's hand," Krutch said. His blue eyes shifted dramatically toward the photo scrap lying on Brown's desk. "Is that it?"

"What about it?" Brown said.

"I've got another piece. And if you shake down Ehrbach's pad, I'm pretty sure you'll find a *third* piece."

"Do you want to tell it, or do we have to pull teeth?"

"I'm ready to tell it."

"Then tell it."

"Sure. Will you help me?"

"To do what?"

"First, to get the piece in Ehrbach's place."

"Why do you want it?"

"Three pieces are better than one, no?"

"Look, Mr. Krutch," Brown said, "if you've got something to say, say it. Otherwise, it's been nice meeting you, and I hope you sell a lot of insurance policies."

"I don't sell insurance, I investigate claims."

"Fine. I wish you lots of luck. Yes or no? Shit or get off the pot."

Krutch smiled at Carella, as though sharing with him his aversion to such crude language. Carella ignored the smile. He was agreeing with Brown. He hated coy disclosures. The 87th Squad ran a nice little store up here on the second floor of the building, and so far the only thing Krutch was spending in it was time. *Their* time.

Sensing the impatience of the two detectives, Krutch said, "Let me fill you in."

"Please do," Brown said.

"Fade in," Krutch said. "Six . . ."

"What?" Brown asked.

"That's a movie expression. Fade in."

"You involved with movies?" Brown asked, ready to confirm the suspicion he'd harbored from the moment Krutch walked in.

"No."

"Then why the movie expression?"

"Everybody says 'Fade in,'" Krutch explained.

"*I* don't say 'Fade in,'" Brown replied.

"Okay, so we *won't* fade in," Krutch said, and shrugged. "Six years ago, in this city, in broad daylight on a rainy afternoon in August, four men held up the Culver Avenue branch of N.S.L.A. and got away with seven hundred and fifty thousand dollars. That's a lot of kale. The branch, incidentally, is located in this precinct."

"Go on," Carella said.

"You remember the case now?" Krutch asked. "Meyer and O'Brien were working on it."

"I remember it," Carella said. "Go ahead."

"Do *you* remember it, Detective Brown?"

"Yes," Brown said.

"I don't think I got your name," Krutch said, turning to Carella.

"Carella."

"Nice to meet you. Are you Italian?"

"Yes."

"The leader of the gang was Italian. Fellow named Carmine Bonamico, record as long as your arm. In fact, he'd just got out of Castleview after serving a five-and-dime there. First thing he did, while he was still on parole, was knock over the bank. You remember any of this?"

"I remember *all* of it," Carella said.

"Are my facts correct so far?"

"They are."

"My facts are *always* correct," Krutch said, and smiled. Nobody smiled with him. "The wheelman was a young punk named Jerry Stein, a Jewish kid from Riverhead, his first job. The two guns were both ex-cons, Lou D'Amore from Majesta and Pete Ryan, also from Riverhead, a regular little United Nations they had on that job. They came in just before closing time, grabbed as much as they could from the vault, shot one of the tellers, and then drove off, presumably heading for Calm's Point, which is where Bonamico lived with his wife. It was raining; did I mention it was raining?"

"You mentioned it."

"They got onto the River Road, and had almost reached the Calm's Point Bridge, when the car went into a skid, hit another car, and caused a traffic tie-up. Two patrolmen from the Three-six pulled up in a squad car, and Bonamico and his pals opened fire. All four of them were killed inside of five minutes. The great mystery is why they began shooting at all. The car was clean. It was later searched from top to bottom, but the bank loot wasn't in it. Not a dime of it." Krutch paused. "Okay, dissolve . . ."

Brown looked at him.

"Trans-American gets called in, Irving Krutch investigating." He grinned. "That's me. Result? Two years of intensive search for that money, and no trace of it. We finally settled the claim in full, seven hundred and fifty G's from our coffers to N.S.L.A.'s." Krutch paused. "That's bad. I don't have to tell you how bad that is."

"How bad is it?" Brown asked.

"Bad. Bad for Trans-American, and especially bad for Irving Krutch who couldn't find the money. Irving Krutch was up for a promotion at the time. Instead, Irving Krutch is now handling minor claims, at the same salary he was getting six years ago. Krutch is an ambitious fellow. He doesn't like dead-end jobs."

"Why doesn't Krutch *change* his job?" Carella suggested.

"Because the field's a narrow one, and losing seven hundred and fifty thousand dollars is the kind of word that gets around very fast. Besides, Krutch has an inordinate amount of pride in his work."

"Do you always talk about yourself in the third person?" Carella asked. "Like your own biographer?"

"It helps me to be objective. It's hard to be objective about losing seven hundred and fifty thousand dollars for the company, especially when the case has been officially closed by your squad."

"Who told you that?" Carella said.

"You got the thieves, didn't you?"

"The case is still in our Open File."

"How come?"

"Let's say we *also* have an inordinate amount of pride in our work," Carella said. "The money wasn't in the car. Okay, the River Road is some three miles from the bank. Which means that somewhere along the escape route, the money could have changed hands. If that happened, then the rest of the gang is still at large, just itching to spend all that cash. We'd like to get them."

"Forget it."

"What do you mean?"

"The money wasn't turned over to *anybody*. If you're keeping the case open in hope of finding the rest of the gang, forget it. There were only four of them, and they're all dead."

"Do you know that for a fact?"

"Yes. I got it from Bonamico's sister-in-law." Krutch paused. "You mind if I tell it in order?"

"Any order you like," Brown said, "so long as you *tell* it."

"Okay, dissolve. Krutch is still bugged by the loss of that money. It keeps him awake nights. His company has settled the claim, not to mention his future, but it still bugs him. Where can the money be? Who's got it? Bonamico is no master criminal, mind you, but neither is he stupid enough to throw that kind of cash out the window of a getaway car. So where the hell is it? Krutch keeps wondering about it. Krutch keeps tossing and turning at night . . ."

"Krutch should be writing mystery stories," Carella said.

". . . obsessed with the thought of locating that cash and becoming a contender again."

"A contender?"

"At Trans-American."

"Oh, I thought maybe you also did a little boxing on the side," Brown said.

"Matter of fact, I used to box in the Navy," Krutch said. "Middleweight division." He paused, eyed them both shrewdly, and said, "You guys don't like me much, do you?"

"We're civil servants," Brown said, "soliciting information from a private citizen who may or may not possess knowledge of a crime. We are patiently waiting. If we have to wait much longer, we'll be forced to rent you office space."

"I like your sense of humor," Krutch said, and smiled.

"My wife doesn't," Brown said. "We're still waiting, Mr. Krutch. We are getting old and gray waiting."

"Okay. Two months ago, I got lucky."

"You mean you were still working on this thing?"

"Not officially. Only on my own time. Pride, remember? Ambition. Tenacity. Krutch the would-be contender. I opened the paper one morning two months ago and learned that a woman named Alice Bonamico had died of cancer at the Sacred Heart Hospital in Calm's Point. No one would have noticed her passing, of course, if she hadn't incidentally been the widow of one Carmine Bonamico who had knocked over a bank six years earlier and caused the loot to magically disappear. I knew the lady because I'd talked to her often when I was investigating the claim. She was a nice type, quiet, pretty in a dark Sicilian way, you'd never think she'd been married to a cheap hood. Anyway, the newspaper item said that she was survived by a sister named Lucia Feroglio. I made a mental note, and later discovered she was a spinster, also living in Calm's Point."

"How much later was this?"

"A week or so. As soon as Alice Bonamico's will was filed in Surrogate's Court. It was a very interesting will. Aside from leaving her entire estate to her sister Lucia, it also left her, and I quote, 'Certain mementos, documents, photographs, and photographic segments considered to be of value by the deceased.' I immediately got on my horse and went to visit Lucia Feroglio in Calm's Point."

"This was two months ago?"

"Right. The third day of April. A Friday. Lucia Feroglio is an old lady in her seventies, memory failing, barely speaking English, partially deaf. You ever try to talk to a deaf woman?"

Carella said nothing.

"Anyway, I talked to her. I convinced her that her brother-in-law had taken out a very small policy on his wife's life, naming Lucia Feroglio as beneficiary, and that a check for one thousand dollars would be issued to her as soon as the conditions of the policy were met. I invented the conditions, of course."

"What were they?"

"That she satisfy my company that she was indeed in possession of the 'Certain mementos, documents, photographs, and photographic segments considered to be of value by the deceased.' Even deaf old ladies who hardly speak English can understand a thousand dollars. She patiently went through all the crap her sister had left her—family pictures, birth certificates, even the caul Alice had been born with, carefully wrapped in a square of pink satin; that's supposed to be good luck, you know, if you're born with a caul. And in the midst of all this crap was exactly what I hoped would be there."

"Which was?"

"A list of names. Or at least a partial list of names. And a piece of a photograph," Krutch paused. "Would you like to see them?"

"Yes," Carella said.

Krutch opened his dispatch case. Resting on top of a sheaf of Trans-American claim forms was a legal-sized white envelope. Krutch opened the envelope and took out a scrap of paper. He put it on the desktop, and both detectives looked at it.

"Those names are in Carmine Bonamico's handwriting," Krutch said. "I'm quite familiar with it."

"Seven of them," Carella said.

"Or maybe more," Krutch answered. "As you can see, the list is torn."

"How'd it get torn?"

"I don't know. That's the way Lucia turned it over to me. It may have been accidentally damaged, or another piece of it may be in someone else's hands. Considering what Bonamico did with the photograph, that's a likely possibility."

"Let's see the picture," Carella said.

Krutch dipped into the envelope again. He took out a piece of a glossy photograph and put it on the desktop, alongside the scrap they had found clutched in Ehrbach's hand.

"How do we know these are pieces of the same photograph?" Carella asked.

"They're both cut like a jigsaw puzzle," Krutch said. "That can't be accidental. Nor can it be accidental that you found *your* piece in the hand of one of the men listed here in Bonamico's handwriting. Or that the *other* dead man is *also* on the list." Krutch paused. "Ehrbach's a better burglar than I am. I've been in and out of Renninger's place a dozen times in the past two months, and I never found a thing."

"You're admitting to breaking and entry, Mr. Krutch?"

"Shall I send for my lawyer?" Krutch asked, and grinned.

"Did you shake down Ehrbach's place as well?"

"I did. And found nothing. *His* piece is probably as carefully hidden as Renninger's was."

Carella looked at the list again. "Who's Albert Weinberg?"

"One of Stein's close buddies. Jerry Stein, the kid who drove the getaway car. Beginning to make sense?"

"Not much."

"Weinberg's a hood in his own right. So are the other two, in case you don't already know."

"Which other two?"

"Renninger and Ehrbach. Renninger was busted eight years ago for pushing junk. He was in Caramoor at the time of the holdup, got out of prison only two years ago. Ehrbach was busted twice for burglary, one more time and they'd have thrown away the key. Makes the risk he took seem even more meaningful, doesn't it? He was taking the chance of a third fall, and for what? Unless that picture means something, he was a goddam fool to break into Renninger's place.'"

"You're better than the I.B.," Brown said. "Assuming this is straight goods."

"As I told you," Krutch said, smiling, "my facts are *always* correct."

"What about the other names on this list?"

"I've been through the telephone book a hundred times. You know how many Geraldines there are? Don't ask. As for Dorothy, she could be Dorothy *Anybody*. And the R-o-b? That could be Robert, or Roberta, or Robin, or even Robespierre, who knows? It was easy to fill in the 'Renninger' because the name was almost complete. And I doped out the 'Ehrbach' because of the 'Eugene E.' They're both listed in the Isola directory. Alice is Alice Bonamico, of course. But I have no idea who the others are, and no idea whether there are more than seven. I hope not. *Seven* pieces of a puzzle are more than enough."

"And when you assemble this puzzle," Krutch said, "I will have the exact location of the seven hundred and fifty thousand dollars stolen from N.S.L.A. six years ago."

"How do you know that?"

"Lucia Feroglio told me. Oh, it took some time to get it out of her, believe me. As I told you, her memory is failing, and she's partially deaf, and her English is of the *Mama mia* variety. But she *finally* remembered that her sister had told her the photograph showed where the treasure was. That was the exact word she used. Treasure."

"She said that in English?" Carella asked. "She said 'treasure'?"

"No. She said *tesoro*. In Italian."

"Maybe she was only calling you 'darling,' " Carella said.

"I doubt it."

"You speak Italian, do you?"

"A girlfriend of mine told me what it meant. *Tesoro*. Treasure."

"So now there are two pieces," Brown said. "What do you want from us?"

"I want you to help me find the other *five* pieces. Or however many more there are." Krutch smiled. "I'm getting too well known, you see. Toward the end there, both Renninger and Ehrbach knew I was on to them. I wouldn't be surprised if Ehrbach *got* to Renninger merely by tailing *me*."

"You make it sound very complicated, Mr. Krutch."

"It *is* complicated. I'm sure that Weinberg knows I've been watching *him,* too. And frankly, I can't risk getting busted on a burglary rap. Which might happen if I keep breaking into places." He smiled again. The smile had lost none of its dazzle.

"So you want *us* to break into places for you, huh?"

"It's been done before."

"It's against the law, even for cops."

"*Lots* of things are against the law. There's seven hundred and fifty G's involved here. I'm sure the Eighty-seventh wouldn't mind locating it. Be quite a feather in your cap, after all these years."

"Yes, it might be," Carella said.

"So do it," Krutch said simply.

"Do *what?*" Brown asked.

"First of all, go over Ehrbach's place with a fine comb. You can do that legally. He's the victim of a homicide, and you're conducting an investigation."

"Okay, let's say we shake down Ehrbach's place."

"Yes, and you find the third piece of that picture."

"Assuming we do, *then* what?"

"Then you go after Weinberg."

"How? What's our legal excuse *there,* Krutch?"

"You don't have one. You couldn't approach him as fuzz, anyway. He's been in trouble before. He's not likely to co-operate with The Law."

"What kind of trouble?"

"Assault. He beat a woman half to death with his fists. He's enormous, must weigh at least two hundred and fifty pounds. He could break either one of you in half with just a dirty look, believe me." Krutch paused. "What do you say?"

"It might be worth our time," Carella said.

"We'll have to talk it over with the lieutenant."

"Yeah, you talk it over with him. I think *he* might understand how nice it would be to recover that bank loot." Krutch smiled again. "Meanwhile, I'll leave the list and the picture with you."

"Won't you need them?"

"I've got copies," Krutch said.

"How come somebody so smart needs our help?" Carella asked.

"That smart I ain't," Krutch said. He took a card from his wallet and placed it on the desk. "That's my home number," he said. "Don't try to reach me at Trans-American. Let me know what you decide."

"We will indeed," Carella said.

"Thank you," Krutch said. He offered his hand to Brown. "Detective Brown?" He retrieved his hand, shook hands next with Carella. "Detective Carella?" Then he smiled his dazzling smile and went out of the squadroom.

"What do you think?" Brown said.

"I don't know. What do *you* think?" Carella said.

"I don't know. Let's see what the lieutenant thinks."

3

LIEUTENANT BYRNES looked at the list of names, and then turned his attention to the two pieces of the photograph:

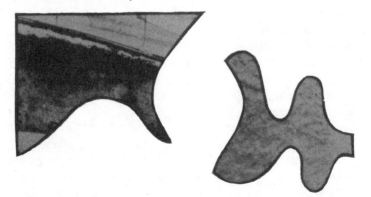

"Don't even look like they *belong* together," he muttered.

They had filled him in on Krutch's story, and he had listened intently, head cocked slightly to one side, blue eyes shifting from Carella's face to Brown's as they alternately picked up threads of the narrative. He was a thickset man, Byrnes, with heavy hands, the backs of which were sprinkled with liver spots. His hair was going white, and he had a bald patch barely beginning to show at the back of his head. But there was a sense of contained power about him, the certain knowledge that he had broken many a hood's nose before being promoted to his present desk job. Impatiently, he looked at the photograph segments again, turning each one on his desktop, trying to fit them together, and then giving up the job.

"Guy comes in here with a story," Byrnes said, "what does he expect us to do? Drop everything and go on a goddamn treasure hunt?'

"Well," Carella said, "there's a possibility he's right."

"A pretty *slim* possibility, if you ask me. Where'd you say he got this story? From an old lady who hardly speaks English, right?"

"That's right."

"But she told him in Italian," Brown said. "She told him the picture shows where *il tresoro* is buried."

"Il te soro," Carella corrected.

"Did she say that? Buried?"

"No. I don't know. Hidden, I think she said. What'd she say, Steve?"

"Just that the picture shows where the treasure *is,* I think. That's all."

"She didn't say buried, huh?"

"I don't think so."

"I just hate to put a man on this, and then . . ." Byrnes shook his head. "It's not as if we've got nothing else to do around here, you know."

The detectives were silent.

"Let's say we search Ehrbach's place," Byrnes said. "And let's say we *do* find a third piece of this picture, then what?"

"Then Krutch's story begins to sound a little better," Carella said.

"Yes, but where do we go from there?" Byrnes asked. "I'm willing to put you on it . . . okay, we don't find anything, we've only wasted a day. But suppose we *do* find something, *then* what? This fellow . . . what's his name?" Byrnes consulted the list again. "Weinberg. Albert Weinberg. He's the next logical step. But Krutch says the man's got an assault record, which means he can smell The Law six blocks away. Whoever we send after him would have to use a cover, and I'd need a second man for a contact and drop. That's two men out of action, maybe on a wild-goose chase." He shook his head again. "I don't know." He looked down at the photograph segments and then up at Carella. "What's your caseload like, Steve?"

"I've got that dry-cleaning store holdup, and the muggings over on Ainsley . . . six in the past two weeks, same m.o. I've also got a lead I want to run down on the pusher who's been working the junior high school on Seventeenth. And there're two cases coming to trial this month. I have to be in court on Tuesday, matter of fact."

"What about you, Artie?"

"I forgot to mention . . ." Carella said.

"Yeah?"

"Couple of burglaries over in Smoke Rise. We've been getting a lot of static on those because the sister of a municipal judge lives in the neighborhood."

"Yeah, so let Hizzoner go find the burglar," Byrnes said dryly. "Artie?"

"A hit-and-run, a jewelry store holdup, and a knifing. I'm supposed to be in court tomorrow on the knifing. It'll be a quick trial—the guy stabbed his wife when he found her in bed with another man."

"You want to take a crack at this Weinberg character? Assuming we find anything in Ehrbach's apartment?"

"Sure," Brown said.

"Does Weinberg live in the precinct? Would he be likely to spot you as a cop?"

"I don't know."

"Check him out with the I.B., see if they've got an address for him."

"Right."

"You'd better find out where he's operated, too, which cities, and pick your cover accordingly. Don't make it anything too big, Artie, don't say you're a mob gun from Chicago or anything like that. Be too simple for him to check if he's got any connections at all. Make it a numbers runner, a small-time pusher, something unimportant. You stumbled on your piece of the picture, you think Weinberg's got another piece, and you want to team up with him. Keep it as simple as that."

"Right."

"Steve, you'll have to be the outside man at the skunk works."

"Fine."

"Arrange a drop, and keep your contacts as few as possible. This guy Weinberg doesn't sound like a customer to fool around with. And let's not go overboard on this thing, okay? Let's handle it in easy stages. If we don't turn up anything at Ehrbach's place, that's it, back to the salt mines. If we hit pay dirt, we move on to Weinberg, stay with him a day or two. If it looks like he's got a piece of the picture, we stick with him. Otherwise, we thank Krutch for his information and we drop the whole damn thing." He looked up at the two men. "Anything else?"

"Just one thing," Carella said. "The I.B. called a few minutes ago and verified everything Krutch said about the two dead men."

"So?"

"So maybe he's right about what we'll find in Ehrbach's apartment, too."

"Maybe," Byrnes said.

Judging from Eugene Edward Ehrbach's apartment, the man had been a highly successful burglar. One could, of course, argue that anyone who had already taken two falls for burglary could not, by any stretch of the imagination, be considered a *successful* burglar. But the fact remained that Ehrbach lived in a luxury apartment close to Silvermine Oval; neither of the detectives who shook down the place could have afforded anything even remotely similar to it on their salaries.

The doorman was not pleased to see them.

He had been hired to check on any and all strangers entering the building, his job being to prevent tenants from getting strangled in the elevator, and incidentally to call taxis for them on rainy nights. It didn't matter that *these* two strangers identified themselves as detectives from the 87th Squad. The doorman liked detectives as much as he liked stranglers or burglars. He had no way of knowing, naturally, that Eugene Edward Ehrbach had been a burglar, and undoubtedly a highly successful one. He told the detectives that he would have to check with the manager of the building, and even though they told him they were investigating a murder, he insisted on making his telephone call. When he got off the phone, he said, "It's okay, but don't go making a mess up there," which was exactly what they *intended* to make up there.

Ehrbach had lived on the tenth floor of the building, in an apartment at the end of the corridor. There were three other apartments on the floor. Ehrbach's was the choice apartment since it overlooked the River Harb. There were two rivers flanking Isola, the Harb on the north and the Dix on the south. Apartments overlooking either of these waterways were considered very desirable, even though the view of the next state across the Harb featured a big housing development and the roller coaster of an amusement park, and the view of the Dix revealed a grimy gray hospital on an island, mid-river, a collection of spiny bridges leading to Calm's Point and Sands Spit, and a house of detention on another island out beyond Devil's Causeway. From Ehrbach's living room window (in addition to the roller coaster, the housing development, and an insistently blinking SPRY sign), you could also see all the way uptown to the Hamilton Bridge.

Carella and Brown entered the apartment with a passkey provided by the doorman, and found themselves in a carpeted foyer. Their reflected images looked back at them from a gilt-framed mirror hanging on the wall facing the door. A long narrow table was against that wall, just below the mirror. The apartment ran off to the right and left of the foyer. They made a perfunctory check of the place, discovering that there were four rooms in all: living room, kitchen, den, and bedroom. A small bathroom was off the entrance foyer, and another bathroom adjoined the bedroom. That was it, and very nice indeed. They divided the apartment in half, Carella taking the foyer, the small bathroom, the kitchen and the den; Brown taking the bedroom, the living room, and the second bathroom. With all the expertise and *sang-froid* of a demolition crew, they started searching for the scrap of photo Irving Krutch was certain Ehrbach had possessed. They began the job at noon. At midnight, they were still looking.

They had made two trips downstairs for sandwiches and coffee, Carella going out at 2 P.M. and Brown going out at seven. Aside from slashing up the mattresses and upholstered furniture, a license not granted to them, they had done a thorough and painstaking job, but had found nothing. They sat now in the living room, exhausted, Brown in an easy chair near a standing floor lamp, Carella straddling the piano bench. The lamp was on, it cast a warm and cozy glow over the moss-green wall-to-wall carpeting.

"Maybe we ought to take it up," Brown said.

"Take what up?" Carella asked.

"The carpet."

"That's a big job."

"The way they lay this stuff," Brown said, "is they've got these strips of wood with tacks sticking up out of it. They nail that to the floor all around the room, and then hook the carpet onto it. You ever see these guys work?"

"Yeah," Carella said.

"You got wall-to-wall carpeting in your house?" Brown asked.

"No."

"Me neither. A hood like Ehrbach has wall-to-wall carpeting, and all I've got is a ten-by-twelve in the living room. How do you figure it?"

"Guess we're in the wrong racket," Carella said. "Did you check out all these books?"

"Every page."

"How about the switch plates? Did you unscrew them?"

"Yep."

"Nothing scotch-taped to the backs, huh?"

"Nothing."

Carella glanced at the floor lamp. "Did you take off that shade?"

"Yeah, zero. It'd show, anyway, with the light on."

"How about the ball in the toilet tank?" Brown asked. "They're hollow, you know. He might have . . ."

"I pried it open," Carella said. "Nothing."

"Maybe we *ought* to take up this damn carpet," Brown said.

"Be here all night," Carella said. "If we have to do that, we'd better get a crew in tomorrow. Did you look in the piano?"

"Yeah, *and* the piano bench."

"How about the clock-radio in the bedroom?"

"Unscrewed the back. Nothing. The television in the den?"

"Same thing." Carella smiled. "Maybe we ought to do what my son does when he loses one of his toys."

"What does he do?"

"Well, he starts by saying 'Where would *you* be if you were a fire truck'?"

"Okay, where would *you* be if you were a photograph?"

"In an album," Carella said.

"You find any picture albums around?"

"Nope."

"So where *else* would you be?"

"We're looking for something maybe this big," Carella said, curling his thumb and forefinger into a C some two inches wide. "Maybe even smaller. He could have hidden it anywhere."

"Um-huh," Brown said, and nodded. "Where?"

"Did you look in those cereal boxes in the kitchen?"

"All of them. He sure liked cornflakes."

"Maybe it *is* under the carpet," Carella said.

"Would *you* put it under the carpet?"

"No. Too much trouble checking on it."

"That's what I figure. Have to move the furniture around and pull up the whole damn rug everytime you wanted to make sure the picture was still there."

"So where *would* you be?" Carella said.

"Home asleep," Brown answered.

"Okay, where *wouldn't* you be?"

"I wouldn't be in plain sight of two cops coming to look for me."

"It sure as hell ain't in plain sight," Carella said.

"Probably right under our noses, though, and we haven't yet spotted it," Brown said. "Maybe we need a little more light on the subject." He rose from the easy chair, sighed heavily, and walked to the piano. A lamp with a brass base rested on the burled walnut top. Brown switched it on. "There," he said, "how's that?"

"The better to see you with, my dear," Carella said.

"You want to look around a little more, or shall we come back in the morning and rip up the carpet?"

"Let's give it another whirl," Carella said. He got off the piano bench, walked to the middle of the room, looked around, and said "So where the hell is it?"

"You don't think he could have rolled it up and stuck it inside a cigarette or something?" Brown asked.

"Why not? Did you check out that cigarette box?"

"I looked inside it, but I didn't slit any of the cigarettes."

"Try it," Carella said. "We may get lucky." He walked to the standing floor lamp and started to unscrew the shade.

"I've already done that," Brown said.

"Right, I'm getting punchy," Carella said. He looked down into the lamp, said, "One of the bulbs is out," and then walked across the room to where Brown was slitting cigarettes open with his thumbnail.

"Just 'cause the man's a burglar," Brown said, "that don't mean he's got to be a bulb-snatcher, too."

"Course not." Carella said. "How we doing there?"

"I may get cancer of the thumb," Brown said.

He looked up at Carella. Their eyes met, and instant recognition flashed onto both their faces at the same moment, leaping the distance between them like heat lightning.

"Yeah!" Carella said, and started moving back toward the floor lamp.

"You thinking what I'm thinking?" Brown said, following him instantly.

"Oh, you *know* it," Carella said.

There were three electric light bulbs in the lamp. Two of them were illuminated, and the third one was out. Carella reached in through the open top of the shade and unscrewed the one bulb that was not burning.

"There it is," he said. "Unplug this damn thing before we electro-cute ourselves."

"Talk about a light bulb going on over a man's head," Brown said, and pulled the plug. Carella reached into the open socket with his thumb and forefinger. Neatly folded in half and then in half again, nestled into the bottom of the socket where it had been hidden by the light bulb screwed in on top of it, was the piece of the photo Krutch had promised they would find.

4

THE BUREAU of Criminal Identification was located at Headquarters, downtown on High Street. It was open twenty-four hours a day, its sole reason for existence being the collection, compilation, and cataloguing of any and all information descriptive of criminals. The I.B. maintained a Fingerprint File, a Criminal Index File, a Wanted File, a Degenerate File, a Parolee File, a Released Prisoner File, and Known Gamblers, Known Rapists, Known Muggers, Known You-Name-It files. Its *Modus Operandi* File alone contained more than 100,000 photographs of known criminals. And since all persons charged with and convicted of a crime were photographed and fingerprinted as specified by law, the file was continually growing and continually being brought up to date. The I.B. received and classified some 206,000 sets of prints yearly, and answered requests for more than 250,000 criminal records from police departments all over the country. Arthur Brown's request for information on Albert Weinberg was one of those. The package from the I.B. was waiting on his desk when he got to work that Friday morning.

As Krutch had faithfully reported, Weinberg had indeed been busted several years back. According to the supplementary information enclosed with his yellow sheet, he had started a fist fight in a bar, and then—for no apparent reason—suddenly attacked a little old lady who was sitting on a stool at the end of the bar, knocking her senseless and taking seventeen dollars and eighty-four cents from her purse. He had pleaded guilty to all charges and had served his time at Castleview Prison upstate, from which he had been released two years back. He had not been in any trouble with the law since.

Brown studied the information carefully, glanced up at the clock on the squadroom wall, and decided he had better get his ass down to the Criminal Courts Building. He told Carella where he was going, advised him that he would probably try to contact Weinberg later that day, and then left the office. He thought of the snapshot all the way downtown. There were now three pieces: the one they had found clenched in the dead Ehrbach's fist, and which was shaped somewhat like a dancing girl; the one Irving Krutch had voluntarily delivered to the squadroom, and which was obviously a corner piece; and now the one they had found hidden in Ehrbach's floor lamp, shaped like a drunken amoeba. He kept thinking of those pieces all during the trial.

His testimony was relatively simple. He explained to the assistant district attorney that at the time of the arrest, the defendant Michael Lloyd had been sitting in the kitchen of his home with a bloody bread knife in his hand. His wife was in the bedroom, stabbed in the shoulder. Her lover was no place to be found; he had apparently left in a great hurry, leaving behind his shoes and his socks. Brown testified that the defendant Michael Lloyd had not resisted arrest, and that he had told the arresting officers that he had tried to kill his wife and hoped the bitch was dead. On the basis of his statement and the evidence of the bloody knife in his hands and the wounded woman in the bedroom, he had been charged with attempted murder. In the cross-examination, the defense lawyer asked a lot of questions about Lloyd's "alleged" statement at the time of his arrest, wanting of course to know whether the prisoner had been properly advised of his rights, and Brown testified that everything had been conducted according to Miranda-Escobedo, and the district attorney excused him without a redirect, and called his next witness, the patrolman who had been present in the apartment when Lloyd had made his statement about having wanted to kill his wife. Brown left the Criminal Courts Building at three that afternoon.

Now, at 6 P.M., he sat at a table near the plate-glass front window of a cafeteria called The R&R, and knew that he was being cased from the street outside by none other than Albert Weinberg himself in person. Weinberg was even bigger than Krutch had described him, and certainly bigger than he had looked in the I.B.'s mug shot. At least as tall as Brown, heavier, with tremendous shoulders and powerful arms, a huge barrel chest and massive hands, he walked past the plate-glass window four times before deciding to come into the restaurant. He was wearing a plaid, long-sleeved sports shirt, the sleeves rolled up past his thick wrists. His reddish-blond hair was curly and long, giving his green-eyed face a cherubic look that denied the brute power of his body. He came directly to Brown's table, approaching him with the confident stride most very strong men possess, stood staring down at him, and immediately said, "You look like fuzz."

"So do you," Brown answered.

"How do I know you're not?"

"How do I know *you're* not?" Brown said. "Why don't you sit down?"

"Sure," Weinberg answered. He pulled out a chair, adjusted his body to the seat and back as though he were maneuvering a bulldozer into a tight corner, and then folded his huge hands on the tabletop. "Let's hear it again," he said.

"From the top?"

"From the top," Weinberg said, and nodded. "First, your name."

"Artie Stokes. I'm from Salt Lake City, you ever been there?"

"No."

"Nice city," Brown said. "Do you ski? Supposed to be great powder skiing at Alta."

"Did you call me to talk about the Olympics, or what?" Weinberg said.

"I thought you might be a skier," Brown answered.

"Are *you?*"

"How many Negroes have you ever seen on the ski slopes?"

"I've never been *on* the ski slopes."

"But you get my point."

"I'm still waiting for your story, Stokes."

"I already gave it to you on the phone."

"Give it to me again."

"Why?"

"Let's say we had a poor connection."

"Okay," Brown said, and sighed. "Couple of weeks ago, I bought a piece of a picture and a couple of names from a guy in Salt Lake. I paid two grand for the package. Guy who sold it to me was fresh out of Utah State, and strapped for cash."

"What's his name?"

"Danny Firth. He was doing eight years for armed robbery, got out in April and needed a stake to set up his next job. That's why he was willing to part with what he had."

"What'd he have?"

"I just told you. Two names and a piece of a snapshot."

"And you were willing to pay two grand for *that?*"

"That's right."

"Why?"

"Because Firth told me I could get seven hundred and fifty thousand dollars just by fitting my piece of the snapshot into the whole picture."

"He told you that, huh?"

"That's what he told me."

"I'm surprised he didn't sell you the Calm's Point Bridge while he was at it."

"This ain't the Calm's Point Bridge, Weinberg, and you know it."

Weinberg was silent for a few moments. He kept looking down at his clasped hands. Then he raised his eyes to Brown's and said, "You've a piece of the snapshot, huh?"

"That's right."

"And two names, huh?"

"That's right."

"What're the two names?"

"Yours is one of them."

"And the other one?"

"I'll tell you that after we make a deal."

"And what're these names supposed to be?"

"They're supposed to be the names of two people who've *also* got pieces of that picture."

"And I'm one of them, huh?"

"That's right."

"You're nuts," Weinberg said.

"I told you most of this on the phone," Brown said. "If you think I'm nuts, what're you doing here?"

Weinberg studied him again. He unclasped his hands, took a cigarette from a package in his pocket, offered one to Brown, and then lighted both of them. He let out a stream of smoke, leaned back in his chair, and said, "Did your pal Danny Firth say *how* you could get seven hundred and fifty G's for pasting a picture together?"

"He did."

"How?"

"Weinberg . . . *you* know, and *I* know the full picture shows where Carmine Bonamico dropped the N.S.L.A. loot."

"I don't know what you're talking about."

"You know *exactly* what I'm talking about. Now how about it? You want to keep playing cute, or you want to talk a deal?"

"I want some more information."

"Like what?"

"Like how'd your pal Danny Firth come across his piece?"

"He got it from a guy at Utah State. The guy was doing life, no chance of getting out unless he *busted* out, which he wasn't about to do. Danny promised to look after his wife and kids if he recovered the loot."

"So Danny gets out, and turns right around and sells you his piece, huh?"

"That's right."

"Nice guy, Danny."

"What do you expect?" Brown said, and smiled. "Honor among thieves?"

"Which brings us to you," Weinberg said, returning the smile. "What's *your* bag?"

"I'm in and out of a lot of things."

"Like what?"

"The last thing I was in and out of was San Quentin," Brown said, and smiled again. "I did five years for hanging some paper. It was a bum rap."

"It's *always* a bum rap," Weinberg said. "Let's get back to the picture for a minute. How many pieces *are* there, do you know?"

"I was hoping you'd know."

"I don't."

"We can talk a deal, anyway."

"Maybe," Weinberg said. "Who else knows about this?"

"Nobody."

"You sure you didn't tell your brother all about it? Or some broad?"

"I haven't *got* a brother. And I never tell broads nothing." Brown paused. "Why? Who'd *you* tell?"

"Not a soul. You think I'm crazy? There's big money involved here."

"Oh, all at once you *know* there's big money involved, huh?"

"What's the other name on your list?"

"Do we have a deal?"

"Only if it's a name I don't already have."

"How many do you have?"

"Just one."

"That makes us even."

"Unless it's the same name."

"If it's the same name, neither of us have lost anything. Here's the deal, Weinberg, take it or leave it. I put up the name and the piece *I've* got, you put up the name and the piece *you've* got. If we find the loot, we split it fifty-fifty—*after* deducting expenses. I've already laid out two grand, you know."

"That's your headache," Weinberg said. "I'm willing to share whatever expenses we have from now on, but don't expect me to pay for a *bar mitzvah* when you were thirteen."

"Okay, forget the two grand. Have we got a deal?"

"We've got a deal," Weinberg said and extended his hand across the table. Brown took it. "Let's see your piece of the picture," Weinberg said.

"Amateur night in Dixie," Brown said, shaking his head. "You didn't *really* think I'd have it with me, did you?"

"No harm trying," Weinberg said, and grinned. "Meet me later tonight. We'll put it all on the table then."

"Where?"

"My place?" Weinberg asked.

"Where's that?"

"220 South Kirby. Apartment 36."

"What time?"

"Eleven o'clock okay with you?"

"I'll be there," Brown said.

220 South Kirby was in a slum as rank as a cesspool. Arthur Brown knew such slums well. The overflowing garbage cans in front of the building were quite familiar to him. The front stoop held no surprises; cracked cement steps, the middle riser of which was lettered in white paint with the words NO SITTING ON STOOP; rusted wrought-iron railings; a shattered pane of glass in the entrance door. The locks on the mailboxes in the foyer, where welfare checks were deposited each month, were broken. There was no light in the foyer and only a single naked bulb illuminated the first-floor landing. The hallway smelled of cooking, breathing, eliminating. The stench that assailed Brown as he climbed to the third floor brought back too many memories of a lanky boy lying in bed in his underwear, listening to the sounds of rats foraging in the kitchen. His sister, in the bed next to his, in the same bedroom shared by his mother and father, would whisper in the darkness, "Are they here again, Artie?" and

he would nod wide-eyed and say reassuringly, "They'll go away, Penny."

One night Penny said, "Suppose they don't, Artie?"

He could find no answer. In his mind's eye, he saw himself walking into the kitchen the next morning to discover the room swarming with long-tailed rats, their sharp fangs dripping blood.

Even now, he shuddered at the thought.

Suppose they don't, Artie?

His sister had died at the age of seventeen, from an overdose of heroin administered in a cellar club by a teenage girl who, like Penny, was one of the debs in a street gang called The Warrior Princes. He could remember a time when one of the boys painted the name of the gang in four-foot-high letters on the brick wall of a housing project—THE WARRIOR PRINCES.

In the darkness of the third-floor landing, Brown rapped on the door to 36, and heard Weinberg say from within, "Yes, who is it?"

"Me," he answered. "Stokes."

"It's open, come in," Weinberg said.

He opened the door.

Something warned him a second too late. As he opened the door, he could see through into the kitchen, but Weinberg was nowhere in sight. And then the warning came, the knowledge that Weinberg's voice had sounded very near to the closed door. He turned to his right, started to bring up his hand in protection against the coming blow—but too late. Something hard hit him on the side of his head, just below the temple. He fell sideways, almost blacked out, tried to get to his knees, stumbled, and looked up into the muzzle of a .38 Special.

"Hello there, Stokes," Weinberg said, and grinned. "Keep your hands flat on the floor, don't make a move or I'll kill you. That's it."

He stepped gingerly around Brown, reached under his jacket from behind, and pulled his gun from the shoulder holster there.

"I hope you've got a license for this," he said, grinned again, and tucked the gun into the waistband of his trousers. "Now get up."

"What do you hope to accomplish?" Brown said.

"I hope to get what I want without having to make any cocka-mamie deals."

"And when you've got it? Then what?"

"I move on to bigger and better things. With*out* you."

"You'd better move far and fast," Brown said. "I'm sure as hell going to find you."

"Not if you're dead, you won't."

"You'd cool me in your own apartment? Who're you trying to kid?"

"It's *not* my apartment," Weinberg said, and grinned again.

"I checked the address with . . ." Brown started, and shut his mouth before he'd said, "the Identification Bureau."

"Yeah, with what?"

"With your name in the phone book. Don't try to con me, Weinberg. This is your pad, all right."

"Used to be, only *used* to be. I moved out two months ago, kept the same phone number."

"Then how'd you get in here tonight?"

"The super's a wino. A bottle of Thunderbird goes a long way in this building."

"What about whoever lives here now?"

"He's a night watchman. He leaves here at ten and doesn't get home until six in the morning. Any other questions?"

"Yeah," Brown said. "What makes you think I'm in this alone?"

"What difference does it make?"

"I'll tell you what difference it makes. You can take my piece of the snapshot—oh, sure, I've got it with me—but if I *am* in this with another guy, or *two* other guys, or a *dozen* other guys, you can bet your ass they've all got prints of it. So where does that leave you? I'm dead, and you've got the picture, but so have they. You're right back where you started."

"If there's anybody else in it with you."

"Right. And if there's anybody else, they know who you are, pal, believe me. You pull that trigger, you'd better start running. Fast."

"You told me nobody knew about this."

"Sure. You told *me* we had a deal."

"Maybe you're full of shit this time, too."

"Or maybe not. You ready to chance it? You know the kind of heat you'd be asking for? Oh, not only from the cops—homicide's still against the law, you know. But also from . . ."

"The cops don't bother me. They'll go looking for the guy who lives here."

"Unless one of my friends tells them you and I had a meeting here tonight."

"It sounds very good, Stokes. But only if you've *really* got some friends out there. Otherwise, it ain't worth a nickel."

"Consider another angle then. You kill me, and you get my piece of the picture, sure. But you don't get that name you want. That's up *here,* Weinberg." He tapped his temple with his forefinger.

"I hadn't thought of that," Weinberg said.

"Think about it now," Brown said. "I'll give you five minutes."

"You'll give *me* five minutes?" Weinberg said, and burst out laughing. *"I'm* holding the gun, and *you're* giving me five minutes."

"Always play 'em like you've got 'em, my daddy used to tell me," Brown said, and smiled.

"Your daddy ever get hit with a slug from a .38?"

"No, but he *did* get hit with a baseball bat one time," Brown said, and Weinberg burst out laughing again.

"Maybe you wouldn't make such a bad partner after all," he said.

"So what do you think?"

"I don't know."

"Put up the gun. Give mine back, and we'll be on equal terms again. Then let's cut the crap and get on with the goddamn business."

"How do I know you won't try to cold-cock me?"

"Because maybe *you've* got friends, too, same as me."

"Always play 'em like you've got 'em," Weinberg said, and chuckled.

"Yes or no?"

"Sure," Weinberg said. He took Brown's gun from his waistband and handed it to him muzzle first. Brown immediately put it back into his holster. Weinberg hesitated a moment, and then put his own gun into a holster on his right hip. "Okay," he said. "Do we shake hands all over again?"

"I'd like to," Brown said.

The two men shook hands.

"Let's see your piece of the picture," Weinberg said.

"Let's see yours," Brown said.

"The Mutual Faith and Trust Society," Weinberg said. "Okay, we'll do it together."

Together, both men took out their wallets. Together, both men removed from plastic compartments the glossy segments of the larger photograph. The piece Brown placed on the tabletop was the one he and Carella had found hidden in Ehrbach's floor lamp. The piece Weinberg placed beside it was a corner piece unlike any the police already had in their possession.

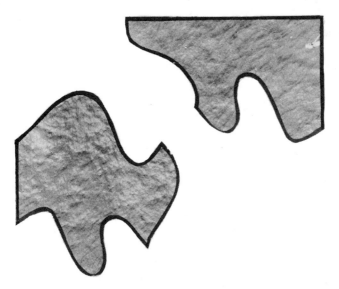

Both men studied the pieces. Weinberg began moving them around on the tabletop. A grin cracked across his face. "We're gonna make good partners," he said. "Look at this. They *fit*."

Brown looked.

Then he smiled. He smiled because the pieces sure as hell did fit. But he also smiled because, heh-heh, unbeknownst to his new partner

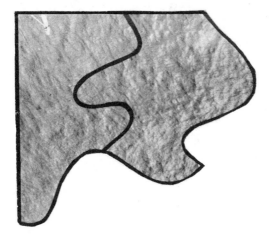

and straight man, there were two additional pieces of the picture in the top drawer of his desk back at the squadroom, and two and two make four, and who knew what *these* two pieces and *those* two pieces together might reveal, who indeed? So Brown smiled and Weinberg smiled, and everybody was having just a wonderful old time putting together the pieces of this old jigsaw puzzle.

"Now the names," Weinberg said, sounding very much like the M.C. at the Annual Academy Awards Presentations.

"Eugene Edward Ehrbach," Brown said, smiling.

"Geraldine Ferguson," Weinberg said, smiling.

"Ehrbach's dead," Brown said, and the smile dropped from Weinberg's face.

"What?" he shouted. "What the hell kind of . . . ?"

"He was killed Wednesday night. The cops found . . ."

"Dead?" Weinberg shouted. *"Dead?"*

"Dead," Brown said. "But the cops found . . ."

"Is this a double cross? Is that what this is? Some kind of a double cross?"

"You've got to learn to calm down," Brown said.

"I'll calm down! I'll break your head in a million pieces, that's what I'll do."

"He was carrying a piece of the picture," Brown said softly.

"What? Who?"

"Ehrbach."

"A piece of *our* picture?"

"That's right."

"Why didn't you say so? Where is it?"

"The cops have it."

"The cops! Jesus Christ, Stokes . . ."

"Cops can be bought," Brown said, "same as anybody else. Ehrbach's dead and anything they found on him is probably in a brown paper bag someplace being watched by a police clerk. All we got to do is find out where, and then cross a few palms."

"I don't like negotiating with fuzz," Weinberg said.

"Who does? But to survive in this city, you *got* to deal with them every now and then."

"Biggest fuckin' thieves in the world," Weinberg said.

"Look," Brown said, "if even a felony can be squared for a couple of bills, we should be able to lay our hands on Ehrbach's piece for maybe fifty, sixty bucks. All we got to do is find out where it is."

"How do we do that? Call the cops and ask?"

"Maybe. I got to think about it a little. Now what about this Geraldine what's-her-name?"

"Ferguson. She runs an art gallery on Jefferson Avenue. I've busted into her apartment maybe six or seven times already, couldn't find the picture. I wouldn't be surprised she stuck it up her twat," Weinberg said, and burst out laughing. Brown laughed with him. They were still good old buddies and still thrilled and amazed by the fact that their two separate pieces fit together as neatly as Yin and Yang.

"Have you got a print of this?" Brown asked.

"Naturally," Weinberg said. "And you?"

"Naturally."

"You want to exchange pieces, is that it?"

"That's it."

"Done," Weinberg said, and picked up the section Brown had placed on the tabletop. Brown picked up the remaining section, and both men grinned again. "Now let's go down for a drink," Weinberg said. "We got a lot of strategy to work out."

"Right," Brown said. As they went toward the front door, he said—casually, he thought—"By the way, how'd you happen to *get* your piece of the snapshot?"

"Be happy to tell you," Weinberg said.

"Good."

"As soon as you tell me how you *really* got yours," Weinberg added, and began chuckling.

Brown suddenly wondered which of them was the straight man.

5

IT WAS all happening too quickly and too easily.

If getting seven hundred and fifty thousand dollars was always this simple, Brown was definitely in the wrong racket. He almost wished that he and Weinberg were truly partners. There was something about the big man that Brown liked, despite the fact that he was a felon. He did not leave Weinberg until two o'clock the next morning. By that time, each of the men had consumed a fifth of Scotch between them, and were calling each other Artie and Al. They had also decided that Brown should be the one who made the next approach to Geraldine Ferguson. Weinberg had been to her gallery several times with offers to buy the segment he was certain she possessed, but each time she had professed ignorance of the photograph, segmented or otherwise. Weinberg told Brown that he *knew* the girl had the goods they were after, but he would not reveal *how* he knew. Brown said that was a hell of a way to start a partnership, and Weinberg said Brown had started in an even *worse* way, giving him all that bullshit about a lifer at Utah State, man, that was straight out of Mickey Mouse, had Brown expected him to believe it? Brown said Well, I guess we both got our reasons for not wanting our sources known, and Weinberg said Well, maybe when we get to know each other better, and Brown said I hope so, and Weinberg said Man, I never thought I'd be partners with a spade.

Brown looked at him.

It was hip these days, he knew, for white men to call Negroes "spades," but to Brown this was simply another of the words which had once been considered—and which he *still* considered—derogatory. Weinberg was smiling in a boozy happy friendly way, and Brown was certain the slur had been unintentional. And yet, the word rankled, the whole fucking thing rankled.

"That bother you?" he asked.

"What bother me?" Weinberg said.

"My being a *spade,*" Brown said, hitting the word hard.

Weinberg looked him square in the eye. "Did I say that? Did I call you that?"

"You did," Brown said, and nodded.

"Then I'm sorry. I didn't mean it." He extended his hand across the table. "I'm sorry, Artie," he said.

Brown took his hand. "Forget it."

"I may be a shit," Weinberg said. "I may go around beating up people and doing rotten things, but I like you, Artie, and I wouldn't hurt you by saying no dumb thing like that."

"Okay."

Weinberg was just gathering steam. "I may be the crumbiest guy ever walked the earth, I may have done some filthy things, but one thing I wouldn't do is call you no spade, Artie, not if I wasn't so piss-ass drunk and didn't know what I was saying that might hurt a good friend of mine and a partner besides."

"Okay," Brown said.

"Okay, excuse it, Artie. Excuse it. I mean it."

"Okay."

"Okay," Weinberg said. "Let's go home, Artie. Artie, I think we better go home. I always get in fights in bars, and I don't want to get in no trouble when we got our little deal cooking, okay?" He winked. "Okay?" He winked again. "Tomorrow morning, you got to go visit little Geraldine Ferguson. Tell her she don't give us that picture, we'll come around and do something terrible to her, okay?" Weinberg smiled. "I can't think of nothing terrible right now, but I'll think of something in the morning, okay?"

On Saturday morning, Brown put the new photo scrap into an envelope together with Geraldine Ferguson's name and address, sealed the envelope, and dropped it into a mailbox in the hallway of 1134 Culver Avenue, three blocks from the precinct. The name on the box was Cara Binieri, which was Steve Carella's little joke, *carabinieri* meaning fuzz in Italian. They had decided between them that Brown was to stay away from the squadroom, and whereas he hoped to call Carella later in the day, he wanted the information to be waiting for him in the mailbox this morning, when he would pick it up on his way to work.

Brown's own day started somewhat more glamorously.

It also ended in a pretty glamorous way.

Geraldine Ferguson was a white woman, petite, with long straight black hair and brown eyes and a generous mouth. She was in her early thirties, wearing purple bell-bottom slacks and a man-tailored shirt done in lavender satin. She had big golden hoops looped into her ear lobes, and she greeted Brown with a smile nothing less than radiant.

"Good morning," she said. "Isn't it a *beautiful* morning?"

"It's a lovely morning," Brown said.

"Are you here for the Gonzagos?" she asked.

"I don't think so," Brown said. "What *are* the gonzagos?"

"Luis Gonzago," she said, and smiled again. "He's a painter. I thought you might have wanted to see his stuff, but we've already taken it down. Will you be going to Los Angeles?"

"No, I hadn't planned to," Brown said.

"Because he'll be having a show at the Herron Gallery out there starting next Tuesday. On Sepulveda."

"No, I won't be going to Los Angeles."

"That's a shame," she said, and smiled.

She was perhaps five-two or five-three, with a perfectly proportioned figure for her size. She moved with a swift feminine grace that he found delightful, her brown eyes flashing in the sunlight that streamed through the front plate-glass window. The smile breaking as sharp and as fast as a curve ball. She threw her arms wide, and said, "But we've got loads of other stuff, so if you'd like me to help you, I'd be happy to. Or you can just look around on your own, if you like. What were you interested in? Paintings or sculpture?"

"Well," Brown said, and hesitated, wondering exactly how he should play this. "Is this your own gallery?" he asked, stalling.

"Yes, it is," she said.

"Then you're Miss Ferguson. I mean, this *is* the Ferguson Gallery, so I guess . . ."

"Well, *Mrs.* Ferguson, really," she said. "But *not* really," she added, and the smile broke again, swift and clean. "I was married to Mr. Ferguson, Mr. *Harold* Ferguson, but Mr. Ferguson and I are no longer sharing bed and board, and so whereas I'm still Geraldine Ferguson, I am no longer *Mrs.* Ferguson. Oh hell," she said, "why don't you just call me Gerry? What's *your* name?"

"Arthur Stokes," he said.

"Are you a cop, Arthur?" she asked flatly.

"No," he said. "What gave you that idea?"

"You're big like a cop," she said, and shrugged. "Also you carry a gun."

"Do I?"

"Mm-huh. Right there," she said, and pointed.

"I didn't think it showed."

"Well, Harold was in the diamond business, and he had a carry-permit, and he used to wear this *enormous* revolver in a shoulder holster, right where yours is. So I guess when your husband wears a gun all the time, you get used to the way it looks, and that's how I spotted yours right away. Why do you wear a gun, Arthur? Are you in the diamond business?"

"No," he said, "I'm in the insurance business."

He figured that was a fair enough beginning, even though he had borrowed the occupation from Irving Krutch who, to his knowledge, did *not* carry a gun.

"Oh, do insurance men wear guns?" Gerry asked. "I didn't know that."

"Yes," he said, "if they're insurance investigators."

"Don't *tell* me!" she squealed. "Someone's had a painting stolen! You're here to check on authenticity."

"Well, no," he said. "Not exactly."

"Arthur," she said. "I think you're a cop, I really do."

"Now why would a cop be visiting *you,* Miss Ferguson?"

"Gerry. Maybe because I charge such exorbitant prices," she said, and smiled. "I don't really. Yes, I do really. Would you like to see some pictures while you decide if you're a cop or not?"

She led him around the gallery. The walls were white, with recessed overhead lighting fixtures that illuminated the hanging paintings and standing pieces of sculpture. Her taste in paintings was a bit far-out for Brown, wildly colorful, non-objective geometric tangles that overpowered the eye and defied analysis. The sculpture was of the junkyard variety, automobile headlights welded to Stillson wrenches, a plumber's red-cupped plunger wired to the broken handle and frayed-stray brush of a broom.

"I can see we're hardly eliciting any wild response," Gerry said, and smiled. "What kind of art do you like?"

"Well, I did have a specific picture in mind," Brown said.

"Did someone see it here?" she asked. "Would it have been in the Gonzago exhibit?"

"I don't think so."

"What kind of a painting is it?"

"It isn't a painting. It's a photograph."

Gerry shook her head. "It couldn't have been here. We've never had a photographic show, not since I've owned the gallery, anyway—and that's close to five years."

"It's not even a *whole* photograph," Brown said, and watched her.

"Oh-*ho,*" she said. This time, she didn't smile. "What happened to the other guy?"

"What other guy?"

"The guy who's been in here three or four thousand times in the past two months. He's *yay* tall, and he's got blondish curly hair, and he said his name was Al Reynolds the first time he came in, and then forgot what he'd told me and said his name was Al *Randolph* the second time around. Is *he* a cop, too?"

"We're neither of us cops."

"Mr. Stark . . ."

"Stokes," Brown said.

"Just checking," Gerry said, and grinned. "Mr. Stokes . . ."

"Arthur . . ."

"Arthur, I don't have what you're looking for. Believe me. If I had it, I'd sell it to you. Assuming the price was right."

"The price can be made right."

"How right is right?"

"You name a figure," Brown said.

"Well, do you see that Albright on the wall there? It's approximately four feet square, and the gallery gets ten thousand dollars for it. The smaller painting next to it, the Sandrovich, costs five thousand. And the tiny *gouache* on the far wall costs three thousand. How large is your photograph, Arthur?"

"I have no idea. Are we talking about the *whole* picture now, or just the piece you have?"

"The whole picture."

"Five by seven? Six by eight? I'm guessing."

"Then you've never seen the whole picture?"

"Have you?"

"I haven't even seen the tiny piece you're after."

"Then how do you know it's tiny?" Brown asked.

"How much is it worth to you and your friend, Arthur? Tiny or otherwise?"

"Have you got it?"

"If I told him no, why should I tell you yes?"

"Maybe I'm more persuasive."

"Sure, look at Superspade," Gerry said, and smiled. "Faster than a rolling watermelon, able to leap tall honkies in a single bound . . ."

". . . who is in reality," Brown continued, "mild-mannered Arthur Stokes of *Ebony* magazine."

"Who are you *really* in reality, Arthur?"

"An insurance investigator, I told you."

"Your friend Reynolds or Randolph or whoever-the-hell doesn't look or sound like an insurance investigator."

"No two insurance investigators look or sound alike."

"That's right. Only cops and crooks look and sound alike. Are you and your friend cops, Arthur? Or crooks? Which?"

"Maybe one of us is a cop and the other's a crook."

"Either way, I don't have what you want."

"I think you have."

"You're right," a voice said from the rear of the gallery. "She has."

"Oh, hell," Gerry said.

Brown turned to where a blue door had opened in the otherwise white wall. A blond man in a brown suit stood in the open doorway, his hand still on the knob. He was about five feet ten inches tall, wearing a vest under the suit jacket, gold-rimmed eyeglasses, a brown-and-gold striped tie. He walked briskly to where they were standing, offered his hand to Brown and said, "Bramley Kahn, how do you do?"

"Bram, you're a pain in the ass," Gerry said.

"Arthur Stokes," Brown said. "Pleased to meet you."

"If we're going to talk business . . ."

"We are *not* going to talk business," Gerry interrupted.

"I suggest," Kahn continued in his mild voice, "that we go into the office." He paused, glanced at Gerry, looked back at Brown, and said, "Shall we?"

"Why not?" Brown said.

They walked to the rear of the gallery. The office was small and simply decorated—a Danish modern desk, a single naturalistic painting of a nude on the wall opposite the desk, a thick gray rug, white walls, a white Lucite hanging light globe, several leather-and-chrome easy chairs. Gerry Ferguson, pouting, sat nearest Kahn's desk, folding her legs up under her and cupping her chin in her hand. Brown took the seat opposite Kahn, who sat behind the desk in an old-fashioned swivel chair that seemed distinctly out of place in such svelte surroundings.

"I'm Gerry's partner," Kahn explained.

"Only in the *gallery,*" Gerry snapped.

"I'm also her business adviser."

"I've got some advice for *you,*" Gerry said heatedly, "Keep your nose . . ."

"Gerry has a temper," Kahn said.

"Gerry has a jerk for a partner," Gerry said.

"Oh, my," Kahn said, and sighed.

Brown watched him, trying to determine whether he was a fag or not. His manner was effete, but not quite feminine; his voice was gently modulated, but there was no evidence in it of characteristic homosexual cadences; his gestures were small and fluid, but he neither dangled a limp wrist, nor used his hands and shoulders like a dancer's. Brown couldn't tell. The biggest queen he'd ever known had been built like a wrestler and moved with all the subtle grace of a longshoreman.

"What about the picture?" Brown asked.

"She has it," Kahn said.

"I *haven't*," Gerry said.

"Maybe I ought to leave you two alone for a while," Brown said.

"How much are you willing to pay for it, Mr. Stokes?" Kahn asked.

"That depends."

"On what?"

Brown said nothing.

Kahn said, "On whether or not it's a piece you already have, isn't that the answer?"

Brown still said nothing.

"You *do* have a piece, don't you? Or *several* pieces?"

"Is it for sale or not?" Brown asked.

"No," Gerry said.

"Yes," Kahn said. "But you still haven't made an offer, Mr. Stokes."

"Let me see it first," Brown said.

"No," Kahn said.

"No," Gerry said, just a beat behind him.

"How many pieces do you have, Mr. Stokes?"

No answer.

"Is the other gentleman your partner? Do you have more than one piece?"

No answer.

"Do you know what the picture is supposed to reveal?"

"Let *me* ask a few," Brown said.

"Please," Kahn said, and offered him the floor with an open-handed, palm-up gesture.

"Miss Ferguson . . ."

"I thought it was Gerry."

"Gerry . . . where did you get the piece you now have?"

"You're both dreaming," Gerry said. "I don't know what either one of you is talking about."

"My client . . ."

"Your client, my ass," Gerry said. "You're a cop. Who are you trying to kid, Arthur?"

"Are you a policeman, Mr. Stokes?"

"No."

"The fuzz stench is overpowering," Gerry said.

"How do you come to be so familiar with that stench?" Brown asked.

"May I answer that one?" Kahn asked.

"Keep your mouth shut, Bram," Gerry warned.

"Mrs. Ferguson's sister is a girl named Patty D'Amore," Kahn said. "Does that mean anything to you?"

"Not a thing," Brown said.

"Her husband was a cheap gangster named Louis D'Amore. He was killed some six years ago, following a bank holdup."

"I don't keep track of such things," Brown said.

"No, I'll just *bet* you don't," Gerry said. "He's a cop, Bram. And *you're* a fool."

"Sicilian blood is much, *much* thicker than water," Kahn said, and smiled. "I would imagine that in your childhood, there was plenty of talk concerning the 'stench of fuzz' while the lasagna was being served, eh, Geraldine?"

"How would you like to hear a choice Sicilian expression?" Gerry asked.

"I'd love to."

"Va fon gool," Gerry said.

"Even *I* know what that means," Brown said.

"Sounds Chinese," Kahn said.

"About the picture . . ."

"We have it, and we'll sell it," Kahn said. "That's our business. Selling pictures."

"Have you got any customers who'll buy a picture sight unseen?" Brown asked.

"Have you got any customers who'll buy a picture sight unseen?" exist?" Gerry asked.

"Well," Brown said, "why don't you give me a ring when you've settled this between you, huh?"

"Where can we reach you, Mr. Stokes?"

"I'm staying at the Selby Arms. It's a fleabag on North Founders, just off Byram Lane."

"Are you an out-of-towner, Mr. Stokes?"

"Room 502," Brown said.

"You didn't answer my question."

"You didn't answer any of mine, either," Brown said. He smiled, rose, turned to Gerry and said, "I hope you'll reconsider, Miss Ferguson."

This time, she didn't ask him to call her Gerry.

On the street outside, Brown looked for a phone booth. The first phone he tried had the dial missing. The receiver on the next phone had been severed from its metal-covered cord, undoubtedly with a wire cutter. The third booth he found seemed okay. He put a dime into the phone and got nothing, no dial tone, no static, no nothing. He jiggled the hook. His dime did not come back. He hung up the receiver. His dime did not come back. He hit the phone with his fist. Nothing. He went out of the booth swearing, wondering when the city was going to crack down on the illegal gambling devices the telephone company had installed all over the city and labeled "Public Telephones." He supposed a Gaylord Ravenal type would have enjoyed this kind of action—you put your money in the slot and either lost it, or else hit the jackpot and a shower of coins came out of the return chute—but Brown merely wanted to make a telephone call, and the Las Vegas aspects of such an endeavor left him absolutely cold. He finally found a working telephone in a restaurant off Tyler. With a glance heavenward, he put his dime into the slot. He got a dial tone immediately.

The number he dialed was Albert Weinberg's. Weinberg had given him his new address the night before, a rooming house on North Colman, close to Byram Lane, which was why Brown had checked into the Selby Arms, only three blocks away from Weinberg's place. When Weinberg came onto the line, Brown related his encounter with the owners of the Ferguson Gallery and said he hoped to hear from them later in the day, was in fact heading back to the hotel right this minute.

"That's the Selby Arms, right?" Weinberg said.

"Yeah, on North Founders. How'd *you* make out?"

"I've been doing a little asking around," Weinberg said, "and the way I understand it, whenever some guy's been knocked off, the cops take his clothes and his belongings downtown to what they call the Property Clerk's Office. The stuff can be claimed by a relative after the medics, and the lab, and the bulls on the case are finished with it. You think I could pass for Ehrbach's brother?"

"*I* sure as hell couldn't," Brown said.

"Might be worth a try, save ourselves a few bucks."

"A fix is safer," Brown said.

"Let me go on the earie a bit longer," Weinberg said, "try to find out who runs that office."

"Okay. You know where to reach me."

"Right. Let me know if Ferguson or her pansy partner get in touch."

"I will," Brown said, and hung up.

In the cloistered stillness of the squadroom (telephones jangling, typewriters clanging, teletype clattering, a prisoner screaming his head off in the detention cage across the room), Steve Carella spread the four pieces of the photograph on his desktop and tried to fit them together.

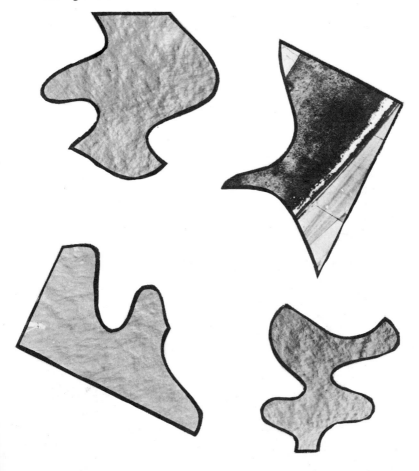

He was not very good at working jigsaw puzzles.

The way he looked at it, and there were *many* ways of looking at it, the right-angle pieces were obviously corner pieces, which meant that either of them could go in any one of four places, most rectangles having four and only four corners, brilliant deduction. The simplest of these two corner pieces looked like nothing more than a dark rough surface with something jutting into it from above or below, depending on whether the corner was a top corner or a bottom corner. The something jutting into the dark rough surface strongly resembled a phallus with a string around it. (He doubted very much that it was actually a phallus. If it was, they had an entirely different kind of case on their hands.) The second corner piece, the one with the sweeping curves, seemed to be a section of a wall or a building or a handball court. Which brought him to the two remaining pieces, both with the same rough gray surface. It was the surface that troubled Carella. The more he looked at it, the more it looked like water—but how could that tie in with the wall or building or handball court in the corner piece?

He was not very good at working jigsaw puzzles.

After ten minutes of study, he finally managed to fit two of the pieces together, a task Albert Weinberg had completed in thirty seconds. Ten minutes later, he had fitted another piece into the puzzle. Twenty minutes after that, he was convinced that the fourth piece did not fit against any of the other three. He looked at what he now had:

It could have been anything, anywhere.

In the city June worked its balmy Saturday afternoon magic.

On Third and Folger, two seventeen-year-old boys stopped a younger boy and asked him if he had any money. This being Saturday, the younger boy had no school carfare, and no lunch money. All he had was an overriding fear that transmitted itself to the older boys like animal musk in a virgin forest. When they discovered he was broke, they beat him up. It is probable that all they wanted to do was beat him up in the first place. They left him senseless, his nose shattered, four teeth knocked out of his mouth. All they took from him was a Ban-the-Bomb button he was wearing on his jacket. Then they went to a movie where John Wayne was starring in *The Green Berets*.

June.

In Grover Park, an old lady sat on a bench feeding the pigeons. She was wearing a flowered housedress and a woolen shawl. She kept feeding the pigeons and cooing to them gently. Her bag was on the bench beside her. From its open top, a half-completed gray sweater and a pair of knitting needles protruded. A college student with long hair and a straggly beard ambled over, and sat on the bench beside her. He was wearing blue jeans and a sweat shirt and scuffed desert boots. He opened a copy of Plato's *Republic* and began reading in the sunshine.

The old lady glanced at him.

She threw a handful of bread crumbs to the pigeons, cooed at them, and glanced again at the boy, who was absorbed in his book.

"Don't you look at *me* that way," she said suddenly.

The boy looked sharply to his right, not sure at first that he was being addressed.

"You heard me, you little shit," the old lady said. "Don't look at *me* that way, you bastard."

The boy stared at the woman for a moment, decided she was crazy, closed his book, and was rising from the bench when she reached into her bag, pulled out one of the knitting needles and stuck it clear through his eye to the back of his neck. At her feet, the pigeons pecked at the bread crumbs and gently cooed.

June, croon.

On a rooftop several miles away, the sunshine beat down on tar already growing sticky, and four boys held the twelve-year-old girl down against the black melting stuff while a fifth boy pulled off her panties and stuffed them into her mouth so that she could not scream. The girl could not move either, because they had her spreadeagled, arms and legs wide. A boy standing near the closed door of the roof whispered, "Hurry it up, Doc," and the boy named Doc, the one who had taken off her panties and who now stood over her, tall and large against the blinding sun, unzipped his fly, displayed his masculinity to her terror-ridden eyes, and then plunged himself deep inside her, against the protest of her tearing flesh. The boy standing near the closed door danced an impatient little jig while they took turns with the little girl. By the time it was his turn, they decided they'd better get out of there before somebody caught them. The little girl, bleeding and unconscious, still lay spreadeagled against the melting tar, her panties in her mouth. The boy who had been lookout complained all the way down the stairs to the street. "You bastards," he kept saying, "you promised I'd get some, too, you promised, you promised."

June, croon, spoon.

As the afternoon waned, a sweet intoxicating breeze blew in off the River Harb and insinuated itself through the narrow canyons of the city. Dusk was upon the horizon now, the sounds of the day were beginning to blend with the sounds of approaching night. The sky to the west turned blood-red and then swam the color spectrum through purple to blue to black. A thin sliver of moon curled against the stars like a pale lemon rind. In an apartment on a side street not far from the river, a man sat in undershirt and trousers, watching television. His wife, wearing a half-slip and a brassiere padded in from the kitchen carrying two open bottles of beer and two glasses. She put one beer and one glass down in front of the man, and then poured the other beer into a glass for herself. The crescent moon shone palely through the open back-yard window. The woman looked at the television screen and said, *"That* again?"

"Yeah," the man said, and picked up his bottle of beer.

"I hate that show," his wife said.

"I like it," he said.

Without a word, the woman went to the set, and turned the channel selector. Without a word, her husband got out of his chair, walked up to her swiftly and hit her eleven times with his beer bottle, twice while she was standing, twice as she slumped to the floor, and another seven times after she was unconscious and bleeding. He turned the television set back to the channel he'd been watching, and he did not call the police until the show was over, forty-five minutes later.

June, croon, spoon, moon.

In a hotel room at the Selby Arms, sixteen blocks to the west,

Arthur Brown made three telephone calls in succession, and then sat back to wait for contact from Ferguson and/or Kahn. The first call he made was to his wife Caroline who deplored the fact that they'd had to cancel a dinner date, and then went on to tell Brown that she missed him and that their daughter Connie was coming down with a cold. Brown told his wife he missed her also, to which she replied, "So why don't you come home and do something about it?"

"Duty calls," he said.

"Foo," she answered.

They hung up billing and cooing and humming June, croon, spoon, moon songs.

Brown opened his notebook to the page on which he had jotted Weinberg's address and telephone number. Weinberg answered on the third ring. As soon as they had exchanged hellos, Weinberg said, "Anything?"

"Not yet."

"You think they'll try to reach you?"

"I'm still hoping."

"I ain't had much luck, either," Weinberg said. "You know that Property Clerk's Office I was telling you about?"

"Yeah?"

"First of all, there must be forty or fifty guys working there, most of them civilians. They get crap from all over the city, anything that's been involved in accidents or crimes, anything not claimed at station houses—it's like a regular goddamn warehouse down there."

"No kidding," Brown said, as if he didn't already know.

"Yeah. There's also *cops* working there, because naturally they got a lot of weapons in the place, you dig?"

"Um-huh."

"In order to claim anything after they're done with it, you got to be a *prime* relative. It don't matter if you're a third cousin, so long as you're the closest living relative, you dig?"

"That sounds good for us," Brown said. "You could easily pass yourself off as . . ."

"Wait a second. You got to get a release from the D.A. first. You got to go to the D.A.'s *office* and get a goddamn *release.*"

"That's bad," Brown said.

"That stinks," Weinberg said.

"Who runs the whole show down there?"

"I don't know yet."

"Try to find out. He's the man we've got to reach." Brown paused. "Unless you'd like to try breaking in some night."

"Ha!" Weinberg said. "Call me later, will you? Let me know if anything happens."

"Will you be there all night?"

"All night. I got a sweet bottle of bourbon, and I intend to kill it."

"Don't let it kill *you,*" Brown said, and hung up.

The next person he called was Irving Krutch.

"Well, well," Krutch said, "this is a pleasant surprise."

"We've decided to make the investigation," Brown said.

"I thought you would," Krutch answered. "You found what you were looking for in Ehrbach's apartment, didn't you?"

"Yes. But even better than that."

"What do you mean?"

"We made contact with Weinberg. He has another piece of the picture, and he gave me a copy of it."

"That's *marvelous!*" Krutch said. "When can I have a look?"

"Not tonight. Can you drop by the squadroom tomorrow morning?"

"The squadroom?"

"Yes. Why? What's wrong with the squadroom?"

"Nothing. I just forgot for a minute that you guys work on Sunday."

"Ten o'clock or thereabouts," Brown said. "I won't be there, but Carella can show you the stuff."

"Fine," Krutch said. "Where can I reach *you* if I need you?"

"I'm at the Selby Arms, room 502."

"I'll jot that down, just in case." There was a pause on the line. "Selby Arms." Krutch repeated, obviously writing, "room 502, fine. Well," he said, "we're certainly off to a good start. I can't tell you how much I appreciate this."

"We all stand to gain," Brown said. "I've got to get off the phone. I'm expecting a call."

"Oh? Another lead?"

"Yes. The 'Geraldine' on your list is a Geraldine Ferguson, sister-in-law of the late Louis D'Amore. She runs an art gallery on Jefferson Avenue."

"Who gave you that?"

"Weinberg."

"Has she got anything?"

"I think so, but I'm not sure. That's what I'm waiting to hear."

"Will you let me know?"

"As soon as anything jells."

"Good. Listen, thanks again for calling. This is great news, really."

"Right, so long," Brown said, and hung up.

His telephone did not ring that night, nor did Saturday end glamorously for him until close to midnight. He had dozed in the armchair near the telephone when a knock sounded at the door. He was instantly awake.

"Yes?" he said.

"Mr. Stokes?"

"Yes."

"Desk clerk. Woman just delivered a message for you downstairs."

"Just a second," he answered. He had taken off his shoes and socks, and he padded to the door now in his bare feet and opened it just a crack.

The door flew wide, and the glamorous part of Saturday night began.

The man was wearing a glamorous nylon stocking pulled up over his face, flattening his nose, distorting his features. He was holding a glamorous pistol in his gloved right hand and as he shoved the door open with his left shoulder, he swung the gun at Brown's head, hitting him over the eye and knocking him to the floor. The man was wearing glamorous, highly polished black shoes, and he kicked Brown in the head the moment he was down. A glamorous shower of rockets went off inside Brown's skull, and then he went unconscious.

6

IT IS BAD to get hit on the head, any doctor can tell you that. It is even worse to get kicked in the head after you have been hit on the head, even your *mother* can tell you that. If a person gets hit on the head and loses consciousness, the doctors examining him will usually insist that he remain in the hospital for a period of at least one week, since unconsciousness precludes concussion, and concussion *can* mean internal hemorrhaging.

Brown regained consciousness twenty minutes later, and went into the bathroom to vomit. The room was a mess. Whoever had creamed him had also shaken down the place as thoroughly as the late Eugene Edward Ehrbach had shaken down the apartment of the late Donald Renninger. Brown was not too terribly concerned with the wreckage, not at the moment. Brown was concerned with staggering to the telephone, which he managed, and lifting the receiver, which he also managed. He gave the desk clerk Steve Carella's home number in Riverhead, waited while the phone rang six times, and then spoke to Fanny, the Carella housekeeper, who advised him that Mr. Carella was in Isola with his wife and was not expected home until one o'clock or thereabouts. He left a message for Carella to call him at the Selby Arms, hung up, thought he had better contact the squad immediately, and was trying to get the desk clerk again when a wave of dizziness washed over him. He stumbled over to the bed, threw himself full-length upon it, and closed his eyes. In a little while, he went into the bathroom to throw up a second time. When he got back to the bed, he closed his eyes and was either asleep or unconscious again within the next minute.

The morning hours of the night were beginning.

Steve Carella reached him a half-hour later. He knocked on the door to room 502, got no answer, and opened it immediately with a skeleton key. He picked his way through the debris on the floor, went directly to the bed where Brown lay unconscious on the slashed and mutilated mattress, saw the swollen lump over his partner's eye, said, "Artie?", received no reply, and went directly to the telephone. He was waiting for the desk clerk to answer the switchboard when Brown mumbled, "I'm okay."

"Like hell you are," Carella said, and jiggled the receiver-rest impatiently.

"Cool it, Steve. I'm okay."

Carella replaced the receiver, went back to the bed, and sat on the edge of it. "I want to get a meat wagon over here," he said.

"And put me out of action for a week, huh?"

"You're growing another head the size of your first one," Carella said.

"I hate hospitals," Brown said.

"How do you like comas?" Carella asked.

"I'm not in coma. Do I look like I'm in coma?"

"Let me get some ice for that lump. Jesus, that's some lump."

"The man hit me with a truck," Brown said.

Carella was jiggling the receiver-rest again. When the desk clerk came on, he said, "I didn't wake you, did I?"

"What?" the desk clerk said.

"Get some ice up here on the double. Room 502."

"Room service is closed," the desk clerk said.

"Open it. This is the police."

"Right away," the desk clerk said, and hung up.

"Some people sure pick ratty dumps to stay in," Carella said.

"Some people try to lend credence to their cover," Brown said, and attempted a smile. It didn't work. He winced in pain, and closed his eyes again.

"Did you see who did it?" Carella asked.

"I saw him, but he had a stocking over his face."

Carella shook his head. "Ever since the first movie where a guy had a stocking over his face, we get nothing but guys with stockings over their faces." He looked around the room. "Did a nice job on the room, too."

"Beautiful," Brown said.

"We're lucky he left you alive."

"Why wouldn't he? He wasn't after me, he was after the picture."

"Who do you think it was, Artie?"

"My partner," Brown said. "Albert Weinberg."

A knock sounded on the door. Carella went to answer it. The

desk clerk was standing there in his shirt sleeves, a soup dish full of ice cubes in his hands. "I had to go to the restaurant up the block for these," he complained.

"Great, thanks a lot," Carella said.

The desk clerk kept standing there. Carella reached into his pocket and handed him a quarter.

"Thanks," the desk clerk said sourly.

Carella closed the door, went into the bathroom, wrapped a towel around the ice cubes and then went back to Brown. "Here," he said, "put this on that lump."

Brown nodded, accepted the ice pack, pressed it to his swollen eye, and winced again.

"How do you know it was Weinberg?"

"I don't, for sure."

"Was he a big guy?"

"They all look big when they're about to hit you," Brown said.

"What I mean is did you get a good look at him?"

"No, it all happened . . ."

". . . in a split second," Carella said, and both men smiled. Brown winced again. "So what makes you think it was Weinberg?"

"I had him on the phone tonight," Brown said. "Told him we'd scored."

"Who else did you talk to?"

"Irving Krutch."

"So it could have been Krutch."

"Sure. It also could have been my wife Caroline. I talked to her, too."

"She pretty good with a blunt instrument?"

"As good as most," Brown said.

"How's that eye feel?"

"Terrible."

"I think I'd *better* get a meat wagon."

"No, you don't," Brown said, "We've got work to do."

"You're not the only cop in this city," Carella said.

"I'm the only one who got clobbered in this room tonight," Brown said.

Carella sighed. "One consolation, anyway," he said.

"What's that?"

"He didn't get what he came after. *That's* in my desk drawer, back at the ranch."

It was decided over Brown's protests (actually Brown only did the protesting; Carella did all the deciding) that he would be taken to Saint Catherine's Hospital a dozen blocks away, for examination and treatment in the Emergency Room. Carella left him there at 2 A.M., still grumbling, and caught a taxi over to Weinberg's apartment on North Colman. At that hour of the morning, the neighborhood resembled a lunar landscape. Weinberg's rooming house was the only building on the street that had not already been abandoned by its owners, those entrepreneurs having decided the buildings were too expensive to maintain in accordance with the city's laws; those respectable businessmen also having discovered that no one was willing to buy such white elephants; those wheeler-dealers having merely pulled out, leaving a row of run-down tenements as a gift to the city, lucky city.

There was a time, and this not too long ago, when hippies and runaways had moved into these buildings en masse, painting their colorful flower designs on the brick fronts, sleeping on mattresses spread wall-to-wall, puffing pot, dropping acid, living the happy carefree life of the commune-dweller. The regular residents of this run-down slum area, forced to live here because of certain language and racial barriers the city raised against some of its citizens, could not understand why anyone would come to live here of his own free will and choice—but they certainly knew pigeons when they saw them. The hippies, the runaways, the carefree happy commune-dwellers had no need for telephones, being in touch as they were with nature. The only time they might have needed Mr. Bell's invention was when the restless natives of the ghetto came piling into the apartment to beat up the boys and rape the girls and take whatever meager possessions were worth hocking. The hippies and the runaways decided that perhaps this wasteland was not for them, it becoming more and more difficult to repeat the word "Love" when a fist was being crashed into the mouth or a girl was screaming on the mattress in the other room. The ghetto regulars had struck back at a society that forced them to live in such surroundings, little realizing that the people they were harassing had themselves broken with the same society, a society that *allowed* such ghettos to exist. It was a case of poor slob beating up on poor slob, while five blocks away, a fashionable discotheque called Rembrandt's bleated its rock-and-roll music, and ladies in sequined slacks and men in dancing slippers laughed away the night. The hippies were gone now, the flower designs on the building fronts faded by the sun or washed away by the rain. The slum dwellers had reclaimed their disputed turf, and now their only enemies were the rats that roamed in the deserted tenement shells.

Weinberg lived in a rooming house on a street that looked as if it had suffered a nuclear attack. It stood with shabby pride in the middle of the block, a single light burning on the second floor of the building. Aside from that, its somber face was dark. Carella climbed to the top floor, trying to ignore the rustle of rats on the staircase, the hackles rising at the back of his neck. When he reached the fourth floor, he struck a match, found 4C at the far end of the hall and put his ear to the door, listening. To any casual passerby unfamiliar with the working ways of the police—and there were likely to be, oh, just *scores* of such passersby on a pitch-black landing at two o'clock in the morning—Carella might have looked like an eavesdropper, which is just what he was. He had been with the police department for a good many years, though, and he could not recall *ever* knocking on a door behind which there might be a criminal without first listening. He listened now for about five minutes, heard nothing, and only then knocked.

There was no answer.

He had decided together with Brown that his visit to Weinberg should not come as a visit from a cop. Instead, he was to pose as one of the "friends" Brown had hinted at, here to seek retribution for the beating Weinberg had possibly administered. The only problem seemed to be that no one was answering the door. Carella knocked again. Weinberg had earlier told Brown that he was about to curl up with a bottle of bourbon. Was it possible he had gone over to the Selby Arms, kicked Brown and the room around a little, and then returned here to his own little palace to knock off the bottle of cheer? Carella banged on the door a third time.

A door at the other end of the hall opened.

"Who is it there?" a woman's voice said.

"Friend of Al's," Carella answered.

"What you doing knocking down the door in the middle of the night?"

"Have to see him about something," Carella said. The landing was dark, and no light came from the woman's apartment. He strained to see her in the gloom, but could make out only a vague shape in the doorway, clothed in what was either a white nightgown or a white robe.

"He's probably asleep," the woman said, "same as everybody else around here."

"Yeah, why don't you just go do that yourself, lady?" Carella said.

"Punk," the woman replied, but she closed the door. Carella heard a lock being snapped, and then the heavy bar of a Fox lock being wedged against the door, solidly hooked into the steel plate that was screwed to the floor inside. He fished into his pocket, took out a penlight, flashed it onto Weinberg's lock, and then pulled out his ring of keys. He tried five keys before he found the one that opened the door. He slipped the key out of the lock, put the ring back into his pocket, gently eased the door open, went into the apartment, closed the door softly behind him, and stood breathing quietly in the darkness.

The room was as black as the landing had been.

A water tap dripped into a sink somewhere off on his left. On the street outside, a fire engine siren wailed into the night. He listened. He could see nothing, could hear nothing. Cupping his penlight in his hand, he flashed it only a few feet ahead of him and began moving into the room, vaguely making out a chair, a sofa, a television set. At the far end of the room, there was a closed door, presumably leading to the bedroom. He turned off the flash, stood silent and motionless for several moments while his eyes readjusted to the darkness, and then started for the bedroom door. He had moved not four feet when he tripped and fell forward, his hands coming out immediately to break his fall. His right hand sank to the wrist into something soft and gushy. He withdrew it immediately, his left hand thumbing the flash into light. He was looking into the wide-open eyes of Albert Weinberg. The something soft and gushy was a big bloody hole in Weinberg's chest.

Carella got to his feet, turned on the lights, and went into the small bathroom off the kitchen. When he turned on the lights there, an army of cockroaches scurried for cover. Fighting nausea, Carella washed his bloody right hand, dried it on a grimy towel hanging on a bar over the sink, and then went into the other room to call the precinct. A radio motor-patrol car arrived some five minutes later. Carella filled in the patrolmen, told them he'd be back shortly, and then headed crosstown and uptown to Irving Krutch's apartment. He did not get there until 3:15 A.M., two and a half hours before dawn.

Krutch opened the door the moment Carella gave his name. He was wearing pajamas, his hair was tousled, even his mustache looked as if it had been suddenly awakened from a very deep sleep.

"What's the matter?" he asked.

"Just a few questions, Mr. Krutch," Carella said.

"At three in the morning?"

"We're both awake, aren't we?"

"I wasn't two minutes ago," Krutch said. "Besides . . ."

"This won't take long," Carella said. "Did you speak to Arthur Brown tonight?"

"I did. Why? What . . . ?"

"When was that?"

"Must have been about . . . eight o'clock? Eight-thirty? I really can't say for sure."

"What'd you talk about, Mr. Krutch?"

"Well Brown told me you'd found a piece of that photograph in Ehrbach's apartment, and he said you'd also got another piece from Weinberg. I was supposed to come up to the squadroom tomorrow morning and see them. In fact, *you* were supposed to show them to me."

"But you couldn't wait, huh?"

"What do you mean, I couldn't . . ."

"Where'd you go after you spoke to Brown?"

"Out to dinner."

"Where?"

"The Ram's Head. The top of 777 Jefferson."

"Anybody with you?"

"Yes."

"Who?"

"A friend of mine."

"Man or woman?"

"A girl."

"What time'd you leave the restaurant?"

"About ten-thirty, I guess."

"Where'd you go?"

"For a walk. We looked in the store windows along Hall Avenue. It was a beautiful night and . . ."

"Where were you along about midnight, Mr. Krutch?"

"Here," Krutch said.

"Alone?"

"No."

"The girl came back here with you?"

"Yes."

"So she was with you between what time and what time?" Carella said.

"She was here when Brown called at eight—or whenever it was." Krutch paused. "She's still here."

"Where?"

"In bed."

"Get her up."

"Why?"

"One man's been assaulted and another's been killed," Carella said. "I want her to tell me where you were when all this was happening. That all right with you?"

"Who was killed?" Krutch asked.

"You sound as if you *know* who was *assaulted*," Carella said quickly.

"No. No, I don't."

"Then why'd you only ask who was killed? Aren't you interested in who was beaten up?"

"I'm . . ." Krutch paused. "Let me get her. She can clear this up in a minute."

"I hope so," Carella said.

Krutch went into the bedroom. Carella heard voices behind the closed door. The bedsprings creaked. There were footsteps. The door opened again. The girl was a young blonde, her long hair trailing down her back, her brown eyes wide and frightened. She was wearing a man's bathrobe belted tightly at the waist. Her hands fluttered like butterflies on an acid trip.

"This is Detective Carella," Krutch said. "He wants to know . . ."

"I'll ask her," Carella said. "What's your name, Miss?"

"Su . . . Su . . . Suzie," she said.

"Suzie what?"

"Suzie Endicott."

"What time did you get here tonight, Miss Endicott?"

"About . . . seven-thirty," she said. "Wasn't it seven-thirty, Irving?"

"About then," Krutch said.

"What time did you go out to dinner, Miss Endicott?"

"Eight or eight-thirty."

"Where'd you eat?"

"The Ram's Head."

"And where'd you go afterwards?"

"We walked for a little while, and then came here."

"What time was that?"

"I guess we got here at about eleven."

"Have you been here since?"

"Yes," she said.

"Did Mr. Krutch leave you at any time between seven-thirty and now?"

"Yes, when he went to the men's room at the restaurant," Suzie said.

"Happy now?" Krutch asked.

"Overjoyed," Carella answered. "Are you familiar with time-tables, Mr. Krutch?"

"What do you mean? *Train* timetables?"

"No, *investigating* timetables. You're an insurance investigator, I thought you might . . ."

"I'm not sure I'm following you."

"I want you to work up a timetable for me. I want you to list everything you did and the exact time you did it from 6 P.M. until right this minute," Carella said, and paused. "I'll wait," he added.

7

THERE'S nothing like a little homicide to give an investigation a shot in the arm. Or the chest, as the case may be. Albert Weinberg had been shot in the chest at close range with a .32-caliber pistol. His demise caused Brown to have a heated argument with the hospital intern who kept insisting he should be kept there under observation, and who refused to give him back his trousers. Brown called Carella, who brought his partner a pair of pants, a clean shirt, and his own spare gun. The two men had a hurried consultation while Brown dressed, deciding that Carella should go out to Calm's Point for a chat in Italian with Lucia Feroglio, the late Carmine Bonamico's sister-in-law. In the meantime, Brown would go over to the Ferguson Gallery, presumably closed on a Sunday, let himself into the place (against the law, but what the hell), and do a little snooping around. The nurse came in as Brown was zipping up his fly.

"What are you doing out of bed?" she asked.

"I'll get back in, if you'll join me," Brown said, grinning lecherously, and the nurse fled down the corridor, calling for the intern. By the time the intern got to the room, the detectives were in the main lobby downstairs, setting up plans for contacting each other later in the day. They nodded to each other briefly, and went out into the June sunshine to pursue their separate pleasures.

Carella's pleasure was the Church of the Holy Spirit on Inhurst Boulevard in Calm's Point. He had first stopped at Lucia Feroglio's garden apartment where he was told by her neighbors that the old lady went to nine o'clock Mass every Sunday morning. He had then driven over to the church, where Mass was in progress, and asked the sexton if he knew Lucia Feroglio, and if he would mind pointing her out when Mass broke. The sexton seemed not to understand any English until Carella put five dollars in the box in

218 JIGSAW

the narthex. The sexton then admitted that he knew Lucia Feroglio very well, and would be happy to identify her when she came out of the church.

Lucia must have been a beauty in her youth; Carella could not understand how or why she had remained a spinster. A woman in her seventies now, she still walked with a tall, erect pride, her hair snowy white, her features recalling those of ancient Roman royalty, the aquiline nose, the full sensuous mouth, the high brow and almond-shaped eyes. The sexton nodded toward her as she came down the broad sunwashed steps. Carella moved to her side immediately and said, *"Scusi, Signorina Feroglio?"*

The woman turned with a faint half-smile on her mouth, her eyebrows lifting in mild curiosity, *"Sí, che cosa?"* she asked.

"Mi chiamo Steve Carella," he answered. *"Sono un agente investigativo, dal distretto ottanta-sette."* He opened his wallet and showed her his detective's shield.

"Sí che vuole?" Lucia asked. "What do you want?"

"Possiamo parlae?" Carella asked. "Can we talk?"

"Certo," she said, and they began to walk away from the church together.

Lucia seemed to have no aversion to holding a conversation with a cop. She was warm, open, and co-operative, speaking in a Sicilian dialect Carella understood only incompletely, promising him she would tell him everything she knew about the photographic segment she had inherited from her sister. As it turned out, though, she knew nothing at *all* about it.

"I do not understand," Carella said in Italian. "Did you not tell the insurance investigator that the full picture reveals where the treasure is?"

"Ma che tesoro?" Lucia asked. "What treasure?"

"The treasure," Carella repeated. "Did you not tell Mr. Krutch about a treasure? When you gave him the list and the photograph?"

"I know nothing of a treasure," Lucia said. "And *what* list? I gave him only the little piece of picture."

"You did *not* give him a list with names on it?"

"No. Nor has Mr. Krutch given me the thousand dollars he promised. Do you know this man?"

"Yes, I know him."

"Would you ask him, please, to send me my money? I gave him the picture, and now it is only fair to expect payment. I am not a wealthy woman."

"Let me understand this, Miss Feroglio," Carella said. "Are you telling me that you did *not* give Mr. Krutch a list of names?"

"Never. *Mai*. Never."

"And you did *not* tell Mr. Krutch about a treasure?"

"If I did not know it, how could I have told him?" She turned to him suddenly, and smiled warmly and quite seductively for a woman in her seventies. *"Is* there a treasure, *signore?"* she asked.

"God only knows, *signorina,"* Carella answered, and returned the smile.

The best burglars in the world are cops.

There are three types of alarm systems in general use, and the one on the back door of the Ferguson Gallery was a closed-circuit system, which meant that it could not be put out of commission merely by cutting the wires, as could be done with the cheapest kind. A weak current ran constantly through the wires of the closed-circuit system; if you cut them, breaking the current, the alarm would sound. So Brown cross-contacted the wires, and then opened the door with a celluloid strip. It was as simple as that, and it took him no longer than ten minutes. In broad daylight.

The gallery was empty and still.

Sunshine slanted silently through the wide plate-glass windows fronting Jefferson Avenue. The white walls were pristine and mute. The only screaming in the place came from the colorful paintings on the walls. Brown went immediately to the blue door on the far wall, opened it and stepped into Bramley Kahn's office.

He started with Kahn's desk. He found letters to and from artists, letters to patrons, a rough mock-up of a brochure announcing the gallery's one-man show to come in August, memos from Kahn to himself, a letter from a museum in Philadelphia, another from the Guggenheim in New York, a hardbound copy of *Story of O* (the first few pages of which Brown scanned, almost getting hooked, almost forgetting why he had come here), a trayful of red pencils and blue pencils, and in the bottom drawer a locked metal cash-box—and a .32-caliber Smith & Wesson. Brown tented his handker-chief over the revolver, picked it up by the butt, and sniffed the barrel. Despite the fact that Albert Weinberg, his late partner, had been slain with a .32-caliber weapon, this gun did not seem to have been fired lately. Brown rolled out the cylinder. There were six cartridges in the pistol, one in each chamber. He closed the gun, put it back into the drawer, and was reaching for the cash-box when the telephone rang. He almost leaped out of Steve

Carella's borrowed trousers. The phone rang once, twice, again, again, again. It stopped suddenly.

Brown kept watching the instrument.

It began ringing again. It rang eight times. Then it stopped.

Brown waited.

The phone did not ring again.

He lifted the gray metal cashbox from the bottom drawer. The lock on it was a simple one; he opened the cashbox in thirty seconds. It contained anything but cash. He found a partnership agreement between Kahn and Geraldine Ferguson, a certificate for two hundred shares of IBM stock, Kahn's last will and testament, three United States Savings Bonds in fifty-dollar denominations, and a small, white, unmarked, unsealed envelope.

Brown opened the envelope. There was a slip of white paper in it:

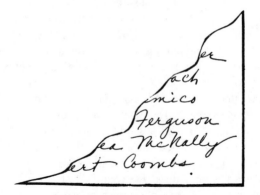

However lousy a bank robber Carmine Bonamico may have been, he was sure good at cutting out paper dolls. If this wasn't the second half of the list Krutch had brought to the squadroom, Brown would eat the list, the photograph, the first chapter of *Story of O,* and maybe O herself. He quickly copied the names in his notebook, replaced the fragment in its envelope, put the envelope and everything else back into the cashbox, locked the box, and replaced it in the bottom drawer of the desk. His attention was captured by the painting of the nude on the opposite wall. He went to it, lifted one edge, and peeked behind it. Reaching up with both hands, he took the heavy painting off the wall. There was a small black safe behind it. Brown knew that people who used safes or combination locks with any frequency would often leave the dial just a notch or two to the right or left of the last number. This facilitated constant opening, since all you then had to do was give the dial a single twist each time, rather than going through the whole, boring rigmarole. He was moving the dial a notch to the left of the number showing when he heard the back door of the gallery being opened. Swiftly, he moved behind the door of Kahn's office, and threw back his jacket.

The butt of Carella's borrowed .38 protruded from a holster at his waist. He drew the gun now and stood silently listening to the footsteps that clattered across the white tile floor toward Kahn's office. The footsteps stopped just outside the open door. Brown held his breath. The man was in the doorway now, his shadow falling into the room across the gray rug. Brown did not want a suit filed against the city; Brown did not want to get kicked off the force; Brown did not want to be smothered again by the ghetto he had escaped.

The first things that registered were the thick handlebar mustache and the glinting blue eyes.

"Hello Krutch," Brown said.

Irving Krutch whirled.

"Hey," he said. "Hi."

"Didn't you see that decal on the back door? 'These premises are protected by the Buckley Alarm System.' "

"I cross-contacted the wiring," Krutch said.

"That makes two of us. Was it you who called ten minutes ago?"

"Yes. I wanted to make sure nobody was here."

"Somebody *was* here," Brown said.

"So I see."

"What do you want, Krutch?"

"The same thing you want. We're in this together, remember?"

"I thought you were letting *us* handle it."

"I figured you might need a hand."

Brown holstered the gun, went to the safe again, moved the dial a notch to the left, then two notches, then three, trying to open it after each move, and getting no results. He tried the same sequence to the right, and when he got nothing, he turned to Krutch and said, "I *do* need a hand. Grab one end of this painting."

"Have you found anything?" Krutch asked.

Brown hesitated. "No," he said.

They lifted the painting and hung it in place. Brown stepped back from it, walked over to the wall again, and tilted one corner of the frame.

"A little to the other side," Krutch said.

"How's that?"

"Perfect."

"Let's go," Brown said.

"I'd sure like to know what's in that safe," Krutch said.

"So would I. What's your guess?"

"A little piece of a picture."

"How are you on safecracking?"

"Lousy."

"So am I. Let's go."

"Where are we going?" Krutch asked.

"*You're* going to fix those alarm wires. *I'm* going to visit Geraldine Ferguson."

"Fix the wires? I can get arrested if I'm caught doing that."

"I may arrest you, anyway," Brown said. "You're in here illegally."

"So are you."

"An off-duty cop on the prowl. Cruising by, saw the back door ajar, came in and discovered a burglary in progress."

"I'm your *partner,*" Krutch protested.

"I had another partner, too. Albert Weinberg, who right now is on ice downtown."

"I had nothing to do with that," Krutch said.

"Who suggested you did?"

"Carella."

"Well, maybe he's just a suspicious person," Brown said.

"How about *you?* What do *you* think?"

"I think you were with a young lady named Suzie Endicott from seven-thirty until whenever it was Carella came to see you. That's what you told him, isn't it?"

"Yes."

"So why would I have any reason to doubt you?"

"Look, Brown . . ."

"I'm looking."

"I want that lost N.S.L.A. money; I want it very badly. But not badly enough to kill for it. *Nothing's* worth that much. Not even my career."

"Okay."

"I just want to get that straight between us."

"It's straight," Brown said. "Now let's get the hell out of here."

Geraldine Ferguson was in her pajamas when she opened the door.

"Oh, hell," she said.

"That's right, Miss Ferguson," Brown said. "Here come de fuzz."

"He's *admitting* it," she said in surprise, and then smiled. "Come in. I admire honest men."

The living room resembled an annex to the gallery—white walls, muted furniture, huge canvases glaring with color, twisted sculptured shapes on pedestals. Gerry swayed across the rug like a dancer, tight little behind jiggling in the blue silk pajama bottoms, black hair caught in a pony tail that bounced between her shoulder blades.

"Would you like a drink?" she asked. "Or is it too early?"

"It's almost one o'clock," Brown said.

"Name it."

"I'm on duty.'"

"So? When did cops get so lily-white, you should pardon the expression?"

"I like to keep a clear head when I'm working," Brown said.

"Okay, keep a clear head," Gerry said, and shrugged. *"I'll* have a drink, though, if you don't mind. I find Sundays very boring. Once I've read the comics and Martin Levin, there's just nothing exciting left to do."

"Who's Martin Levin?" Brown asked.

Gerry went to a bar over which hung a white canvas slashed with jagged black streaks of paint. She poured a liberal shot of bourbon onto the ice in a short glass, lifted the glass, said, "Here's to improved race relations," and drank, eying him steadily over the glass.

"Miss Ferguson . . ."

"Gerry," she corrected.

"Gerry, a man was killed last night . . ."

"Who?" she said immediately, and put the glass down on the bartop.

"The man who visited you several times. The one who said he was Al Reynolds. Or Al Randolph."

"What was his real name?"

"Albert Weinberg." Brown paused. "Ever hear of him?"

"No," Gerry said, and picked up her glass again. "What's *your* real name?"

"Arthur Brown."

"You're putting me on," she said, and smiled.

"No, that's it. Detective Second/Grade, 87th Squad. Want to see my shield?"

"Why?"

"You're supposed to ask for identification."

"I don't like to do anything I'm *supposed* to do," Gerry said.

"On Wednesday night . . ."

"How'd we get back to Wednesday?"

"I just took us there," Brown said impatiently. "On Wednesday night, two men killed each other in a brawl . . ."

"Who?"

"That's not important, Gerry. What *is* important is that one of them had a piece of photograph in his hand . . ."

"Are we going to start on *that* again? I already told you . . ."

"Miss Ferguson," Brown said, "I've got some questions to ask you concerning murder and armed robbery. I'd like to ask those questions here in comfortable surroundings, but I can just as easily ask them uptown, in the squadroom."

"What's that, a threat?"

"No, it's a realistic appraisal of the situation."

"After I was nice enough to offer you a drink," Gerry said, and smiled. "Go on, I promise to be quiet."

"Thank you. We have good reason to believe that the fragment in the dead man's hand was part of a larger photograph showing the location of the money stolen from the National Savings & Loan Association six years ago. We also have good reason to believe that *you* have another piece of that picture, and *we* want it. It's as simple as that."

"What smoked you out, Arthur?" she asked. "What made you drop the phony cover? Are you afraid somebody else might get killed?"

"It's possible, yes."

"Me?"

"Possibly. *Whoever's* got a piece of that picture is in danger. For your own safety . . ."

"Bullshit," Gerry said.

"I beg your pardon?"

"The day the cops start worrying about anybody's *safety* is the day . . ." She banged the glass down on the bar top. "Who do you think you're kidding, Arthur?"

"Miss Ferguson, I'm not . . ."

"And make up your goddamn mind! It's either Miss Ferguson or it's Gerry. You can't have it both ways."

"Then I think I'd prefer Miss Ferguson."

"Why? Are you afraid of me or something? Big strong Superspade afraid of a snippety little girl?"

"Let's knock off the 'Superspade' crap, shall we?" Brown said.

"You ever been to bed with a white girl?" Gerry asked suddenly.

"No."

"Want to try?"

"No."

"Why not?"

"Believe it or not, Miss Ferguson, my fantasies don't include a big black Cadillac and a small white blonde."

"I'm not a blonde."

"I know that. I was merely . . ."

"Stop getting so nervous. I'll bet your palms are wet."

"My palms are dry," Brown said evenly.

"Mine aren't," Gerry said, and turned away from him to pour herself another drink. The living room was silent. "You married?" she asked.

"I am."

"That's okay. I've been to bed with married spades, too."

"I don't like that expression, Miss Ferguson."

"Which? Married?" she asked, and turned to face him, leaning on the bar. "Grow up, Arthur."

Brown rose from the sofa. "I think maybe we'd *better* head uptown," he said. "You want to get dressed, please?"

"No, I don't," Gerry said, and smiled, and sipped at her bourbon. "What'll the charge be? Attempted rape?"

"I don't have to charge you with anything, Miss Ferguson. I'm conducting a murder investigation, and I'm entitled . . ."

"All right, all right, don't start spouting legalities. Sit down, Arthur. Oh, *do* sit down. I'd much rather talk here than in some stuffy old squadroom."

Brown sat.

"There, isn't that better? Now—what would you like to know?"

"Do you have a piece of the photograph?"

"Yes."

"Where'd you get it?"

"My brother-in-law gave it to me."

"Louis D'Amore?"

"Yes."

"When?"

"Just before the holdup."

"What'd he say about it?"

"Only that I should hold onto it."

"How come he gave it to you, and not your sister?"

"My sister's a scatterbrain, always was. Lou knew who the smart one was."

"Did he give you the list, too?"

"What list?"

"The list of names."

"I don't know anything about a list of names."

"That's a lie, Gerry."

"No, I swear. What list?"

"A list that has your name on it, among others."

"I've never seen it."

"You're lying Gerry. Your partner has half of that list. Where'd he get it?"

"I don't know anything *about* a list. What's it supposed to be?"

"Forget it," Brown said. "Where's your part of the snapshot?"

"In the gallery safe."

"Will you turn it over to us?"

"No."

"I thought you said . . ."

"I said I'd answer your questions. Okay. I've done that. There's no law that says I have to give personal property to the police."

"I can think of one," Brown said.

"Yeah, which one?"

"How about Section 1308 of the Penal Law? *A person who conceals, withholds, or aids in concealing or withholding any property, knowing the same to have been stolen . . .*"

"Is the photograph stolen property?"

"It indicates the *location* of stolen property."

"How do I know that? Lou gave me a tiny little corner of a photograph and asked me to hold onto it. That's all I know."

"Okay, I'm *telling* you the photograph shows the location of the N.S.L.A. loot. Now you know."

"Can you prove it?" Gerry said, and smiled. "I don't think so, Arthur. Until you find the money, you can't say for sure it even *exists*. And you *won't* find the money until you put the whole picture together. Tch, tch, such a dilemma. Why don't we go into the other room and ball a little?"

"I'd rather not, thanks."

"I'd drive you out of your mind, Arthur."

"You already have," Brown said, and left.

8

THE DILEMMA was not quite so horned as Geraldine Ferguson imagined. All Brown had to do was find himself a Supreme Court judge, swear to the judge that upon reliable information and personal knowledge, there was probable cause to believe that a safe at the Ferguson Gallery at 568 Jefferson Avenue contained evidence that could lead to the solution of a crime, and request from the judge a warrant and order of seizure to open the safe, search it, and appropriate the evidence. He couldn't do that today because it was Sunday, and in the city for which Brown worked. Supreme Court judges were entitled to a day of rest; only the direst of emergencies would have been considered cause for shaking a man out of his bed and requesting a search warrant. Brown was confident, though, that Gerry would not rush down to the gallery and take the photograph out of the safe. He had done nothing to disabuse her notion that he was helpless to open that safe, and he felt certain the photograph would still be there come morning when, armed with his legal paper, he would force her to produce it.

At 3 P.M. Sunday afternoon, he met with Carella in the squadroom and went over what they now had. By combining Krutch's half of the list (which *he* claimed to have received from Lucia Feroglio, but which *she* claimed she had not given him) with the half found in Kahn's cashbox (which Geraldine Ferguson claimed she knew nothing about), they were able to piece together seven names:

ALBERT WEINBERG

DONALD RENNINGER

EUGENE E. EHRBACH

ALICE BONAMICO

GERALDINE FERGUSON

DOROTHEA McNALLY

ROBERT COOMBS

The first four people on the list were already dead. The fifth person had admitted having a piece of the photograph, and they hoped to get that from her in the morning. Now, with the telephone directories for the five sections of the city spread open before them, they began searching for the remaining two names.

There was a Robert Coombs in Riverhead, and another Robert Coombs in Bethtown.

There were a hundred and sixty-four McNallys scattered all over the city, more than enough to have started a revival of the clan, but none of them were named Dorothea, and there was only one listing for a *McNally, D.*—on South Homestead, off Skid Row."

"How do you want to hit them?" Carella asked.

"Let's save Bethtown till tomorrow morning. Have to take a ferry to get out there, and God knows how they run on Sundays."

"Okay," Carella said. "Why don't I take the Coombs in Riverhead, and go straight home from there?"

"Fine. I'll take the McNally woman."

"How come you're getting all the girls lately?"

"It's only fair," Brown said. "We *never* get them on television."

It was a city of contrasts.

Follow Esplanade Avenue uptown to where the Central & Northeastern railroad tracks came up out of the ground and, within the length of a city block, the neighborhood crumbled before your eyes, buildings with awnings and doormen giving way to grimy brick tenements, well-dressed affluent citizens miraculously transformed into shabby, hungry, unemployed victims of poverty. Take any crosstown street that knifed through the 87th Precinct, follow it across Mason, and Culver, and Ainsley, and you passed through slums that spread like cancers and then abruptly shriveled on the fringes of fancy Silvermine Road, with luxurious, exclusive, wooded, moneyed Smoke Rise only a stone's throw away. Head all the way downtown to The Quarter, and find yourself a bustling middle-class bohemian community with its fair share of faggots and artsy-craftsy leather shops, its little theaters and renovated brownstones glistening with sandblasted facades and freshly painted balustrades and fire escapes, shuttered windows, cobblestoned alleys, spring flowers hanging in gaily colored pots over arched doorways with shining brass knobs and knockers. Then follow your nose west into Little Italy, a ghetto as dense as those uptown, but of a different hue, take a sniff of coffee being brewed in *espresso* machines, savor the rich smells of a transplanted Neapolitan cuisine merged with the aroma of roasting pork wafting over from Chinatown, not a block away, where the telephone booths resembled miniature pagodas and where the phones—like their uptown cousins—rarely worked. (How nice to have an emergency number with which to dial the police, three fast digits and a cop was on your doorstep—if only the phones would work.) Then walk a few blocks south, crossing the wide avenue where the elevated train structure used to stand, its shadow gone now, the flophouses and soup kitchens, the wholesale lighting fixture, restaurant supply, factory reject, party favor, and office equipment establishments draped with winos and exposed in all their shabby splendor to the June sunshine.

D. McNally lived in a building two blocks south of the wide avenue that ran for better than half a mile, the city's skid row, a graveyard for vagrants and drunks, a happy hunting ground for policemen anxious to fill arrest quotas—pull in a bum, charge him with vagrancy or disorderly conduct, allow him to spend a night or two or more in jail, and then turn him out into the street again, a much better person for his experience. Brown walked past two drunks who sat morosely on the front stoop. Neither of the men looked up at him. Sitting on the curb in front of the building, his feet in the gutter, was a third man. He had taken off his shirt, black with lice, and he delicately picked the parasites from the cloth now, squashing them with his thumbnail against the curbstone. His skin was a pale sickly white in the glare of the sunshine, his back and arms covered with sores.

The entryway was dark; after the brilliant sunshine outside, it hit the eyes like a closed fist. Brown studied the row of broken mailboxes and found one with a hand-crayoned card that read D. McNally, Apt. 2A. He climbed the steps, listened outside the apartment door for several moments, and then knocked.

"Yes?" a woman's voice said.

"Miss McNally?"

"Yes?" she said, and before Brown could announce that he was The Law, the door opened. The woman standing in the doorway was perhaps fifty years old. Her hair had been dyed a bright orange, and it exploded about her chalk-white face like Fourth-of-July fireworks, erupting from her scalp in every conceivable direction, wildly unkempt, stubbornly independent. Her eyes were a faded blue, their size emphasized by thick black liner. Her lashes had been liberally stroked with mascara, her brows had been darkened with pencil, her mouth had been enlarged with lipstick the color of human blood. She wore a silk flowered wrapper belted loosely at the waist. Pendulous white breasts showed in the open top of the wrapper. Near the nipple of one breast, a human bite mark was clearly visible, purple against her very white skin. She was a short, dumpy woman with an overabundance of flabby flesh, and she looked as though she had deliberately dressed for the role of the unregenerate old whore in the local amateur production of *Seven Hookers East.*

"I don't take niggers," she said immediately, and started to close the door. Brown stuck his foot out, and the closing door collided with his shoe. Through the narrow open crack, D. McNally said again, emphatically this time, "I told you I don't take niggers." Brown didn't know whether to laugh himself silly or fly into an offended rage. Here was a run-down old prostitute who would probably flop with anyone and everyone for the price of a bottle of cheap wine, but she would not take Negroes. He decided to find it amusing.

"All I want's a blow job," he said.

"No," D. McNally said, alarmed now. "No. Go away!"

"A friend of mine sent me," he said.

From behind the door, D. McNally's voice lowered in suspicion. "Which friend?" she asked. "I don't suck no niggers."

"Lieutenant Byrnes," Brown said.

"A soldier?"

"No, a policeman," Brown said, and decided to end the game. "I'm a detective, lady, you want to open this door?"

"You ain't no detective," she said.

Wearily, Brown dug into his pocket and held his shield up to the crack between door and jamb.

"Why didn't you say so?" D. McNally asked.

"Why? Do you suck nigger *detectives?*"

"I didn't mean no offense," she said, and opened the door. "Come in."

He went into the apartment. It consisted of a tiny kitchen and a room with a bed. Dishes were piled in the sink, the bed was unmade, there was the stale stink of human sweat and cheap booze and cheaper perfume.

"You the Vice Squad?" she asked.

"No."

"I ain't hooking no more," she said. "That's why I told you to go away. I been out of the game, oh, must be six, seven months now."

"Sure," Brown said. "Is your name Dorothea McNally?"

"That's right. I put 'D. McNally' in the phone book and in the mailbox downstairs because there's all kinds of crazy nuts in this city, you know? Guys who call up and talk dirty, you know? I don't like that kind of dirty shit."

"No, I'll bet you don't."

"When I was hooking, I had a nice clientele."

"Mm-huh."

"Gentlemen."

"But no niggers."

"Look, you didn't take offense at that, did you?"

"No, of course not. Why should I take offense at a harmless little remark like that?"

"If you're going to make trouble just because I said . . ."

"I'm not going to make any trouble, lady."

"Because if you *are,* look, I'll go down on you right this minute, you know what I mean? A cock's a cock," Dorothea said, "white *or* black."

"Or even purple," Brown said.

"Sure, even purple. Just don't make trouble for me, that's all." She paused. "You want me to?"

"No. Thanks a lot," Brown said.

"Well," she said, and shrugged, "if you should change your mind . . ."

"I'll let you know. Meanwhile, I'm here to talk about a photograph."

"Yeah, well come on in," she said, gesturing toward the bedroom. "No sense standing here with the dirty dishes, huh?"

They walked into the other room. Dorothea sat on the bed and crossed her legs. Brown stood at the foot of the bed, looking down at her. She had allowed the silk wrapper to fall open again. The bite mark near her nipple looked angry and swollen, the outline of the teeth stitched across her flabby breast in a small elongated oval.

"A photograph, huh?" Dorothea said.

"That's right."

"Man, you guys sure know how to bring up ancient history," she said. "I thought you weren't going to make trouble for me."

"I'm not."

"I musta posed for those pictures twenty years ago. You mean to tell me one of them's still around?" She shook her head in amazement. "I was *some* little piece in those days. I had guys coming to see me all the way from San Francisco. They'd get in town, pick up the phone, 'Hello there, Dorothea, this is old Bruce, you ready to go, honey?' I was always ready to go in those days. I knew how to show a man a good time." she looked up at Brown. "I *still* do, I mean I'm not exactly what you'd call an old hag, you know. Not that I'm in the game any more. I mean, I'm just saying."

"When was your last arrest for prostitution?" Brown asked.

"I told you, musta been six or seven . . ."

"Come on, I can check it."

"All right, last month. But I've been clean since. This is no kind of life for a person like me. So, you know, when you come around bringing up those pictures, Jesus, I can get in real trouble for something like that, can't I?" She smiled suddenly. "Why don't you just come on over here, sweetie, and we'll forget all about those pictures, okay?"

"The picture I'm talking about isn't pornography," Brown said.

"No? What then?"

"A picture that may have come into your possession six years ago."

"Jesus, who can remember six years ago?"

"You just now had no trouble remembering *twenty* years ago."

"Yeah, but that was . . . you know, a girl remembers something like that. That's the only time I ever done anything like that, you know, pose for pictures with some guy. I only let them take one roll, that was all, just *one,* and I got fifty bucks for it, which was more than I'd have got if I was just turning a trick without them taking pictures, you understand?"

"Sure," Brown said. "What do you know about the National Savings & Loan Association holdup six years ago?"

"Oh, man, now we're jumping around real fast," Dorothea said. "First it's hooking, then it's dirty pictures, now it's armed robbery. The stakes keep getting higher all the time."

"What do you know about that holdup?"

"I think I remember reading about it."

"What do you remember reading?"

"Look . . . I got your word you ain't going to make trouble?"

"You've got it."

"My nephew was one of the guys who pulled that job."

"What's his name?"

"Peter Ryan. He's dead now. They *all* got killed on that job, some bank robbers," she said, and grimaced.

"And the picture?"

"What picture? I don't know what . . ."

"A piece of a snapshot. From what you've just told me, your nephew might have given it to you. Before the job. Would you remember anything like that?"

"Jesus, that was six years ago."

"Try to remember."

"When was the job? Do you remember what month it was?"

"August."

"August. Six years ago. Let me see . . ." She grimaced again. "I wasn't even living here at the time. God knows *where* the hell I was."

"Think, Dorothea."

"I think better when I'm drinking," she said.

"Have you got anything in the house?"

"Yeah, but that's like my insurance, you know? The Johns are few and far between these days."

Brown reached into his wallet. "Here's ten dollars," he said. "Drink up your insurance and get yourself another bottle later."

"And if I remember about the picture?"

"What about it?"

"How much is it worth to you?"

"Another twenty."

"Make it fifty. You're taking up a lot of my time, you know."

"I don't see a line of guys outside the door," Brown said.

"Well, they come and go, come and go," Dorothea said. "I'd hate to have to send a trick away just because I'm busy in here with a cop." She paused, and then smiled. "Fifty?"

"Thirty-five."

"It's a deal." She went into the kitchen, took a bottle of cheap rye from the shelf, poured herself a half tumblerful, looked up, and said. "You want some of this piss? Makes you go blind, I understand."

"No, thanks," Brown said.

"Here's looking up your whole family," Dorothea said, and drained the glass. "Whooo," she said, "that's poison, absolute poison." She poured the glass full to the brim and carried it back into the bedroom with her. "I don't remember any snapshot," she said shaking her head.

"Where were you living at the time?"

"Up on the North Side, I think. I think I had a room in a hotel up there." She sipped at the rye thoughtfully. "Six years ago. That's like a whole century, you know?"

"Think."

"I'm thinking, just shut up. My nephew was in and out all the time; who remembers whether he ever gave me a snapshot?"

"This would be just a *portion* of a snapshot. Not the whole picture."

"Better yet," Dorothea said, "Even if he *did* give it to me, you know how many times I moved in the past six years? Don't ask. Between The Law and the rent collector, I'm a very busy lady."

"Where do you keep your valuables?"

"*What* valuables?"

"Where do you keep important papers?"

"Are you kidding me?"

"Things like your birth certificate, your Social Security card . . ."

"Oh, yeah. I got them around someplace," Dorothea said, and sipped at the drink again.

"Where?"

"I don't keep much junk, you know. I don't like memories. Too many fucking memories," she said, and this time she took a healthy swallow of the drink, draining the glass. She got up from the bed, walked into the kitchen, and poured the glass full again. "You ever hear of a fighter named Tiger Willis?" she asked, coming back into the bedroom.

"No."

"This was before your time, I guess. Twenty-five years ago, maybe even longer. He was a middleweight."

"What about him?"

"I used to live with him. He had a *shlong* on him, man, it musta been a yard long." Dorothea shook her head. "He got killed in the ring. This kid from Buenos Aires killed him. Hit him so hard, he . . . I was there that night, at ringside, you know. Freddie—that was his real name, Freddie Willis, the 'Tiger' shit was just for the ring— Freddie always got me a ringside seat for his fights, I was something in those days, I was real merchandise. This kid from Buenos Aires, he brought one up from the floor, almost knocked Freddie's head off. And Freddie went down, he went down like a stone, he hit that canvas so hard . . ." She swallowed more rye and looked away from Brown. "Well, those are the old times," she said.

"About the photograph," Brown said gently.

"Yeah, yeah, the fucking photograph. Let me see what's in the closet here."

She went across the room, and opened the door to the closet. A black cloth coat hung on a wire hanger. Beside it was a blue satin dress. Nothing else was hanging on the wooden bar. On the floor of the closet, there were two pairs of high-heeled pumps. A cardboard box and a candy tin were on the shelf over the bar. Dorothea reached up, and came back to the bed with the candy tin in her hands. She pried off the lid.

"Not much here," she said. "I don't like to keep things."

"There was a birth certificate, a marriage certificate (Dorothea Pierce to Richard McNally), a snip of hair in a cheap gold-plated locket, a *Playbill* for an opening night long long ago, a photograph of a very young girl sitting on a swing behind a clapboard house, a faded valentine card, and a copy of *Ring* magazine with a picture of Tiger Willis on the cover.

"That's all of it," Dorothea said.

"Want to dump it all on the bed here?" Brown suggested. "What we're looking for may be very small." He picked up the *Playbill* and shook out its pages. Nothing. He picked up the copy of *Ring* magazine.

"Be careful with that," Dorothea warned.

He gave it a single shake. The pages fluttered apart, and a glossy black-and-white photograph scrap fell onto the soiled sheets.

"Is that what you're looking for?" Dorothea asked.

"That's what I'm looking for," Brown said.

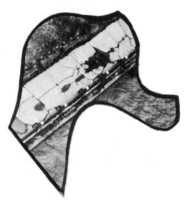

"It resembles Donald Duck," she said. "Or Woody Woodpecker."

"Or the extinct dodo bird," Brown said.

"I don't remember Petey giving it to me," Dorothea said, and shook her head. "I suppose he must have, but I really don't remember." Her look hardened. She held out her hand to Brown, and said. "That's thirty-five bucks, mister."

The address for the Robert Coombs who lived in Riverhead was 6451 Avondale, two miles from Carella's house. Carella got there at about four-thirty, pulling into the tree-lined street just behind a Good Humor ice-cream truck, the first he had seen this season. The houses on the block were mostly two-family homes. The community gave an appearance of neat lower-middle-class respectability. This was Sunday afternoon, and the Riverhead burghers were out on their front stoops reading their newspapers or listening to transistor radios. Carella counted twelve kids on bicycles as he drove up the street searching for 6451.

The house was on the corner of Avondale and Birch, a big brick-and-clapboard building on a comfortable plot. As Carella stepped out of the car, he smelled the aroma of cooking steak. He had eaten only a hamburger for lunch, and he was hungry as hell. A small black sign on the front lawn was lettered in white with the name R. COOMBS. Carella went up the walk to the front door, rang the bell, and waited. There was no answer. He rang again. He waited several moments more, and then walked around toward the back of the house. A man in a white apron was standing near an outdoor grille, a long fork in his right hand. Another man and two women were sitting at a redwood picnic table opposite the grille. The foursome was in conversation as Carella came around the side of the house, but they stopped talking the moment they saw him.

"I'm looking for Robert Coombs," Carella said.

"Yes, I'm Coombs," the man at the grille said.

"Sorry to intrude like this, Mr. Coombs," Carella said, walking over to him. "I'm Detective Carella of the 87th Squad. I wonder if I might talk to you privately."

"What is it, Bobby?" one of the women said, and rose immediately from where she was sitting at the picnic table. She was a tall woman wearing a blond fall, a snug blue cashmere sweater, tight navy-blue slacks. Her eyes were a shade lighter than the sweater, and she squinted them in suspicion, if not open hostility, as she approached the grille. "I'm *Mrs.* Coombs," she said, as if she were announcing exactly who ran this household. "What is it you want?"

"He's a detective, hon," Coombs said.

"A detective? What is it? What's the matter?"

"Nothing, Mrs. Coombs," Carella said. "I simply wanted to ask your husband some questions."

"What about? Are you in some kind of trouble, Bobby?"

"No, no, hon, I . . ."

"He's not in any trouble, Mrs. Coombs. This has to do with . . ."

"Then it can wait," Mrs. Coombs said. "The steaks are almost done. You just come back later, Detective . . ."

"Coppola," Coombs said.

"Carella," Carella said.

"We're about to eat," Mrs. Coombs said. "You come back later, do you hear?"

"Can you come back in an hour?" Coombs asked gently.

"Make it an hour and a half," Mrs. Coombs snapped.

"Honey, an hour's more time than . . ."

"I don't want to rush through my Sunday dinner," Mrs. Coombs said flatly. "An hour and a half, Detective Coppola."

"Carella," he said, *"bon appétit,"* and walked out of the yard, the aroma of the cooking steak nearly destroying him forever. He found an open luncheonette on Birch, ordered a cup of coffee and a cheese Danish, and then went out for a stroll around the neighborhood. Four little girls on the sidewalk ahead were skipping rope, chanting their ritualistic ditty, "Double-ee-Dutch, double-ee-Dutch," and from the open lot on the corner, there came the crack of a bat against a baseball, and a shout went up from the middle-aged men in shirt sleeves who were watching their sons play. The sky, magnificently blue all day long, virtually cloudless, was succumbing to the pale violet of dusk. The balmy afternoon breeze was turning a bit cooler. All up and down the street, he could hear mothers calling their children in to dinner. It was the time of day when a man wanted to be home with his family. Carella looked at his watch and sighed.

Isabel Coombs was a ventriloquist, of that Carella was certain.

The Coombs's guests had gone indoors the moment he'd returned, and he could see them now through the rear sliding glass doors of the house, standing near the record player and browsing through the album collection. He sat with Mr. and Mrs. Coombs at the redwood table and even though Robert Coombs occasionally tried to answer a question, he was really only the dummy in the act, and Isabel Coombs was doing most of the talking.

"Mr. Coombs," Carella said, "I'll make this as brief as I can. We found your name on a list allegedly . . ."

"His name?" Isabel said. "You found *Bobby's* name on some list?"

"Yes, ma'am," Carella said, "a list . . ."

"His name is not on any list," Isabel said.

"Well, maybe it is, hon," Robert said.

"It is *not,"* Isabel said. "Detective Caretta . . ."

"Carella."

"Yes, perhaps before we talk any further, we'd better get a lawyer."

"Well, that's entirely up to you, of course," Carella said, "but there's no intention here of charging your husband with any crime. We're merely seeking information about . . ."

"Then why is his name on a *list?"* Isabel demanded.

Carella's wife was a deaf mute. He looked at Isabel Coombs now, wearing her blond fall and her brassy voice, and silently contrasted her with Teddy—black hair and brown eyes, voiceless, gentle, beautiful.

Mrs. Coombs's blue eyes flashed. "Well?" she said.

"Mrs. Coombs," Carella said patiently, "maybe it'd be better if you just let me *ask* the questions before you decide what they're going to be."

"What's that supposed to mean?"

"It's supposed to mean that this can take ten minutes or ten hours. We can do it right here in your back yard, or I can request that your husband accompany me . . ."

"You're going to *arrest* him?"

"No, ma'am, I'm only going to ask him some questions."

"Then why don't you?"

Carella was silent for a moment. Then he said only, "Yes, ma'am," and fell silent again. He had forgotten for a moment just what it was he wanted to ask Coombs. He kept thinking of Teddy and wishing he were home in bed with her. "Well," he said, "Mr. Coombs, would you have any knowledge of a robbery that took place . . . ?"

"I thought you said there wasn't any crime being investigated," Isabel said.

"I didn't say that. I said we had no intention of charging your *husband* with any crime."

"You just now mentioned a robbery."

"Yes, six years ago." He turned to Robert and said, "Would you know anything about such a robbery, Mr. Coombs?"

"I don't know," Robert said. "Who was robbed?"

"The National Savings & Loan Association."

"What's that?"

"A bank."

"Where?"

"In this city," Carella said. "Downtown."

"Six years ago," Isabel said flatly, "we were living in Detroit."

"I see," Carella said. "And when did you move here?"

"Just before Christmas," Robert said.

"That'd be . . . about six months ago."

"Almost six months ago exactly," Robert said.

"Mr. Coombs, did anyone ever give you or did you ever come into possession in any way whatsoever . . ."

"This has to do with the robbery, doesn't it?" Isabel said shrewdly.

". . . a piece of a photograph?" Carella continued, ignoring her.

"What do you mean?" Robert asked.

"A section of a picture."

"A picture of *what?*" Isabel asked.

"We don't know. That is, we're not sure."

"Then how would my husband know whether or not he has it?"

"If he has it, I guess he would know he has it," Carella said. "Do you have it?"

"No," Robert said.

"Do any of these names mean anything to you? Carmine Bonamico, Louis D'Amore . . ."

"No."

"Jerry Stein . . ."

"No."

"Pete Ryan?"

"No."

"Never heard of any of them?"

"No. Who are they?"

"How about these names? Albert Weinberg, Donald Renninger, Alice Bonamico . . ."

"No, none of them."

"Dorothea McNally? Geraldine Ferguson?"

Robert shook his head.

"Eugene Ehrbach?"

"No, I'm sorry."

"Well, then," Carella said. "I guess that's it. Thank you very much for your time." He rose, nodded briefly at Isabel Coombs, and started out of the yard.

Behind him, Isabel said, "Is that all?"

She sounded disappointed.

Carella did not get home until eight o'clock that night.

His wife Teddy was sitting at the kitchen table with Arthur Brown. She smiled as he entered, brown eyes engulfing him, one delicate hand brushing a strand of black hair away from her face.

"Hey, this is a surprise," he said to Brown. "Hello, honey," he said to Teddy, and bent to kiss her.

"How'd you make out?" Brown asked.

"He's not our man. Moved here from Detroit six months ago, doesn't know a thing about the photograph, and never even *heard* of National Savings & Loan." Carella suddenly turned to his wife. "I'm sorry, honey," he said, "I didn't realize my back was turned." He repeated what he had just told Brown, watching Teddy's eyes for confirmation that she was reading his lips. She nodded when he fin-

ished, and then rapidly moved her fingers in the hand alphabet he
understood, telling him that Arthur had found another section of the
photograph.

"Is that right?" Carella said, turning to Brown. "You've got another piece?"

"That's why I'm here, baby," Brown said. He reached into his
jacket pocket, pulled out a glassine envelope, opened it, and emptied
five pieces of the snapshot onto the tabletop. The men stared blankly
at the collection. Teddy Carella—who lived in a soundless, speech-
less, largely visual and tactile universe—studied the twisted shapes
on the tabletop. Her hands moved out swiftly. In less time than it
had taken Carella to assemble the four pieces that had been in their
possession yesterday, she now put together the five pieces before
her:

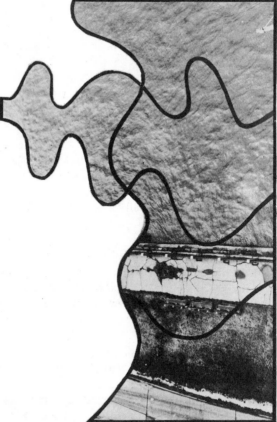

"Hey!" Brown said. *"Now* we're getting there!"
"Yeah," Carella said, "but where?"

9

NEVER let it be bruited about that just because a homicide victim also happens to be an ex-con, the police will devote less time and energy to finding out who has done him in. Perish the thought! In this fair and democratic land of ours, the rich and the poor, the powerful and the meek, the honest citizen and the wrongdoer are all afforded equal protection under the law, even after they're dead. So, boy oh boy, did those guys work hard trying to find out who had left the hole in Albert Weinberg's chest!

To begin with, there are a lot of people who have to be informed when someone inconsiderately gets himself knocked off. Just *informing* all these different people takes a lot of time. Imagine having to call the Police Commissioner, *and* the Chief of Detectives, *and* the District Commander of the Detective Division, *and* Homicide, *and* the Squad and Precinct Commanding Officers of the precinct where the body was found, *and* the Medical Examiner, *and* the District Attorney, *and* the Telegraph, Telephone and Teletype Bureau at Headquarters, *and* the Police Laboratory, not to mention the police photographers and stenographers—the list alone is longer than the average laundry list, and just try phoning in a dirty shirt to the local laundryman. All that vast machinery of law enforcement ground into immediate action the moment it was discovered that Albert Weinberg had a hole in his chest; all those oiled gears smoothly meshed and rotated in the cause of justice; all those relentless preventers of crime and pursuers of criminals called upon their enormous reservoir of physical courage and stamina, their mental acumen, their experience, intelligence, their *brilliance* even—and all in an attempt to discover who had shot and killed the man who once upon a time had beat up a little old lady for the sum of seventeen dollars and thirty-four cents.

Actually, most of the physical courage and stamina, the mental

acumen, the experience, intelligence and brilliance was being ex-
pended by Detectives Meyer Meyer and Cotton Hawes of the 87th
Squad; Carella (who had discovered the corpse) being elsewhere
occupied. Meyer and Hawes did not have much trouble taking apart
the apartment; whoever killed Weinberg had already done a very
good job of that. They decided after a thorough search of the place
that Brown's surmise was a correct one. The killer had been after
Weinberg's pieces of the photograph, and had apparently been successful in finding them. Meyer and Hawes questioned all of the
tenants in the building and discovered that three of them had heard a
very loud noise shortly after midnight. None of these people thought
it either necessary or advisable to call the police. In this neighborhood, policemen were not exactly looked upon as benefactors of the
people, and besides the sounds of gunfire were somewhat common-
place, day *or* night. So both detectives went back to the squadroom
to consult the timetable Irving Krutch had so thoughtfully typed up
for Steve Carella:

```
6:00 P.M.   -- Arrived home from work. Talked to door-
               man downstairs about fine weather.
6:05 P.M.   -- Entered apartment. Called Suzanne
               Endicott, reminded her of our date.
6:15 P.M.   -- Ran bath, mixed martinis, caught last
               part of Six O'clock News on television
               while waiting for tub to fill.
6:30 P.M.)  -- Bathed, shaved, dressed, mixed another
    to   )     pitcherful of martinis.
7:30 P.M.)
7:30 P.M.)  -- Suzie arrived at apartment. We each had
               two martinis.
8:00 P.M.   -- Arthur Brown called to advise me of new
               developments on case.
8:25 P.M.   -- Called downstairs, asked doorman to get
               me a taxicab.
8:30 P.M.   -- Suzie and I went downstairs, taxi wait-
               ing, took taxi to The Ram's Head, 777
               Jefferson Avenue. (Reservation for 8:45
               P.M. made by my secretary, Donna Hogan,
               earlier in day.)
8:45 P.M.)  -- Dinner at The Ram's Head. Headwaiter
    to   )     Maurice suggested the Chateau Bouscaut
10:30 P.M.)    '64.
10:30 P.M.) -- Walked up Hall Avenue looking in shop
    to   )     windows, and finally hailed taxi.
11:30 P.M.)
```

11:45 P.M.	—	Taxi dropped us at Apartment. Came upstairs. I had a cognac, Suzie had a creme de menthe on the rocks. Watched Johnny Carson for approximately a half-hour. Buddy Hackett guest star.
12:15 A.M.	—	Went to bed.
3:15 A.M.	—	Awakened by knocking on door. Detective Steve Carella in hallway outside.
3:15 A.M.) to) 3:25 A.M.)	—	Talked to Detective Carella.
3:25 A.M.	—	Typed timetable for Detective Carella.
3:30 A.M.	—	Detective Carella left. Went back to bed.

The day doorman outside Krutch's apartment building corroborated that Krutch had come home from work at about 6 P.M., and that they had had a brief discussion about the wonderful weather, so different from last June's weather, when the city was sweltering in the grip of a ninety-degree heat wave. He put Meyer and Hawes in touch with the night doorman who stated that Krutch had called down for a taxi at approximately eight-thirty, and had left the building with a young lady shortly thereafter. He had personally given Krutch's destination to the cab driver: The Ram's Head at 777 Jefferson Avenue. He further reported that Krutch and the young lady had come back to the apartment shortly before midnight and that he had not seen either of them leaving again at any time during his tour of duty, which ended at 8 A.M. Meyer and Hawes went over the building's entrances very carefully, though, and discovered that anyone who chose not to be seen by either the doorman or the elevator operator had only to take the service steps down to the basement and leave the building through the side-street exit door, where the garbage cans were stacked.

The reservations book for The Ram's Head noted a reservation for "Irving Krutch, 2" at 8:45 P.M. on the night Albert Weinberg was murdered. The headwaiter, a man named Maurice Duchene recalled Mr. Krutch and a young lady being there, and also recalled recommending the Chateau Bouscaut '64 to them. He said that Mr. Krutch had ordered a bottle and had commented that the wine was delicious. Mr. Krutch had tipped him three dollars when he left the restaurant at about ten-thirty.

A call to the local affiliate of the National Broadcasting Company ascertained the fact that one of Johnny Carson's guests that night had been Buddy Hackett and that he had come on almost immediately after the monologue, sometime before midnight.

There was nothing left to do but talk to Suzanne Endicott.

Ask any cop whom he would rather interview, an eighty-year-old lady with varicose veins or a twenty-two-year-old blonde wearing a see-through blouse, just ask any cop.

Suzanne Endicott worked in a swinging boutique called The Nickel Bag, and she was wearing a leather mini-skirt and a blouse through which her breasts were clearly visible. Her attire was very disconcerting, especially to policemen who were rather more used to eighty-year-old ladies with varicose veins. Detective Meyer Meyer was a married man. Cotton Hawes was a single man, but he, too, seemed to be having difficulty concentrating on the questions. He kept thinking he should ask Suzanne Endicott to go to a movie with him. Or something. The shop was thronged with young girls similarly though not identically dressed, mini-skirts and tights, headbands and shiny blouses, a veritable aviary of chirping young birds—Meyer Meyer hadn't even enjoyed the Hitchcock film. Suzanne Endicott fluttered here and there, helping this young lady with a pants suit, that one with a crocheted dress, the next with a sequined vest. Between flutterings and chirpings and quick glimpses of nipples and thighs, the detectives tried to ask their questions.

"You want to tell us exactly what happened that night?" Meyer asked.

"Oh, sure, I'd be happy to," Suzie said. She had the faintest trace of a Southern accent in her speech, Hawes noticed.

"Where are you from originally?" he asked, thinking to put her at ease, and also thinking he would definitely ask her to go to a movie or something.

"Oh my, does my accent still show?" Suzie said.

"Just a little," Hawes said, and tried a gentle understanding smile which did not seem appropriate to his massive height, nor his fiery red mane, nor the white streak in the hair over his left temple, the result of a knifing many years back.

"I'm from Georgia," she said. "The Peach State."

"It must be lovely down there in Georgia," Hawes said.

"Oh yes, just lovely," Suzie said. "Excuse me, just one teeny little minute, won't you?" she said, and dashed off to where a striking brunette was coming out of one of the dressing rooms. The brunette had on bright red velvet hip-huggers. Hawes thought he might go over and ask *her* to go to a movie or something.

"I feel as if I'm backstage at the Folies-Bergère," Meyer whispered.

"Have you ever *been* backstage at the Folies-Bergère?" Hawes whispered back.

"No, but I'm sure it's just like this."

"Better," Hawes said.

"Have *you* ever been?"

"Never."

"Well, here I am, back again," Suzie said, and smiled, and tossed her long blond hair and added, "I think they were a bit too snug, don't you?"

"What's that?" Meyer said.

"The pants she had on."

"Oh, sure, a little too snug," Meyer said. "Miss Endicott, about the night Weinberg was killed . . ."

"Oh, yes, that was just dreadful, wasn't it?" Suzie said.

"Yes, it was," Hawes said gently and tenderly.

"Although I understand he was a criminal. Weinberg, I mean."

"Who told you that?"

"Irving did. *Was* he a criminal?"

"He paid his debt to society," Hawes said tenderly and gently.

"Oh, yes, I suppose he did," Suzie answered. "But still."

"In any event," Meyer said, passing a hand over his bald pate and rolling his china-blue eyes, "he *was* killed, and we're conducting an investigation into his murder, and we'd like very much to ask you some questions about that night, if it's not too much trouble, Miss Endicott."

"Oh, it's no trouble at all," Suzie said. "Would you please excuse me for just one teeny minute?" she said, and went over to the cash register where a leggy redhead was standing with several sweaters in her arms, waiting to pay for them.

"We'll *never* get out of this joint," Meyer said.

"That wouldn't be too bad," Hawes said.

"For *you,* maybe it wouldn't be too bad. For *me,* if I don't get home in time for dinner, Sarah'll kill me."

"Why don't you run on along then?" Hawes said, and grinned. "I think I can handle this alone."

"Oh, I'm sure you can," Meyer said. "Trouble is, you see, we're supposed to find out who killed Weinberg. That's the trouble, you see."

"Well, here I am back again," Suzie said, and smiled, and tossed her long blond hair. "I've asked Michelle to spell me, so I don't think we'll be interrupted again."

"That's very kind of you, Suzie," Hawes said.

"Oh, not at all," she answered, and smiled again.

"About that night . . ."

"Yes," she said, alert, and responsive, and eager to co-operate. "What would you like to know?"

"First, what time did you get to Irving Krutch's apartment?"

"It must have been about seven-thirty," Suzie said.

"How long have you known Mr. Krutch?" Hawes said.

"We've practically been living together for four years," Suzie answered, her big brown eyes opened wide.

"Oh," Hawes said.

"Yés."

"I see."

"We have separate apartments, of course."

"Of course."

Meyer cleared his throat. "What . . . uh . . . what was I saying?" he said, turning to Hawes.

"Time she got there," Hawes said.

"Oh yes. Seven-thirty, is that right?"

"That's right," Suzie said.

"And what did you do when you got there?"

"Irving gave me a martini. Two martinis, in fact. I love martinis. Don't you just adore martinis?" she asked Hawes.

"Mmm," Hawes said.

"Were there any visitors while you were there?"

"None."

"Any phone calls?"

"Yes."

"Would you happen to know from whom?"

"From a detective. Irving seemed very happy when he hung up."

"Are you engaged or something?" Hawes asked. "Is that it?"

"To be married, do you mean?"

"Yes, to be married."

"Oh, no, don't be silly," Suzie said.

Meyer cleared his throat again. "What time did you *leave* the apartment?" he asked.

"About eight-thirty. I think it was eight-thirty. It could have been a teeny bit earlier or a teeny bit later. But I think it was *around* eight-thirty."

"And where did you go?"

"To The Ram's Head." She smiled up at Hawes. "That's a restaurant. Have you ever been there?"

"No. No, I haven't."

"It's very nice."

"What time did you leave the restaurant, Miss Endicott?"

"About ten-thirty. Again, as I said, it might have been a teeny bit . . ."

"Yes, but it was *around* ten-thirty."

"Yes."

"And then what did you do?"

"We went for a walk on Hall Avenue, and looked in all the store windows. We saw some marvelous lounging pajamas in Kilkenny's. Italian, I think they were. Just, oh so colorful."

"How long did you walk on Hall Avenue?"

"An hour or so? I guess it was an hour or so."

"And then what did you do?"

"We went back to Irving's apartment. What we do, you see, is we either go to Irving's apartment or to my apartment. I live downtown in The Quarter," she said looking up at Hawes. "Do you know Chelsea Street?"

"Yes, I do," Hawes said.

"12½ Chelsea Street," she said, "apartment 6B. That's because of hard luck."

"What is?"

"The 12½. It should be 13, but the owner of the building is superstitious."

"Yes, there are lots of buildings in the city like that," Hawes said.

"Lots of buildings don't even have a thirteenth *floor,*" Suzie said. "That is, they *have* a thirteenth floor, but it's called the *fourteenth* floor."

"Yes, I know."

"12½ Chelsea Street," she said, "apartment 6B, Hampton 4-8100." She paused. "That's my telephone number."

"So you went back to Mr. Krutch's apartment at about eleven-thirty," Meyer said, "and then what did you do?"

"We watched television for a while. Buddy Hackett was on. He's a scream. Don't you just adore Buddy Hackett?" she said, looking up at Hawes.

"I adore him, yes," Hawes said, and Meyer gave him a peculiar look. "He's very comical," Hawes said, ignoring the look.

"He's just adorable," Suzie said.

"What did you do after watching television?" Meyer said.

"We made love," Suzie said.

Meyer cleared his throat.

"Twice," Suzie added.

Meyer cleared his throat again.

"Then we went to sleep," she said, "and in the middle of the night this Italian detective knocked on the door and started asking all sorts of questions about where we were and what we were doing. Is he allowed to do something like that, come around in the middle of the night, and bang on the door, and ask dumb questions?"

"Yes, he is," Hawes said.

"I think that's awful," Suzie said. "Don't you think that's awful?" she asked Hawes.

"Well, it's a job," Hawes said, and smiled weakly, and tried to avoid Meyer's glance again.

"Did either of you leave the apartment at any time between 11:30 and 3 A.M.?" Meyer asked.

"Oh, no. I told you. First we watched television, and then we made love, and then we went to sleep."

"You were there all the time?"

"Yes."

"*Both* of you."

"Yes."

"Mr. Krutch didn't leave the apartment at all."

"No."

"If you were asleep, how do you know whether he left or not?"

"Well, we didn't go to sleep until about maybe two o'clock. Things take *time,* you know."

"You were awake until 2 A.M.?"

"Yes."

"And Mr. Krutch did not leave the apartment?"

"No."

"Did he leave the bedroom?"

"No."

"Not at any time during the night?"

"Not at any time during the night."

"Okay," Meyer said. "You got anything else, Cotton?"

"Is that your name?" Suzie asked. "I had an uncle named Cotton."

"That's my name," Hawes said.

"After Cotton Mather?"

"That's right."

"Isn't that a coincidence?" Suzie said. "I think that's a marvelous coincidence."

"You got anything else to ask?" Meyer said again.

"Well . . . yes," Hawes said, and looked at Meyer.

"I'll wait for you outside," Meyer said.

"Okay," Hawes said.

He watched as Meyer picked his way through the milling girls in the shop, watched as Meyer opened the front door and stepped out onto the sidewalk.

"I have only one further question, Suzie," he said.

"Yes, what's that?"

"Would you like to go to a movie with me? Or something?"

"Oh, no," Suzie said. "Irving wouldn't like that." She smiled and looked up at him with her big brown eyes. "I'm terribly sorry," she said. "really I am, but Irving simply wouldn't like that at all."

"Well, uh, thanks a lot for your co-operation, Miss Endicott," Hawes said. "Thank you very much, I'm sorry we—uh—broke into your day this way, thanks a lot."

"Not at all," Suzie said, and rushed off to another beautiful brunette who was emerging from yet another dressing room. Hawes looked at the brunette, decided not to risk further rejection, and went outside to where Meyer was waiting on the sidewalk.

"Did you score?" Meyer asked.

"Nope."

"How come? I thought it was a sure thing."

"So did I. I guess she thinks Krutch is just adorable."

"I think *you're* just adorable," Meyer said.

"Up yours," Hawes answered, and both men went back to the squadroom. Hawes typed up the report and then went out to talk to a grocery store owner who had a complaint about people stealing bottles of milk from boxes stacked up in back of the store, this in the wee hours of the morning before the store was opened for business. Meyer went to talk to an assault victim and to show him some mug shots for possible identification. They had worked long and hard on the Weinberg Case, yeah, and it was now in the Open File, pending further developments.

Meanwhile, on the ferry to Bethtown, two other cops were working very hard at sniffing the mild June breezes that blew in off the River Harb. Coatless, hatless, Carella and Brown stood at the railing and watched Isola's receding skyline, watched too the busy traffic on the river, tugboats and ocean liners, a squadron of Navy destroyers, barges and scows, each of them tooting and chugging and sounding bells and sending up steam and leaving a boiling, frothy wake behind.

"This is still the cheapest date in the city," Brown said. "Five cents for a forty-five minute boat ride—who can beat it?"

"I wish *I* had a nickel for all the times I rode this ferry with Teddy, before we were married," Carella said.

"Caroline used to love it," Brown said. "She never wanted to sit inside, winter or summer. We always stood here on the bow, even if it meant freezing our asses off."

"The poor man's ocean cruise," Carella said.

"Moonlight and sea breezes . . ."

"Concertina playing . . ."

"Tugboats honking . . ."

"Sounds like a Warner Brothers movie."

"I sometimes thought it *was*," Brown said wistfully. "There were lots of places I couldn't go in this city, Steve, either because I couldn't afford them or because it was made plain to me I wasn't wanted in them. On the Bethtown ferry, though, I could be the hero of the movie. I could take my girl out on the bow and we could feel the wind on our faces, and I could kiss her like a colored Humphrey Bogart. I love this goddamn ferry, I really do."

"Yeah," Carella said, and nodded.

"Sure," Robert Coombs said, "I used to have a piece of that picture."

"*Used* to have?" Brown asked.

"*Used* to have, correct," Coombs said, and spat on the sidewalk in front of the hot-dog stand. He was a man of about sixty, with a weather-beaten face, spikes of yellow-white hair sticking up out of his skull like withered stalks of corn, an altogether grizzled look about him as he sat on one of the stools in front of his establishment (Bob's Roadside) and talked to the two detectives. The hot-dog stand was on Route 24, off the beaten path; it was unlikely that a dozen automobiles passed the place on any given day, in either direction.

"Where'd you get it?" Carella asked.

"Petey Ryan give it to me before the holdup," Coombs said. His eyes were a pale blue, fringed with blond lashes, overhung with blond-white brows. His teeth were the color of his brows. He spat again on the sidewalk. Brown wondered what it was like to eat food prepared at Bob's Roadside.

"Why'd Ryan give it to you?" Carella asked.

"We was good friends," Coombs said.

"Tell us all about it," Brown suggested.

"What for? I already told you I ain't got the picture no more."

"Where is it now?"

"Christ knows," Coombs said, and shrugged, and spat.

"How long before the holdup?" Carella said.

"How long *what?*"

"When he gave you the picture."

"Three days."

"Petey came to you . . ."

"Correct."

"And handed you a piece of a snapshot . . ."

"Correct."

"And said what?"

"Said I should hang onto it till after the hit."

"And then what?"

"Then he'd come collect it from me."

"Did he say why?"

"In case he got busted."

"He didn't want to have the picture on him if the police caught him, is that it?"

"Correct."

"What did you think about all that?" Brown asked.

"What should I think? A good friend asks me to do a favor, I do it. What was there to think?"

"Did you have any idea what the picture meant?"

"Sure."

"What did it mean?"

"It showed where they was ditching the loot. You think I'm a dope?"

"Did Petey say how many pieces there were in the complete photograph?"

"Nope."

"Just told you to hang onto this little piece of it until he came to collect it?"

"Correct."

"Okay, where's the piece now?"

"I threw it in the garbage," Coombs said.

"Why?"

"Petey got killed. Cinch he wasn't going to come back for the piece, so I threw it out."

"Even though you knew it was part of a bigger picture? A picture that showed where they were dropping the N.S.L.A. loot?"

"Correct."

"When did you throw it out?"

"Day after the hit. Soon as I read in the paper that Petey got killed."

"You were in a pretty big hurry to get rid of it, huh?"

"A pretty big hurry, correct."

"Why?"

"I didn't want to get hooked into the holdup. I figured if the picture was hot, I didn't want no part of it."

"But you accepted it from Petey to begin with, didn't you?"

"Correct."

"Even though you knew it showed where they planned to hide the proceeds of a robbery."

"I only *guessed* that. I didn't know for sure."

"When did you find out for sure?"

"Well, I *still* don't know for sure."

"But you became sufficiently alarmed *after* the robbery to throw away the scrap Petey had given you."

"Correct."

"This was six years ago, right, Mr. Coombs?"

"Correct."

"You threw it in the garbage."

"In the garbage, correct."

"Where was the garbage?"

"Where was the *what?*"

"The garbage."

"In the back."

"Out back there?"

"Correct."

"You want to come back there with us, and show us where you threw it in the garbage?"

"Sure," Coombs said, and got off the stool, and spat, and then led them around to the rear side of the hot-dog stand. "Right there," he said, pointing. "In one of them garbage cans."

"You carried that little tiny piece of the photograph out back here, and you lifted the lid of the garbage can and dropped it in, is that right?"

"Correct."

"Show us how you did it," Brown said.

Coombs looked at him curiously. Then he shrugged, pinched an imaginary photograph segment between his thumb and forefinger, carried it to the nearest garbage can, lifted the lid, deposited the non-existent scrap inside the can, covered the can, turned to the cops, and said, "Like that. That's how I done it."

"You're lying," Brown said flatly.

Neither of the two detectives, of course, knew whether or not Coombs was lying, nor had their little charade with the garbage can proved a damn thing. But public relations has a lot to do with criminal investigation and detection. There is not a red-blooded citizen of the U.S. of A. who does not know through constant exposure to television programs and motion pictures that cops are always asking trick questions and doing trick things to trap a person in a lie. Coombs had seen his share of movies and television shows, and he knew now, knew with heart-stopping, face-blanching, teeth-jarring certainty that he had done something wrong when he walked over to the garbage can, and lifted the lid, and dropped in the imaginary photo scrap, something that had instantly told these two shrewd investigators that he was lying.

"Lying?" he said. "Me? Lying?" He tried to spit again, but his throat muscles wouldn't respond, and he almost choked, and then began coughing violently.

"You want to come along with us?" Carella said, sternly and pompously, and in his most legal-sounding voice.

"Wh . . . wh . . . wh . . . ?" Coombs said, and coughed again, his face turning purple, and then put one hand flat against the rear wall of the hot-dog stand, head bent, and leaned against it, and tried to catch his breath and recover his wits. They had him cold, he knew, but he couldn't figure what the charge would be, and he tried to buy time now while the big black cop reached into his back pocket and pulled out a pair of handcuffs with vicious-looking saw-toothed edges—oh Jesus, Coombs thought, I am busted. But for what?

"What's the crime," he said, "the charge," he said, "what's the, what's the, what did I do?"

"You know what you did, Mr. Coombs," Carella said, coldly. "You destroyed evidence of a crime."

"That a felony," Brown said, lying.

"Section 812 of the Penal Law," Carella said.

"Look, I . . ."

"Come along, Mr. Coombs," Brown said, and held out the handcuffs.

"What if I . . . what if I hadn't thrown out the thing, the picture?" Coombs asked.

"Did you?"

"I didn't. I got it. I'll give it to you. Jesus, I'll give it to you."

"Get it," Brown said.

A ferryboat is a good place for speculation. It is also a good place for listening. So on the way back to Isola, Carella and Brown each did a little speculating and a little listening.

"Four guys in the holdup," Brown said. "Carmine Bonamico, who masterminded the job . . ."

"Some mastermind," Carella said.

"Jerry Stein, who drove the getaway heap, and two guns named Lou D'Amore and Pete Ryan. Four altogether."

"So?"

"So figure it out. Pete Ryan gave one piece of the snapshot to his aunt Dorothea McNally and another piece to his good old pal Robert Coombs . . ."

"Of Bob's Famous Roadside Emporium," Carella said.

"Correct," Brown said. "Which means, using a method known as arithmetical deduction, that Ryan was at one time in possession of *two* pieces of the snapshot."

"Correct," Carella said.

"Is it not reasonable to assume, therefore, that *each* member of the gang was *likewise* in possession of two pieces of the snapshot?"

"It is reasonable, but not necessarily exclusive," Carella said.

"How do you mean, Holmes?"

"Elementary. You are assuming there are only *eight* pieces of the full photograph. However, using other multiples of four, we can equally reason that there are twelve pieces, or sixteen pieces, or indeed . . ."

"My guess is eight," Brown said.

"Why the magic number eight?"

"If you were planning a heist, would you go cutting a picture into twelve parts? Or sixteen?"

"Or twenty?" Carella said.

"Would you?"

"I think it's a goofy idea to begin with," Carella said. "I wouldn't cut up a photograph at *all.*"

"My guess is eight. Four guys, two pieces each. We've now got six of them. My guess is we'll find number seven in Gerry Ferguson's safe. That'll leave only one piece to go. One, baby. One more piece and we're home free."

As Robert Burns, that sage Scottish poet once remarked, however, the best laid plans . . .

That afternoon, they went down to the Ferguson Gallery with a warrant obliging Geraldine Ferguson to open her safe. And though they searched it from top to bottom and found a lot of goodies in it, none of which were related to any crime, they did *not* find another piece of the photograph. By the end of that Monday, they still had only six pieces.

Six.

Count 'em.

Six.

As they studied these assembled pieces in the midnight silence of the squadroom, something struck them as being terribly wrong. There was no sky in the picture. And because there was no sky, neither was there an up nor a down, a top nor a bottom. They were looking at a landscape without perspective, and it made no sense.

10

THE NYLON stocking was wrapped tightly around her throat, embedded in the soft flesh of her neck. Her eyes were bulging, and she lay grotesque in death upon the turquoise-colored rug in her bedroom, wearing a baby-doll nightgown and bikini panties, the bedsheets trailing off the bed and tangled in one twisted leg.

Geraldine Ferguson would never again swear in Italian, never again proposition married spades, never again charge exorbitant prices for a painting or a piece of sculpture. Geraldine Ferguson lay robbed of life in a posture as angularly absurd as the geometric designs that had shrieked from the walls of her gallery, death silent and shrill in that turquoise-matted sanctuary, the bedroom a bedlam around her, a tired reprise of the havoc wreaked in the rooms of Donald Renninger and Albert Weinberg, the searcher run amok, the quest for seven hundred and fifty G's reaching a climax of desperation. The police had not found what they'd wanted in Gerry's safe, and they wondered now if whoever had demolished Gerry's apartment and strangled her into the bargain had had any better luck than they.

Arthur Brown went out into the hallway and, oddly, wondered if Gerry had ever roller-skated on a city sidewalk.

They picked up Bramley Kahn in a gay bar that night.

He was wearing a brocade Nehru jacket over white linen hip-huggers. His hand was resting on the shoulder of a curly-haired young man in a black leather jacket. A sculpted gold ring set with a gray freshwater pearl was on Kahn's left pinky.

He was slightly drunk, and decidedly campy, and he seemed surprised to see the police. Everywhere around him, men danced with men, men whispered to men, men embraced men, but Kahn was nonetheless surprised to see the police because this was the most permissive city in the world, where private homosexual clubs could expressly prohibit policemen from entering (unless of course they, too, were members) and where everyone looked the other way unless a six-year-old boy was being buggered by a flying queen in a dark alley. This was just a run-of-the-mill gay bar, never any trouble here, never any strident jealous arguments, never anything more than consenting adults quietly doing their thing— Kahn was very surprised to see the police.

He was even more surprised to learn that Geraldine Ferguson was dead.

He kept telling the police how surprised he was.

This was a Tuesday, he kept telling the police, and Tuesday was normally Gerry's day off; she took Tuesdays, he took Wednesdays. He had not expected to see her at the gallery and was not surprised when she did not show up for work. He had closed the gallery at six, had gone for a quiet dinner with a close friend, and then had come down here to The Quarter for a nightcap before turning in. Arthur Brown asked him if he would mind coming uptown to the squadroom, and Kahn said he could see no objection to that, though perhaps he had better first consult his lawyer. Brown said he was entitled to a lawyer, and in fact didn't have to answer any questions at all if he didn't want to, lawyer or no lawyer, and then went into the whole Miranda-Escobedo bit, advising Kahn of his rights while Kahn listened intently, and then decided that he had *better* call his lawyer and have him come up to the squadroom to be present during the interrogation, murder being a somewhat serious occurrence, even in a city as permissive as this one.

The lawyer was a man named Anatole Petitpas, and he asked Brown to do the whole Miranda-Escobedo song and dance one more time for the benefit of the people in the cheaper seats. Brown patiently explained Kahn's rights to him again, and Kahn said that he understood everything, and Petitpas seemed satisfied that all was being conducted in a proper legal manner, and then he signaled to the detectives that it was now all right to ask his client whatever questions they chose to ask. There were four detectives standing in a loose circle around Kahn, but their weight of numbers was offset by the presence of Petitpas, who could be counted on to leap into the fray if ever the questioning got too rough. This was murder they were fooling around with here, and nobody was taking any chances.

They asked all the routine questions (almost putting even themselves to sleep) such as WHERE WERE YOU AT 2 A.M. LAST NIGHT? (the time established by the M.E. as the probable time

of Gerry's death) and WHO WAS WITH YOU? and WHERE
DID YOU GO? and WERE YOU SEEN BY ANYONE?, all the
usual police crap, the questions coming alternately from Brown,
Carella, Meyer, and Hawes working smoothly and efficiently as a
team. And then finally they got back to the photograph, everything
always got back to the photograph because it was obvious to each
of the cops in that squadroom that four people had been killed
so far and that all of them had been in possession of a piece or
pieces of a picture showing the location of the N.S.L.A. loot, and if
a motive were any more evident than that, each of them would
have tripped over it with his big flat feet.

"When I talked to you at the gallery Saturday," Brown said,
"you told me Gerry Ferguson was in possession of a certain piece
of a photograph. When you said this, were you . . ."

"Just a second," Petitpas interrupted. "Have you talked to my
client before this?"

"I talked to him, yes."

"Did you advise him of his rights?"

"I was conducting a field investigation," Brown said wearily.

"He didn't tell me he was a cop," Kahn said.

"Is that true?" Petitpas asked.

"It's true."

"It may be significant."

"Not necessarily," Brown said, and smiled. The other detectives
smiled with him. They were thinking of thousands of social agency
reports in triplicate where, for example, a young man would be
described as having been arrested at the age of fourteen for possession
of narcotics, at sixteen for possession with intent to sell, and at
eighteen for smuggling in twelve kilos of heroin in a brown paper
bag, all of which damning criminal history would be followed by
the words, typewritten in upper case,

"Go on," Petitpas said.

"I wanted to ask your client whether he knew for certain that
Miss Ferguson had a piece of that photograph."

"I knew for certain," Kahn said.

"Miss Ferguson told us the piece was in the gallery safe," Carella
said. "Was that your impression as well?"

"It was my impression."

"As you know, however, when we opened the safe, we did not
find the photograph."

"I know that."

"Where did you think it was then?" Hawes asked.

"I don't understand your question."

"When you found out it wasn't in the safe, when we opened the safe yesterday and the picture wasn't in it, where did you think it might be?"

"I had no idea."

"Did you think it was in Miss Ferguson's apartment?" Meyer asked.

"He has already told you he had no idea where it was," Petitpas said. "You're asking him to speculate . . ."

"Let's save it for the courtroom, counselor," Carella said. "There's nothing out of line here so far, and you know it. A woman's been killed. If your client can satisfy us on certain points, he'll walk out of here in ten minutes. If not . . ."

"Yes, Mr. Canella?"

"Carella. If not, I think you're as well aware of the possibilities as we are."

"Are you threatening him with a murder charge?"

"Did anyone mention a murder charge?"

"The implication was clear."

"So was Detective Meyer's question. Mr. Kahn, did you or did you not think the photograph might be in Miss Ferguson's apartment?"

"May I answer that?" Kahn asked his lawyer.

"Yes, go ahead, go ahead," Petitpas said, annoyed.

"I guess I thought it could have been there, yes."

"Did you go there looking for it?" Brown asked.

"That's it, I'm afraid," Petitpas said. "I feel I must advise my client at this point that it would not be to his benefit to answer any further questions."

"Do you want us to book him, counselor, is that it?"

"You may do as you wish. I know I don't have to remind you that murder is a serious . . ."

"Oh, man, what bullshit," Brown said. "Why don't you just play ball with us, Petitpas? Has your man got something to hide?"

"I've got nothing to hide, Anatole," Kahn said.

"Then let him answer the goddamn questions," Carella said.

"I can answer the questions," Kahn said, and looked at Petitpas.

"Very well, go ahead," Petitpas said.

"I didn't kill her, Anatole."

"Go ahead, go ahead."

"I really didn't. I have nothing to hide."

"Okay, counselor?"

"I have already indicated that he may answer your questions."

"Thank you. Did you go to Gerry Ferguson's apartment last night?"

"No."

"Or any time yesterday?"

"No."

"Did you see her yesterday?"

"Yes, at the gallery. I left before she did. This was sometime after you'd opened the safe."

"Sometime after you knew the picture wasn't in the safe?"

"That's right, yes."

"And sometime after you thought it might be in Miss Ferguson's apartment?"

"Yes."

"Let's talk about the list, Mr. Kahn."

"What?"

"The list."

"What list?"

"The torn list of names you keep in a little cashbox in the bottom drawer of your office desk."

"I . . . I don't know what you mean," Kahn said.

"Four people on that list have already been killed, Mr. Kahn."

"What list does he mean, Bram?" Petitpas asked.

"I don't know."

"It's a list of names, Mr. Petitpas," Brown said, "presumably of people who possess or once possessed portions of a photograph alleging to show the location of certain monies stolen from the National Savings & Loan Association six years ago. Does that clearly identify the nature of the list, Mr. Kahn?"

Petitpas stared at his client. Kahn stared back at him.

"Well, answer it," Petitpas said.

"It clearly identifies the nature of the list, yes," Kahn said.

"Then the list *does* exist?"

"It exists."

"And a torn portion of it is indeed in your cashbox?"

"It is, yes, but how . . . ?"

"Never mind how. Where'd you get that list?"

"Gerry gave it to me for safekeeping."

"Where'd *she* get it?"

"I don't know."

"Mr. Kahn, try to help us," Meyer said gently.

"I didn't kill her," Kahn said.

"Somebody did," Carella said.

"It wasn't me."

"We're not suggesting it was."

"All right. As long as you know."

"Who gave her the list?"

"Carmine."

"Bonamico?"

"Yes. Carmine Bonamico. He gave half of the list to his wife, and half to Geraldine."

"Why Geraldine?"

"They were having a thing."

"They were lovers?"

"Yes."

"Did he also give her a piece of the photograph?"

"No. She got that from her brother-in-law, Lou D'Amore. There were four men on the holdup. Bonamico cut the picture into eight parts, a wiggly line across the middle horizontally, three wiggly lines vertically, eight pieces in all. He gave two pieces to each of the men, and kept two for himself. He asked the men to distribute the pieces to people they could trust. It was an insurance policy, so to speak. The beneficiaries were the people who held sections of the photograph. The trustees were Alice Bonamico and Gerry Ferguson, the only two people who could put togther the list and collect the photograph segments and uncover the loot."

"Who told you all this?"

"Gerry."

"How'd she know?"

"Pillow talk. Bonamico told her everything. I don't think his wife knew who had the other half of the list. But Gerry sure as hell knew."

"So Gerry was in possession of half of the list as well as one piece of the photograph."

"Yes."

"Why didn't she put the list together and go after the other pieces?"

"She tried to."

"What stopped her?"

"Alice." Kahn paused. "Well, after all, would *your* wife co-operate with your mistress?"

"I don't have a mistress," Carella said.

"Here's a typewritten copy of the list," Brown said. "Take a look at it."

"Is it all right to look at it?" Kahn asked his lawyer.

"Yes," Petitpas said. He turned to the police stenographer and said. "Let the record indicate that Mr. Kahn is being shown a list with such-and-such names on it; record all the names as they appear on the list."

"May I see the list?" the stenographer asked.

Brown handed it to him. The stenographer studied it, noted the names, and then handed it back to Brown.

"All right, Mr. Kahn, would you now please look at this list?"

Kahn accepted the list.

ALBERT WEINBERG

DONALD RENNINGER

EUGENE E. EHRBACH

ALICE BONAMICO

GERALDINE FERGUSON

DOROTHEA McNALLY

ROBERT COOMBS

"I've looked at it," he said, and handed it back to Brown.

"Which of those names are familiar to you?"

"Only three of them."

"Which?"

"Gerry, of course, Alice Bonamico, and Donald Renninger. He's the other person who got a piece of the picture from Lou D'Amore."

"How come?"

"They were cellmates at Caramoor. In fact, Lou mailed the piece to him there. He was still behind bars at the time of the robbery."

"What about these other names?"

"I don't know any of them."

"Robert Coombs?"

"Don't know him."

"His name was on the half of the list you had in your possession. Didn't you ever try to contact him?"

"Gerry may have. I didn't."

"You weren't at all curious about him, is that right?"

"Oh, I was *curious,* I suppose, but not curious enough to go all the way out to . . ." Kahn suddenly stopped.

"Out to where, Mr. Kahn?"

"All right, Bethtown. I *did* go to see him. He wouldn't give up the piece. I offered him twelve hundred dollars for it, but he wouldn't give it up."

"How about some of these other names? Did you ever try to contact any of them?"

"How could I? I only had half the list."

"There are only seven names on this list, Mr. Kahn."

"Yes, I noticed that."

"You said the picture had been divided into eight pieces."

"That's what Gerry told me."

"Who's got the eighth piece?"

"I don't know."

"How about this first name on the list, Mr. Kahn? Albert Weinberg? Are you trying to say you've never heard of him?"

"Never."

"Don't you read the newspapers?"

"Oh, you mean his murder. Yes, of course, I read about his murder. I thought you were referring . . ."

"Yes?"

"To my having some knowledge of him *before* then."

"Did you kill Albert Weinberg?"

"Just a second, Mr. Brown . . ."

"It's all right, Anatole," Kahn said. "No, I did *not* kill him, Mr. Brown. In fact, before the night of his murder, I didn't even know he *existed*."

"I see," Brown said. "Even though he'd been in the gallery several times to inquire about the photograph?"

"Yes, but always using an assumed name."

"I see."

"I had nothing to do with either murder."

"Did you have anything to do with beating me up?"

"I should say not!"

"Where were you at the time?"

"Home in bed!"

"When?"

"The night you were beat up."

"How do you know it happened at night?"

"Just a second, Mr. Brown . . ."

"No, it's all right, Anatole," Kahn said. "Gerry told me."

"Who told Gerry?"

"Why, *you* I would guess."

"No, I didn't tell her anything about it."

"Then she must have known some other way. Maybe she was involved in it. Maybe she hired someone to go to your hotel . . ."

"How do you know that's where it happened?"

"She . . . she said so."

"She said I'd been attacked by two men in my hotel room?"

"Yes, she told me about it the next day."

"She couldn't have told you there were *two* men, Mr. Kahn, because I just made that up. There was only *one* man, wearing a stocking over his face."

"Well, it wasn't *me!*" Kahn shouted.

"Then who was it?" Brown shouted back. "You just said you learned about Albert Weinberg on the night of his murder. How?"

"The morning after, I meant. The newspapers . . ."

"You said 'the *night* of his murder,' you said you didn't even know he existed until that night. How'd you find *out* about his existence, Mr. Kahn? From my open notebook by the telephone?"

"Just a second, just a second," Petitpas shouted.

"I didn't kill him!" Kahn shouted.

"What'd you do, go after him the minute you left me?"

"No!"

"Just a second!"

"Walk the three blocks to his room . . ."

"No!"

"You killed him, Kahn, admit it!"

"No!"

"You attacked me . . ."

"Yes, no, NO!"

"Yes or no?"

Kahn had half-risen from his chair, and now he collapsed back into it, and began sobbing.

"Yes or no, Mr. Kahn?" Carella asked gently.

"I didn't want to . . . to hit you, I deplore violence," Kahn said, sobbing, not looking up at Brown. "I intended only to . . . to force you to give me the piece you had . . . to . . . to threaten you with the gun. And then . . . when you opened the door, I . . . you looked so *big* . . . and . . . and in that split second, I . . . I decided to . . . to strike out at you. I was very frightened, so frightened. I . . . I was afraid you might hurt me."

"Book him," Brown said. "First Degree Assault."

"Just a second," Petitpas said.

"Book him," Brown said flatly.

11

It was time to put on that old thinking cap.

It was time for a little plain and fancy deduction.

Nothing can confuse a person (cops included) more than a lot of names and a lot of pieces and a lot of corpses. Stop any decent law-abiding citizen on the street and ask him which he would prefer, a lot of names and pieces and corpses or a simple hatchet murder, and see what he says. Oh, you can safely bet six-to-five he'll take that hatchet in the head any day of the week, Thursday included, and Thursdays are no prizes, except when they fall on Thanksgiving.

Here's the way they saw it.

Fact: Renninger killed Ehrbach and Ehrbach killed Renninger— a simple uncomplicated mutual elimination, which was only fair.

Fact: Bramley Kahn kayoed Arthur Brown in one point four seconds of the first round, using the .32 Smith & Wesson Brown later found in the bottom drawer of Kahn's desk, and using as well his own feet—not for nothing was Kahn renowned as one of the fanciest dancers in gay bars all along The Quarter's glittering Kublenz Square.

Fact: Somebody killed Albert Weinberg.

NOT NECESSARILY SIGNIFICANT.

Fact: Somebody killed Geraldine Ferguson.

NOT NECESSARILY SIGNIFICANT.

(The "somebody," it was decided after intensive questioning was definitely *not* Bramley Kahn, who had gone directly home to the arms of a forty-four-year-old closet queen after battering Brown senseless.)

Fact(s): There were seven names on the list in Carmine Bonamico's handwriting. Carmine had skillfully dissected the list, giving one-half of it to his late wife, Alice Bonamico, and the other half to his late mistress, Geraldine Ferguson. Thoughtful fellow he, sharing his bed, his board, and also his contemplated ill-gotten gains with the two fairest flowers in his life. More's the pity the two broads could not have put their heads and their halves together and thereafter reaped the rewards of Carmine's professional acumen. Crime does not pay if you're fooling around with another woman.

Fact(s): There were eight pieces to the picture that revealed the location of the N.S.L.A. loot. Carmine had given two pieces to each of his associates, and had presumably kept two pieces for himself, he being the founder and beloved leader of the doomed band of brigands.

Fact: Petey Ryan, a gun on the ill-fated caper, had given one of his pieces to Dorothea McNally, woman about town, and another to Robert Coombs, restaurateur extraordinaire.

Fact: Lou D'Amore, the second gun, had given one of his pieces to Geraldine Ferguson, art appreciator, and the other to Donald Renninger, ex-cellmate.

Fact: Carmine Bonamico, mastermind, had given one of his pieces to Alice, his aforementioned wife.

Theory: Was it possible that Jerry Stein, Jewish driver of the misbegotten getaway car, had given one of his pieces to Albert Weinberg, and another to Eugene Edward Ehrbach, both of them likewise Jewish, rather than handing them over, say, to some passing Arab?

NOT NECESSARILY SIGNIFICANT.

Question: To whom had Carmine Bonamico given the eighth piece of the picture, the piece for which no name had been listed?

Or (to break things down into list form, which the police were very fond of doing):

PETE RYAN	-- DOROTHEA MCNALLY	(1)
	ROBERT COOMBS	(2)
LOU D'AMORE	-- GERALDINE FERGUSON	(3)
	DONALD RENNINGER	(4)
JERRY STEIN	-- ALBERT WEINBERG-?	(5)
	EUGENE E. EHRBACH-?	(6)
CARMINE BONAMICO	-- ALICE BONAMICO	(7)
	??????????????	(8)

But there was more, oh there was yet more, a policeman's lot is not a happy one. For example, was it not Irving Krutch, the *pro-*

vocateur, who had told the police that Alice Bonamico's piece, together with a torn list of names, had been willed to her sister, Lucia Feroglio, from whose dainty Sicilian hands Krutch had acquired both items, having faithlessly promised that good lady a thousand dollars in return for them? And had he not also said that Lucia had told him the assembled photograph would reveal the location of *"il tesoro,"* and had not Lucia delicately denied ever having said this to him? Or, for that matter, ever having given him a list of names? Ah so. And if he had *not* received his information from Lucia, then from whom exactly had it come? The person in possession of the eighth piece? The person who had gone unlisted by Carmine Bonamico?

On the night of Weinberg's murder, Brown had talked to three people: his wife Caroline, whom he could safely discount as a suspect; Weinberg, himself, who had been speedily dispatched to that great big photo lab in the sky; and Irving Krutch, to whom he had reported having struck pay dirt with Weinberg.

It seemed about time to talk to Irving Krutch again.

If Krutch was lying about having received the list of names from Lucia Feroglio, he could also be lying about having spent that night of the murder in his apartment with Suzanne Endicott. It was worth a try. When you're running out of suspects, it's even worth talking to the local Welsh terrier. Brown put on his sunglasses in preparation for the insurance investigator's dazzling smile.

Krutch was not smiling.

"The old bag's lying," he said. "It's as simple as that."

"Or maybe you are," Brown said.

"Why should I be? For Christ's sake, I'm the one who *came* to you with all this stuff. I'm as anxious to locate that money as you are. It's my *career* here that's at stake, don't you realize that?"

"Okay, I'll ask you again," Brown said patiently. "Why would a nice old deaf lady who hardly speaks English and who's incidentally waiting for you to fork over a thousand bucks . . ."

"I'll pay her, don't you worry. Krutch doesn't welsh."

"Why would this nice old lady deny having told you anything about a treasure? Or about having given you a list of names?"

"How do I know? Go ask *her.* I'm telling you she gave me the list, a piece of the picture, and the information that tied them together."

"She says she only gave you the picture."

"She's a liar. Sicilians are liars."

"Okay, Krutch," Brown said, and sighed. "One other thing I'd like to know."

"What's that?"

"I want to know where you were on Monday night when Geraldine Ferguson got killed."

"What? Why the hell do you want to know *that?*"

"Because we'd already told you we struck out on Gerry's safe. And maybe you decided to have a look around her apartment, the way you've had a look around a few other apartments."

"No," Krutch said, and shook his head. "You've got the wrong customer."

"Okay, so tell me where you were."

"I was in bed with Suzanne Endicott."

"You're *always* in bed with Suzanne Endicott, it seems."

"Wouldn't *you* be?" Krutch said, and flashed his brilliant grin.

"And, of course, she'll corroborate that."

"Go ask her. I've got nothing to hide," Krutch said.

"Thanks, partner," Brown said.

When he got back to the squadroom, Carella told him that there had been a call from Bramley Kahn, who had been arraigned, released on bail, and—while awaiting trial—was back selling art at the same old stand. Brown returned his call at once.

"I want to talk a deal," Kahn said.

"I'll be right over," Brown answered.

When he got to the gallery, Kahn was waiting in his office, seated in the old-fashioned swivel chair behind his desk, facing the painting of the nude on the wall opposite. Brown took a seat on one of the leather-and-chrome chairs. Kahn took a long time getting started. Brown waited. At last, Kahn said, "Suppose . . ." and hesitated.

"Yes, suppose what?"

"Suppose I know where Gerry's piece of the picture is?"

"Do you?"

"I'm saying suppose."

"Okay, suppose you do?"

"Suppose I didn't tell you everything I know about that picture?"

"Okay, go ahead, we're still supposing."

"Well, what would it be worth to you?"

"I can't make any promises," Brown said.

"I understand that. But you *could* talk to the district attorney, couldn't you?"

"Oh, sure. He's a very nice fellow, the D.A., always eager for a little chat."

"I've heard that the D.A.'s office is the bargain basement of the law," Kahn said. "Well, I want a bargain."

"Your lawyer pleaded 'Not Guilty' to Assault One, didn't he?"

"That's right."

"Okay, let's suppose you're willing to co-operate, and let's suppose I can catch the D.A.'s ear, and let's suppose he allowed you to plead guilty to a lesser charge, how would that sound to you?"

"A lesser charge like what?"

"Like Assault Two."

"What's the penalty for that?"

"A maximum of five years in prison, or a thousand-dollar fine, or both."

"That's steep," Kahn said.

"The penalty for Assault One is even steeper."

"What is it?"

"A maximum of ten years."

"Yes, but Anatole feels I can win my case."

"Anatole's dreaming. You confessed to the crime in the presence of your own lawyer, four detectives, and a police stenographer. You haven't got a chance in hell of beating this rap, Kahn."

"Still, he feels we can do it."

"In which case, I would suggest that you change your lawyer."

"How about *Third* Degree Assault? Is there such a thing?"

"Yes, there is, but forget it. The D.A. wouldn't even listen to such a suggestion."

"Why not?"

"He's got a sure conviction here. He may not even want to reduce it to Second Degree. It all depends on how valuable your information is. And on whether or not he had a good breakfast on the morning I go to talk to him."

"I think my information is *very* valuable," Kahn said.

"Let me hear it, and I'll tell you how valuable it is."

"First, what's the deal?"

"I told you, I can't make any promises. If I think your information is really worth something, I'll talk to the D.A. and see what he thinks. He may be willing to accept a plea of guilty to Assault Two."

"That sounds very nebulous."

"It's all I've got to sell," Brown said, and shrugged. "Yes or no?"

"Suppose I told you . . ." Kahn said, and hesitated.

"I'm listening."

"Let's start with the picture."

"Okay, let's start with the picture."

"There are eight pieces, right?"

"Right."

"But only seven names on the list."

"Right."

"Suppose I know where that eighth piece went?"

"Let's stop supposing," Brown said. *"Do* you know?"

"Yes."

"Okay, where'd it go?"

"To Alice Bonamico."

"We already know that, Kahn. Her husband gave her half of the list and one piece of the photograph. If that's all you're . . ."

"No, he gave her *two* pieces of the photograph."

"Two," Brown said.

"Two," Kahn repeated.

"How do you know?"

"Gerry tried to bargain with her, remember? But Alice was dealing from a position of strength. Her husband had given his *mistress* only half of the list. But to Alice, his *wife,* he had given the other half of the list plus two pieces of the photo. That can make a woman feel very important."

"Yes, that was very thoughtful of him," Brown said. He was remembering that Irving Krutch claimed to have received half of the list and only one piece of the picture from Lucia Feroglio. If Alice Bonamico had indeed possessed *two* pieces of the picture, why had she willed only *one* of those pieces to her sister? And where was the missing piece now, the eighth piece? He decided to ask Kahn.

"Where *is* that eighth piece now?" he asked.

"I don't know," Kahn said.

"Well, that's certainly very valuable information," Brown said. "When I talk to the D.A., he might even be willing to reduce the charge to Spitting on the Sidewalk, which is only a misdemeanor."

"But I *do* know where Gerry's piece is," Kahn said, unperturbed. "And believe me, it's a *key* piece. I don't think Bonamico realized how important a piece it was, or he wouldn't have entrusted it to a dumb gunsel like D'Amore."

"Okay," Brown said, "where *is* Gerry's piece?"

"Right behind you," Kahn said.

Brown turned and stared at the wall.

"We've already looked in the safe," he said.

"Not in the safe," Kahn said.

"Then where?"

"Give me a hand, will you?" Kahn said, and walked to the painting of the nude. Together, they lifted the painting from the wall, and placed it face-down on the rug. The canvas was backed with what appeared to be brown wrapping paper. Kahn lifted one corner of the backing and plucked a shining black-and-white scrap from where it was wedged between the frame and the canvas.

"*Voilà*," he said, and handed the scrap to Brown.

"Well," Kahn said, "what do you think now?"
"I think you're right," Brown answered. "It *is* a key piece."

It was a key piece because it gave perspective to the photograph. There was no sky, they now realized, because the picture had been taken from *above,* the photographer shooting *down* at what now revealed itself as a road running beside a footpath. The Donald Duck segment of the picture, now that the perspective was defined, showed three benches at the back of the fowl's head, a broken patch in the cement forming the bird's eye, a series of five fence posts running vertically past its bill. The bill jutted out into . . .

Not mud, not cement, not stucco, not fur, but *water.*

Cool, clear water.

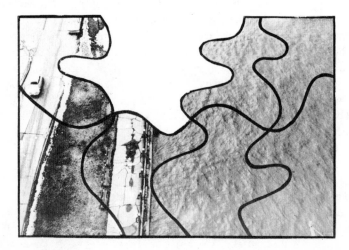

Or, considering the fact that Carmine Bonamico and his inept band had tried to make their escape along the River Road, perhaps water that was *not* quite so clear, perhaps water that was slightly polluted, but water nonetheless, the water of the River Dix that ran along the southern bank of Isola. Carella and Brown had a hurried conversation in the squadroom, and decided between them that Donald Duck should be easy to spot from the air.

He was not all that easy to spot.

They boarded a police helicopter at the heliport downtown and flew above the River Road for close to three hours, up and down its winding length, swooping low wherever a side street entered the road. The upper left-hand corner of the picture indicated just such a side street entering *somewhere,* and they hoped now to find the elusive duck with its telltale eye just below one of those entrances. The footpath with its benches and its guardrail ran the length of the river. There were thirty-four side streets entering the road, spaced at ten-block intervals. Their only hope of finding the *right* side street was to find the broken patch of cement.

But the robbery had taken place six years ago.

And whereas the city was sometimes a trifle slow in repairing broken sections of footpaths, they had done a damn good job on Donald Duck's eye.

Without the missing eighth piece, nobody knew where *nothing* was.

12

You can sometimes solve a mystery by the simple process of elimination, which is admittedly undramatic, but where does it say that a cop has to get hit on the head every day of the week? Cops may be dumb, but not *that* dumb. When everything has already narrowed itself down into the skinny end of the funnel, when nearly everybody's either dead or obviously innocent, then it merely becomes a matter of trying to figure out who is lying and why. There are lots of things cops don't understand, but lies they understand very well.

They don't understand, for example, why thieves will spend so much time and energy devising and executing a crime (with all its attendant risks) when that same amount of time and energy devoted to a legal pursuit would probably net much larger returns in the long run. It was the belief of every detective on the 87th Squad that the *real* motive behind half the crimes being committed in the city was *enjoyment,* plain and simple—the *fun* of playing Cops and Robbers. Forget gain or profit as motivation, forget passion, forget rebellion, it all came down to Cops and Robbers.

What had Carmine Bonamico been doing, if not playing Cops and Robbers? Took his little camera, dear boy, and went out to photograph the River Road from an airplane or something, and then drew his squiggly little lines across the print, and cut it apart, and handed out pieces to his gang, all hush-hush, top-secret, tip-toey, clever-crook stuff—Cops and Robbers. Why the hell hadn't he just whispered the location to each of his hoods, and asked them to whisper it in turn to their friends and loved ones? Ah, but no. That would have taken from the crime one of its essential elements, known to gumshoes far and wide as The Game Aspect. Take the fun out of criminal activity, and all the prisons in the world would be empty. Who can figure crooks? Certainly not cops. They couldn't even figure

why Irving Krutch had had the audacity to come to them for assistance in locating the loot, unless this too was tied in with The Game
Aspect, the sheer enjoyment of playing Cops and Robbers.

They *did* figure, however, that Krutch was not telling them the
truth about his whereabouts on the nights Albert Weinberg and
Geraldine Ferguson were murdered; when a man's lying, it comes
over like a supersonic missile streaking through the atmosphere,
and you don't have to be working for NASA to spot it. Krutch's
alibi, of course, was a broad he'd been laying since the year One,
hardly the most reliable sort of witness to bring to your defense in a
courtroom. But Suzanne Endicott's credibility as a witness was
academic unless they could get Krutch *into* a courtroom. Logical
deduction aside, the fact remained that he claimed to have been in
bed with Suzie while both murders were being committed, and
Suzie backed his story, and it is quite a trick to be out killing people
while you are home in your apartment making love to a sweet li'l ol'
Georgia peach. These days, it was getting more and more difficult
to arrest a person even if you caught him with a hacksaw in his
bloody hands, standing over a dissected corpse. How could you arrest a mustache-twirling villain who had an alibi as long as a penin-
sula?

How indeed?

It was Carella who first got the idea.

He discussed it with Hawes, and Hawes thought it was too risky.
Carella insisted that it was a good idea, considering the fact that
Suzie Endicott was from Georgia. Hawes said he thought Brown
might take offense if they even *suggested* the idea to him, and Carella
said he thought Brown would go along with the idea wholeheartedly.
Hawes protested that the notion was pretty far-out to begin with:
Suzie had been living in the north for at least four years now,
spending half that time in bed with Krutch (to hear her tell it),
and had probably been pretty well assimilated into the culture; it was
a bad idea. Carella informed Hawes that certain prejudices and
stereotypes died very hard deaths, as witness Hawes' own reluctance
to even *broach* the idea to Brown. Hawes took offense at that, saying he was as tolerant a man as ever lived, in fact it was his very
tolerance that *caused* his reluctance, he simply didn't want to offend
Brown by suggesting an idea that probably wouldn't work anyway.
Carella raised his voice and demanded to know how they could
possibly crack Suzie's story; *he* had tried to crack it, *Hawes* had
tried to crack it, the only way they could get to her was to scare hell
out of her. Hawes shouted that Brown's feelings were more im-

portant to him and to the well-being of the squad than solving any goddamn murder case, and Carella shouted back that prejudice was certainly a marvelous thing when a white man couldn't even explore an excellent idea with a Negro for fear of hurting his feelings.

"Okay, *you* ask him," Hawes said.

"I will," Carella answered.

They came out of the Interrogation Room together and walked to where Brown was sitting at his desk, studying the photograph for the seven-hundredth time.

"We've got an idea, Artie," Carella said.

"He's got an idea," Hawes said, "It's *his* idea, Artie."

"What's the idea?" Brown said.

"Well, you know," Carella said, "we're all pretty much agreed on this Krutch character, right?"

"Right."

"I mean, he wants that seven hundred and fifty G's so bad, his hands are turning green. And you can't tell me his *career* has anything to do with it."

"Me neither," Brown said.

"He wants that *money,* period. The minute he gets it, he'll probably take Suzie and head straight for Brazil."

"Okay, how do we get to him?" Brown asked.

"We go to Suzie."

"We've *been* to Suzie," Brown said. *"You* talked to her, *Meyer* talked to her, *Cotton* talked to her. She alibis Krutch right down the line."

"Sure, but she's been sleeping with the guy for four years," Hawes said, still annoyed by the thought.

"Another three years, and they're man and wife in the eyes of the law," Carella said. "You expect her *not* to back his alibis?"

"Okay, let's say she's lying," Brown said.

"Let's say she's lying. Let's say Krutch *did* leave that apartment once to kill Weinberg, and again to kill Gerry Ferguson."

"Okay, let's say it. How we going to prove it?"

"Well, let's say that we drop in on Krutch sometime tonight and ask him a few more questions. Just to keep him busy, you understand? Just to make sure he doesn't climb into the sack with li'l Suzie again."

"Yeah?"

"Yeah, and let's say about two o'clock in the morning, somebody knocks on li'l Suzie's door and starts getting rough with her."

"Come on, Steve, we can't do that," Brown said.

"I don't mean we actually push her around," Carella said.

"I told you he wouldn't buy it," Hawes said.

"I mean we just let her *think* we're getting rough."

"Well, why would she think that?" Brown asked. "If we're *not* going to push her around . . ."

"She's from Georgia," Carella said.

The squadroom was silent. Hawes looked at his shoes.

"Who's going to hit Krutch?" Brown asked.

"I thought Cotton and I might do that."

"And who'll go scare Suzie?"

The squadroom went silent again. The clock on the wall was ticking too loudly.

"Don't tell me," Brown said, and broke into a wide grin. "Man, I love it."

Hawes glanced at Carella uncertainly.

"You'll do it?" Carella said.

"Oh, man, I *love* it," Brown said, and fell into a deliberately broad dialect. "We goan send a big black nigger man to scare our Georgia peach out'n her skin! Oh, man, it's delicious!"

Prejudice is a wonderful thing.

Stereotypes are marvelous.

At two o'clock in the morning, Suzie Endicott opened her door to find that the most terrifying of her Southern fantasies had materialized in the gloom, a Nigra come to rape her in the night, just as her mother had warned her time and again. She started to close the door, but her rapist suddenly shouted, "You jes' hole it right there, Missy. This here's the law! Detective Arthur Brown of d'87th Squad. I got some questions to ast you."

"Wh . . . wh . . . it's . . . the middle of the night," Suzie said.

Brown flashed his shield. "This hunk o' tin here doan respec' no time o' day nor night," he said, and grinned. "You goan let me in, Missy, or does I start causin' a ruckus here?" Suzie hesitated. Brown suddenly wondered if he were playing it too broadly, and then decided he was doing just fine. Without waiting for an answer, he shoved past her into the apartment, threw his fedora onto the hall table, looked around appreciatively, whistled, and said, "Man, this's *some* nice place you got here. Ain't never *been* inside no fancy place like this one."

"Wh . . . wh . . . what did you want to ask me?" Suzie said. She was wearing a robe over her nightgown, and her right hand was clutched tightly into the collar of the robe.

"Well now, ain' no hurry, is there?" Brown asked.

"I . . . I have to go to work in the mor . . . morning," Suzie said. "I . . . I . . . I . . . have to get some sleep," she said, and realized instantly she had made a mistake by even mentioning anything even remotely suggesting bed. "I mean . . ."

"Oh, I *knows* whut you mean," Brown said, and grinned lewdly. "Sit down, Missy."

"Wh . . . what did you want to ask?"

"I *said* sit down! You jes' do whut I tells you to do, okay, an' we goan get along fine. Otherwise . . ."

Suzie sat instantly, tucking the flaps of her robe around her.

"Those're nice legs," Brown said. He narrowed his eyes. "Mighty fine white legs, I can tell you that, honey."

Suzie wet her lips and then swallowed. Brown was suddenly afraid she might pass out cold before he got to the finale of his act. He decided to push on regardless.

"We busted yo' li'l playmate half an hour ago," he said. "So if you're thinkin *he* goan help you, you can jes' f'get it."

"Who? What? What did you say?"

"Irving Krutch, yo' lover boy," Brown said. "You shunt'a lied to us, Missy. That ain't goan sit too well with the D.A."

"I didn't lie to . . . to . . . anybody," Suzie said.

" 'Bout bein' in bed there all the time? 'Bout making love there when two people was being murdered. Tsk, tsk, Missy, them was outright lies. I'm really sprised at you."

"We did, we were, we did do that, we . . ." Suzie started, and realized they were talking about making love, and suddenly looked into Brown's eyes, and saw the fixed, drooling stare of a sex-crazed maniac and wondered how she would ever get out of this alive. She should have listened to her mother who had warned her never to wear a tight skirt walking past any of these people because it was so easy to arouse animal lust in them.

"You in serious trouble," Brown said.

"I didn't . . ."

"Real serious trouble."

". . . lie to anybody, I swear."

"Only one way to get out of that trouble now," Brown said.

"But I didn't . . ."

"Only *one* way, Missy."

". . . really. I didn't lie, really. Really, officer," she heard herself saying to this black man, "officer, I really didn't, I swear. I don't know what Irving told you, but I honestly did not lie to anyone, if anyone was lying, it was him. I had no idea of anything, of it, of anything. I mean that, officer, you can check that out if you want to. I certainly wouldn't lie to the police, not to those nice policemen who . . ."

"Only *one* way to save yo' sweet ass now," Brown said, and saw her face go pale.

"Wh . . . what's that?" Suzie said. *"What* way? What?"

"You can tell d'troof," Brown said, and rose out of his chair to his full monstrous height, muscles bulging, eyes glaring, shoulders heaving, rose like a huge black gorilla, and hulked toward her with his arms dangling at his sides, hands curled like an ape's, towered over her where she sat small and white and trembling on the edge of her chair, and repeated in his most menacing nigger-in-the-alley voice, "You can tell d'troof *now,* Missy, unless you cares to work it out some *other* way!"

"Oh my good Lord Jesus," Suzie shouted, "he left the apartment, he left both times, I don't know where he went, I don't know anything else, if he killed these people, I had nothing to do with it!"

"Thank you, Miss Endicott," Brown said. "Would you put on some clothes now, I'd like you to accompany me to the squadroom."

She stared at him in disbelief. Where had the rapist gone? Who was this polite nuclear physicist standing in his place? And then his charade dawned upon her, and her eyes narrowed, and her lips drew back over her teeth, and she said, "Boy, you say *please* when you ask *me* to go any place."

"Go to *hell,*" Brown said. "Please."

"The rotten bitch," Krutch said.

He could have been talking about Suzie Endicott, but he wasn't. He was railing, instead, against the late Alice Bonamico. The departed gang leader's departed wife, it seemed, had cheated Krutch. In his investigation of the robbery, he had learned from Carmine's widow that she was in possession of "certain documents and photographic segments" purporting to show the hiding place of the N.S.L.A. loot. He had bargained with her for months, and they had finally agreed on a purchase price. She had turned over to him the half of the list in her possession as well as the piece of the photo he had originally shown the police.

"But I didn't know she had yet *another* piece," Krutch said. "I didn't learn that until I read about her will, and contacted her sister. That's when I got *this* piece. The eighth piece of the puzzle. The *important* one. The one that bitch held out on me."

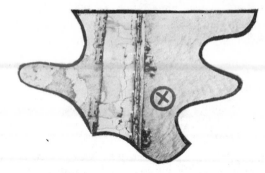

"Which, naturally, you didn't give to us," Brown said.

"Naturally. It shows the exact location of the loot. Do you think I'm an idiot?"

"Why'd you come to us in the first place?"

"I *told* you why. Krutch needed help. Krutch couldn't handle it alone any more. Krutch figured what better way to get help on an investigation than by calling in experts?"

"You got more than you bargained for," Brown said.

"Except from Alice Bonamico, that bitch. I paid her ten thousand dollars for half of the list and a meaningless piece of the picture. Ten thousand bucks! It was every penny I had."

"But, of course, you were going for very big money."

"It was an investment," Krutch said. "Krutch looked upon it as an investment."

"Well," Brown said, "now Krutch can look upon it as a capital loss. Why'd you kill Weinberg?"

"Because you told me he had another piece, and I wanted it. Look, I was running a race with you guys. I knew I was ahead of you because *I* had the piece with the X on it, but suppose you got cute somewhere along the line and refused to show me anything else? I'm in the insurance business, you know. Getting Weinberg's piece was insurance, plain and simple."

"And Gerry Ferguson's?"

"Same thing. Insurance. I went in there looking for it because you'd already told me it wasn't in the safe. So where *else* could it be? Had to be in her apartment, right? I wasn't going to kill her, but she started screaming the minute I came in. I was too close then to let anybody stop me. You don't *know* how close I came to putting this whole thing together. You guys were helping me more than you realized. I almost had it made."

"You've got balls, all right," Brown said, shaking his head. "You come to the police for help in locating the proceeds from a bank robbery. That takes real balls."

"Real *brains,*" Krutch corrected.

"Oh, yes," Brown said.

"It wasn't easy to think this up."

"You'll have plenty of time to do a lot more thinking," Brown said.

"What do you mean?"

"You figure it out."

"In prison, do you mean?" Krutch asked.

"Now you've got the picture," Brown said.

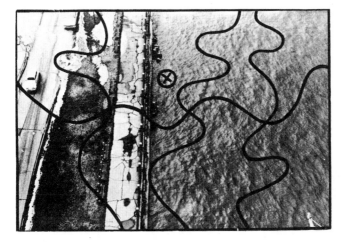

This time, the helicopter ride was a joyous one. For whereas there were thirty-four side streets entering the River Road, only one of those side streets was opposite a twin cluster of offshore rocks. Coincidentally, the rocks were just west of the Calm's Point Bridge, from which vantage point Bonamico must have snapped the picture, standing on the bridge's walkway some fifty feet above the surface of the water. They landed the chopper close to where Donald Duck's eye must have been before the city's Highway Maintenance Department had repaired it, and then they walked toward the rocks and looked down into the filthy waters of the River Dix and saw nothing. Carmine Bonamico's "X" undoubtedly marked the spot, but water pollution triumphed over the naked eye, and there was nary a treasure to be seen. They did not uncover the loot until they dredged the river close to the bank, and found an old leather suitcase, green with slime, water-logged, badly deteriorated. Seven hundred and fifty thousand dollars in good American currency was ensconced in that bag, slightly damp to be sure, but nonetheless negotiable.

It was a good day's pay.

Arthur Brown got home in time for dinner.

His wife met him at the door and said, "Connie's got a fever. I had the doctor here a half-hour ago."

"What'd he say?"

"He thinks it's just the flu. But she's *so* uncomfortable, Artie."

"Did he give her anything?"

"I'm waiting for it now. The drug store said they'd deliver."

"She awake?"

"Yes."

"I'll go talk to her. How're *you?*" he said, and kissed her.

"Forgot what you looked like," Caroline answered.

"Well, here's what I look like," he said and smiled.

"Same old handsome devil," Caroline said.

"That's me," he said, and went into the bedroom.

Connie was propped against the pillows, her eyes wet, her nose running. "Hello, Daddy," she said in her most miserable-sounding voice.

"I thought you were sick," he said.

"I *am,*" she answered.

"You can't be sick," he said, "you look too beautiful." He went to the bed and kissed her on the forehead.

"Oh, Daddy, please be careful," Caroline said, "you'll catch the bug."

"I'll catch him and stomp him right under my foot," Brown said, and grinned.

Connie giggled.

"How would you like me to read you a story?" he asked.

"Yes," she said. "Please."

"What would you like to hear?"

"A good mystery," Connie said. "One of the Nancy Drews."

"One of the Nancy Drews it is," Brown said, and went to the bookcase. He was crouched over, searching the shelves for Connie's favorite, when he heard the urgent shriek of a police siren on the street outside.

"Do you like mysteries, Daddy?" Connie asked.

Brown hesitated a moment before answering. The siren faded into the distant city. He went back to the bed and gently touched his daughter's hair, and wondered again, oddly, if Geraldine Ferguson had ever roller-skated on a city sidewalk. Then he said, "No, honey, I don't care for mysteries too much," and sat on the edge of the bed, and opened the book, and began reading aloud.

FUZZ

The city in these pages is imaginary.
The people, the places are all fictitious.
Only the police routine is based on estab-
lished investigatory technique.

This is for my father-in-law,
HARRY MELNICK,
who inspired *The Heckler,*
and who must therefore take
at least partial blame for this one.

1

OH BOY, what a week.

Fourteen muggings, three rapes, a knifing on Culver Avenue, thirty-six assorted burglaries, and the squadroom was being painted.

Not that the squadroom didn't *need* painting.

Detective Meyer Meyer would have been the first man to admit that the squadroom definitely needed painting. It merely seemed idiotic for the city to decide to paint it now, at the beginning of March, when everything outside was rotten and cold and miserable and dreary, and when you had to keep the windows shut tight because you never could get enough damn heat up in the radiators, and as a result had the stink of turpentine in your nostrils all day long, not to mention two painters underfoot and overhead, both of whom never would have made it in the Sistine Chapel.

"Excuse me," one of the painters said, "could you move that thing?"

"What thing?" Meyer said.

"That thing."

"That thing," Meyer said, almost blowing his cool, "happens to be our Lousy File. *That* thing happens to contain information on known criminals and troublemakers in the precinct, and *that* thing happens to be invaluable to the hard-working detectives of this squad."

"Big deal," the painter said.

"Won't he move it?" the other painter asked.

"You move it," Meyer said. "You're the painters, *you* move it."

"We're not supposed to move nothing," the first painter said.

"We're only supposed to paint," the second painter said.

"I'm not supposed to move things, either," Meyer said. "I'm supposed to detect."

"Okay, so don't move it," the first painter said, "it'll get all full of green paint."

"Put a dropcloth on it," Meyer said.

"We got our dropcloths over there on those desks there," the second painter said, "that's all the dropcloths we got."

"Why is it I always get involved with vaudeville acts?" Meyer asked.

"Huh?" the first painter said.

"He's being wise," the second painter said.

"All I know is I don't plan to move that filing cabinet," Meyer said. "In fact, I don't plan to move *any*thing. You're screwing up the whole damn squadroom, we won't be able to find anything around here for a week after you're gone."

"We do a thorough job," the first painter said.

"Besides, we didn't ask to come," the second painter said. "You think we got nothing better to do than shmear around up here? You think this is an interesting job or something? This is a *boring* job, if you want to know."

"It is, huh?" Meyer said.

"Yeah, it's boring," the second painter said.

"It's boring, that's right," the first painter agreed.

"Everything apple green, you think that's interesting? The ceiling apple green, the walls apple green, the stairs apple green, that's some interesting job, all right."

"We had a job last week at the outdoor markets down on Council Street, *that* was an interesting job."

"That was the most interesting job we ever had," the second painter said. "Every stall was a different pastel color, you know those stalls they got? Well, every one of them was a different pastel color, *that* was a *good* job."

"*This* is a *crappy* job," the first painter said.

"It's boring and it's crappy," the second painter agreed.

"I'm still not moving that cabinet," Meyer said, and the telephone rang. "87th Squad, Detective Meyer," he said into the receiver.

"Is this Meyer Meyer in person?" the voice on the other end asked.

"Who's this?" Meyer asked.

"First please tell me if I'm speaking to Meyer Meyer himself?"

"This is Meyer Meyer himself."

"Oh God, I think I may faint dead away."

"Listen, who . . ."

"This is Sam Grossman."

"Hello, Sam, what's . . ."

"I can't tell you how thrilled I am to be talking to such a famous person," Grossman said.

"Yeah?"

"Yeah."

"Okay, what is it? I don't get it."

"You mean you don't know?"

"No, I don't know. What is it I'm supposed to know?" Meyer asked.

"I'm sure you'll find out," Grossman said.

"There's nothing I hate worse than a mystery," Meyer said, "so why don't you just tell me what you're talking about and save me a lot of trouble?"

"Ah-ha," Grossman said.

"You I need today," Meyer said, and sighed.

"Actually, I'm calling about a man's sports jacket, size thirty-eight, color red-and-blue plaid, label Tom's Town and Country, analysis of suspect stain on the left front flap requested. Know anything about it?"

"I requested the test," Meyer said.

"You got a pencil handy?"

"Shoot."

"Blood negative, semen negative. Seems to be an ordinary kitchen stain, grease or oil. You want us to break it down?"

"No, that won't be necessary."

"This belong to a rape suspect?"

"We've had three dozen rape suspects in here this week. We also have two painters."

"I beg your pardon?"

"Forget it. Is that all?"

"That's all. It certainly was a pleasure talking to you, Mr. Meyer Meyer, you have no idea how thrilled I am."

"Listen, what the hell . . . ?" Meyer started, but Grossman hung up. Meyer held the receiver in his hand a moment longer, looking at it peculiarly, and then put it back onto the cradle. He noticed that there were several spatters of apple green paint on the black plastic. "Goddamn slobs," he muttered under his breath, and one of the painters said, "What?"

"Nothing."

"I thought you said something."

"Listen, what department are you guys from, anyway?" Meyer asked.

"Public Works," the first painter said.

"Maintenance and Repair," the second painter said.

"Whyn't you come paint this damn place last summer, instead of now when all the windows are closed?"

"Why? What's the matter?"

"It stinks in here, that's what's the matter," Meyer said.

"It stunk in here even before we got here," the first painter said, which was perhaps true. Meyer sniffed disdainfully, turned his back on the two men, and tried to locate the filing cabinet containing last week's D.D. reports, which cabinet seemed to have vanished from sight.

If there was one thing (and there were *many* things) Meyer could not abide, it was chaos. The squadroom was in a state of utter, complete, and total chaos. Stepladders, dropcloths, newspapers, closed paint cans, open paint cans, used paint brushes, clean paint brushes, cans of turpentine and cans of thinner, mixing sticks, color samples (all in various lovely shades of apple green), rollers, rolling trays, rolls of masking tape, coveralls, stained rags were strewn, thrown, draped, scattered, leaning against, lying upon, spread over and balanced precariously on desks, cabinets, floors, walls, water coolers, window sills, and anything inanimate. (Yesterday, the painters had almost thrown a dropcloth over the inert form of Detective Andy Parker who was, as usual asleep in the swivel chair behind his desk, his feet propped up on an open drawer.) Meyer stood in the midst of this disorder like the monument to patience he most certainly was, a sturdy man with china blue eyes and a bald head, speckled now (he didn't even realize it) with apple green paint. There was a pained look on his round face, his shoulders slumped with fatigue, he seemed disoriented and dis-combobulated, and he didn't know where the hell anything *was!* Chaos, he thought, and the telephone rang again.

He was standing closest to Carella's desk, so he groped around under the dropcloth for the ringing telephone, came away with a wide apple green stain on his jacket sleeve, and bounded across the room to the phone on his own desk. Swearing, he lifted the receiver.

"87th Squad, Detective Meyer," he said.

"Parks Commissioner Cowper will be shot to death tomorrow night unless I receive five thousand dollars before noon," a man's voice said. "More later."

"What?" Meyer said.

The line went dead.

He looked at his watch. It was four-fifteen P.M.

At four-thirty that afternoon, when Detective Steve Carella got to the squadroom, Lieutenant Byrnes asked him to come to his office for a moment. He was sitting behind his desk in the two-windowed room, puffing on a cigar and looking very much like a boss (which he was) in his gray pin-striped suit, a shade darker than his close-cropped hair, a black-and-gold silk rep tie on his white shirt (tiny spatter of apple green on one cuff), college ring with maroon stone on his right ring finger, wedding band on his left. He asked Carella if he wanted a cup of coffee, and Carella said yes, and Byrnes buzzed Miscolo in the Clerical Office and asked him to bring in another cup of coffee, and then asked Meyer to fill Carella in on the telephone call. It took Meyer approximately ten seconds to repeat the content of the conversation.

"Is that it?" Carella asked.

"That's it."

"Mmm."

"What do you think, Steve?" Byrnes asked.

Carella was sitting on the edge of Byrnes' scarred desk, a tall slender man who looked like a vagrant at the moment because as soon as it got dark he would take to the streets, find himself an alley or a doorway and lie there reeking of wine and hoping somebody would set fire to him. Two weeks ago, a *real* vagrant had been set ablaze by some fun-loving youngsters, and last week another bum had supplied fuel for a second bonfire, a fatal one this time. So Carella had been spending his nights lying in assorted doorways simulating drunkenness and wishing for arson. He had not shaved for three days. There was a bristly stubble on his jaw, the same color as his brown hair, but growing in sparsely and patchily and giving his face a somewhat incomplete look, as though it had been hastily sketched by an inexpert artist. His eyes were brown (he liked to think of them as penetrating), but they appeared old and faded now through association with the scraggly beard and the layers of unadulterated dirt he had allowed to collect on his forehead and his cheeks. What appeared to be a healing cut ran across the bridge of his nose, collodion and vegetable dye skillfully applied to resemble congealing blood and pus and corruption. He also looked as if he had lice. He made Byrnes a little itchy. He made everybody in the room a little itchy. He blew his nose before answering the lieutenant's question, and the handkerchief he took from the back pocket of his greasy pants looked as if it had been fished from a nearby sewer. He blew his fluidly (there's such a thing as carrying an impersonation *too* far, Meyer thought), replaced the handkerchief in his trouser pocket, and then said, "He ask to talk to anyone in particular?"

"Nope, just began talking the minute I said who I was."

"Could be a crank," Carella said.

"Could be."

"Why *us?*" Byrnes said.

It was a good question. Assuming the man was *not* a crank, and assuming he *did* plan to kill the commissioner of parks unless he got his five thousand dollars by noon tomorrow, why call the Eight-Seven? There were a great many squadrooms in this fair city, none of which (it was safe to assume) were in the midst of being painted that first week in March, all of which contained detectives every bit as hard-working and determined as the stalwart fellows who gathered together now to sip their afternoon beverages and while away the deepening hours, all of whom doubtless knew the commissioner of parks as intimately as did these very minions of the law—so why the Eight-Seven?

A good question. Like most good questions, it was not immediately answered. Miscolo came in with a cup of coffee, asked Carella when he planned to take a bath, and then went back to his clerical duties. Carella picked up the coffee cup in a filth-encrusted hand, brought it to his cracked and peeling lips, sipped at it, and then said, "We ever having anything to do with Cowper?"

"How do you mean?"

"I don't know. Any special assignments, anything like that?"

"Not to my recollection," Byrnes said. "Only thing I can think of is when he spoke at that P.B.A. thing, but every cop in the city was invited to that one."

"It must be a crank," Carella said.

"Could be," Meyer said again.

"Did he sound like a kid?" Carella asked.

"No, he sounded like a grown man."

"Did he say when he'd call again?"

"No. All he said was 'More later.' "

"Did he say when or where you were supposed to deliver the money?"

"Nope."

"Did he say where you were supposed to *get* it?"

"Nope."

"Maybe he expects us to take up a collection," Carella said.

"Five grand is only five hundred and fifty dollars less than I make in a year," Meyer said.

"Sure, but he's undoubtedly heard how generous the bulls of the 87th are."

"I admit he sounds like a crank," Meyer said. "Only one thing bothers me about what he said."

"What's that?"

"Shot to death. I don't like that, Steve. Those words scare me."

"Yeah. Well," Carella said, "why don't we see if he calls again, okay? Who's relieving?"

"Kling and Hawes should be in around five."

"Who's on the team?" Byrnes asked.

"Willis and Brown. They're relieving on post."

"Which case?"

"Those car snatches. They're planted on Culver and Second."

"You think it's a crank, Meyer?"

"It could be. We'll have to see."

"Should we call Cowper?"

"What for?" Carella said. "This may turn out to be nothing. No sense alarming him."

"Okay," Byrnes said. He looked at his watch, rose, walked to the hatrack in the corner, and put on his overcoat. "I promised Harriet I'd take her shopping, the stores are open late tonight. I should be home around nine if anybody wants to reach me. Who'll be catching?"

"Kling."

"Tell him I'll be home around nine, will you?"

"Right."

"I hope it's a crank," Byrnes said, and went out of the office.

Carella sat on the edge of the desk, sipping his coffee. He looked very tired. "How does it feel to be famous?" he asked Meyer.

"What do you mean?"

"Carella looked up. "Oh, I guess you don't know yet."

"Don't know *what* yet?"

"About the book."

"What book?"

"Somebody wrote a book."

"So?"

"It's called *Meyer Meyer.*"

"What?"

"Yeah. *Meyer Meyer.* It was reviewed in today's paper."

"Who? What do you mean? Meyer *Meyer,* you mean?"

"It got a nice review."

"Meyer Meyer?" Meyer said. "That's *my* name."

"Sure."

"He can't do that?"

"She. A woman."

"Who?"

"Her name's Helen Hudson."

"She can't do that!"

"She's already done it."

"Well, she *can't.* I'm a *person,* you can't go naming some character after a *person."* He frowned and then looked at Carella suspiciously. "Are you putting me on?"

"Nope, God's honest truth."

"Is this guy supposed to be a cop?"

"No, I think he's a teacher."

"A *teacher,* Jesus Christ!"

"At a university."

"She can't do that!" Meyer said again. "Is he bald?"

"I don't know. He's short and plump, the review said."

"Short and plump! She can't use my name for a short plump person. I'll sue her."

"So sue her," Carella said.

"You think I won't? Who published that goddamn book?"

"Dutton."

"Okay!" Meyer said, and took a pad from his jacket pocket. He wrote swiftly on a clean white page, slammed the pad shut, dropped it to the floor as he was putting it back into his pocket, swore, stooped to pick it up, and then looked at Carella plaintively and said, "After all, *I* was here first."

The second call came at ten minutes to eleven that night. It was taken by Detective Bert Kling, who was catching, and who had been briefed on the earlier call before Meyer left the squadroom.

"87th Squad," he said, "Kling here."

"You've undoubtedly decided by now that I'm a crank," the man's voice said. "I'm not."

"Who is this?" Kling asked, and motioned across the room for Hawes to pick up the extension.

"I was quite serious about what I promised," the man said. "Parks Commissioner Cowper will be shot to death sometime tomorrow night unless I receive five thousand dollars by noon. This is how I want it. Have you got a pencil?"

"Mister, why'd you pick on *us?*" Kling asked.

"For sentimental reasons," the man said, and Kling could have sworn he was smiling on the other end of the line. "Pencil ready?"

"Where do you expect us to get five thousand dollars?"

"Entirely your problem," the man said. *"My* problem is killing Cowper if you fail to deliver. Do you want this information?"

"Go ahead," Kling said, and glanced across the room to where Hawes sat hunched over the other phone. Hawes nodded.

"I want the money in singles, need I mention they must be unmarked?"

"Mister, do you know what extortion is?" Kling asked suddenly.

"I know what it is," the man said. "Don't try keeping me on the line. I plan to hang up long before you can effect a trace."

"Do you know the penalty for extortion?" Kling asked, and the man hung up.

"Son of a bitch," Kling said.

"He'll call back. We'll be ready next time," Hawes said.

"We can't trace it through automatic equipment, anyway."

"We can try."

"What'd he say?"

"He said 'sentimental reasons.' "

"That's what I thought he said. "What's that supposed to mean?"

"Search me," Hawes said, and went back to his desk, where he had spread a paper towel over the dropcloth, and where he had been drinking tea from a cardboard container and eating a cheese Danish before the telephone call interrupted him.

He was a huge man, six feet two inches tall and weighing two hundred pounds, some ten pounds more than was comfortable for him. He had blue eyes and a square jaw with a cleft chin. His hair was red, except for a streak over his left temple where he had once been knifed and where the hair had curiously grown in white after the wound healed. He had a straight unbroken nose, and a good mouth with a wide lower lip. Sipping his tea, munching his Danish, he looked like a burly Captain Ahab who had somehow been trapped in a civil service job. A gun butt protruded from the holster under his coat as he leaned over the paper towel and allowed the Danish crumbs to fall onto it. The gun was a big one, as befitted the size of the man, a Smith & Wesson .357 Magnum, weighing 44½ ounces, and capable of putting a hole the size of a baseball in your head if you happened to cross the path of Cotton

Hawes on a night when the moon was full. He was biting into the Danish when the telephone rang again.

"87th Squad, Kling here."

"The penalty for extortion," the man said, "is imprisonment not exceeding fifteen years. Any other questions?"

"Listen . . ." Kling started.

"*You* listen," the man said. "I want five thousand dollars in unmarked singles. I want them put into a metal lunch pail, and I want the pail taken to the third bench on the Clinton Street footpath into Grover Park. More later," he said, and hung up.

"We're going to play Fits and Starts, I see," Kling said to Hawes.

"Yeah. Shall we call Pete?"

"Let's wait till we have the whole picture," Kling said, and sighed and tried to get back to typing up his report. The phone did not ring again until eleven-twenty. When he lifted the receiver, he recognized the man's voice at once.

"To repeat," the man said, "I want the lunch pail taken to the third bench on the Clinton Street footpath into Grover Park. If the bench is watched, if your man is not alone, the pail will not be picked up, and the commissioner will be killed."

"You want five grand left on a park bench?" Kling asked.

"You've got it," the man said, and hung up.

"You think that's all of it?" Kling asked Hawes.

"I don't know," Hawes said. He looked up at the wall clock. "Let's give him till midnight. If we don't get another call by then, we'll ring Pete."

"Okay," Kling said.

He began typing again. He typed hunched over the machine, using a six-finger system that was uniquely his own, typing rapidly and with a great many mistakes, overscoring or erasing as the whim struck him, detesting the paperwork that went into police work, wondering why anyone would want a metal pail left on a park bench where any passing stranger might pick it up, cursing the decrepit machine provided by the city, and then wondering how anyone could have the unmitigated gall to demand five thousand dollars *not* to commit a murder. He frowned as he worked, and because he was the youngest detective on the squad, with a face comparatively unravaged by the pressures of his chosen profession, the only wrinkle in evidence was the one caused by the frown, a deep cutting ridge across his smooth forehead. He was a blond man, six feet tall, with hazel eyes and an open countenance. He wore a yellow sleeveless pullover, and his brown sports jacket was draped over the back of his chair. The Colt .38 Detective's Special he usually wore clipped to his belt was in its holster in the top drawer of his desk.

He took seven calls in the next half-hour, but none of them were from the man who had threatened to kill Cowper. He was finishing his report, a routine listing of the persons interrogated in a mugging on Ainsley Avenue, when the telephone rang again. He reached for the receiver automatically. Automatically, Hawes lifted the extension.

"Last call tonight," the man said. "I want the money before noon tomorrow. There are more than one of us, so don't attempt to arrest the man who picks it up or the commissioner will be killed. If the lunch pail is empty, or if it contains paper scraps or phony bills or marked bills, or if for any reason or by any circumstance the money is not on that bench before noon tomorrow, the plan to kill the commissioner will go into effect. If you have any questions, ask them now."

"You don't really expect us to hand you five thousand dollars on a silver platter, do you?"

"No, in a lunch pail," the man said, and again Kling had the impression he was smiling.

"I'll have to discuss this with the lieutenant," Kling said.

"Yes, and he'll doubtless have to discuss it with the parks commissioner," the man said.

"Is there any way we can reach you?" Kling asked, taking a wild gamble, thinking the man might hastily and automatically reveal his home number or his address.

"You'll have to speak louder," the man said. "I'm a little hard of hearing."

"I said is there any way . . ."

And the man hung up.

The bitch city can intimidate you sometimes by her size alone, but when she works in tandem with the weather she can make you wish you were dead. Cotton Hawes wished he was dead on that Tuesday, March 5. The temperature as recorded at the Grover Park Lake at seven A.M. that morning was twelve degrees above zero, and by nine A.M.—when he started onto the Clinton Street footpath—it had risen only two degrees to stand at a frigid fourteen above. A strong harsh wind was blowing off the River Harb to the north, racing untrammeled through the narrow north-south corridor leading directly to the path. His red hair whipped fitfully about his hatless head, the tails of his overcoat were flat against the backs of his legs. He was wearing gloves and carrying a black lunch pail in his left hand. The third button of his overcoat, waist high, was open, and the butt of his Magnum rested just behind the gaping flap, ready for a quick right-handed, spring-assisted draw.

The lunch pail was empty.

They had awakened Lieutenant Byrnes at five minutes to twelve the night before, and advised him of their subsequent conversations with the man they now referred to as The Screwball. The lieutenant had mumbled a series of grunts into the telephone and then said, "I'll be right down," and then asked what time it was. They told him it was almost midnight. He grunted again, and hung up. When he got to the squadroom, they filled him in more completely, and it was decided to call the parks commissioner to apprise him of the threat against his life, and to discuss any possible action with him. The parks commissioner looked at his bedside clock the moment the phone rang and immediately informed Lieutenant Byrnes that it was half past midnight, wasn't this something that could wait until morning?

Byrnes cleared his throat and said, "Well, someone says he's going to shoot you."

The parks commissioner cleared his throat and said, "Well, why didn't you say so?"

The situation was ridiculous.

The parks commissioner had never heard of a more ridiculous situation, why this man had to be an absolute maniac to assume anyone would pay him five thousand dollars on the strength of a few phone calls. Byrnes agreed that the situation was ridiculous, but that nonetheless a great many crimes in this city were committed daily by misguided or unprincipled people, some of whom were doubtless screwballs, but sanity was not a prerequisite for the successful perpetration of a criminal act.

The situation was unthinkable.

The parks commissioner had never heard of a more unthinkable situation, he couldn't even understand why they were bothering him with what were obviously the rantings of some kind of lunatic. Why didn't they simply forget the entire matter?

"Well," Byrnes said, "I hate to behave like a television cop, sir, I would really *rather* forget the entire thing, as you suggest, but the possibility exists that there *is* a plan to murder you, and in all good conscience I cannot ignore that possibility, not without discussing it first with you."

"Well, you've discussed it with me," the parks commissioner said, "and I say forget it."

"Sir," Byrnes said, "we would like to try to apprehend the man who picks up the lunch pail, and we would also like to supply you with police protection tomorrow night. Had you planned on leaving the house tomorrow night?"

The parks commissioner said that Byrnes could do whatever he thought fit in the matter of apprehending the man who picked up the lunch pail, but that he did indeed plan on going out tomorrow night, was in fact invited by the mayor to attend a performance of Beethoven's *Eroica* given by the Philharmonic at the city's recently opened music and theater complex near Remington Circle, and he did not want or need police protection.

Byrnes said, "Well, sir, let's see what results we have with the lunch pail, we'll get back to you."

"Yes, get back to me," the parks commissioner said, "but not in the middle of the night again, okay?" and hung up.

At five A.M. on Tuesday morning while it was still dark, Detectives Hal Willis and Arthur Brown drank two fortifying cups of coffee in the silence of the squadroom, donned foul-weather gear requisitioned from an Emergency Squad truck, clipped on their holsters, and went out onto the arctic tundra to begin a lonely surveillance of the third bench on the Clinton Street footpath into Grover Park. Since most of the park's paths meandered from north to south and naturally had entrances on either end, they thought at first there might be some confusion concerning the Clinton Street footpath. But a look at the map on the precinct wall showed that there was only one entrance to this particular path, which began on Grover Avenue, adjacent to the park, and then wound through the park to end at the band shell near the lake. Willis and Brown planted themselves on a shelf of rock overlooking the suspect third bench, shielded from the path by a stand of naked elms. It was very cold. They did not expect action, of course, until Hawes dropped the lunch pail where specified, but they could hardly take up posts after the event, and so it had been Byrnes' brilliant idea to send them out before anyone watching the bench might observe them. They did windmill exercises with their arms, they stamped their feet, they continuously pressed the palms of their hands against portions of their faces that seemed to be going, the telltale whiteness of frostbite appearing suddenly and frighteningly in the bleak early morning hours. Neither of the two men had ever been so cold in his life.

Cotton Hawes was almost, but not quite, as cold when he entered the park at nine A.M. that morning. He passed two people on his way to the bench. One of them was an old man in a black overcoat, walking swiftly toward the subway kiosk on Grover Avenue. The other was a girl wearing a mink coat over a long pink nylon night-gown that flapped dizzily about her ankles, walking a white poodle wearing a red wool vest. She smiled at Hawes as he went by with his lunch pail.

The third bench was deserted.

Hawes took a quick look around and then glanced up and out of the park to the row of apartment buildings on Grover Avenue. A thousand windows reflected the early morning sun. Behind any one of those windows, there might have been a man with a pair of binoculars and a clear unobstructed view of the bench. He put the lunch pail on one end of the bench, moved it to the other end, shrugged, and relocated it in the exact center of the bench. He took another look around, feeling really pretty stupid, and then walked out of the park and back to the office. Detective Bert Kling was sitting at his desk, monitoring the walkie-talkie operated by Hal Willis in the park.

"How you doing down there?" Kling asked.

"We're freezing our asses off," Willis replied.

"Any action yet?"

"You think anybody's crazy enough to be out in this weather?" Willis said.

"Cheer up," Kling said, "I hear the boss is sending you both to Jamaica when this is over."

"Fat Chance Department," Willis said. "Hold it!"

There was silence in the squadroom. Hawes and Kling waited. At last, Willis' voice erupted from the speaker on Kling's box.

"Just a kid," Willis said. "Stopped at the bench, looked over the lunch pail, and then left it right where it was."

"Stay with it," Kling said.

"We have to stay with it," Brown's voice cut in. "We're frozen solid to this goddamn rock."

There were people in the park now.

They ventured into the bitch city tentatively, warned by radio and television forecasters, further cautioned by the visual evidence of thermometers outside apartment windows, and the sound of the wind whipping beneath the eaves of old buildings, and the touch of the frigid blast that attacked any exploratory hand thrust outdoors for just an instant before a window slammed quickly shut again.

They dressed with no regard to the dictates of fashion, the men wearing ear muffs and bulky mufflers, the women bundled into layers of sweaters and fur-lined boots, wearing woolen scarves to protect their heads and ears, rushing at a quick trot through the park, barely glancing at the bench or the black lunch pail sitting in the center of it. In a city notorious for its indifference, the citizens were more obviously withdrawn now, hurrying past each other without so much as eyes meeting, insulating themselves, becoming tight private cocoons that defied the cold. Speech might have made them more vulnerable, opening the mouth might have released the heat they had been storing up inside, commiseration would never help to diminish the wind that tried to cut them down in the streets, the saberslash wind that blew in off the river and sent newspapers wildly soaring into the air, fedoras wheeling into the gutter. Speech was a precious commodity that cold March day.

In the park, Willis and Brown silently watched the bench.

The painters were in a garrulous mood.

"What have you got going, a stakeout?" the first painter asked.

"Is that what the walkie-talkie's for?" the second painter asked.

"Is there gonna be a bank holdup?"

"Is that why you're listening to that thing?"

"Shut up," Kling said encouragingly.

The painters were on their ladders, slopping apple green paint over everything in sight.

"We painted the D.A.'s office once," the first painter said.

"They were questioning this kid who stabbed his mother forty-seven times."

"Forty-*seven* times."

"In the belly, the head, the breasts, everyplace."

"With an icepick."

"He was guilty as sin."

"He said he did it to save her from the Martians."

"A regular bedbug."

"Forty-*seven* times."

"How could that save her from the Martians?" the second painter said.

"Maybe Martians don't like ladies with icepick holes in them," the first painter said, and burst out laughing. The second painter guffawed with him. Together, they perched on their ladders, helpless with laughter, limply holding brushes that dripped paint on the newspapers spread on the squadroom floor.

The man entered the park at ten A.M.

He was perhaps twenty-seven years old, with a narrow cold-pinched face, his lips drawn tight against the wind, his eyes watering. He wore a beige car coat, the collar pulled up against the back of his neck, buttoned tight around a green wool muffler at his throat. His hands were in the slash pockets of the coat. He wore brown corduroy trousers, the wale cut diagonally, and brown high-topped workman's shoes. He came onto the Clinton Street footpath swiftly, without looking either to the right or the left, walked immediately and directly to the third bench on the path, picked up the lunch pail, tucked it under his arm, put his naked hand back into his coat pocket, wheeled abruptly, and was starting out of the park again, when a voice behind him said, "Hold it right there, Mac."

"He turned to see a tall burly Negro wearing what looked like a blue astronaut's suit. The Negro was holding a big pistol in his right hand. His left hand held a wallet which fell open to reveal a gold and blue shield.

"Police officer," the Negro said. "We want to talk to you."

2

MIRANDA-ESCOBEDO sounds like a Mexican bullfighter.

It is not.

It is the police shorthand for two separate Supreme Court decisions. These decisions, together, lay down the ground rules for the interrogation of suspects, and cops find them a supreme pain in the ass. There is not one working cop in the United States who thinks Miranda-Escobedo is a good idea. They are all fine Americans, these cops, and are all very concerned with the rights of the individual in a free society, but they do not like Miranda-Escobedo because they feel it makes their job more difficult. Their job is crime prevention.

Since the cops of the 87th had taken a suspect into custody and intended to question him, Miranda-Escobedo immediately came into play. Captain Frick, who was in charge of the entire precinct, had issued a bulletin to his men shortly after the Supreme Court decision in 1955, a flyer printed on green paper and advising every cop in the precinct, uniformed and plainclothes, on the proper interrogation of criminal suspects. Most of the precinct's uniformed cops carried the flyer clipped inside their notebooks where it was handy for reference whenever they needed it. The detectives, on the other hand, normally questioned more people than their uniformed colleagues, and had committed the rules to memory. They used them now with easy familiarity, while continuing to look upon them with great distaste.

"In keeping with the Supreme Court decision in *Miranda v. Arizona,*" Hal Willis said, "we're required to advise you of your rights, and that's what I'm doing now. First, you have the right to remain silent if you choose, do you understand that?"

"I do."

"Do you also understand that you need not answer any police questions?"

"I do."

"And do you also understand that if you *do* answer questions, your answers may be used as evidence against you?"

"Yes, I understand."

"I must also inform you that you have the right to consult with an attorney before or during police questioning, do you understand that?"

"I understand."

"And if you decide to exercise that right but do not have the funds with which to hire counsel, you are entitled to have a lawyer appointed without cost, to consult with him before or during questioning. Is that clear?"

"Yes."

"You understand all of your rights as I have just explained them to you?"

"I do."

"Are you willing to answer questions without the presence of an attorney?"

"Gee, I don't know," the suspect said. "Should I?"

Willis and Brown looked at each other. They had thus far played Miranda-Escobedo by the book, warning the suspect of his privilege against self-incrimination, and warning him of his right to counsel. They had done so in explicit language, and not by merely making references to the Fifth Amendment. They had also made certain that the suspect understood his rights before asking him whether or not he wished to waive them. The green flyer issued by Captain Frick had warned that it was not sufficient for an officer simply to give the warnings and then proceed with an interrogation. It was necessary for the prisoner to *say* he understood, and that he was willing to answer questions without counsel. Only then would the court find that he had waived his constitutional rights.

In addition, however, the flyer had warned all police officers to exercise great care in avoiding language which could later be used by defense attorneys to charge that the officer had "threatened, tricked, or cajoled" the defendant into waiving. The officer was specifically cautioned against advising the suspect not to bother with a lawyer, or even implying that he'd be better off without a lawyer. He was, in short, supposed to inform the defendant of his privilege against self-incrimination and his right to counsel, period. Both Willis and Brown knew that they could not answer the suspect's question. If either of the two had advised him to answer questions without an attorney present, any confession they thereafter took would be inadmissible in court. If, on the other hand, they advised him *not* to answer questions, or advised him to consult with an attorney, their chances of getting a confession would be substantially lessened.

So Willis said, "I've explained your rights, and it would be improper for me to give you any advice. The decision is yours."

"Gee, I don't know," the man said.

"Well, think it over," Willis said.

The young man thought it over. Neither Willis nor Brown said a word. They knew that if their suspect refused to answer questions, that was it, the questioning would have to stop then and there. They also knew that if he began answering questions and suddenly decided he didn't want to go on with the interrogation, they would have to stop immediately, no matter what language he used to express his wishes—"I claim my rights," or "I don't want to say nothing else," or "I demand a mouthpiece."

So they waited.

"I got nothing to hide," the young man said at last.

"Are you willing to answer questions without the presence of an attorney?" Willis asked again.

"I am."

"What's your name?" Willis said.

"Anthony La Bresca."

"Where do you live, Anthony?"

"In Riverhead."

"Where in Riverhead, Anthony?" Brown said.

Both detectives had automatically fallen into the first-name basis of interrogation that violated only human dignity and not human rights, having nothing whatever to do with Miranda-Escobedo, but having everything in the world to do with the psychological unsettling of a prisoner. Call a man by his first name without allowing him the return courtesy and:

(a) You immediately make him a subordinate, and

(b) You instantly rob the familiarity of any friendly connotation, charging its use with menace instead.

"Where in Riverhead, Anthony?" Willis said.

"1812 Johnson."

"Live alone?"

"No, with my mother."

"Father dead?"

"They're separated."

"How old are you, Anthony?"

"Twenty-six."

"What do you do for a living?"

"I'm unemployed at the moment."

"What do you normally do?"

"I'm a construction worker."

"When's the last time you worked?"

"I was laid off last month."

"Why?"

"We completed the job."

"Haven't worked since?"

"I've been looking for work."

"But didn't have any luck, right?"

"That's right."

"Tell us about the lunch pail."

"What about it?"

"Well, what's *in* it, first of all?"

"Lunch, I guess," La Bresca said.

"Lunch, huh?"

"Isn't that what's usually in lunch pails?"

"We're asking *you,* Anthony."

"Yeah, lunch," La Bresca said.

"Did you call this squadroom yesterday?" Brown asked.

"No."

"How'd you know where that lunch pail would be?"

"I was told it would be there."

"Who told you?"

"This guy I met."

"What guy?"

"At the employment agency."

"Go on," Willis said, "let's hear it."

"I was waiting on line outside this employment agency on Ainsley, they handle a lot of construction jobs, you know, and that's where I got my last job from, so that's where I went back today. And this guy is standing on line with me, and all of a sudden he snaps his fingers and says, 'Jesus, I left my lunch in the park.' So I didn't say nothing, so he looks at me and says, 'How do you like that, I left my lunch on a park bench.' So I said that's a shame, and all, I sympathized with him, you know. What the hell, poor guy left his lunch on a park bench."

"So then what?"

"So he tells me he would run back into the park to get it, except he has a bum leg. So he asks me if I'd go get it for him."

"So naturally you said yes," Brown said. "A strange guy asks you to walk all the way from Ainsley Avenue over to Grover and into the park to pick up his lunch pail, so naturally you said yes."

"No, naturally I said no," La Bresca said.

"Then what were you you doing in the park?"

"Well, we got to talking a little, and he explained how he got his leg hurt in World War II fighting against the Germans, picked up shrapnel from a mortar explosion, he had a pretty rough deal, you know?"

"So naturally you decided to go for the lunch pail after all."

"No, naturally I still didn't decide to do nothing."

"So how *did* you finally end up in the park?"

"That's what I've been trying to tell you."

"You took pity on this man, right? Because he had a bum leg, and because it was so cold outside, right?" Willis said.

"Well, yes and no."

"You didn't want him to have to walk all the way to the park, right?" Brown said.

"Well, yes and no. I mean, the guy was a stranger, why the hell should I care if he walked to the park or not?"

"Look, Anthony," Willis said, beginning to lose his temper, and trying to control himself, reminding himself that it was exceptionally difficult to interrogate suspects these days of Miranda-Escobedo when a man could simply refuse to answer at any given moment, Sorry, boys, no more questions, just shut your dear little flatfoot mouths or run the risk of blowing your case. "Look, Anthony," he said more gently, "we're only trying to find out how *you* happened to walk to the park and go directly to the third bench to pick up that lunch pail.

"I know," La Bresca said.

"You met a disabled war veteran, right?"

"Right."

"And he told you he left his lunch pail in the park."

"Well, he didn't say lunch *pail* at first. He just said *lunch.*"

"When did he say lunch *pail?*"

"After he gave me the five bucks."

"Oh, he offered you five dollars to go get his lunch pail, is that it?"

"He didn't offer it to me, he *handed* it to me."

"He handed you five bucks and said, 'Would you go get my lunch pail for me?'"

"That's right. And he told me it would be on the third bench in the park, on the Clinton Street footpath. Which is right where it was."

"What were you supposed to do with this lunch pail after you got it?"

"Bring it back to him. He was holding my place in line."

"Mm-huh," Brown said.

"What's so important about that lunch pail, anyway?" La Bresca asked.

"Nothing," Willis said. "Tell us about this man. What did he look like?"

"Ordinary-looking guy."

"How old would you say he was?"

"Middle thirties, thirty-five, something like that."

"Tall, short, or average?"

"Tall. About six feet, I would say, give or take."

"What about his build? Heavy, medium, or slight?"

"He was built nice. Good shoulders."

"Heavy?"

"Husky, I would say. A good build."

"What color was his hair?"

"Blond."

"Was he wearing a mustache or a beard?"

"No."

"What color were his eyes, did you notice?"

"Blue."

"Did you notice any scars or identifying marks?"

"No."

"Tattoos?"

"No."

"What sort of voice did he have?"

"Average voice. Not too deep. Just average. A good voice."

"Any accent or regional dialect?"

"No."

"What was he wearing?"

"Brown overcoat, brown gloves."

"Suit?"

"I couldn't see what he had on under the coat. I mean, he was wearing pants, naturally, but I didn't notice what color they were, and I couldn't tell you whether they were part of a suit or whether . . ."

"Fine, was he wearing a hat?"

"No hat."

"Glasses?"

"No glasses."

"Anything else you might have noticed about him?"

"Yeah," La Bresca said.

"What?"

"He was wearing a hearing aid."

The employment agency was on the corner of Ainsley Avenue and Clinton Street, five blocks north of the entrance to the park's Clinton Street footpath. On the off-chance that the man wearing the hearing aid would still be waiting for La Bresca's return, they checked out a sedan and drove over from the station house. La Bresca sat in the back of the car, willing and eager to identify the man if he was still there.

There was a line of men stretching halfway around the corner of Clinton, burly men in work clothes and caps, hands thrust into coat pockets, faces white with cold, feet moving incessantly as they shuffled and jigged and tried to keep warm.

"You'd think they were giving away dollar bills up there," La Bresca said. "Actually, they charge you a whole week's pay. They got good jobs, though. The last one they got me paid real good, and it lasted eight months."

"Do you see your man anywhere on that line?" Brown asked.

"I can't tell from here. Can we get out?"

"Yeah, sure," Brown said.

They parked the car at the curb. Willis, who had been driving, got out first. He was small and light, with the easy grace of a dancer and the steady cold gaze of a blackjack dealer. He kept slapping his gloved hands together as he waited for Brown. Brown came out of the car like a rhinoceros, pushing his huge body through the door frame, slamming the door behind him, and then pulling his gloves on over big-knuckled hands.

"Did you throw the visor?" Willis asked.

"No. We'll only be a minute here."

"You'd better throw it. Goddamn eager beavers'll give us a ticket sure as hell."

Brown grunted and went back into the car.

"Boy, it's cold out here," La Bresca said.

"Yeah," Willis said.

In the car, Brown lowered the sun visor. A hand-lettered card-board sign was fastened to the visor with rubber bands. It read:

POLICE DEPARTMENT VEHICLE

The car door slammed again. Brown came over and nodded, and together, they began walking the line of men standing on the sidewalk. Both detectives unbuttoned their overcoats.

"Do you see him?" Brown asked La Bresca.

"Not yet," La Bresca said.

They walked the length of the line slowly.

"Well?" Brown asked.

"No," La Bresca said. "He ain't here."

"Let's take a look upstairs," Willis suggested.

The line of job seekers continued up a flight of rickety wooden steps to a dingy second-floor office. The lettering on a frosted glass door read:

MERIDIAN EMPLOYMENT AGENCY

JOBS OUR SPECIALTY

"See him?" Willis asked.

"No," La Bresca said.

"Wait here," Willis said, and the two detectives moved away from him, toward the other end of the corridor.

"What do you think?" Brown asked.

"What can we hold him on?"

"Nothing."

"So *that's* what I think."

"Is he worth a tail?"

"It depends on how serious the loot thinks this is."

"Why don't you ask him?"

"I think I will. Hold the fort."

Brown went back to La Bresca. Willis found a pay phone around the bend in the corridor, and dialed the squadroom. The lieutenant listened carefully to everything he had to report, and then said, "How do you read him?"

"I think he's telling the truth."

"You think there really *was* some guy with a hearing aid?"

"Yes."

"Then why'd he leave before La Bresca got back with the pail?"

"I don't know, Pete. I just don't make La Bresca for a thief."

"Where'd you say he lived?"

"1812 Johnson. In Riverhead."

"What precinct would that be?"

"I don't know."

"I'll check it out and give them a ring. Maybe they can spare a man for a tail. Christ knows we can't."

"So shall we turn La Bresca loose?"

"Yeah, come on back here. Give him a little scare first, though, just in case."

"Right," Willis said, and hung up, and went back to where La Bresca and Brown were waiting.

"Okay, Anthony," Willis said, "you can go."

"Go? Who's *going* anyplace? I got to get back on that line again. I'm trying to get a job here."

"And remember, Anthony, if anything happens, we know where to find you."

"What do you mean? What's gonna happen?"

"Just remember."

"Sure," La Bresca said. He paused and then said, "Listen, you want to do me a favor?"

"What's that?"

"Get me up to the front of the line there."

"How can we do that?"

"Well, you're cops, ain't you?" La Bresca asked, and Willis and Brown looked at each other.

When they got back to the squadroom, they learned that Lieutenant Byrnes had called the 115th in Riverhead and had been informed they could not spare a man for the surveillance of Anthony La Bresca. Nobody seemed terribly surprised.

That night, as Parks Commissioner Cowper came down the broad white marble steps outside Philharmonic Hall, his wife clinging to his left arm, swathed in mink and wearing a diaphanous white scarf on her head, the commissioner himself resplendent in black tie and dinner jacket, the mayor and his wife four steps ahead, the sky virtually starless, a bitter brittle dryness to the air, that night as the parks commissioner came down the steps of Philharmonic Hall with the huge two-story-high windows behind him casting warm yellow light onto the windswept steps and pavement, that night as the commissioner lifted his left foot preparatory to placing it on the step below, laughing at something his wife said in his ear, his laughter billowing out of his mouth in puffs of visible vapor that whipped away on the wind like comic strip balloons, that night as he tugged on his right-hand glove with his already gloved left hand, that night two shots cracked into the plaza, shattering the wintry stillness, and the commissioner's laugh stopped, the commissioner's hand stopped, the commissioner's foot stopped, and he tumbled headlong down the steps, blood pouring from his forehead and his cheek, and his wife screamed, and the mayor turned to see what was the matter, and an enterprising photographer on the sidewalk caught the toppling commissioner on film for posterity.

He was dead long before his body rolled to a stop on the wide white bottom step.

3

CONCETTA ESPOSITA LA BRESCA had been taught only to dislike and distrust all Negroes. Her brothers, on the other hand, had been taught to dismember them if possible. They had learned their respective lessons in a sprawling slum ghetto affectionately and sarcastically dubbed Paradiso by its largely Italian population. Concetta, as a growing child in this dubious garden spot, had watched her brothers and other neighborhood boys bash in a good many Negro skulls when she was still just a *piccola ragazza*. The mayhem did not disturb her. Concetta figured if you were stupid enough to be born a Negro, and were further stupid enough to come wandering into Paradiso, why then you deserved to have your fool black head split wide open every now and then.

Concetta had left Paradiso at the age of nineteen, when the local iceman, a fellow *Napolitano* named Carmine La Bresca moved his business to Riverhead and asked the youngest of the Esposito girls to marry him. She readily accepted because he was a handsome fellow with deep brown eyes and curly black hair, and because he had a thriving business of which he was the sole owner. She also accepted because she was pregnant at the time.

Her son was born seven months later, and he was now twenty-seven years old, and living alone with Concetta in the second-floor apartment of a two-family house on Johnson Street. Carmine La Bresca had gone back to Pozzuoli, fifteen miles outside of Naples, a month after Anthony was born. The last Concetta heard of him was a rumor that he had been killed during World War II, but, knowing her husband, she suspected he was king of the icemen somewhere in Italy, still fooling around with young girls and getting them pregnant in the icehouse, as was her own cruel misfortune.

Concetta Esposita La Bresca still disliked and distrusted all Negroes and she was rather startled—to say the least—to find one on her doorstep at 12:01 A.M. on a starless, moonless night.

"What is it?" she shouted. "Go away."

"Police officer," Brown said, and flashed the tin, and it was then that Concetta noticed the other man standing with the Negro, a white man, short, with a narrow face and piercing brown eyes, *madonna mia*, it looked as if he was giving her the *malocchio*.

"What do you want, go away," she said in a rush, and lowered the shade on the glass-paneled rear door of her apartment. The door was at the top of a rickety flight of wooden steps (Willis had almost tripped and broken his neck on the third one from the top) overlooking a back yard in which there was a tar-paper-covered tree. (Doubtless a fig tree, Brown remarked on their way up the steps.) A clothesline stiff with undergarments stretched from the tiny back porch outside the glass-paneled door to a pole set diagonally at the other end of the yard. The wind whistled around the porch and did its best to blow Willis off and down into the grape arbor covering the outside patio below. He knocked on the door again, and shouted, "Police officers, you'd better open up, lady."

"*Sta zitto!*" Concetta said, and unlocked the door. "You want to wake the whole neighbor? *Ma che vergogna!*"

"Is it all right to come in, lady?" Willis asked.

"Come in, come in," Concetta said, and stepped back into the small kitchen, allowing Willis and then Brown to pass her.

"So what you want two o'clock in the morning?" Concetta said, and closed the door against the wind. The kitchen was narrow, the stove, sink, and refrigerator lined up against one wall, an enamel-topped table on the opposite wall. A metal cabinet, its door open to reveal an array of breakfast cereals and canned foods, was on the right-angled wall, alongside a radiator. There was a mirror over the sink and a porcelain dog on top of the refrigerator. Hanging on the wall over the radiator was a picture of Jesus Christ. A light bulb with a pull chain and a large glass globe hung in the center of the kitchen. The faucet was dripping. An electric clock over the range hummed a steady counterpoint.

"It's only midnight," Brown said. "Not two o'clock."

There was an edge to his voice that had not been there on the long ride up to Riverhead, and Willis could only attribute it to the presence of Mrs. La Bresca, if indeed that was who the lady was. He wondered for perhaps the hundredth time what radar Brown possessed that enabled him to pinpoint unerringly any bigot within a radius of a thousand yards. The woman was staring at both men with equal animosity, it seemed to Willis, her long black hair pinned into a bun at the back of her head, her brown eyes slitted and defiant. She was wearing a man's bathrobe over her nightgown, and he saw now that she was barefoot.

"Are you Mrs. La Bresca?" Willis asked.

"I am Concetta La Bresca, who wants to know?" she said.

"Detectives Willis and Brown of the 87th Squad," Willis said. "Where's your son?"

"He's asleep," Concetta said, and because she was born in Naples and raised in Paradiso, immediately assumed it was necessary to provide him with an alibi. "He was here with me all night," she said, "you got the wrong man."

"You want to wake him up, Mrs. La Bresca?" Brown said.

"What for?"

"We'd like to talk to him."

"What for?"

"Ma'am, we can take him into custody, if that's what you'd like," Brown said, "but it might be easier all around if we just asked him a few simple questions right here and now. You want to go fetch him, ma'am?"

"I'm up," La Bresca's voice said from the other room.

"You want to come out here, please, Mr. La Bresca?" Willis said.

"Just a second," La Bresca said.

"He was here all night," Concetta said, but Brown's hand drifted nonetheless toward the revolver holstered at his waist, just in case La Bresca had been out pumping two bullets into the commissioner's head instead. He was a while coming. When he finally opened the door and walked into the kitchen, he was carrying nothing more lethal in his hand than the sash of his bathrobe, which he knotted about his waist. His hair was tousled, and his eyes were bleary.

"What now?" he asked.

Since this was a field investigation, and since La Bresca couldn't conceivably be considered "in custody," neither Willis nor Brown felt it necessary to advise him of his rights. Instead, Willis immediately said, "Where were you tonight at eleven-thirty?"

"Right here," La Bresca said.

"Doing what?"

"Sleeping."

"What time'd you go to bed?"

"About ten."

"You always hit the sack so early?"

"I do when I gotta get up early."

"You getting up early tonorrow?"

"Six A.M.," La Bresca said.

"Why?"

"To get to work."

"We thought you were unemployed."

"I got a job this afternoon, right after you guys left me."

"What kind of a job?"

"Construction work. I'm a laborer."

"Meridian get you the job?"

"That's right."

"Who with?"

"Erhard Engineering."

"In Riverhead?"

"No, Isola."

"What time'd you get home tonight?" Brown asked.

"I left Meridian, it musta been about one o'clock, I guess. I went up the pool hall on South Leary and shot a few games with the boys. Then I came home here, it musta been about five or six o'clock."

"What'd you do then?"

"He ate," Concetta said.

"Then what?"

"I watched a little TV, and got into bed," La Bresca said.

"Can anybody besides your mother verify that story?"

"Nobody was here, if that's what you mean."

"You get any phone calls during the night?"

"No."

"Just your word then, right?"

"And *mine,*" Concetta said.

"Listen, I don't know what you guys want from me," La Bresca said, "but I'm telling you the truth, I mean it. What's going on, anyway?"

"Did you happen to catch the news on television?"

"No, I musta fell asleep before the news went on. Why? What happened?"

"I go in his room and turn off the light at ten-thirty," Concetta said.

"I wish you guys would believe me," La Bresca said. "Whatever it is you've got in mind, I didn't have nothing to do with it."

"I believe you," Willis said. "How about you, Artie?"

"I believe him, too," Brown said.

"But we have to ask questions," Willis said, "you understand?"

"Sure, I understand," La Bresca said, "but I mean, it's the middle of the night, you know? I gotta get up tomorrow morning."

"Why don't you tell us about the man with the hearing aid again," Willis suggested gently.

They spent at least another fifteen minutes questioning La Bresca and at the end of that time decided they'd either have to pull him in and charge him with something, or else forget him for the time being. The man who'd called the squadroom had said, "There are more than one of us," and this information had been passed from Kling to the other detectives on the squad, and it was only this nagging knowledge that kept them there questioning La Bresca long after they should have stopped. A cop can usually tell whether he's onto real meat or not, and La Bresca did not seem like a thief. Willis had told the lieutenant just that only this afternoon, and his opinion hadn't changed in the intervening hours. But if there *was* a gang involved in the commissioner's murder, wasn't it possible that La Bresca was one of them? A lowly cog in the organization, perhaps, the gopher, the slob who was sent to pick up things, the expendable man who ran the risk of being caught by the police if anything went wrong? In which case, La Bresca was lying.

Well, if he was lying, he did it like an expert, staring out of his baby blues and melting both those hardhearted cops with tales of the new job he was anxious to start tomorrow morning, which is why he'd gone to bed so early and all, got to get a full eight hours' sleep, growing mind in a growing body, red-blooded second-generation American, and all that crap. Which raised yet another possibility. If he *was* lying—and so far they hadn't been able to trip him up, hadn't been able to find a single discrepancy between the story he'd told that afternoon and the one he was telling now—but if he *was* lying, then wasn't it possible the caller and La Bresca were one and the same person? *Not* a gang at all, that being a figment of his own imagination, a tiny falsehood designed to lead the police into believing this was a well-organized group instead of a single ambitious hood trying to make a killing. And if La Bresca and the caller were one and the same, then La Bresca and the man who'd murdered the commissioner were also one and the same. In which case, it would be proper to take the little liar home and book him for murder. Sure, and then try to find something that would stick, *anything* that would stick, they'd be laughed out of court right at the preliminary hearing.

Some nights you can't make a nickel.

So after fifteen minutes of some very fancy footwork designed to befuddle and unsettle La Bresca, with Brown utilizing his very special logically persistent method of questioning while Willis sniped and jabbed around the edges, they knew nothing more than they had known that afternoon. The only difference was that now the commissioner was dead. So they thanked Mrs. La Bresca for the use of the hall, and they shook hands with her son and apologized for having pulled him out of bed, and they wished him luck at his new job, and then they both said good night again and went out of the house and heard Mrs. La Bresca locking the kitchen door behind them, and went down the rickety wooden steps, and down the pot-holed driveway, and across the street to where they had parked the police sedan.

Then Willis started the car, and turned on the heater, and both men talked earnestly and softly for several moments and decided to ask the lieutenant for permission to bug La Bresca's phone in the morning.

Then they went home.

It was cold and dark in the alley where Steve Carella lay on his side huddled in a tattered overcoat. The late February snow had been shoveled and banked against one brick alley wall, soiled now with the city's grime, a thin layer of soot crusted onto its surface. Carella was wearing two pairs of thermal underwear and a quilted vest. In addition, a hand warmer was tucked into one pocket of the vest, providing a good steady heat inside the threadbare overcoat. But he was cold.

The banked snow opposite him only made him colder. He did not like snow. Oh yes, he could remember owning his own sled as a boy, and he could remember belly-whopping with joyous abandon, but the memory seemed like a totally fabricated one in view of his present very real aversion to snow. Snow was cold and wet. If you were a private citizen, you had to shovel it, and if you were a Department of Sanitation worker, you had to truck it over to the River Dix to get rid of it. Snow was a pain in the ass.

This entire stakeout was a pain in the ass.

But it was also very amusing.

It was the amusing part of it that kept Carella lying in a cold dark alley on a night that wasn't fit for man or beast. (Of course, he had also been *ordered* to lie in a cold dark alley by the lieutenant for whom he worked, nice fellow name of Peter Byrnes, *he* should come lie in a cold dark alley some night.) The amusing part of this particular stakeout was that Carella wasn't planted in a bank hoping to prevent a multimillion dollar robbery, nor was he planted in a candy store someplace, hoping to crack an international ring of narcotics peddlers, nor was he even hidden in the bathroom of a spinster lady's apartment, hoping to catch a mad rapist. He was lying in a cold dark alley, and the amusing part was that two vagrants had been set on fire. That wasn't so amusing, the part about being set on fire. That was pretty serious. The amusing part was that the victims had been vagrants. Ever since Carella could remember, the police had been waging an unremitting war against this city's vagrants, arresting them, jailing them, releasing them, arresting them again, on and on ad infinitum. So now the police had been presented with two benefactors who were generously attempting to rid the streets of any and all bums by setting them aflame, and what did the police do? The police promptly dispatched a valuable man to a cold dark alley to lie on his side facing a dirty snowbank while hoping to catch the very fellows who were in charge of incinerating bums. It did not make sense. It was amusing.

A lot of things about police work were amusing.

It was certainly funnier to be lying here freezing than to be at home in bed with a warm and loving woman; oh God, that was so amusing it made Carella want to weep. He thought of Teddy alone in bed, black hair spilling all over the pillow, half-smile on her mouth, nylon gown pulled back over curving hip, God, I could freeze to death right here in this goddamn alley, he thought, and my own wife won't learn about it till morning. My own passionate wife! She'll read about it in the papers! She'll see my name on page four! She'll—

There were footsteps at the other end of the alley.

He felt himself tensing. Beneath the overcoat, his naked hand moved away from the warmer and dropped swiftly to the cold steel butt of his service revolver. He eased the gun out of its holster, lay hunched on his side with the gun ready, and waited as the footsteps came closer.

"Here's one," a voice said.

It was a young voice.

"Yeah," another voice answered.

Carella waited. His eyes were closed, he lay huddled in the far corner of the alley, simulating sleep, his finger curled inside the trigger guard now, a hair's-breadth away from the trigger itself.

Somebody kicked him.

"Wake up!" a voice said.

He moved swiftly, but not swiftly enough. He was shoving himself off the floor of the alley, yanking the revolver into firing position, when the liquid splashed onto the front of his coat.

"Have a drink!" one of the boys shouted, and Carella saw a match flare into life, and suddenly he was in flames.

His reaction sequence was curious in that his sense of smell supplied the first signal, the unmistakable aroma of gasoline fumes rising from the front of his coat, and then the flaring match, shocking in itself, providing a brilliant tiny explosion of light in the nearly black alley, more shocking in combination with the smell of the gasoline. Warning slammed with physical force into his temples, streaked in a jagged electric path to the back of his skull, and suddenly there were flames. There was no shock coupled with the fire that leaped up toward his face from the front of his coat. There was only terror.

Steve Carella reacted in much the same way Cro-Magnon must have reacted the first time he ventured too close to a raging fire and discovered that flames can cook people as well as saber-toothed tigers. He dropped his weapon, he covered his face, he whirled abruptly, instinctively rushing for the soot-crusted snowbank across the alley, forgetting his attackers, only vaguely aware that they were running, laughing, out of the alley and into the night, thinking only in a jagged broken pattern fire run burn fire out fire fire and hurling himself full length onto the snow. His hands were cupped tightly to his face, he could feel the flames chewing angrily at the backs of them, could smell the terrifying stench of burning hair and flesh, and then heard the sizzle of fire in contact with the snow, felt the cold and comforting snow, was suddenly enveloped in a white cloud of steam that rose from the beautiful snow, rolled from shoulder to shoulder in the glorious marvelous soothing beneficial white and magnificent snow, and found tears in his eyes, and thought nothing, and lay with his face pressed to the snow for a long while, breathing heavily, and still thinking nothing.

He got up at last and painfully retrieved his discarded revolver and walked slowly to the mouth of the alley and looked at his hands in the light of the street lamp. He caught his breath, and then went to the call box on the next corner. He told Sergeant Murchison at the desk that the fire bugs had hit, and that his hands had been burned and he would need a meat wagon to get him over to the hospital. Murchison said, "Are you all right?" and Carella looked at his hands again, and said, "Yes, I'm all right, Dave."

4

DETECTIVE BERT KLING was in love, but nobody else was.

The mayor was not in love, he was furious. The mayor called the police commissioner in high dudgeon and wanted to know what kind of a goddamn city this was where a man of the caliber of Parks Commissioner Cowper could be gunned down on the steps of Philharmonic Hall, what the hell kind of a city was this, anyway?

"Well, sir," the police commissioner started, but the mayor said, "Perhaps you can tell me why adequate police protection was not provided for Commissioner Cowper when his wife informs me this morning that the police *knew* a threat had been made on his life, perhaps you can tell me that," the mayor shouted into the phone.

"Well, sir," the police commissioner started, but the mayor said, "Or perhaps you can tell me why you still haven't located the apartment from which those shots were fired, when the autopsy has already revealed the angle of entrance and your ballistics people have come up with a probable trajectory, perhaps you can tell me that."

"Well, sir," the police commissioner started, but the mayor said, "Get me some results, do you want this city to become a laughingstock?"

The police commissioner certainly didn't want the city to become a laughingstock, so he said, "Yes, sir, I'll do the best I can," and the mayor said, "You had better," and hung up.

There was no love lost between the mayor and the police commissioner that morning. So the police commissioner asked his secretary, a tall wan blond man who appeared consumptive and who claimed his constant hacking cough was caused by smoking three packs of cigarettes a day in a job that was enough to drive anyone utterly mad, the police commissioner asked his secretary to find out what the mayor had meant by a threat on the parks commissioner's life, and report back to him immediately. The tall wan blond secretary got to work at once, asking around here and there, and discovering that the 87th Precinct had indeed logged several telephone calls from a mysterious stranger who had threatened to kill the parks commissioner unless five thousand dollars was delivered to him by noon yesterday. When the police commissioner received this information, he said, "Oh, *yeah?*" and immediately dialed Frederick 7-8024, and asked to talk to Detective-Lieutenant Peter Byrnes.

Detective-Lieutenant Peter Byrnes had enough headaches that morning, what with Carella in the hospital with second-degree burns on the backs of both hands, and the painters having moved from the squadroom into his own private office, where they were slopping up everything in sight and telling jokes on their ladders. Byrnes was not overly fond of the police commissioner to begin with, the commissioner being a fellow who had been imported from a neighboring city when the new administration took over, a city which, in Byrnes' opinion, had an even larger crime rate than this one. Nor was the new commissioner terribly fond of Lieutenant Byrnes, because Byrnes was the sort of garrulous Irishman who shot off his mouth at Police Benevolent Association and Emerald Society functions, letting anyone within earshot know what he thought of the mayor's recent whiz-kid appointee. So there was hardly any sweetness and light oozing over the telephone wires that morning between the commissioner's office at Headquarters downtown on High Street, and Byrnes' paint-spattered corner office on the second floor of the grimy station house on Grover Avenue.

"What's this all about, Byrnes?" the commissioner asked.

"Well, sir," Byrnes said, remembering that the *former* commissioner used to call him Pete, "we received several threatening telephone calls from an unidentified man yesterday, which telephone calls I discussed personally with Parks Commissioner Cowper."

What did you do about those calls, Byrnes?"

"We placed the drop site under surveillance, and apprehended the man who made the pickup."

"So what happened?"

"We questioned him and released him."

"Why?"

"Insufficient evidence. He was also interrogated after the parks commissioner's murder last night. We did not have ample grounds for an arrest. The man is still free, but a telephone tap went into effect this morning, and we're ready to move in if we monitor anything incriminating."

"Why wasn't the commissioner given police protection?"

"I offered it, sir, and it was refused."

"Why wasn't your suspect put under surveillance *before* a crime was committed?"

"I couldn't spare any men, sir, and when I contacted the 115th in Riverhead, where the suspect resides, I was told they could not spare any men either. Besides, as I told you, the commissioner did not *want* protection. He felt we were dealing with a crackpot, sir, and I must tell you that was our opinion here, too. Until, of course, recent events proved otherwise."

"Why hasn't that apartment been found yet?"

"What apartment, sir?"

"The apartment from which the two shots were fired that killed Parks Commissioner Cowper."

"Sir, the crime was not committed in our precinct. Philharmonic Hall, sir, is in the 53rd Precinct and, as I'm sure the commissioner realizes, a homicide is investigated by the detectives assigned to the squad in the precinct in which the homicide was committed."

"Don't give me any of that bullshit, Byrnes," the police commissioner said.

"That is the way we do it in this city, sir," Byrnes said.

"This is your case," the commissioner answered. "You got that, Byrnes?"

"If you say so, sir."

"I say so. Get some men over to the area, and find that goddamn apartment."

"Yes, sir."

"And report back to me."

"Yes, sir," Byrnes said, and hung up.

"Getting a little static, huh?" the first painter said.

"Getting your ass chewed out, huh?" the second painter said.

Both men were on their ladders, grinning and dripping apple green paint on the floor.

"Get the hell out of this office!" Byrnes shouted.

"We ain't finished yet," the first painter said.

"We don't leave till we finish," the second painter said.

"That's our orders," the first painter said.

"We don't work for the Police Department, you know."

"We work for the Department of Public Works."

"Maintenance and Repair."

"And we don't quit a job till we finish it."

"Stop dripping paint all over my goddamn floor!" Byrnes shouted, and stormed out of the office. "Hawes!" he shouted. "Kling! Willis! Brown! Where the hell *is* everybody?" he shouted.

Meyer came out of the men's room, zipping up his fly. "What's up, Skipper?" he said.

"Where were you?"

"Taking a leak. Why, what's up?"

"Get somebody over to the area!" Byrnes shouted.

"What area?"

"Where the goddamn commissioner got shot!"

"Okay, sure," Meyer said. "But why? That's not our case."

"It is now."

"Oh?"

"Who's catching?"

"I am."

"Where's Kling?"

"Day off."

"Where's Brown?"

"On that wire tap."

"And Willis?"

"He went to the hospital to see Steve."

"And Hawes?"

"He went down for some Danish."

"What the hell am I running here, a resort in the mountains?"

"No, sir. We . . ."

"Send Hawes over there! Send him over the minute he gets back. Get on the phone to Ballistics. Find out what they've got. Call the M.E.'s office and get that autopsy report. Get cracking, Meyer!"

"Yes, *sir!*" Meyer snapped, and went immediately to the telephone.

"This goddamn racket drives me crazy," Byrnes said, and started to storm back into his office, remembered that the jolly green painters were in there slopping around, and stormed into the Clerical Office instead.

"Get those files in order!" he shouted. "What the hell do you do in here all day, Miscolo, make coffee?"

"Sir?" Miscolo said, because that's exactly what he was doing at the moment.

Bert Kling was in love.

It was not a good time of the year to be in love. It is better to be in love when flowers are blooming and balmy breezes are wafting in off the river, and strange animals come up to lick your hand. There's only one good thing about being in love in March, and that's that it's better to be in love in March than not to be in love at all, as the wise man once remarked.

Bert Kling was madly in love.

He was madly in love with a girl who was twenty-three years old, full-breasted and wide-hipped, her blond hair long and trailing midway down her back or sometimes curled into a honey conch shell at the back of her head, her eyes a cornflower blue, a tall girl who came just level with his chin when she was wearing heels. He was madly in love with a scholarly girl who was studying at night for her master's degree in psychology while working during the day conducting interviews for a firm downtown on Shepherd Street; a serious girl who hoped to go on for her Ph.D., and then pass the state boards, and then practice psychology; a nutty girl who was capable of sending to the squadroom a six-foot high heart cut out of plywood and painted red and lettered in yellow with the words Cynthia Forrest Loves Detective 3rd/Grade Bertram Kling, So Is That A Crime?, as she had done on St. Valentine's Day just last month (and which Kling had still not heard the end of from all his comical colleagues); an emotional girl who could burst into tears at the sight of a blind man playing an accordion on The Stem, to whom she gave a five-dollar bill, merely put the bill silently into the cup, soundlessly, it did not even make a rustle, and turned away to weep into Kling's shoulder; a passionate girl who clung to him fiercely in the night and who woke him sometimes at six in the morning to say, "Hey, Cop, I have to go to work in a few hours, are you interested?" to which Kling invariably answered, "No, I am not interested in sex and things like that," and then kissed her until she was dizzy and afterwards sat across from her at the kitchen table in her apartment, staring at her, marveling at her beauty and once caused her to blush when he said, "There's a woman who sells *pidaguas* on Mason Avenue, her name is Illuminada, Cindy. You fill the room with light."

Boy, was he in love.

But, it being March, and the streets still banked high with February snow, and the winds howling, and the wolves growling and chasing civilians in troikas who cracked whips and huddled in bear rugs, it being a bitter cold winter which seemed to have started in September and showed no signs of abating till next August, when possibly, but just possibly, all the snow might melt and the flowers would bloom—it being that kind of a treacherous winter, what better to do than discuss police work? What better to do than rush along the frozen street on Cindy's lunch hour with her hand clutched tightly in the crook of his arm and the wind whipping around them and drowning out Kling's voice as he tried to tell her of the mysterious circumstances surrounding the death of Parks Commissioner Cowper.

"Yes, it *sounds* very mysterious," Cindy said, and brought her hand out of her pocket in an attempt to keep the wind from tearing the kerchief from her head. "Listen, Bert," she said, "I'm really very tired of winter, aren't you tired of it?"

"Yeah," Kling said. "Listen, Cindy, you know who I hope this isn't?"

"Hope who isn't?" she said.

"The guy who made the calls. The guy who killed the commissioner. You know who I hope we're not up against?"

"Who?" she asked.

"The deaf man," he said.

"What?" she said.

"He was a guy we went up against a few years back, it must have been maybe seven, eight years ago. He tore this whole damn city apart trying to rob a bank. He was the smartest crook we ever came up against."

"Who?" Cindy said.

"The deaf man," Kling said again.

"Yes, but what's his name?"

"We don't know his name. We never caught him. He jumped in the river and we thought he drowned, but maybe he's back now. Like Frankenstein."

"Like Frankenstein's monster, you mean," Cindy said.

"Yeah, like him. Remember he was supposed to have died in that fire, but he didn't."

"I remember."

"That was a scary picture," Kling said.

"I wet my pants when I saw it," Cindy said. "And that was on television."

"You wet your pants on *television?*" Kling said. "In front of forty million *people?*"

"No, I saw *Frankenstein* on television," Cindy said, and grinned and poked him.

"The deaf man," Kling said. "I hope it's not him."

It was the first time any man on the squad had voiced the possibility that the commissioner's murderer was the man who had given them so much trouble so many years ago. The thought was somewhat numbing. Bert Kling was a young man, and not a particularly philosophical one, but he intuitively understood that the deaf man (who had once signed a note L. Sordo, very comical, El Sordo meaning "The Deaf One" in Spanish) was capable of manipulating odds with computer accuracy, of spreading confusion and fear, of juggling permutations and combinations in a manner calculated to upset the strict and somewhat bureaucratic efficiency of a police precinct, making law enforcers behave like bumbling Keystone cops in a yellowing ancient film, knew instinctively and with certainty that if the commissioner's murderer was indeed the deaf man, they had not yet heard the end of all this. And because the very thought of what the deaf man might and *could* do was too staggering to contemplate, Kling involuntarily shuddered, and he knew it was not from the cold.

"I hope it isn't him," he said, and his words were carried away on the wind.

"Kiss me," Cindy said suddenly, "and then buy me a hot chocolate, you cheapskate."

The boy who came into the muster room that Wednesday afternoon was about twelve years old.

He was wearing his older brother's hand-me-down ski parka which was blue and three sizes too large for him. He had pulled the hood of the parka up over his head, and had tightened the drawstrings around his neck, but the hood was still too big, and it kept falling off. He kept trying to pull it back over his head as he came into the station house carrying an envelope in the same hand with which he wiped his runny nose. He was wearing high-topped sneakers with the authority of all slum kids who wear sneakers winter and summer, all year round, despite the warnings of podiatrists. He walked to the muster desk with a sneaker-inspired bounce, tried to adjust the parka hood again, wiped his dripping nose again, and then looked up at Sergeant Murchison and said, "You the desk sergeant?"

"I'm the desk sergeant," Murchison answered without looking up from the absentee slips he was filling out from that morning's muster sheet. It was 2:10 P.M., and in an hour and thirty-five minutes the afternoon shift of uniformed cops would be coming in, and there'd be a new roll call to take, and new absentee slips to fill out, a regular rat race, he should have become a fireman or a postman.

"I'm supposed to give you this," the kid said, and reached up to hand Murchison the sealed envelope.

"Thanks," Murchison said, and accepted the envelope without looking at the kid, and then suddenly raised his head and said, "Hold it just a second."

"Why, what's the matter?"

"Just hold it right there a second," Murchison said, and opened the envelope. He unfolded the single sheet of white paper that had been neatly folded in three equal parts, and he read what was on the sheet, and then he looked down at the kid again and said, "Where'd you get this?"

"Outside."

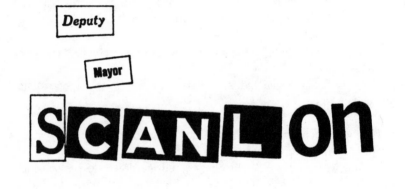

"Where?"

"A guy gave it to me."

"What guy?"

"A tall guy outside."

"Outside where?"

"Near the park there. Across the street."

"Gave you this?"

"Yeah."

"What'd he say?"

"Said I should bring it in here and give it to the desk sergeant."

"You know the guy?"

"No, he gave me five bucks to bring it over here."

"What'd he look like?"

"A tall guy with blond hair. He had a thing in his ear."

"What kind of a thing?"

"Like he was deaf," the kid said, and wiped his hand across his nose again.

That was what the note read.

So they studied the note, being careful not to get any more fingerprints on it than Sergeant Murchison had already put there, and then they stood around a runny-nosed twelve-year-old kid wearing a blue ski parka three sizes too large for him, and fired questions at him as though they had captured Jack the Ripper over from London for the weekend.

They got nothing from the kid except perhaps his cold.

He repeated essentially what he had told Sergeant Murchison, that a tall blond guy wearing a thing in his ear (A hearing aid, you mean, kid?) yeah, a thing in his ear, had stopped him across the street from the police station and offered him five bucks to carry an envelope in to the desk sergeant. The kid couldn't see nothing wrong with bringing an envelope into the police station, so he done it, and that was all, he didn't even know who the guy with the thing in his ear was. (You mean a hearing aid kid?) Yeah, a thing in his ear, he didn't know who he was, never even seen him around the neighborhood or nothing, so could he go home now because he had to make a stop at Linda's Boutique to pick up some dresses for his sister who did sewing at home for Mrs. Montana? (He was wearing a hearing aid, huh, kid?) Yeah, a thing in his ear, the kid said.

So they let the kid go at two-thirty without even offering him an ice cream cone or some gumdrops, and then they sat around the squadroom handling the suspect note with a pair of tweezers and decided to send it over to Lieutenant Sam Grossman at the police lab in the hope that he could lift some latent prints that did not belong to Sergeant Murchison.

None of them mentioned the deaf man.

Nobody likes to talk about ghosts.

Or even *think* about them.

"Hello, Bernice," Meyer said into the telephone, "is your boss around? Yeah, sure, I'll wait."

Patiently, he tapped a pencil on his desk and waited. In a moment, a bright perky voice materialized on the line.

"Assistant District Attorney Raoul Chabrier," the voice insisted.

"Hello, Rollie, this is Meyer Meyer up here at the 87th," Meyer said. "How's every little thing down there on Chelsea Street?"

"Oh, pretty good, pretty good," Chabrier said, "what have you got for us, a little homicide up there perhaps?"

"No, nothing like that, Rollie," Meyer said.

"A little ax murder perhaps?" Chabrier said.

"No, as a matter of fact, this is something personal," Meyer said.

"Oh-*ho!*" Chabrier said.

"Yeah. Listen, Rollie, what can you do if somebody uses your name?"

"What do you mean?" Chabrier asked.

"In a book."

"Oh-*ho!*" Chabrier said. "Did somebody use your name in a book?"

"Yes."

"In a book about the workings of the police department?"

"No."

"Were you mentioned specifically?"

"No. Well, yes *and* no. What do you mean?"

"Did the book specifically mention Detective 3rd/Grade Meyer Meyer . . ."

"Detective *2nd*/Grade," Meyer corrected.

"It specifically mentioned Detective 2nd/Grade Meyer Meyer of the . . ."

"No."

"It *didn't* mention you?"

"No. Not that way."

"I thought you said somebody used your name."

"Well, they did. She did."

"Meyer, I'm a busy man," Chabrier said. "I've got a case load here that would fell a brewer's horse, now would you please tell me what's on your mind?"

"A novel," Meyer said. "It's a novel named *Meyer Meyer.*"

"That is the title of the novel?" Chabrier asked.

"Yes. Can I sue?"

"I'm a criminal lawyer," Chabrier said.

"Yes, but . . ."

"I am not familiar with the law of literary property."

"Yes, but . . ."

"Is it a good book?"

"I don't know," Meyer said. "You see," he said, "I'm a *person,* and this book is about some college professor or something, and he's a short plump fellow . . ."

"I'll have to read it," Chabrier said.

"Will you call me after you've read it?"

"What for?"

"To advise me."

"On what?"

"On whether I can sue or not."

"I'll have to read the law," Chabrier said. "Do I owe you a favor, Meyer?"

"You owe me *six* of them," Meyer said somewhat heatedly, "as for example the several times I could have got you out of bed at three o'clock in the morning when we had real meat here in the squadroom and at great risk to myself I held the suspect until the following morning so you could get your beauty sleep on nights when you had the duty. Now, Rollie, I'm asking a very tiny favor, I don't want to go the expense of getting some fancy copyright lawyer or whatever the hell, I just want to know whether I can sue somebody who used my name that's on a record in the Department of Health on a birth certificate, can I sue this person who uses my name as the title of a novel, and for a *character* in a novel, when here I am a real *person,* for Christ's sake!"

"Okay, don't get excited," Chabrier said.

"Who's excited?" Meyer said.

"I'll read the law and call you back."

"When?"

"Sometime."

"Maybe if we got somebody in the squadroom sometime when you've got the duty, I'll fly in the face of Miranda-Escobedo again and hold off till morning so you can peacefully snore the night . . ."

"Okay, okay, I'll get back to you tomorrow." Chabrier paused. "Don't you want to know what *time* tomorrow?"

"What time tomorrow?" Meyer asked.

The landlady had arthritis, and she hated winter, and she didn't like cops too well, either. She immediately told Cotton Hawes that there had been other policemen prowling around ever since that big mucky-muck got shot last night, why couldn't they leave a lady alone? Hawes, who had been treated to similar diatribes from every landlady and superintendent along the street, patiently explained that he was only doing his job, and said he knew she would want to co-operate in bringing a murderer to justice. The landlady said the city was rotten and corrupt, and as far as she was concerned they could shoot *all* those damn big mucky-mucks, and she wouldn't lose no sleep over any of them.

Hawes had thus far visited four buildings in a row of identical slum tenements facing the glittering glass and concrete structure that was the city's new Philharmonic Hall. The building, a triumph of design (the acoustics weren't so hot, but what the hell) could be clearly seen from any one of the tenements, the wide marble steps across the avenue offering an unrestricted view of anyone who happened to be standing on them, or coming down them, or going up them. The man who had plunked two rifle slugs into Cowper's head could have done so from *any* of these buildings. The only reason the police department was interested in the exact source of the shots was that the killer may have left some evidence behind him. Evidence is always nice to have in a murder case.

The first thing Hawes asked the landlady was whether she had rented an apartment or a room recently to a tall blond man wearing a hearing aid.

"Yes," the landlady said.

That was a good start. Hawes was an experienced detective, and he recognized immediately that the landlady's affirmative reply was a terribly good start.

"Who?" he asked immediately. "Would you know his name?"

"Yes."

"What's his name?"

"Orecchio. Mort Orecchio."

Hawes took out his pad and began writing. "Orecchio," he said, "Mort. Would you happen to know whether it was Morton or Mortimer or exactly what?"

"Just Mort," the landlady said. "Mort Orecchio. He was Eye-talian."

"How do you know?"

"Anything ending in O is Eye-talian."

"You think so? How about Shapiro?" Hawes suggested.

"What are you, a wise guy?" the landlady said.

"This fellow Orecchio, which apartment did you rent him?"

"A *room,* not an apartment," the landlady said. "Third floor front."

"Facing Philharmonic?"

"Yeah."

"Could I see the room?"

"Sure why not? I got nothing else to do but show cops rooms."

They began climbing. The hallway was cold and the air shaft windows were rimed with frost. There was the commingled smell of garbage and urine on the stairs, a nice clean old lady this landlady. She kept complaining about her arthritis all the way up to the third floor, telling Hawes the cortisone didn't help her none, all them big mucky-muck doctors making promises that didn't help her pain at all. She stopped outside a door with the brass numerals 31 on it, and fished into the pocket of her apron for a key. Down the hall, a door opened a crack and then closed again.

"Who's that?" Hawes asked.

"Who's who?" the landlady said.

"Down the hall there. The door that just opened and closed."

"Musta been Polly," the landlady said, and unlocked the door to 31.

The room was small and cheerless. A three-quarter bed was against the wall opposite the door, covered with a white chenille bedspread. A framed print was over the bed. It showed a logging mill and a river and a sheepdog looking up at something in the sky. A standing floor lamp was on the right of the bed. The shade was yellow and soiled. A stain, either whiskey or vomit, was on the corner of the bedspread where it was pulled up over the pillows. Opposite the bed, there was a single dresser with a mirror over it. The dresser had cigarette burns all the way around its top. The mirror was spotted and peeling. The sink alongside the dresser had a big rust ring near the drain.

"How long was he living here?" Hawes asked.

"Took the room three days ago."

"Did he pay by check or cash?"

"Cash. In advance. Paid for a full week. I only rent by the week, I don't like none of these one-night stands."

"Naturally not," Hawes said.

"I know what you're thinking. You're thinking it ain't such a fancy place, I shouldn't be so fussy. Well, it may not be fancy," the landlady said, "but it's clean."

"Yes, I can see that."

"I mean it ain't got no *bugs,* mister."

Hawes nodded and went to the window. The shade was torn

and missing its pull cord. He grabbed the lower edge in his gloved hand, raised the shade and looked across the street.

"You hear any shots last night?"

"No."

He looked down at the floor. There were no spent cartridge cases anywhere in sight.

"Who else lives on this floor?"

"Polly down the hall, that's all."

"Polly who?"

"Malloy."

"Mind if I look through the dresser and the closet?"

"Go right ahead. I got all the time in the world. The way I spend my day is I conduct guided tours through the building."

Hawes went to the dresser and opened each of the drawers. They were all empty, except for a cockroach nestling in the corner of the bottom drawer.

"You missed one," Hawes said, and closed the drawer.

"Huh?" the landlady said.

Hawes went to the closet and opened it. There were seven wire hangers on the clothes bar. The closet was empty. He was about to close the door when something on the floor caught his eye. He stooped for a closer look, took a pen light from his pocket, and turned it on. The object on the floor was a dime.

"If that's money," the landlady said, "it belongs to me."

"Here," Hawes said, and handed her the dime. He did so knowing full well that even if the coin *had* belonged to the occupant of the room, it was as impossible to get latent prints from money as it was to get reimbursed by the city for gasoline used in one's private car on police business.

"Is there a john in here?" he asked.

"Down the hall. Lock the door behind you."

"I only wanted to know if there was another room, that's all."

"It's clean, if that's what you're worrying about."

"I'm sure it's spotless," Hawes said. He took another look around. "So this is it, huh?"

"This is it."

"I'll be sending a man over to dust that sill," Hawes said.

"Why?" the landlady said. "It's clean."

"I mean for fingerprints."

"Oh." The landlady stared at him. "You think that big mucky-muck was shot from this room?"

"It's possible," Hawes said.

"Will that mean trouble for me?"

"Not unless you shot him," Hawes said, and smiled.

"You got some sense of humor," the landlady said.

They went out of the apartment. The landlady locked the door behind her. "Will that be all," she asked, "or did you want to see anything else?"

"I want to talk to the woman down the hall," Hawes said, "but I won't need you for that. Thank you very much, you were very helpful."

"It breaks the monotony," the landlady said, and he believed her.

"Thank you again," he said, and watched her as she went down the steps. He walked to the door marked 32 and knocked. There was no answer. He knocked again and said, "Miss Malloy?"

The door opened a crack.

"Who is it?" a voice said.

"Police officer. May I talk to you?"

"What about?"

"About Mr. Orecchio."

"I don't know any Mr. Orecchio," the voice said.

"Miss Malloy . . ."

"It's *Mrs.* Malloy, and I don't know any Mr. Orecchio."

"Could you open the door, ma'am?"

"I don't want any trouble."

"I won't . . ."

"I know a man got shot last night, I don't want any trouble."

"Did you hear the shots, Miss Malloy?"

"Mrs. Malloy."

"Did you?"

"No."

"Would you happen to know if Mr. Orecchio was in last night?"

"I don't know who Mr. Orecchio is."

"The man in 31."

"I don't know him."

"Ma'am, could you please open the door?"

"I don't want to."

"Ma'am, I can come back with a warrant, but it'd be a lot easier . . ."

"Don't get me in trouble," she said. "I'll open the door, but please don't get me in trouble."

Polly Malloy was wearing a pale green cotton wrapper. The wrapper had short sleeves. Hawes saw the hit marks on her arms the moment she opened the door, and the hit marks explained a great deal about the woman who was Polly Malloy. She was perhaps twenty-six years old, with a slender youthful body and a face that would have been pretty if it were not so clearly stamped with knowledge. The green eyes were intelligent and alert, the mouth vulnerable. She worried her lip and held the wrapper closed about her naked body, and her fingers were long and slender, and the hit marks on her arms shouted all there was to shout.

"I'm not holding," she said.

"I didn't ask."

"You can look around if you like."

"I'm not interested," Hawes said.

"Come in," she said.

He went into the apartment. She closed and locked the door behind him.

"I don't want trouble," she said. "I've had enough trouble."

"I won't give you any. I only want to know about the man down the hall."

"I know somebody got shot. Please don't get me involved in it."

They sat opposite each other, she on the bed, he on a straight-backed chair facing her. Something shimmered on the air between them, something as palpable as the tenement stink of garbage and piss surrounding them. They sat in easy informality, comfortably aware of each other's trade, Cotton Hawes detective, Polly Malloy addict. And perhaps they knew each other better than a great many people ever get to know each other. Perhaps Hawes had been inside too many shooting galleries not to understand what it was like to be this girl, perhaps he had arrested too many hookers who were screwing for the couple of bucks they needed for a bag of shit, perhaps he had watched the agonized writhings of too many cold turkey kickers, perhaps his knowledge of this junkie or any junkie was as intimate as a pusher's, perhaps he had seen too much and knew too much. And perhaps the girl had been collared too many times, had protested too many times that she was clean, had thrown too many decks of heroin under bar stools or down sewers at the approach of a cop, had been in too many different squadrooms and handled by too many different bulls, been offered the Lexington choice by too many different magistrates, perhaps her knowledge of the law as it applied to narcotics addicts was as intimate as any assistant district attorney's, perhaps she too had seen too much and knew too much. Their mutual knowledge was electric, it generated a heat lightning of its own, ascertaining the curious symbiosis of lawbreaker and enforcer, affirming the interlocking subtlety of crime and punishment. There was a secret bond in that room, an affinity —almost an empathy. They could talk to each other without any bullshit. They were like spent lovers whispering on the same pillow.

"Did you know Orecchio?" Hawes asked.

"Will you keep me clean?"

"Unless you had something to do with it."

"Nothing."

"You've got my word."

"A cop?" she asked, and smiled wanly.

"You've got my word, if you want it."

"I need it, it looks like."

"You need it, honey."

"I knew him."

"How?"

"I met him the night he moved in."

"When was that?"

"Two, three nights ago."

"Where'd you meet?"

"I was hung up real bad, I needed a fix. I just got out of Caramoor, *that* sweet hole, a week ago. I haven't had time to get really connected yet."

"What were you in for?"

"Oh, hooking."

"How old are you, Polly?"

"Ninteen. I look older, huh?"

"Yes, you look older."

"I got married when I was sixteen. To another junkie like myself. Some prize."

"What's he doing now?"

"Time at Castleview."

"For what?"

Polly shrugged. "He started pushing."

"Okay, what about Orecchio next door?"

"I asked him for a loan."

"When was this?"

"Day before yesterday."

"Did he give it to you?"

"I didn't actually ask him for a loan. I offered to turn a trick for him. He was right next door, you see, and I was pretty sick, I swear to God I don't think I coulda made it to the street."

"Did he accept?"

"He gave me ten bucks. He didn't take nothing from me for it."

"Sounds like a nice fellow."

Polly shrugged.

"Not a nice fellow?" Hawes asked.

"Let's say not my type," Polly said.

"Mm-huh."

"Let's say a son of a bitch," Polly said.

"What happened?"

"He came in here last night."

"When? What time?"

"Musta been about nine, nine-thirty."

"After the symphony started," Hawes said.

"Huh?"

"Nothing, I was just thinking out loud. Go on."

"He said he had something nice for me. He said if I came into his room, he would give me something nice."

"Did you go?"

"First I asked him what it was. He said it was something I wanted more than anything else in the world."

"But did you go into his room?"

"Yes."

"Did you see anything out of the ordinary?"

"Like what?"

"Like a high-powered rifle with a telescopic sight."

"No, nothing like that."

"All right, what was this 'something nice' he promised you?"

"Hoss."

"He had heroin for you?"

"That's what he said."

"And that's why he asked you to come into his room? For the heroin?"

"Yes."

"He didn't attempt to sell it to you, did he?"

"No. But . . ."

"Yes?"

"He made me beg for it."

"What do you mean?"

"He showed it to me, and he let me taste it to prove that it was real stuff, and then he refused to give it to me unless I . . . begged for it."

"I see."

"He . . . teased me for . . . I guess for . . . for almost two hours. He kept looking at his watch and making me . . . do things."

"What kind of things?"

"Stupid things. He asked me to sing for him. He made me sing 'White Christmas,' that was supposed to be a big joke, you see, because the shit is white and he knew how bad I needed a fix, so he made me sing 'White Christmas' over and over again, I musta sung it for him six or seven times. And all the while he kept looking at his watch."

"Go ahead."

"Then he . . . he asked me to strip, but . . . I mean, not just take off my clothes, but . . . you know, do a strip for him. And I did it. And he began . . . he began making fun of me, of the way I looked, of my body. I . . . he made me stand naked in front of him, and he just went on and on about how stupid and pathetic I looked, and he kept asking me if I really wanted the heroin, and then looked at his watch again, it was about eleven o'clock by then, I kept saying Yes, I want it, please let me have it, so he asked me to dance for him, he asked me to do the waltz, and then he asked me to do the shag, I didn't know what the hell he was talking about, I never even heard of the shag, have you ever heard of the shag?"

"Yes, I've heard of it," Hawes said.

"So I did that for him, I would have done anything for him, and finally he told me to get on my knees and explain to him why I felt I really needed the bag of heroin. He said he expected me to talk for five minutes on the subject of the addict's need for narcotics, and he looked at his watch and began timing me, and I talked. I was shaking by this time, I had the chills, I needed a shot more than . . ." Polly closed her eyes. "I began crying. I talked and I cried, and at last he looked at his watch and said. 'Your five minutes are up. Here's your poison, now get the hell out of here.' And he threw the bag to me."

"What time was this?"

"It musta been about ten minutes after eleven. I don't have a watch, I hocked it long ago, but you can see the big electric numbers on top of the Mutual Building from my room, and when I was shooting up later it was 11:15, so this musta been about ten after or thereabouts."

"And he kept looking at his watch all through this, huh?"

"Yes. As if he had a date or something."

"He did," Hawes said.

"Huh?"

"He had a date to shoot a man from his window. He was just amusing himself until the concert broke. A nice fellow, Mr. Orecchio."

"I got to say one thing for him," Polly said.

"What's that?"

"It was good stuff." A wistful look came onto her face and into her eyes. "It was some of the best stuff I've had in years. I wouldn't have heard a *cannon* if it went off next door."

Hawes made a routine check of all the city's telephone directories, found no listing for an Orecchio—Mort, Morton, or Mortimer—and then called the Bureau of Criminal Identification at four o'clock that afternoon. The B.C.I., fully automated, called back within ten minutes to report that they had nothing on the suspect. Hawes then sent a teletype to the F.B.I. in Washington, asking them to check their voluminous files for any known criminal named Orecchio, Mort or Mortimer or Morton. He was sitting at his desk in the paint-smelling squadroom when Patrolman Richard Genero came up to ask whether he had to go to court with Kling on the collar they had made jointly and together the week before. Genero had been walking his beat all afternoon, and he was very cold, so he hung around long after Hawes had answered his question, hoping he would be offered a cup of coffee. His eye happened to fall on the name Hawes had scribbled onto his desk pad when calling the B.C.I., so Genero decided to make a quip.

"Another Italian suspect, I see," he said.

"How do you know?" Hawes asked.

"Anything ending in O is Italian," Genero said.

"How about Munro?" Hawes asked.

"What are you, a wise guy?" Genero said, and grinned. He looked at the scribbled name again, and then said, "I got to admit *this* guy has a very funny name for an Italian."

"Funny how?" Hawes asked.

"Ear," Genero said.

"What?"

"Ear. That's what Orecchio means in Italian. Ear."

Which when coupled with Mort, of course, could mean nothing more or less than Dead Ear.

Hawes tore the page from the pad, crumpled it into a ball, and threw it at the wastebasket, missing.

"I said something?" Genero asked, knowing he'd never get his cup of coffee now.

5

THE BOY who delivered the note was eight years old, and he had instructions to give it to the desk sergeant. He stood in the squadroom now surrounded by cops who looked seven feet tall, all of them standing around him in a circle while he looked up with saucer-wide blue eyes and wished he was dead.

"Who gave you this note?" one of the cops asked.

"A man in the park."

"Did he pay you to bring it here?"

"Yeah. Yes. Yeah."

"How much?"

"Five dollars."

"What did he look like?"

"He had yellow hair."

"Was he tall?"

"Oh, yeah."

"Was he wearing a hearing aid?"

"Yeah. A *what?*"

"A thing in his ear."

"Oh, yeah," the kid said.

Everybody tiptoed around the note very carefully, as though it might explode at any moment. Everybody handled the note with tweezers or white cotton gloves. Everybody agreed it should be sent at once to the police lab. Everybody read it at least twice. Everybody studied it and examined it. Even some patrolmen from downstairs came up to have a look at it. It was a very important document. It demanded at least an hour of valuable police time before it was finally encased in a celluloid folder and sent downtown in a manila envelope.

Everybody decided that what this note meant was that the deaf

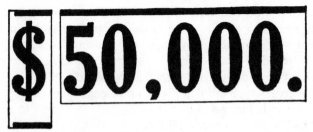

man (who they now reluctantly admitted was once again in their midst) wanted fifty thousand dollars in lieu of killing the deputy mayor exactly as he had killed the parks commissioner. Since fifty thousand dollars was considerably more than the previous demand for five thousand dollars, the cops of the 87th were quite rightfully incensed by the demand. Moreover, the audacity of this criminal somewhere out there was something beyond the ken of their experience. For all its resemblance to a kidnaping, with its subsequent demand for ransom, this case was *not* a kidnaping. No one had been abducted, there was nothing to ransom. No, this was very definitely extortion, and yet the extortion cases they'd dealt with over the years had been textbook cases involving "a wrongful use of force or fear" in an attempt to obtain "property from another." The key word was "another." "Another" was invariably the person against whom mayhem had been threatened. In this case, though, their extortionist didn't seem to care *who* paid the money so long as someone did. *Any*one. Now how were you supposed to deal with a maniac like that?

"He's a maniac," Lieutenant Byrnes said. "Where the hell does he expect us to get fifty thousand dollars?"

Steve Carella, who had been released from the hospital that afternoon and who somewhat resembled a boxer about to put on gloves, what with assorted bandages taped around his hands, said, "Maybe he expects the deputy mayor to pay it."

"Then why the hell didn't he *ask* the deputy mayor?"

"We're his intermediaries," Carella said. "He assumes his demand will carry more weight if it comes from law enforcement officers."

Byrnes looked at Carella.

"Sure," Carella said. "Also, he's getting even with us. He's sore because we fouled up his bank-robbing scheme eight years ago. This is his way of getting back."

"He's a maniac," Byrnes insisted.

"No, he's a very smart cookie," Carella said. "He knocked off Cowper after a measly demand for five thousand dollars. Now that we know he can do it, he's asking ten times the price not to shoot the deputy mayor."

"Where does it say 'shoot'?" Hawes asked.

"Hmmm?"

"He didn't say anything about *shooting* Scanlon. The note yesterday just said 'Deputy Mayor Scanlon Goes Next.'"

"That's right," Carella said. "He can poison him or bludgeon him or stab him or . . ."

"Please," Byrnes said.

"Let's call Scanlon," Carella suggested. "Maybe he's got fifty grand laying around he doesn't know what to do with."

They called Deputy Mayor Scanlon and advised him of the threat upon his life, but Deputy Mayor Scanlon did not have fifty grand laying around he didn't know what to do with. Ten minutes later, the phone on Byrnes' desk rang. It was the police commissioner.

"All right, Byrnes," the commissioner said sweetly, "what's this latest horseshit?"

"Sir," Byrnes said, "we have had two notes from the man we suspect killed Parks Commissioner Cowper, and they constitute a threat upon the life of Deputy Mayor Scanlon."

"What are you doing about it?" the commissioner asked.

"Sir," Byrnes said, "we have already sent both notes to the police laboratory for analysis. Also, sir, we have located the room from which the shots were fired last night, and we have reason to believe we are dealing with a criminal known to this precinct?"

"Who?"

"We don't know."

"I thought you said he was known . . ."

"Yes, sir, we've dealt with him before, but to our knowledge, sir he is unknown."

"How much money does he want this time?"

"Fifty thousand dollars, sir."

"When is Scanlon supposed to be killed?"

"We don't know, sir."

"When does this man want his money?"

"We don't know, sir."

"Where are you supposed to deliver it?"

"We don't know, sir."

"What the hell *do* you know, Byrnes?"

"I know, sir, that we are doing our best to cope with an unprecedented situation, and that we are ready to put our entire squad at the deputy mayor's disposal, if and when he asks for protection. Moreover, sir, I'm sure I can persuade Captain Frick who, as you may know, commands this entire precinct . . ."

"What do you mean, *as* I may know, Byrnes?"

"That is the way we do it in this city, sir."

"That is the way they do it in *most* cities, Byrnes."

"Yes, sir, of course. In any case, I'm sure I can persuade him to release some uniformed officers from their regular duties, or perhaps to call in some off-duty officers, if the commissioner feels that's necessary."

"I feel it's necessary to protect the life of the deputy mayor."

"Yes, of course, sir, we all feel that," Byrnes said.

"What's the matter, Byrnes, don't you like me?" the commissioner asked.

"I try to keep personal feelings out of my work, sir," Byrnes said. "This is a tough case. I don't know about you, but I've never come up against anything like it before. I've got a good team here, and we're doing our best. More than that, we can't do."

"Byrnes," the commissioner said, "you may *have* to do more."

"Sir . . ." Byrnes started, but the commissioner had hung up.

Arthur Brown sat in the basement of Junior High School 106, with a pair of earphones on his head and his right hand on the start button of a tape recorder. The telephone at the La Bresca house diagonally across the street from the school had just rung for the thirty-second time that day, and as he waited for Concetta La Bresca to lift the receiver (as she had done on thirty-one previous occasions) he activated the recorder and sighed in anticipation of what was to come.

It was very clever of the police to have planted a bug in the La

Bresca apartment, that bug having been installed by a plainclothes cop from the lab who identified himself as a telephone repairman, did his work in the La Bresca living room, and then strung his overhead wires from the roof of the La Bresca house to the telephone pole outside, and from there to the pole on the school sidewalk, and from there to the roof of the school building, and down the side wall, and into a basement window, and across the basement floor to a tiny room containing stacked textbooks and the school's old sixteen-millimeter sound projector, where he had set up Arthur Brown's monitoring station.

It was also very clever of the police to have assigned Arthur Brown to this eavesdropping plant because Brown was an experienced cop who had conducted wiretaps before and who was capable of separating the salient from the specious in any given telephone conversation.

There was only one trouble.

Arthur Brown did not understand Italian, and Concetta La Bresca spoke to her friends exclusively in Italian. For all Brown knew, they might have plotted anything from abortion to safe cracking thirty-one times that day, and for all he knew were about to plot it yet another time. He had used up two full reels of tape because he hadn't understood a word that was said, and he wanted each conversation recorded so that someone—probably Carella—could later translate them.

"Hello," a voice said in English.

Brown almost fell off his stool. He sat erect, adjusted the headset, adjusted the volume control on the tape recorder, and began listening.

"Tony?" a second voice asked.

"Yeah, who's this?" The first voice belonged to La Bresca. Apparently he had just returned home from work. The second voice . . .

"This is Dom."

"Who?"

"Dominick."

"Oh, hi, Dom, how's it going?"

"Great."

"What's up, Dom?"

"Oh, nothing," Dom said. "I was just wondering how you was, that's all."

There was silence on the line. Brown tilted his head and brought his hand up to cover one of the earphones.

Again, there was silence.

"I'm fine," La Bresca said at last.

"Good, good," Dom said.

"Well, if that was all you wanted," La Bresca said, "I guess . . ."

"Actually, Tony, I was wondering . . ."

"Yeah?"

"I was wondering if you could lend me a couple of bills till I get myself organized here."

"Organized doing what?" La Bresca asked.

"Well, I took a big loss on that fight two weeks ago, you know, and I still ain't organized."

"You never been organized in your life," La Bresca said.

"That ain't true, Tony."

"Okay, it ain't true. What *is* true is I ain't got a couple of bills to lend you."

"Well, I heard different," Dom said.

"Yeah? What'd you hear?"

"The rumble is you're coming into some very big loot real soon."

"Yeah? Where'd you hear *that* shit?"

"Oh, I listen around here and there, I'm always on the earie."

"Well, this time the rumble is wrong."

"I was thinking maybe just a few C-notes to tide me over for the next week or so. Till I get organized."

"Dom, I ain't seen a C-note since Hector was a pup."

"Tony . . ."

There was a slight hesitation, only long enough to carry the unmistakable weight of warning. Brown caught the suddenly ominous note and listened expectantly for Dom's next words.

"I *know,*" Dom said.

There was another silence on the line. Brown waited. He could hear one of the men breathing heavily.

"What do you know?" La Bresca asked.

"About the caper."

"What caper?"

"Tony, don't let me say it on the phone, huh? You never know who's listening these days."

"What the hell are you trying to do?" La Bresca asked. "Shake me down?"

"No, I'm trying to borrow a couple of hundred is all. Until I get organized. I'd hate like hell to see all your planning go down the drain, Tony. I'd really hate to see that happen."

"You blow the whistle, pal, and we'll know just who done it."

"Tony, if *I* found out about the caper, there's lots of other guys also know about it. It's all over the street. You're lucky the fuzz aren't onto you already."

"The cops don't even know I exist," La Bresca said. "I never took a fall for nothing in my life."

"What you took a fall for and what you done are two different things, right, Tony?"

"Don't bug me, Dom. You screw this up . . ."

"I ain't screwing nothing up. I'm asking for a loan of two hundred bucks, now yes or no, Tony. I'm getting impatient here in this goddamn phone booth. Yes or no?"

"You're a son of a bitch," La Bresca said.

"Does that mean yes?"

"Where do we meet?" La Bresca asked.

Lying in the alleyway that night with his bandaged hands encased in woolen gloves, Carella thought less often of the two punks who had burned him, and also burned him up, than he did about the deaf man.

As he lay in his tattered rags and mildewed shoes, he was the very model of a modern major derelict, hair matted, face streaked, breath stinking of cheap wine. But beneath that torn and threadbare coat, Carella's gloved right hand held a .38 Detective's Special. The right index finger of the glove had been cut away to the knuckle, allowing Carella to squeeze the finger itself inside the trigger guard. He was ready to shoot, and this time he would not allow himself to be cold-cocked. Or even pan-broiled.

But whereas his eyes were squinted in simulated drunken slumber while alertly he watched the alley mouth and listened for tandem footsteps, his thoughts were on the deaf man. He did not like thinking about the deaf man because he could remember with painful clarity the shotgun blast fired at him eight years ago, the excruciating pain in his shoulder, the numbness of his arm and hand, and then the repeated smashing of the shotgun's stock against his face until he fell senseless to the floor. He did not like thinking about how close he had come to death at the hands of the deaf man. Nor did he enjoy thinking of a criminal adversary who was really quite smarter than any of the detectives on the 87th Squad, a schemer, a planner, a brilliant bastard who juggled life and death with the dexterity and emotional sang-froid of a mathematician. The deaf man—somewhere out there—was a machine, and Carella was terrified of things that whirred with computer precision, logical but unreasoning, infallible and aloof, cold and deadly. He dreaded the thought of going up against him once again, and yet he knew this stakeout was small potatoes, two punks itching to get caught, two punks who *would* be caught because they assumed all their intended victims were defenseless and did not realize that one of them could be a detective with his finger curled around the trigger of a deadly weapon. And once they were caught, he would move from the periphery of the deaf man case into the very nucleus of the case itself. And perhaps, once again, come face to face with the tall blond man who wore the hearing aid.

He thought it oddly coincidental and perfectly ironic that the person he loved most in the world was a woman named Teddy Carella, who happened to be his wife, and who also happened to be a deaf mute, whereas the person who frightened him most as a cop and as a man was also deaf, or at least purported to be so, advertised it blatantly —or was this only another subterfuge, a part of the overall scheme? The terrifying thing about the deaf man was his confident assumption that he was dealing with a bunch of nincompoops. Perhaps he was. That was *another* terrifying thing about him. He moved with such certainty that his assumptions took on all the aspects of cold fact. If he said that all flatfoots were fools, then by God that's exactly what they must be—better pay the man whatever he wants before he kills off every high-ranking official in the city. If he could outrageously outline a murder scheme and then execute it before the startled eyes of the city's finest, how could he possibly be stopped from committing the *next* murder, or the one after that, or the one after that?

Carella did not enjoy feeling like a fool.

There were times when he did not necessarily enjoy police work (like right now, freezing his ass off in an alley) but there were never times when he lacked respect for what he did. The concept of law enforcement was simple and clear in his mind. The good guys against the bad guys. He was one of the good guys. And whereas the bad guys in this day and age won often enough to make virtue seem terribly unfashionable sometimes, Carella nonetheless felt that killing people (for example) was not a very nice thing. Nor was breaking into someone's dwelling place in the nighttime overly considerate. Nor was pushing dope quite thoughtful. Nor were mugging, or forging, or kidnaping, or pimping (or spitting on the sidewalk, for that matter) civilized acts designed to uplift the spirit or delight the soul.

He was a cop.

Which meant that he was stuck with all the various images encouraged by countless television shows and motion pictures: the dim-witted public servant being outsmarted by the tough private eye; the overzealous jerk inadvertently blocking the attempts of the intelligent young advertising executive in distress; the insensitive dolt blindly encouraging the young to become adult criminals. Well, what're you gonna do? You got an image, you got one. (He wondered how many television writers were lying in an alley tonight waiting for two hoods to attack.) The damn thing about the deaf man, though, was that he made all these stereotypes seem true. Once he appeared on the scene, every cop on the squad *did* appear dim-witted and bumbling and inefficient.

And if a man could do that merely by making a few phone calls or sending a few notes, what would happen if—

Carella tensed.

The detective assigned to the surveillance of Anthony La Bresca was Bert Kling, whom he had never seen before. Brown's call to the squadroom had advised the lieutenant that La Bresca had admitted he was involved in a forthcoming caper, and this was reason enough to put a tail on him. So Kling took to the subzero streets, leaving the warmth and generosity of Cindy's apartment, and drove out to Riverhead, where he waited across the street from La Bresca's house, hoping to pick up his man the moment he left to meet Dominick. Brown had informed the lieutenant that the pair had arranged a meeting for ten o'clock that night, and it was now 9:07 by Kling's luminous dial, so he figured he had got here good and early, just in time to freeze solid.

La Bresca came down the driveway on the right of the stucco house at ten minutes to ten. Kling stepped into the shadows behind his parked car. La Bresca began walking east, toward the elevated train structure two blocks away. Just my luck, Kling thought, he hasn't got a car. He gave him a lead of half a block, and then began following him. A sharp wind was blowing west off the wide avenue ahead. Kling was forced to lift his face to its direct blast every so often because he didn't want to lose sight of La Bresca, and he cursed for perhaps the fifty-seventh time that winter the injustice of weather designed to plague a man who worked outdoors. Not that he worked outdoors all of the time. Part of the time, he worked at a desk typing up reports in triplicate or calling victims or witnesses. But *much* of the time (it was fair to say much of the time) he worked outdoors, legging it here and there all over this fair city, asking questions and compiling answers and this was the worst son of a bitch winter he had ever lived through in his life. I hope you're going some-

place nice and warm, La Bresca, he thought. I hope you're going
to meet your friend at a Turkish bath or someplace.

Ahead, La Bresca was climbing the steps to the elevated platform. He glanced back at Kling only once, and Kling immediately
ducked his head, and then quickened his pace. He did not want to
reach the platform to discover that La Bresca had already boarded
a train and disappeared.

He need not have worried. La Bresca was waiting for him near
the change booth.

"You following me?" he asked.

"What?" Kling said.

"I *said* are you following me?" La Bresca asked.

The choices open to Kling in that moment were severely limited.
He could say, "What are you out of your mind, why would I be
following you, you're so handsome or something?" Or he could say,
"Yes, I'm following you, I'm a police officer, here's my shield and my
I.D. card," those were the open choices. Either way, the tail was
blown.

"You looking for a rap in the mouth?" Kling said.

"What?" La Bresca said, startled.

"I said what are you, some kind of paranoid nut?" Kling said,
which wasn't what he had said at all. La Bresca didn't seem to notice
the discrepancy. He stared at Kling in honest surprise, and then
started to mumble something, which Kling cut short with a glowering,
menacing, thoroughly frightening look. Mumbling himself, Kling
went up the steps to the uptown side of the platform. The station
stop was dark and deserted and windswept. He stood on the platform with his coattails flapping about him, and waited until La
Bresca came up the steps on the downtown side. La Bresca's train
pulled in not three minutes later, and he boarded it. The train rattled
out of the station. Kling went downstairs again and found a telephone booth. When Willis picked up the phone at the squadroom,
Kling said, "This is Bert. La Bresca made me a couple of blocks
from his house. You'd better get somebody else on him."

"How long you been a cop?" Willis asked.

"It happens to the best of us," Kling said. "Where'd Brown say
they were meeting?"

"A bar on Crawford."

"Well, he boarded a downtown train just a few minutes ago,
you've got time to plant somebody there before he arrives."

"Yeah, I'll get O'Brien over there right away."

"What do you want me to do, come back to the office or what?"

"How the hell did you manage to get spotted?"

"Just lucky, I guess," Kling said.

It was one of those nights.

They came into the alley swiftly, moving directly toward Carella, both of them boys of about seventeen or eighteen, both of them brawny, one of them carrying a large tin can, the label gone from it, the can catching light from the street lamp, glinting in the alleyway as they approached, that's the can of gasoline, Carella thought.

He started to draw his gun and for the first time ever in the history of his career as a cop, it snagged.

It snagged somewhere inside his coat. It was supposed to be a gun designed for negligible bulk, it was not supposed to catch on your goddamn clothing, the two-inch barrel was not supposed to snag when you pulled it, here we go, he thought, the Keystone cops, and leaped to his feet. He could not get the damn gun loose, it was tangled in the wool of his slipover sweater, the yarn pulling and unraveling, he knew the can of gasoline would be thrown into his face in the next moment, he knew a match or a lighter would flare into life, this time they'd be able to smell burning flesh away the hell back at the squadroom. Instinctively, he brought his left hand down as straight and as rigid as a steel pipe, slammed it down onto the forearm of the boy with the can, hitting it hard enough to shatter bone, hearing the scream that erupted from the boy's mouth as he dropped the can, and then feeling the intense pain that rocketed into his head and almost burst from his own lips as his burned and bandaged hand reacted. This is great, he thought, I have no hands, they're going to beat the shit out of me, which turned out to be a fairly good prediction because that's exactly what they did.

There was no danger from the gasoline now, small consolation, at least they couldn't set fire to him. But his hands were useless, and his gun was snagged somewhere inside there on his sweater—he tried ripping the tangled yarn free, ten seconds, twenty seconds, a millennium—and his attackers realized instantly that they had themselves a pigeon, so they all jumped on him, all forty guys in the alley, and then it was too late. They were very good street fighters, these boys. They had learned all about punching to the Adam's apple, they had learned all about flanking operations, one circling around to his left and the other coming up behind him to clout him on the back of the head with the neatest rabbit's punch he had ever taken, oh, they were nice fighters, these boys, he wondered whether the coffin would be metal or wood. While he was wondering this, one of the boys who had learned how to fight in some clean friendly slum, kicked him in the groin, which can hurt. Carella doubled over, and the other clean fighter behind him delivered a second rabbit punch, rabbit punches doubtless being his specialty, while the lad up front connected with a good hard-swinging uppercut that almost tore off his head. So now he was down on the alley floor, the alley covered with refuse and grime and not a little of his own blood, so they decided to stomp him, which is of course what you must necessarily do when your opponent falls down, you kick him in the head and the shoulders and the chest and everywhere you can manage to kick him. If he's a live one, he'll squirm around and try to grab your feet, but if you happen to be lucky enough to get a pigeon who was burned only recently, why you can have an absolute field day kicking him at will because his hands are too tender to grab at *anything,* no less feet. That's why guns were invented, Carella thought, so that if you happen to have second-degree burns on your hands you don't have to use them too much, all you have to do is squeeze a trigger, it's a shame the gun snagged. It's a shame, too, that Teddy's going to be collecting a widow's dole tomorrow morning, he thought, but these guys are going to kill me unless I do something pretty fast. The trouble is I'm a bumbling god-damn cop, the deaf man is right. The kicks landed now with increasing strength and accuracy, nothing encourages a stomper more than an inert and increasingly more vulnerable victim. I'm certainly glad the gasoline, he thought, and a kick exploded against his left eye. He thought at once he would lose the eye, he saw only a blinding flash of yellow, he rolled away, feeling dizzy and nauseous, a boot collided with his rib, he thought he felt it crack, another kick landed on the kneecap of his left leg, he tried to get up, his hands, "You fucking fuzz," one of the boys said, Fuzz, he thought, and was suddenly sick, and another kick crashed into the back of his skull and sent him falling face forward into his own vomit.

He lost consciousness.

He might have been dead, for all he knew.

It was one of those nights.

Bob O'Brien got a flat tire on the way to the Erin Bar & Grill on Crawford Avenue, where Tony La Bresca was to meet the man named Dom.

By the time he changed the flat, his hands were numb, his temper was short, the time was 10:32, and the bar was still a ten-minute drive away. On the off-chance that La Bresca and his fair-weather friend would still be there, O'Brien drove downtown, arriving at the bar at ten minutes to eleven. Not only were they both gone already, but the bartender said to O'Brien the moment he bellied up, "Care for something to drink, Officer?"

It was one of those nights.

6

ON FRIDAY MORNING March 8, Detective-Lieutenant Sam Grossman of the Police Laboratory called the squadroom and asked to talk to Cotton Hawes. He was informed that Hawes, together with several other detectives on the squad, had gone to Buena Vista Hospital to visit Steve Carella. The man answering the telephone was Patrolman Genero, who was holding the fort until one of them returned.

"Well, do *you* want this information or what?" Grossman asked.

"Sir, I'm just supposed to record any calls till they get back," Genero said.

"I'm going to be tied up later," Grossman said, "why don't I just give this to you?"

"All right, sir," Genero said, and picked up his pencil. He felt very much like a detective. Besides, he was grateful not to be outside on another miserable day like this one. "Shoot," he said, and quickly added, "Sir."

"It's on those notes I received."

"Yes, sir, what notes?"

" 'Deputy Mayor Scanlon goes next,' " Grossman quoted, "and 'Look! A whole new,' et cetera."

"Yes, sir," Genero said, not knowing what Grossman was talking about.

"The paper is Whiteside Bond, available at any stationery store in the city. The messages were clipped from national magazines and metropolitan dailies. The adhesive is rubber cement."

"Yes, sir," Genero said, writing frantically.

"Negative on latent prints. We got a whole mess of smeared stuff, but nothing we could run a make on."

"Yes, sir."

"In short," Grossman said, "you know what you can do with these notes."

"What's that, sir?" Genero asked.

"We only run the tests," Grossman said. *"You* guys are supposed to come up with the answers."

Genero beamed. He had been included in the phrase "You guys" and felt himself to be a part of the elite. "Well, thanks a lot," he said, "we'll get to work on it up here."

"Right," Grossman said. "You want these notes back?"

"No harm having them."

"I'll send them over," Grossman said, and hung up.

Very interesting, Genero thought, replacing the receiver on its cradle. If he had owned a deerstalker hat, he would have put it on in that moment.

"Where's the john?" one of the painters asked.

"Why?" Genero said.

"We have to paint it."

"Try not to slop up the urinals," Genero said.

"We're Harvard men," the painter said. "We never slop up the urinals."

The other painter laughed.

The third note arrived at eleven o'clock that morning.

It was delivered by a high school dropout who walked directly past the muster desk and up to the squadroom where Patrolman Genero was evolving an elaborate mystery surrounding the rubber cement that had been used as an adhesive.

"What's everybody on vacation?" the kid asked. He was seventeen years old, his face sprinkled with acne. He felt very much at home in a squadroom because he had once been a member of a street gang called The Terrible Ten, composed of eleven young men who had joined together to combat the Puerto Rican influx into their turf. The gang had disbanded just before Christmas, not because the Puerto Ricans had managed to demolish them, but only because seven of the eleven called The Terrible Ten had finally succumbed to an enemy common to Puerto Rican and white Anglo-Saxon alike: narcotics. Five of the seven were hooked, two were dead. Of the remaining three, one was in prison for a gun violation, another had got married because he'd knocked up a little Irish girl, and the last was carrying an envelope into a detective squadroom, and feeling comfortable enough there to make a quip to a uniformed cop.

"What do you want?" Genero asked.

"I was supposed to give this to the desk sergeant, but there's nobody at the desk. You want to take it?"

"What is it?"

"Search me," the kid said. "Guy stopped me on the street and give me five bucks to deliver it."

"Sit down," Genero said. He took the envelope from the kid and debated opening it, and then realized he had got his fingerprints all over it. He dropped it on the desk. In the toilet down the hall, the painters were singing. Genero was only supposed to answer the phone and take down messages. He looked at the envelope again, severely tempted. "I said sit down," he told the kid.

"What for?"

"You're going to wait here until one of the detectives gets back, that's what for."

"Up yours, fuzz," the kid said, and turned to go.

Genero drew his service revolver. "Hey," he said, and the boy glanced over his shoulder into the somewhat large bore of a .38 Police Special.

"I'm hip to Miranda-Escobedo," the kid said, but he sat down nonetheless.

"Good, that makes two of us," Genero said.

Cops don't like other cops to get it. It makes them nervous. It makes them feel they are in a profession that is not precisely white collar, despite the paperwork involved. It makes them feel that at any moment someone might hit them or kick them or even shoot them.

It makes them feel unloved.

The two young sportsmen who had unloved Carella so magnificently had broken three of his ribs and his nose. They had also given him a headache, due to concussion caused by a few well-placed kicks to the medulla oblongata. He had gained consciousness shortly after being admitted to the hospital and he was conscious now, of course, but he didn't look good, and he didn't feel good, and he didn't feel much like talking. So he sat with Teddy beside the bed, holding her hand and breathing shallowly because the broken ribs hurt like hell. The detectives did most of the talking, but there was a cheerlessness in their banter. They were suddenly face to face with violence of a most personal sort, not the violence they dealt with every working day of their lives, not an emotionless confrontation with broken mutilated strangers, but instead a glimpse at a friend and colleague who lay in battered pain on a hospital bed while his wife held his hand and tried to smile at their feeble jokes.

The four detectives left the hospital room at twelve noon. Brown and Willis walked ahead of Hawes and Kling, who trailed behind them silently.

"Man, they got him good," Brown said.

The seventeen-year-old dropout was beginning to scream Miranda-Escobedo, quoting rights like a lawyer. Genero kept telling him to shut up, but he had never really understood the Surpreme Court decision too well, despite the flyers issued to every cop in the precinct, and he was afraid now that the kid knew something he didn't know. He was overjoyed to hear the ring of footsteps on the recently painted iron-runged steps leading to the squadroom. Willis and Brown came into view on the landing first. Kling and Hawes were behind them. Genero could have kissed them all.

"These the bulls?" the dropout asked, and Genero said, "Shut up."

"What's up?" Brown asked.

"Tell your friend here about Miranda-Escobedo," the kid said.

"Who're you?" Brown asked.

"He delivered an envelope," Genero said.

"Here we go," Hawes said.

"What's your name, kid?"

"Give me some advice on my rights," the kid said.

"Tell me your name, or I'll kick your ass in," Brown said. "How do you like *that* advice?" He had just witnessed what a pair of young hoods had done to Carella, and he was in no mood to take nonsense from a snotnose.

"My name is Michael McFadden, and I won't answer no questions without a lawyer here," the kid said.

"Can you afford a lawyer?" Brown asked.

"No."

"Get him a lawyer, Hal," Brown said, bluffing.

"Hey, wait a minute, what is this?" McFadden asked.

"You want a lawyer, we'll get you a lawyer," Brown said.

"What do I need a lawyer for? All I done was deliver an envelope."

"*I* don't know why you need a lawyer," Brown said. "*You're* the one who said you wanted one. Hal, call the D.A.'s office, get this suspect here a lawyer."

"Suspect?" McFadden said. *"Suspect?* What the hell did *I* do?"

"I don't know, kid," Brown said, "and I can't find out because you won't let me ask any questions without a lawyer here. You getting him that lawyer, Hal?"

Willis, who had lifted the phone receiver and was listening to nothing more vital than a dial tone, said, "Tie-line's busy, Art."

"Okay, I guess we'll just have to wait then. Make yourself comfortable, kid, we'll get a lawyer up here for you soon as we can."

"Look, what the hell," McFadden said, "I don't need no lawyer."

"You said you wanted one."

"Yeah, but, I mean, like if this is nothing serious . . ."

"We just wanted to ask you some questions about that envelope, that's all."

"Why? What's in it?"

"Let's open the envelope and show the kid what's in it, shall we do that?" Brown said.

"All I done was deliver it," McFadden said.

"Well, let's see what's inside it, shall we?" Brown said. He folded his handkerchief over the envelope, slit it open with a letter opener, and then used a tweezer to yank out the folded note.

"Here, use these," Kling said, and took a pair of white cotton gloves from the top drawer of his desk. Brown put on the gloves, held his hands widespread alongside his face, and grinned.

"Whuffo does a chicken cross de road, Mistuh Bones?" he said, and burst out laughing. The other cops all laughed with him. Encouraged, McFadden laughed too. Brown glowered at him, and the laugh died in his throat. Gingerly, Brown unfolded the note and spread it flat on the desk top:

Now repeat:

same

PARK

sAme

bench

same

pail

before

NOON
tomorrow

OR ELSE

sAme

ASSASSINS

"What's that supposed to mean?" McFadden asked.

"You tell us," Brown said.

"Beats me."

"Who gave you this note?"

"A tall blond guy wearing a hearing aid."

"You know him?"

"Never saw him before in my life."

"He just came up to you and handed you the envelope, huh?"

"No, he came up and offered me a fin to take it in here."

"Why'd you accept?"

"Is there something wrong with bringing a note in a police station?"

"Only if it's an extortion note," Brown said.

"What's extortion?" McFadden asked.

"You belong to The Terrible Ten, don't you?" Kling asked suddenly.

"The club broke up," McFadden said.

"But you *used* to belong."

"Yeah, how do you know?" McFadden asked, a trace of pride in his voice.

"We know every punk in this precinct," Willis said. "You finished with him, Artie?"

"I'm finished with him."

"Good-by, McFadden."

"What's extortion?" McFadden asked again.

"Good-by," Willis said again.

The detective assigned to tailing Anthony La Bresca was Meyer Meyer. He was picked for the job because detectives aren't supposed to be bald, and it was reasoned that La Bresca, already gun shy, would never tip to him. It was further reasoned that if La Bresca was really involved in a contemplated caper, it might be best not to follow him from his job to wherever he was going, but instead to be waiting for him there when he arrived. This presented the problem of second-guessing where he might be going, but it was recalled by one or another of the detectives that La Bresca had mentioned frequenting a pool hall on South Leary, and so this was where Meyer stationed himself at four o'clock that afternoon.

He was wearing baggy corduroy trousers, a brown leather jacket, and a brown watch cap. He looked like a longshoreman or something. Actually, he didn't know what he looked like, he just hoped he didn't look like a cop. He had a matchstick in his mouth. He figured that was a nice touch, the matchstick. Also, because criminal types have an uncanny way of knowing when somebody is heeled, he was not carrying a gun. The only weapon on his person was a longshoreman's hook tucked into the waistband of his trousers. If anyone asked him about the hook, he would say he needed it on the job, thereby establishing his line of work at the same time. He hoped he would not have to use the hook.

He wandered into the pool hall, which was on the second floor of a dingy brick building, said "Hi," to the man sitting behind the entrance booth, and then said, "You got any open tables?"

"Pool or billiards?" the man said. He was chewing on a match-stick, too.

"Pool," Meyer said.

"Take Number Four," the man said, and turned to switch on the table lights from the panel behind him. "You new around here?" he asked, his back to Meyer.

"Yeah, I'm new around here," Meyer said.

"We don't dig hustlers," the man said.

"I'm no hustler," Meyer answered.

"Just make sure you ain't."

Meyer shrugged and walked over to the lighted table. There were seven other men in the pool hall, all of them congregated around a table near the windows, where four of them were playing and the other three were kibitzing. Meyer unobtrusively took a cue from the rack, set up the balls, and began shooting. He was a lousy player. He kept mentally calling shots and missing. Every now and then he glanced at the door. He was playing for perhaps ten minutes when one of the men from the other table sauntered over.

"Hi," the man said. He was a burly man wearing a sports jacket over a woolen sports shirt. Tufts of black hair showed above the open throat of the shirt. His eyes were a deep brown, and he wore a black mustache that seemed to have leaped from his chest onto the space below his nose. The hair on his head was black too. He looked tough and he looked menacing, and Meyer immediately made him for the local cheese.

"You play here before?" the man asked.

"Nope," Meyer said without looking up from the table.

"I'm Tino."

"Hello, Tino," Meyer said, and shot.

"You missed," Tino said.

"That's right, I did."

"You a hustler?" Tino said.

"Nope."

"We break hustlers' arms and throw them down the stairs," Tino said.

"The arms or the whole hustler?" Meyer asked.

"I got no sense of humor," Tino said.

"Me, neither. Buzz off, you're ruining my game."

"Don't try to take nobody, mister," Tino said. "This's a friendly neighborhood pool hall."

"Yeah, you sure make it sound very friendly," Meyer said.

"It's just we don't like hustlers."

"I got your message three times already," Meyer said. "Eight ball in the side." He shot and missed.

"Where'd you learn to shoot pool?" Tino said.

"My father taught me."

"Was he as lousy as you?"

Meyer didn't answer.

"What's that in your belt there?"

"That's a hook," Meyer said.

"What's it for?"

"I use it," Meyer said.

"You work on the docks?"

"That's right."

"Where?"

"On the docks," Meyer said.

"Yeah, *where* on the docks?"

"Look, friend," Meyer said, and put down the pool cue and stared at Tino."

"Yeah?"

"What's it your business where I work?"

"I like to know who comes in here."

"Why? You own the joint?"

"My brother does."

"Okay," Meyer said, "My name's Stu Levine, I'm working the Leary Street docks right now, unloading the S.S. *Agda* out of Sweden. I live downtown on Ridgeway, and I happened to notice there was a pool hall here, so I decided to come in and run off a few racks before heading home. You think that'll satisfy your brother, or do you want to see my birth certificate?"

"You Jewish?" Tino asked.

"Funny I don't look it, right?"

"No, you *do* look it."

"So?"

"So nothing. We get some Jewish guys from around the corner in here every now and then."

"I'm glad to hear it. Is it okay to shoot now?"

"You want company?"

"How do I know *you're* not a hustler?"

"We'll pay for time, how's that?"

"You'll win," Meyer said.

"So what? It's better than playing alone, ain't it?"

"I came up here to shoot a few balls and enjoy myself," Meyer said. "Why should I play with somebody better than me? I'll get stuck with the time, and you'll be doing all the shooting."

"You could consider it a lesson."

"I don't need lessons."

"You need lessons, believe me," Tino said. "The way you shoot pool, it's a disgrace."

"If I need lessons, I'll get Minnesota Fats."

"There ain't no real person named Minnesota Fats," Tino said, "he was just a guy they made up," which reminded Meyer that someone had named a fictitious character after him, and which further reminded him that he had not yet heard from Rollie Chabrier down at the D.A.'s office.

"Looks like I'll never get to shoot, anyway," he said, "if you're gonna stand here and gab all day."

"Okay?" Tino said.

"Go ahead, take a cue," Meyer said, and sighed. He felt he had handled the encounter very well. He had not seemed too anxious to be friendly, and yet he had succeeded in promoting a game with one of the pool hall regulars. When La Bresca walked in, if indeed he ever did, he would find Tino playing with his good old buddy Stu Levine from the Leary Street docks. Very good, Meyer thought, they ought to up me a grade tomorrow morning.

"First off, you hold your cue wrong," Tino said. "Here's how you got to hold it if you expect to sink anything."

"Like this?" Meyer said, trying to imitate the grip.

"You got arthritis or something?" Tino asked, and burst out laughing at his own joke, proving to Meyer's satisfaction that he really did not have a sense of humor.

Tino was demonstrating the proper English to put on the cue ball in order to have it veer to the left after contact, and Meyer was alternately watching the clock and the door when La Bresca walked in some twenty minutes later. Meyer recognized him at once from the description he'd been given, but turned away immediately, not wanting to seem at all interested, and listened to Tino's explanation, and then listened to the meager joke Tino offered, something about the reason it's called English is because if you hit an Englishman in the balls with a stick, they'll turn white just like the cue ball on the table, get it? Tino laughed, and Meyer laughed with him, and that was what La Bresca saw as he approached the table, Tino and his good old buddy from the Leary Street docks, laughing it up and shooting a friendly game of pool in the friendly neighborhood pool hall.

"Hi, Tino," La Bresca said.

"Hi, Tony."

"How's it going?"

"So-so. This here is Stu Levine."

"Glad to meet you," La Bresca said.

"Same here," Meyer said, and extended his hand.

"This here is Tony La Bresca. He shoots a good game."

"Nobody shoots as good as you," La Bresca said.

"Stu here shoots the way Angie used to. You remember Angie who was crippled? That's the way Stu here shoots."

"Yeah, I remember Angie," La Bresca said, and both men burst out laughing. Meyer laughed with them, what the hell.

"Stu's father taught him," Tino said.

"Yeah? Who taught his father?" La Bresca said, and both men burst out laughing again.

"I hear you got yourself a job," Tino said.

"That's right."

"You just getting through?"

"Yeah, I thought I'd shoot a game or two before supper. You see Calooch around?"

"Yeah, he's over there by the windows."

"Thought maybe I'd shoot a game with him."

"Why'nt you join us right here?" Tino said.

"Thanks," La Bresca said, "but I promised Calooch I'd shoot a game with him. Anyway, you're too much of a shark."

"A shark, you hear that, Stu?" Tino said. "He thinks I'm a shark."

"Well, I'll see you," La Bresca said, and walked over to the window table. A tall thin man in a striped shirt was bent over the table, angling for a shot. La Bresca waited until he had run off three or four balls, and then they both went up to the front booth. The lights suddenly came on over a table across the hall. La Bresca and the man named Calooch went to the table, took sticks down, racked up the balls, and began playing.

"Who's Calooch?" Meyer asked Tino.

"Oh, that's Pete Calucci," Tino said.

"Friend of Tony's?"

"Oh, yeah, they know each other a long time."

Calooch and La Bresca were doing a lot of talking. They weren't doing too much playing, but they sure were talking a lot. They talked, and then one of them took a shot, and then they talked some more, and after a while the other one took a shot, and it went like that for almost an hour. At the end of the hour, both men put up their sticks, and shook hands. Calooch went back to the window table, and La Bresca went up front to settle for the time. Meyer looked up at the clock and said, "Wow, look at that, already six o'clock. I better get home, my wife'll murder me."

"Well, Stu, I enjoyed playing with you," Tino said. "Stop in again sometime."

"Yeah, maybe I will," Meyer said.

The street outside was caught in the pale gray grasp of dusk, empty, silent except for the keening of the wind, bitterly cold, forbidding. Anthony La Bresca walked with his hands in the pockets of his beige car coat, the collar raised, the green muffler wound about his neck and flapping in the fierce wind. Meyer stayed far behind him, mindful of Kling's embarrassing encounter the night before and determined not to have the same thing happen to an old experienced workhorse like himself. The cold weather and the resultant empty streets did not help him very much. It was comparatively simple to tail a man on a crowded street, but when there are only two people left alive in the world, the one up front might suddenly turn at the sound of a footfall or a tail-of-the-eye glimpse of something or someone behind him. So Meyer kept his distance and utilized every doorway he could find, ducking in and out of the street, grateful for the frantic activity that helped ward off the cold, convinced he would not be spotted, but mindful of the alternate risk he was running: if La Bresca turned a corner suddenly, or entered a building unexpectedly, Meyer could very well lose him.

The girl was waiting in a Buick.

The car was black, Meyer made the year and make at once, but he could not read the license plate because the car was too far away, parked at the curb some two blocks up the street. The engine was running. The exhaust threw gray plumes of carbon monoxide into the gray and empty street. La Bresca stopped at the car, and Meyer ducked into the closest doorway, the windowed alcove of a pawnshop. Surrounded by saxophones and typewriters, cameras and tennis rackets, fishing rods and loving cups, Meyer looked diagonally through the joined and angled windows of the shop and squinted his eyes in an attempt to read the license plate of the Buick. He could not make out the numbers. The girl had blond hair, it fell loose to the base of her neck, she leaned over on the front seat to open the door for La Bresca.

La Bresca got into the car and slammed the door behind him.

Meyer came out of the doorway just as the big black Buick gunned away from the curb.

He still could not read the license plate.

7

NOBODY likes to work on Saturday.

There's something obscene about it, it goes against the human grain. Saturday is the day before the day of rest, a good time to stomp on all those pressures that have been building Monday to Friday. Given a nice blustery rotten March day with the promise of snow in the air and the city standing expectantly monolithic, stoic, and solemn, given such a peach of a Saturday, how nice to be able to start a cannel coal fire in the fireplace of your three-room apartment and smoke yourself out of the joint. Or, lacking a fireplace, what better way to utilize Saturday than by pouring yourself a stiff hooker of bourbon and curling up with a blonde or a book, spending your time with *War and Peace* or *Whore and Piece,* didn't Shakespeare invent some of his best puns on Saturday, drunk with a wench in his first best bed?

Saturday is a quiet day. It can drive you to distraction with its prospects of leisure time, it can force you to pick at the coverlet wondering what to do with all your sudden freedom, it can send you wandering through the rooms in search of occupation while moodily contemplating the knowledge that the loneliest night of the week is fast approaching.

Nobody likes to work on Saturday because nobody else is working on Saturday.

Except cops.

Grind, grind, grind, work, work, work, driven by a sense of public-mindedness and dedication to humanity, law enforcement officers are forever at the ready, alert of mind, swift of body, noble of purpose.

Andy Parker was asleep in the swivel chair behind his desk.

"Where is everybody?" one of the painters said.

"What?" Parker said. "Huh?" Parker said, and sat bolt upright, and glared at the painter and then washed his huge hand over his face and said, "What the hell's the matter with you, scaring a man that way?"

"We're leaving," the first painter said.

"We're finished," the second painter said.

"We already got all our gear loaded on the truck, and we wanted to say good-by to everybody."

"So where is everybody?"

"There's a meeting in the lieutenant's office," Parker said.

"We'll just pop in and say good-by," the first painter said.

"I wouldn't advise that," Parker said.

"Why not?"

"They're discussing homicide. It's not wise to pop in on people when they're discussing homicide."

"Not even to say good-by?"

"You can say good-by to *me,*" Parker said.

"It wouldn't be the same thing," the first painter said.

"So then hang around and say good-by when they come out. They should be finished before twelve. In fact, they *got* to be finished before twelve."

"Yeah, but *we're* finished *now,*" the second painter said.

"Can't you find a few things you missed?" Parker suggested. "Like, for example, you didn't paint the typewriters, or the bottle on the water cooler, or our guns. How come you missed our guns? You got green all over everything else in the goddamn place."

"You should be grateful," the first painter said. "Some people won't work on Saturday *at all,* even at time and a half."

So both painters left in high dudgeon, and Parker went back to sleep in the swivel chair behind his desk.

"I don't know what kind of a squad I'm running here," Lieutenant Byrnes said, "when two experienced detectives can blow a surveillance, one by getting made first crack out of the box, and the other by losing his man; that's a pretty good batting average for two experienced detectives."

"I was told the suspect didn't have a car," Meyer said. "I was told he had taken a train the night before."

"That's right, he did," Kling said.

"I had no way of knowing a woman would be waiting for him in a car," Meyer said.

"So you lost him," Byrnes said, "which might have been all right

if the man had gone home last night. But O'Brien was stationed outside the La Bresca house in Riverhead, and the man never showed,
which means we don't know where he is today, now do we? We don't
know where a prime suspect is on the day the deputy mayor is
supposed to get killed."

"No, sir," Meyer said, "we don't know where La Bresca is."

"Because *you* lost him."

"I guess so, sir."

"Well, how would you revise that statement, Meyer?"

"I wouldn't, sir. I lost him."

"Yes, very good, I'll put you in for a commendation."

"Thank you, sir."

"Don't get flip, Meyer."

"I'm sorry, sir."

"This isn't a goddamn joke here, I don't want Scanlon to wind up
with two holes in his head the way Cowper did."

"No, sir, neither do I."

"Okay, then learn for Christ's sake how to tail a person, will you?"

"Yes, sir."

"Now what about this other man you say La Bresca spent time
with in conversation, what was his name?"

"Calucci, sir. Peter Calucci."

"Did you check him out?"

"Yes, sir, last night before I went home. Here's the stuff we got
from the B.C.I."

Meyer placed a manila envelope on Byrnes' desk, and then
stepped back to join the other detectives ranged in a military line
before the desk. None of the men was smiling. The lieutenant was in
a lousy mood, and somebody was supposed to come up with fifty
thousand dollars before noon, and the possibility existed that the
deputy mayor would soon be dispatched to that big City Hall in
the sky, so nobody was smiling. The lieutenant reached into the
envelope and pulled out a photocopy of a fingerprint card, glanced
at it cursorily, and then pulled out a photocopy of Calucci's police
record.

Byrnes read the sheet, and then said, "When did he get out?"

"He was a bad apple. He applied for parole after serving a third
of the sentence, was denied, and applied every year after that. He
finally made it in seven."

Byrnes looked at the sheet again.

IDENTIFICATION BUREAU

NAME ____ Peter Vincent Calucci ____

IDENTIFICATION JACKET NUMBER ___ P 421904 ___

ALIAS ____ "Calooch"   "Cooch"   "Kook" ____

____ **COLOR** ___ White ___

RESIDENCE ____ 336 South 91st Street, Isola ____

DATE OF BIRTH ____ October 2, 1938 ____ **AGE** __ 22 __

BIRTHPLACE ____ Isola ____

HEIGHT __ 5'9" __ **WEIGHT** ___ 156 ___ **HAIR** Brown __ **EYES** Brown __

COMPLEXION ___ Swarthy ___ **OCCUPATION** Construction worker __

SCARS AND TATTOOS ___ Appendectomy scar, no tattoos. ___

ARRESTED BY: ____ Patrolman Henry Butler ____

DETECTIVE DIVISION NUMBER: ___ 63-R1-1605-1960 ___

DATE OF ARREST __ 3/14/60 __ **PLACE** 812 North 65 St., Isola

---

CHARGE ____ Robbery ____

BRIEF DETAILS OF CRIME ___ Calucci entered gasoline station at __

__ 812 North 65 Street at or about midnight, threatened __

__ to shoot attendant if he did not open safe. Attendant __

__ said he did not know combination, Calucci cocked __

__ revolver and was about to fire when patrolman Butler __

__ of 63rd Precinct came upon scene and apprehended him. __

PREVIOUS RECORD ___ None ___

INDICTED ____ Criminal Courts, March 15, 1960. ____

FINAL CHARGE ___ Robbery in first degree, Penal Law 2125 __

DISPOSITION ___ Pleaded guilty 7/8/60, sentenced to ten __

____ years at Castleview Prison. ____

"What's he been doing?" Byrnes asked.

"Construction work."

"That how he met La Bresca?"

"Calucci's parole officer reports that his last job was with Abco Construction, and a call to the company listed La Bresca as having worked there at the same time."

"I forget, does this La Bresca have a record?"

"No, sir."

"Has Calucci been clean since he got out?"

"According to his parole officer, yes, sir."

"Now who's this person 'Dom' who called La Bresca Thursday night?"

"We have no idea, sir."

"Because La Bresca tipped to your tailing him, isn't that right, Kling?"

"Yes, sir, that's right, sir."

"Is Brown still on that phone tap?"

"Yes, sir."

"Have you tried any of our stoolies?"

"No, sir, not yet."

"Well, when the hell do you propose to get moving? We're supposed to deliver fifty thousand dollars by twelve o'clock. It's now a quarter after ten, when the hell . . ."

"Sir, we've been trying to get a line on Calucci. His parole officer gave us an address, and we sent a man over, but his landlady says he hasn't been there since early yesterday morning."

"Of course not!" Byrnes shouted. "The two of them are probably shacked up with that blond woman, whoever the hell *she* was, planning how to murder Scanlon when we fail to deliver the payoff money. Get Danny Gimp or Fats Donner, find out if they know a fellow named Dom who dropped a bundle on a big fight two weeks ago. Who the hell was fighting two weeks ago, anyway? Was that the championship fight?"

"Yes, sir."

"All right, get cracking. Does anybody use Gimp besides Carella?"

"No, sir."

"Who uses Donner?"

"I do, sir."

"Then get him right away, Willis."

"If he's not in Florida, sir. He usually goes south in the winter."

"Goddamn stool pigeons go south," Byrnes grumbled, "and we're stuck here with a bunch of maniacs trying to kill people. All right, go on, Willis, get moving."

"Yes, sir," Willis said, and left the office.

"Now what about this other possibility, this deaf man thing? Jesus Christ, I hope it's not him, I hope this is La Bresca and Calucci and the blond bimbo who drove him clear out of sight last night, Meyer . . ."

"Yes, sir . . ."

". . . and not that deaf bastard again. I've talked to the commissioner on this, and I've also talked to the deputy mayor *and* the mayor, and we're agreed that paying the fifty thousand dollars is out of the question. We're to try apprehending whoever picks up that lunch pail and see if we can't get a lead this time. And we're to provide protection for Scanlon and that's all for now. So I want you two to arrange the drop, and saturation coverage of that bench, and I want a suspect brought in here today, and I want him questioned till he's blue in the face, have a lawyer ready and waiting for him in case he screams Miranda-Escobedo, I want a *lead* today, have you got that?"

"Yes, sir," Meyer said.

"Yes, sir," Kling said.

"You think you can set up the drop and cover without fouling it up like you fouled up the surveillance?"

"Yes, sir, we can handle it."

"All right, then get going, and bring me some meat on this goddamn case."

"Yes, sir," Kling and Meyer said together, and then went out of the office.

"Now what's this about a junkie being in that room with the killer?" Byrnes asked Hawes.

"That's right, sir."

"Well, what's your idea, Cotton?"

"My idea is he got her in there to make sure she'd be stoned when he started shooting, that's my idea, sir."

"That's the stupidest idea I've ever heard in my life," Byrnes said. "Get the hell out of here, go help Meyer and Kling, go call the hospital, find out how Carella's doing, go set up another plant for those two punks who beat him up, go do *something,* for Christ's sake!"

"Yes, sir," Hawes said, and went out into the squadroom.

Andy Parker, awakened by the grumbling of the other men,

washed his hand over his face, blew his nose, and then said, "The painters said to tell you good-by."

"Good riddance," Meyer said.

"Also, you got a call from the D.A.'s office."

"Who from?"

"Rollie Chabrier."

"When was this?"

"Half-hour ago, I guess."

"Why didn't you put it through?"

"While you were in there with the loot? No, sir."

"I've been waiting for this call," Meyer said, and immediately dialed Chabrier's number.

"Mr. Chabrier's office," a bright female voice said.

"Bernice, this is Meyer Meyer up at the 87th. I hear Rollie called me a little while ago."

"That's right," Bernice said.

"Would you put him on, please?"

"He's gone for the day," Bernice said.

"Gone for the day? It's only a little after ten."

"Well," Bernice said, "nobody likes to work on Saturday."

The black lunch pail containing approximately fifty thousand scraps of newspaper was placed in the center of the third bench on the Clinton Street footpath into Grover Park by Detective Cotton Hawes, who was wearing thermal underwear and two sweaters and a business suit and an overcoat and ear muffs. Hawes was an expert skier, and he had skied on days when the temperature at the base was four below zero and the temperature at the summit was thirty below, had skied on days when his feet went and his hands went and he boomed the mountain non-stop not for fun or sport but just to get near the fire in the base lodge before he shattered into a hundred brittle pieces. But he had never been this cold before. It was bad enough to be working on Saturday, but it was indecent to be working when the weather threatened to gelatinize a man's blood.

Among the other people who were braving the unseasonable winds and temperatures that Saturday were:

(1) A pretzel salesman at the entrance to the Clinton Street footpath.

(2) Two nuns saying their beads on the second bench into the park.

(3) A passionate couple necking in a sleeping bag on the grass behind the third bench.

(4) A blind man sitting on the fourth bench, patting his seeing eye German shepherd and scattering bread crumbs to the pigeons.

The pretzel salesman was a detective named Stanley Faulk, recruited from the 88th across the park, a man of fifty-eight who wore a gray handlebar mustache as his trademark. The mustache made it quite simple to identify him when he was working in his own territory, thereby diminishing his value on plants. But it also served to strike terror into the hearts of hoods near and wide, in much the same way that the green-and-white color combination of a radio motor patrol car is supposed to frighten criminals and serve as a deterrent. Faulk wasn't too happy about being called into service for the 87th on a day like this one, but he was bundled up warmly in several sweaters over which was a black cardigan-type candy store-owner sweater over which he had put on a white apron. He was standing behind a cart that displayed pretzels stacked on long round sticks. A walkie-talkie was set into the top of the cart.

The two nuns saying their beads were Detectives Meyer Meyer and Bert Kling, and they were really saying what a son of a bitch Byrnes had been to bawl them out that way in front of Hawes and Willis, embarrassing them and making them feel very foolish.

"I feel very foolish right now," Meyer whispered.

"How come?" Kling whispered.

"I feel like I'm in drag," Meyer whispered.

The passionate couple assignment had been the choice assignment, and Hawes and Willis had drawn straws for it. The reason it was so choice was that the other half of the passionate couple was herself quite choice, a policewoman named Eileen Burke, with whom Willis had worked on a mugging case many years back. Eileen had red hair and green eyes, Eileen had long legs, sleek and clean, full-calved, tapering to slender ankles, Eileen had very good breasts, and whereas Eileen was much taller than Willis (who only barely scraped past the five-foot-eight height requirement), he did not mind at all because big girls always seemed attracted to him, and vice versa.

"We're supposed to be kissing," he said to Eileen, and held her close in the warm sleeping bag.

"My lips are getting chapped," she said.

"Your lips are very nice," he said.

"We're supposed to be here on business," Eileen said.

"Mmm," he answered.

"Get your hand off my behind," she said.

"Oh, is that your behind?" he asked.

"Listen," she said.

"I hear it," he said. "Somebody's coming. You'd better kiss me."

She kissed him. Willis kept one eye on the bench. The person passing was a governess wheeling a baby carriage, God knew who would send an infant out on a day when the glacier was moving south. The woman and the carriage passed. Willis kept kissing Detective 2nd/Grade Eileen Burke.

"Mm frick sheb bron," Eileen mumbled.

"Mmm?" Willis mumbled.

Eileen pulled her mouth away and caught her breath. "I *said* I think she's gone."

"What's that?" Willis asked suddenly.

"Do not be afraid, *guapa,* it is only my pistol," Eileen said, and laughed.

"I meant on the path. Listen."

They listened.

Someone else was approaching the bench.

From where Patrolman Richard Genero sat in plainclothes on the fourth bench, wearing dark glasses and patting the head of the German shepherd at his feet, tossing crumbs to the pigeons, wishing for summer, he could clearly see the young man who walked rapidly to the third bench, picked up the lunch pail, looked swiftly over his shoulder, and began walking not *out* of the park, but deeper *into* it.

Genero didn't know quite what to do at first.

He had been pressed into duty only because there was a shortage of available men that afternoon (crime prevention being an arduous and difficult task on any given day, but especially on Saturday), and he had been placed in the position thought least vulnerable, it being assumed the man who picked up the lunch pail would immediately reverse direction and head out of the park again, onto Grover Avenue, where Faulk the pretzel man and Hawes, parked in his own car at the curb, would immediately collar him. But the suspect was coming into the park instead, heading for Genero's bench, and Genero was a fellow who didn't care very much for violence, so he sat there wishing he was home in bed, with his mother serving him hot *minestrone* and singing old Italian arias.

The dog at his feet had been trained for police work, and Genero had been taught a few hand signals and voice signals in the squadroom before heading out for his vigil on the fourth bench, but he was also afraid of dogs, especially big dogs, and the idea of giving this animal a kill command that might possibly be misunderstood filled

Genero with fear and trembling. Suppose he gave the command and the dog leaped for his *own* jugular rather than for the throat of the young man who was perhaps three feet away now and walking quite rapidly, glancing over his shoulder every now and again? Suppose he did that and this beast tore him to shreds, what would his mother say to that? *che bella cosa,* you hadda to become a police, hah?

Willis, in the meantime, had slid his walkie-talkie up between Eileen Burke's breasts and flashed the news to Hawes, parked in his own car on Grover Avenue, good place to be when your man is going the other way. Willis was now desperately trying to lower the zipper on the bag, which zipper seemed to have become somehow stuck. Willis didn't mind being stuck in a sleeping bag with someone like Eileen Burke, who wiggled and wriggled along with him as they attempted to extricate themselves, but he suddenly fantasied the lieutenant chewing him out the way he had chewed out Kling and Meyer this morning and so he really *was* trying to lower that damn zipper while entertaining the further fantasy that Eileen Burke was beginning to enjoy all this adolescent tumbling. Genero, of course, didn't know that Hawes had been alerted, he only knew that the suspect was abreast of him now, and passing the bench now, and moving swiftly beyond the bench now, so he got up and first took off the sun-glasses, and then unbuttoned the third button of his coat the way he had seen detectives do on television, and then reached in for his revolver and then shot himself in the leg.

The suspect began running.

Genero fell to the ground and the dog licked his face.

Willis got out of the sleeping bag and Eileen Burke buttoned her blouse and her coat and then adjusted her garters, and Hawes came running into the park and slipped on a patch of ice near the third bench and almost broke his neck.

"Stop, police!" Willis shouted.

And, miracle of miracles, the suspect stopped dead in his tracks and waited for Willis to approach him with his gun in his hand and lipstick all over his face.

The suspect's name was Alan Parry.

They advised him of his rights and he agreed to talk to them without a lawyer, even though a lawyer was present and waiting for him in case he demanded one.

"Where do you live, Alan?" Willis asked.

"Right around the corner. I know you guys. I see you guys around all the time. Don't you know me? I live right around the corner."

"You make him?" Willis asked the other detectives.

They all shook their heads. They were standing around him in a loose circle, the pretzel man, two nuns, the pair of lovers, and the big redhead with a white streak in his hair and a throbbing ankle in his thermal underwear.

"Why'd you run, Alan?" Willis asked.

"I heard a shot. In this neighborhood, when you hear shooting, you run."

"Who's your partner?"

"What partner?"

"The guy who's in this with you."

"In *what* with me?"

"The murder plot."

"The *what?*"

"Come on, Alan, you play ball with us, we'll play ball with you."

"Hey, man, you got the wrong customer," Parry said.

"How were you going to split the loot, Alan?"

"What loot?"

"The loot in that lunch pail."

"Listen, I never seen that lunch pail before in my life."

"There's thirty thousand dollars in that lunch pail," Willis said, "now come on, Alan, you know that, stop playing it cozy."

Parry either avoided the trap, or else did not know there was supposed to be *fifty* thousand dollars in the black pail he had lifted from the bench. He shook his head and said, "I don't know nothing about no loot, I was asked to pick up the pail, and I done it."

"Who asked you?"

"A big blond guy wearing a hearing aid."

"Do you expect me to believe that?" Willis said.

The cue was one the detectives of the 87th had used many times before in interrogating suspects, and it was immediately seized upon by Meyer, who said, "Take it easy, Hal," the proper response, the response that told Willis they were once again ready to assume antagonistic roles. In the charade that would follow, Willis would play the tough bastard out to hang a phony rap on poor little Alan Parry, while Meyer would play the sympathetic father figure. The other detectives (including Faulk of the 88th, who was familiar with the ploy and had used it often enough himself in his own squad-room) would serve as a sort of nodding Greek chorus, impartial and objective.

Without even so much as a glance at Meyer, Willis said, "What do you mean, take it easy? This little punk has been lying from the minute we got him up here."

"Maybe there really *was* a tall blond guy with a hearing aid," Meyer said. "Give him a chance to tell us, will you?"

"Sure, and maybe there was a striped elephant with pink polka dots," Willis said. "Who's your partner, you little punk?"

"I don't *have* no partner!" Parry said. Plaintively, he said to Meyer, "Will you please tell this guy I ain't *got* a partner?"

"Calm down, Hal, will you?" Meyer said. "Let's hear it, Alan."

"I was on my way home when . . ."

"From where?" Willis snapped.

"Huh?"

"Where were you coming from?"

"From my girl's house."

"Where?"

"Around the corner. Right across the street from my house."

"What were you doing there?"

"Well, you know," Parry said.

"No, we *don't* know," Willis said.

"For God's sake, Hal," Meyer said, "leave the man a little something personal and private, will you please?"

"Thanks," Parry said.

"You went to see your girl friend," Meyer said. "What time was that, Alan?"

"I went up there around nine-thirty. Her mother goes to work at nine. So I went up around nine-thirty."

"You unemployed?" Willis snapped.

"Yes, sir," Parry said.

"When's the last time you worked?"

"Well, you see . . ."

"Answer the question!"

"Give him a chance, Hal!"

"He's stalling!"

"He's trying to answer you!" Gently, Meyer said, "What happened, Alan?"

"I had this job, and I dropped the eggs."

"What?"

"At the grocery store on Eightieth. I was working in the back and one day we got all these crates of eggs, and I was taking them to the refrigerator, and I dropped two crates. So I got fired."

"How long did you work there?"

"From when I got out of high school."

"When was that?" Willis asked.

"Last June."

"Did you graduate?"

"Yes, sir, I have a diploma," Parry said.

"So what have you been doing since you lost the job at the grocery?"

Parry shrugged. "Nothing," he said.

"How old are you?" Willis asked.

"I'll be nineteen . . . what's today?"

"Today's the ninth."

"I'll be nineteen next week. The fifteenth of March."

"You're liable to be spending your birthday in jail," Willis said.

"Now cut it out," Meyer said, "I won't have you threatening this man. What happened when you left your girl friend's house, Alan?"

"I met this guy."

"Where?"

"Outside the Corona."

"The what?"

"The Corona. You know the movie house that's all boarded up about three blocks from here, you know the one?"

"We know it," Willis said.

"Well, there."

"What was he doing there?"

"Just standing. Like as if he was waiting for somebody."

"So what happened?"

"He stopped me and said was I busy? So I said it depended. So he said would I like to make five bucks? So I asked him doing what? He said there was a lunch pail in the park, and if I picked it up for him, he'd give me five bucks. So I asked him why he couldn't go for it himself, and he said he was waiting there for somebody, and he was afraid if he left the guy might show up and think he'd gone. So he said I should get the lunch pail for him and bring it back to him there outside the theater so he wouldn't miss his friend. He was supposed to meet him outside the Corona, you see. You know the place? A cop got shot outside there once."

"I told you we know it," Willis said.

"So I asked him what was in the lunch pail, and he said just his lunch, so I said he could buy *some* lunch for five bucks, but he said he also had a few other things in there with his sandwiches, so I asked him like what and he said do you want this five bucks or not? So I took the five and went to get the pail for him."

"He gave you the five dollars?"

"Yeah."

"Before you went for the pail?"

"Yeah."

"Go on."

"He's lying," Willis said.

"This is the truth, I swear to God."

"What'd you think was in that pail?"

Parry shrugged. "Lunch. And some other little things. Like he said."

"Come on," Willis said, "do you expect us to buy that?"

"Kid, what'd you *really* think was in that pail?" Meyer asked gently.

"Well . . . look . . . you can't do nothing to me for what I *thought* was in there, right?"

"That's right," Meyer said. "If you could lock up a man for what he's thinking, we'd *all* be in jail, right?"

"Right," Parry said, and laughed.

Meyer laughed with him. The Greek chorus laughed too. Everybody laughed except Willis, who kept staring stone-faced at Parry. "So what'd you *think* was in the pail?" Meyer said.

"Junk," Parry said.

"You a junkie?" Willis asked.

"No, sir, never touch the stuff."

"Roll up your sleeve."

"I'm not a junkie, sir."

"Let's see your arm."

Parry rolled up his sleeve.

"Okay," Willis said.

"I told you," Parry said.

"Okay, you told us. What'd you plan to do with that lunch pail?"

"What do you mean?"

"The Corona is three blocks *east* of here. You picked up that pail and started heading *west*. What were you planning?"

"Nothing."

"Then why were you heading *away* from where the deaf man was waiting?"

"I wasn't heading anyplace."

"You were heading *west.*"

"No, I musta got mixed up."

"You got so mixed up you forgot how you came into the park, right? You forgot that the entrance was *behind* you, right?"

"No, I didn't forget where the entrance was."

"Then why'd you head deeper into the park?"

"I told you. I musta got mixed up."

"He's a lying little bastard," Willis said. "I'm going to book him, Meyer, no matter *what* you say."

"Now hold it, just hold it a minute," Meyer said. "You know you're in pretty serious trouble if there's junk in that pail, don't you, Alan?" Meyer said.

"Why? Even if there *is* junk in there, it ain't mine."

"Well, *I* know that, Alan, *I* believe you, but the law is pretty specific about possession of narcotics. I'm sure you must realize that every pusher we pick up claims somebody must have planted the stuff on him, he doesn't know how it got there, it isn't his, and so on. They all give the same excuses, even when we've got them dead to rights."

"Yeah, I guess they must," Parry said.

"So you see, I won't be able to help you much if there really *is* junk in that pail."

"Yeah, I see," Parry said.

"He knows there's no junk in that pail. His partner sent him to pick up the money," Willis said.

"No, no," Parry said, shaking his head.

"You didn't know anything about the thirty thousand dollars, is that right?" Meyer asked gently.

"Nothing," Parry said, shaking his head. "I'm telling you, I met this guy outside the Corona and he gave me five bucks to go get his pail."

"Which you decided to steal," Willis said.

"Huh?"

"Were you going to bring that pail back to him?"

"Well . . ." Parry hesitated. He glanced at Meyer. Meyer nodded encouragingly. "Well, no," Parry said. "I figured if there was junk in it, maybe I could turn a quick buck, you know. There's lots of guys in this neighborhood'll pay for stuff like that."

"Stuff like what?" Willis asked.

"Like what's in the pail," Parry said.

"Open the pail, kid," Willis said.

"No." Parry shook his head. "No, I don't want to."

"Why not?"

"If it's junk, I don't know nothing about it. And if it's thirty G's, I got nothing to do with it. I don't know nothing. I don't want to answer no more questions, that's it."

"That's it, Hal," Meyer said.

"Go on home, kid," Willis said.

"I can go?"

"Yeah, yeah, you can go," Willis said wearily.

Parry stood up quickly, and without looking back headed straight for the gate in the slatted railing that divided the squadroom from the corridor outside. He was down the hallway in a wink. His footfalls clattered noisily on the iron-runged steps leading to the street floor below.

"What do you think?" Willis said.

"I think we did it ass-backwards," Hawes said. "I think we should have followed him out of the park instead of nailing him. He would have led us straight to the deaf man."

"The lieutenant didn't think so. The lieutenant figured nobody would be crazy enough to send a stranger after fifty thousand dollars. The lieutenant figured the guy who made the pickup *had* to be a member of the gang."

"Yeah, well the lieutenant was wrong," Hawes said.

"You know what I think?" Kling said.

"What?"

"I think the deaf man *knew* there'd be nothing in that lunch pail. That's why he could risk sending a stranger for it. He *knew* the money wouldn't be there, and he *knew* we'd pick up whoever he sent."

"If that's the case . . ." Willis started.

"He *wants* to kill Scanlon," Kling said.

The detectives all looked at each other. Faulk scratched his head and said, "Well, I better be getting back across the park, unless you need me some more."

"No, thanks a lot, Stan," Meyer said.

"Don't mention it," Faulk said, and went out.

"I enjoyed the plant," Eileen Burke said, and glanced archly at Willis, and then swiveled toward the gate and out of the squadroom.

"Can it be the breeze . . ." Meyer sang.

"That fills the trees . . ." Kling joined in.

"Go to hell," Willis said, and then genuflected and piously added, "Sisters."

If nobody in the entire world likes working on Saturday, even less people like working on Saturday night.

Saturday night, baby, is the night to howl. Saturday night is the night to get out there and hang ten. Saturday night is when you slip into your satin slippers and your Pucci dress, put on your shirt with the monogram on the cuff, spray your navel with cologne, and laugh too loud.

The bitch city is something different on Saturday night, sophisticated in black, scented and powdered, but somehow not as unassailable, shiveringly beautiful in a dazzle of blinking lights. Reds and oranges, electric blues and vibrant greens assault the eye incessantly, and the resultant turn-on is as sweet as a quick sharp fix in a penthouse pad, a liquid cool that conjures dreams of towering glass spires and enameled minarets. There is excitement in this city on Saturday night, but it is tempered by romantic expectancy. She is not a bitch, this city. Not on Saturday night.

Not if you will love her.

Nobody likes to work on Saturday night, and so the detectives of the 87th Squad should have been pleased when the police commissioner called Byrnes to say that he was asking the D.A.'s Squad to assume the responsibility of protecting Deputy Mayor Scanlon from harm. If they'd had any sense at all, the detectives of the 87th would have considered themselves fortunate.

But the commissioner's cut was deeply felt, first by Byrnes, and then by every man on the squad when he related the news to them. They went their separate ways that Saturday night, some into the streets to work, others home to rest, but each of them felt a corporate sense of failure. Not one of them realized how fortunate he was.

The two detectives from the D.A.'s Squad were experienced men who had handled special assignments before. When the deputy mayor's personal chauffeur arrived to pick them up that night, they were waiting on the sidewalk outside the Criminal Courts Building, just around the corner from the District Attorney's office. It was exactly 8.00 P.M. The deputy mayor's chauffeur had picked up the Cadillac sedan at the municipal garage a half-hour earlier. He had gone over the upholstery with a whisk broom, passed a dust rag over the hood, wiped the windows with a chamois cloth, and emptied all the ashtrays. He was now ready for action, and he was pleased to note that the detectives were right on time; he could not abide tardy individuals.

The drove up to Smoke Rise, which was where the deputy mayor lived, and one of the detectives got out of the car and walked to the front door, and rang the bell, and was ushered into the huge brick house by a maid in a black uniform. The deputy mayor came down the long white staircase leading to the center hall, shook hands with the detective from the D.A.'s Squad, apologized for taking up his time this way on a Saturday night, made some comment about the "damn foolishness of it all," and then called up to his wife to tell her the car was waiting. His wife came down the steps, and the deputy mayor introduced her to the detective from the D.A.'s Squad, and then they all went to the front door.

The detective stepped outside first, scanned the bushes lining the driveway, and then led the deputy mayor and his wife to the car. He opened the door and allowed them to precede him into the automobile. The other detective was stationed on the opposite side of the car, and as soon as the deputy mayor and his wife were seated, both detectives got into the automobile and took positions facing them on the jump seats.

The dashboard clock read 8:30 P.M.

The deputy mayor's personal chauffeur set the car in motion, and the deputy mayor made a few jokes with the detectives as they drove along the gently winding roads of exclusive Smoke Rise on the edge of the city's northern river, and then onto the service road leading to the River Highway. It had been announced in the newspapers the week before that the deputy mayor would speak at a meeting of the B'nai Brith in the city's largest synagogue at nine o'clock that night. The deputy mayor's home in Smoke Rise was only fifteen minutes away from the synagogue, and so the chauffeur drove slowly and carefully while the two detectives from the D.A.'s Squad eyed the automobiles that moved past on either side of the Cadillac.

The Cadillac exploded when the dashboard clock read 8:45 P.M.

The bomb was a powerful one.

It erupted from somewhere under the hood, sending flying steel into the car, tearing off the roof like paper, blowing the doors into the highway. The car screeched out of control, lurched across two lanes, rolled onto its side like a ruptured metal beast and was suddenly ablaze.

A passing convertible tried to swerve around the flaming Cadillac. There was a second explosion. The convertible veered wildly and crashed into the river barrier.

When the police arrived on the scene, the only person alive in either car was a bleeding seventeen-year-old girl who had gone through the windshield of the convertible.

8

ON SUNDAY MORNING, the visiting hours at Buena Vista Hospital were from ten to twelve. It was a busy day, busier than Wednesday, for example, because Saturday night encourages broken arms and legs, bloody pates and shattered sternums. There is nothing quite so hectic as the Emergency Room of a big city hospital on a Saturday night. And on Sunday morning it's only natural for people to visit the friends and relatives who were unfortunate enough to have met with assorted mayhem the night before.

Steve Carella had met with assorted mayhem on Thursday night, and here it was Sunday morning, and he sat propped up in bed expecting Teddy's arrival and feeling gaunt and pale and unshaven even though he had shaved himself not ten minutes ago. He had lost seven pounds since his admission to the hospital (it being singularly difficult to eat and breathe at the same time when your nose is taped and bandaged) and he still ached everywhere, seemed in fact to discover new bruises every time he moved, which can make a man feel very unshaven.

He had had a lot of time to do some thinking since Thursday night, and as soon as he had got over feeling, in sequence, foolish, angry, and murderously vengeful, he had decided that the deaf man was responsible for what had happened to him. That was a good way to feel, he thought, because it took the blame away from two young punks (for Christ's sake, how could an experienced detective get smeared that way by two young punks?) and put it squarely onto a master criminal instead. Master criminals are very handy scapegoats, Carella reasoned, because they allow you to dismiss your own inadequacies. There was an old Jewish joke Meyer had once told him, about the mother who says to her son, *"Trombenik,* go get a job," and the son answers, "I can't, I'm a *trombenik."* The situation now was similar, he supposed, with the question being altered to read, "How can you let a master criminal do this to you?" and the logical answer being, "It's easy, he's a master criminal."

Whether or not the deaf man was a master criminal was perhaps a subject for debate. Carella would have to query his colleagues on the possibility of holding a seminar once he got back to the office. This, according to the interns who'd been examining his skull like phrenologists, should be by Thursday, it being their considered opinion that unconsciousness always meant concussion and concussion always carried with it the possibility of internal hemorrhage with at least a week's period of observation being *de rigueur* in such cases, go argue with doctors.

Perhaps the deaf man wasn't a master criminal at all. Perhaps he was simply smarter than any of the policemen he was dealing with, which encouraged some pretty frightening conjecture. Given a superior intelligence at work, was it even *possible* for inferior intelligences to second-guess whatever diabolical scheme was afoot? Oh, come on now, Carella thought, diabolical indeed! Well, *yeah,* he thought, diabolical. It *is* diabolical to demand five thousand dollars and then knock off the parks commissioner, and it *is* diabolical to demand fifty thousand dollars and then knock off the deputy mayor, and it is staggering to imagine what the next demand might be, or who the next victim would be. There most certainly would be another demand which, if not met would doubtless lead to yet another victim. Or would it? How can you second-guess a master criminal? You can't, he's a master criminal.

No, Carella thought, he's only a human being, and he's counting on several human certainties. He's hoping to establish a pattern of warning and reprisal, he's hoping we'll attempt to stop him each time, but only so that we'll fail, forcing him to carry out his threat. Which means that the two early extortion tries were only preparation for the big caper. And since he seems to be climbing the municipal government ladder, and since he multiplied his first demand by ten, I'm willing to bet his next declared victim will be James Martin Vale, the mayor himself, and that he'll ask for ten times what he asked for the last time: five hundred thousand dollars. That is a lot of strawberries.

Or am I only second-guessing a master criminal?

Am I *supposed* to be second-guessing him?

Is he really preparing the ground for a big killing, or is there quite another diabolical (there we go again) plan in his mind?

Teddy Carella walked into the room at that moment.

The only thing Carella had to second-guess was whether he would kiss her first or vice versa. Since his nose was in plaster, he decided to let her choose the target, which she did with practiced ease, causing him to consider some wildly diabolical schemes of his own, which if executed would have resulted in his never again being permitted inside Buena Vista Hospital.

Not even in a private room.

Patrolman Richard Genero was in the same hospital that Sunday morning, but his thoughts were less erotic than they were ambitious.

Despite a rather tight official security lid on the murders, an enterprising newspaperman had only this morning speculated on a possible connection between Genero's leg wound and the subsequent killing of Scanlon the night before. The police and the city officials had managed to keep all mention of the extortion calls and notes out of the newspapers thus far, but the reporter for the city's leading metropolitan daily wondered in print whether or not the detectives of "an uptown precinct bordering the park" hadn't in reality possessed foreknowledge of an attempt to be made on the deputy mayor's life, hadn't in fact set up an elaborate trap that very afternoon, "a trap in which a courageous patrolman was destined to suffer a bullet wound in the leg while attempting to capture the suspected killer." Wherever the reporter had dug up his information, he had neglected to mention that Genero had inflicted the wound upon himself, due to a fear of dogs and criminals, and due to a certain lack of familiarity with shooting at fleeing suspects.

Genero's father, who was a civil service employee himself, having worked for the Department of Sanitation for some twenty years now, was not aware that his son had accidentally shot himself in the leg. All he knew was that his son was a hero. As befitted a hero, he had brought a white carton of *cannoli* to the hospital, and now he and his wife and his son sat in the semi-private stillness of a fourth floor room and demolished the pastry while discussing Genero's almost certain promotion to Detective 3rd/Grade.

The idea of a promotion had not occurred to Genero before this, but as his father outlined the heroic action in the park the day before, Genero began to visualize himself as the man who had made the capture possible. Without him, without the warning shot he had fired into his own leg, the fleeing Alan Parry might never have stopped. The fact that Parry had turned out to be a wet fuse didn't matter at all to Genero. It was all well and good to realize a man wasn't dangerous *after* the fact, but where were all those detectives when Parry was running straight for Genero with a whole lunch pail full of God-knew-what under his arm, where were they *then,* huh? And how could they have known *then,* while Genero was courageously drawing his pistol, that Parry would turn out to be only another innocent dupe, nossir, it had been impossible to tell.

"You were brave," Genero's father said, licking pot cheese from his lips. "It was *you* who tried to stop him."

"That's true," Genero said, because it *was* true.

"It was *you* who risked your life."

"That's right," Genero said, because it *was* right.

"They should promote you."

"They should," Genero said.

"I will call your boss," Genero's mother said.

"No, I don't think you should, Mama."

"Perchè no?"

"Perchè . . . Mama, please don't talk Italian, you know I don't understand Italian so well."

"Vergogna," his mother said, "an Italian doesn't understand his own tongue. I will call your boss."

"No, Mama, that isn't the way it's done."

"Then how *is* it done?" his father asked.

"Well, you've got to hint around."

"Hint? To who?"

"Well, to people."

"Which people?"

"Well, Carella's upstairs in this same hospital, maybe . . ."

"Ma chi è questa Carella?" his mother said.

"Mama, please."

"Who is this Carella?"

"A detective on the squad."

"Where you work, *sì?"*

"Sì. Please, Mama."

"He is your boss?"

"No, he just works up there."

"He was shot, too?"

"No, he was beat up."

"By the same man who shot you?"

"No, not by the same man who shot me," Genero said, which was also the truth.

"So what does he have to do with this?"

"Well, he's got influence."

"With the boss?"

"Well, no. You see, Captain Frick runs the entire precinct, he's actually the boss. But Lieutenant Byrnes is in charge of the detective squad, and Carella is a detective/2nd, and him and the lieutenant are like this, so maybe if I talk to Carella he'll see how I helped them grab that guy yesterday, and put in a good word for me."

"Let her call the boss," Genero's father said.

"No, it's better this way," Genero said.

"How much does a detective make?" Genero's mother asked.

"A fortune," Genero said.

Gadgets fascinated Detective-Lieutenant Sam Grossman, even when they were bombs. Or perhaps especially when they were bombs. There was no question in anyone's mind (how much question *could* there have been, considering the evidence of the demolished automobile and its five occupants?) that someone had put a bomb in the deputy mayor's car. Moreover, it was mandatory to assume that someone had set the bomb to go off at a specific time, rather than using the ignition wiring of the car as an immediate triggering device. This aspect of the puzzle pleased Grossman enormously because he considered ignition-trigger bombs to be rather crude devices capable of being wired by any gangland ape. This bomb was a time bomb. But it was a very special time bomb. It was a time bomb that had not been wired to the automobile clock.

How did Grossman know this?

Ah-ha, the police laboratory never sleeps, not even on Sunday. And besides, his technicians had found two clock faces in the rubble of the automobile.

One of the faces had been part of the Cadillac's dashboard clock. The other had come from a nationally advertised, popular-priced electric alarm clock. There was one other item of importance found in the rubble: a portion of the front panel of a DC-to-AC inverter, part of its brand name still showing where it was stamped into the metal.

These three parts lay on the counter in Grossman's laboratory like three key pieces to a jigsaw puzzle. All he had to do was fit them together and come up with a brilliant solution. He was feeling particularly brilliant this Sunday morning because his son had brought home a 92 on a high-school chemistry exam only two days ago; it always made Grossman feel brilliant when his son achieved anything. Well, let's see, he thought brilliantly. I've got three parts of a time bomb, or rather *two* parts because I think I can safely eliminate the car's clock except as a reference point. Whoever wired the bomb undoubtedly refused to trust his own wrist watch since a difference of a minute or two in timing might have proved critical—in a minute, the deputy mayor could have been out of the car already and on his way into the synagogue. So he had set the electric clock with the time showing on the dashboard clock. Why an *electric* clock? Simple. He did not want a clock that *ticked*. Ticking might have attracted attention, especially if it came from under the hood of a purring Cadillac. Okay, so let's see what we've got. We've got an electric alarm clock, and we've got a DC-to-AC inverter, which means someone wanted to translate direct current to alternating current. The battery in a Cadillac would *have* to be 12-volts DC, and the electric clock would doubtless be wired for alternating current. So perhaps we can reasonably assume that someone wanted to wire the clock to the battery and needed an inverter to make this feasible. Let's see.

He'd have had to run a positive lead to the battery and a negative lead to any metal part of the automobile, since the car itself would have served as a ground, right? So now we've got a power source to the clock, and the clock is running. Okay, right, the rest is simple, he'd have had to use an electric blasting cap, sure, there'd have been enough power to set one off, most commercial electric detonators can be fired by passing a continuous current of 0.3 to 0.4 amperes through the bridge wire. Okay, let's see, hold it now, let's look at it.

The battery provides our source of power . . .

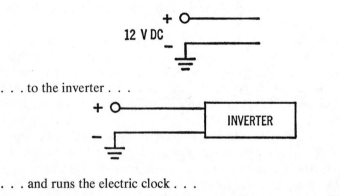

. . . to the inverter . . .

. . . and runs the electric clock . . .

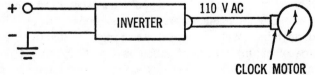

. . . which is in turn set for a specific time, about eight, wasn't it? He'd have had to monkey around with the clock so that instead of the alarm ringing, a switch would close. That would complete the circuit, let's see, he'd have needed a lead running back to the battery, another lead running to the blasting cap, and a lead from the blasting cap to any metal part of the car. So that would look like . . .

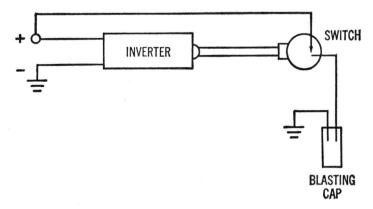

And that's it.

He could have assembled the entire package at home, taken it with him in a tool box, and wired it to the car in a very short time—making certain, of course, that all his wires were properly insulated, to guard against a stray current touching off a premature explosion. The only remaining question is how he managed to get access to the car, but happily that's not my problem.

Whistling brilliantly, Sam Grossman picked up the telephone and called Detective Meyer Meyer at the 87th.

The municipal garage was downtown on Dock Street, some seven blocks from City Hall. Meyer Meyer picked up Bert Kling at ten-thirty. The drive down along the River Dix took perhaps twenty minutes. They parked on a meter across the street from the big concrete and tile structure, and Meyer automatically threw the visor sign, even though this was Sunday and parking regulations were not in force.

The foreman of the garage was a man named Spencer Coyle.

He was reading Dick Tracy and seemed less impressed by the two detectives in his midst than by the fictional exploits of his favorite comic strip sleuth. It was only with a great effort of will that he managed to tear himself away from the newspaper at all.

He did not rise from his chair, though. The chair was tilted back against the tiled wall of the garage. The tiles, a vomitous shade of yellow, decorated too many government buildings all over the city, and it was Meyer's guess that a hefty hunk of graft had influenced some purchasing agent back in the Thirties, either that or the poor bastard had been color-blind. Spencer Coyle leaned back in his chair against the tiles, his face long and gray and grizzled, his long legs stretched out in front of him, the comic section still dangling from his right hand, as though he were reluctant to let go of it completely even though he had stopped lip-reading it. He was wearing the greenish-brown coveralls of a Transportation Division employee, his peaked hat sitting on his head with all the rakish authority of a major in the Air Force. His attitude clearly told the detectives that he did not wish to be disturbed at *any* time, but especially on Sunday.

The detectives found him challenging.

"Mr. Coyle," Meyer said, "I've just had a telephone call from the police laboratory to the effect that the bomb . . ."

"What bomb?" Coyle asked, and spat on the floor, narrowly missing Meyer's polished shoe.

"The bomb that was put in the deputy mayor's Cadillac," Kling said, and hoped Coyle would spit again, but Coyle didn't.

"Oh, *that* bomb," Coyle said, as if bombs were put in every one of the city's Cadillacs regularly, making it difficult to keep track of all the bombs around. "What *about* that bomb?"

"The lab says it was a pretty complicated bomb, but that it couldn't have taken too long to wire to the car's battery, provided it had been assembled beforehand. Now, what we'd like to know . . ."

"Yeah, I'll bet it was complicated," Coyle said. He did not look into the faces of the detectives, but instead seemed to direct his blue-eyed gaze at a spot somewhere across the garage. Kling turned to see what he was staring at, but the only thing he noticed was another yellow tile wall.

"Would you have any idea who installed that bomb, Mr. Coyle?"

"*I* didn't," Coyle said flatly.

"Nobody suggested that you did," Meyer said.

"Just so we understand each other," Coyle said. "All I do is run this garage, make sure the cars are in working order, make sure they're ready to roll whenever somebody up there wants one, that's all I'm in charge of."

"How many cars do you have here?" Meyer asked.

"We got two dozen Caddys, twelve used on a regular basis, and the rest whenever we get visiting dignitaries. We also got fourteen buses and eight motorcycles. And there's also some vehicles that are kept here by the Department of Parks, but that's a courtesy because we got the space."

"Who services the cars?"

"Which ones?"

"The Caddys."

"Which one of the Caddys?" Coyle said, and spat again.

"Did you know, Mr. Coyle," Kling said, "that spitting on the sidewalk is a misdeameanor?"

"This ain't a sidewalk, this is my garage," Coyle said.

"This is city property," Kling said, "the equivalent of a sidewalk. In fact, since the ramp comes in directly from the street outside there, it could almost be considered an extension of the sidewalk."

"Sure," Coyle said. "You going to arrest me for it, or what?"

"You going to keep giving us a hard time?" Kling asked.

"Who's giving you a hard time?"

"We'd like to be home reading the funnies too," Kling said, "instead of out busting our asses on a bombing. Now how about it?"

"None of our mechanics put a bomb in that car," Coyle said flatly.

"How do you know?"

"Because I know all the men who work for me, and none of them put a bomb in that car, that's how I know."

"Who was here yesterday?" Meyer asked.

"I was."

"You were here alone?"

"No, the men were here too."

"Which men?"

"The mechanics."

"How many mechanics?"

"Two."

"Is that how many you usually have on duty?"

"We usually have six, but yesterday was Saturday, and we were working with a skeleton crew."

"Anybody else here?"

"Yeah, some of the chauffeurs were either picking up cars or bringing them back, they're in and out all the time. Also, there was supposed to be an outdoor fishing thing up in Grover Park, so we had a lot of bus drivers in. They were supposed to pick up these slum kids and take them to the park where they were going to fish through the ice on the lake. It got called off."

"Why?"

"Too cold."

"When were the bus drivers here?"

"They reported early in the morning, and they hung around till we got word it was called off."

"You see any of them fooling around near that Cad?"

"Nope. Listen, you're barking up the wrong tree. All those cars got checked out yesterday, and they were in A-number-One shape. That bomb must've been put in there *after* the car left the garage."

"No, that's impossible, Mr. Coyle."

"Well, it wasn't attached here."

"You're sure of that, are you?"

"I just told you the cars were inspected, didn't I?"

"Did you inspect them personally, Mr. Coyle?"

"No, I got other things to do besides inspecting two dozen Caddys and fourteen buses and eight motorcycles."

"Then who *did* inspect them, Mr. Coyle? One of your mechanics?"

"No, we had an inspector down from the Bureau of Motor Vehicles."

"And he said the cars were all right?"

"He went over them from top to bottom, every vehicle in the place. He gave us a clean bill of health."

"Did he look under the hoods?"

"Inside, outside, transmission, suspension, everything. He was here about six hours."

"So he would have found a bomb if one was there, is that right?"

"That's right."

"Mr. Coyle, did he give you anything in writing to the effect that the cars were inspected and found in good condition?"

"Why?" Coyle asked. "You trying to get off the hook?"

"No, we're . . ."

"You trying to pass the buck to Motor Vehicles?"

"We're trying to find out how he could have missed the bomb that was undoubtedly under the hood of that car, that's what we're trying to do."

"It *wasn't,* that's your answer."

"Mr. Coyle, our lab reported . . ."

"I don't care what your lab reported or didn't report. I'm telling you all these cars were gone over with a fine-tooth comb yesterday, and there couldn't have been a bomb in the deputy mayor's car when it left this garage. Now that's *that,*" Coyle said, and spat on the floor again, emphatically.

"Mr. Coyle," Kling said, "did you personally see the deputy mayor's car being inspected?"

"I personally saw it being inspected."

"You personally saw the hood being raised?"

"I did."

"And you'd be willing to swear that a thorough inspection was made of the area under the hood?"

"What do you mean?"

"Did you actually *see* the inspector checking the area under the hood?"

"Well, I didn't stand around looking over his shoulder, if that's what you mean."

"Where were you, actually, when the deputy mayor's car was being inspected?"

"I was right here."

"On this exact spot?"

"No, I was inside the office there. But I could see out into the garage. There's a glass panel in there."

"And you saw the inspector lifting the hood of the deputy mayor's car?"

"That's right."

"There are two dozen Caddys here. How'd you know that one was the deputy mayor's car?"

"By the license plate. It has DMA on it, and then the number. Same as Mayor Vale's car has MA on it for 'mayor,' and then the number. Same as the . . ."

"All right, it was clearly his car, and you definitely saw . . ."

"Look, that guy spent a good half-hour on each car, now don't tell *me* it wasn't a thorough inspection."

"Did he spend a half-hour on the deputy mayor's car?"

"Easily."

Meyer sighed. "I guess we'll have to talk to him personally," he said to Kling. He turned again to Coyle. "What was his name, Mr. Coyle?"

"Who?"

"The inspector. The man from Motor Vehicles."

"I don't know."

"He didn't give you his name?" Kling asked.

"He showed me his credentials, and he said he was here to inspect the cars, and that was that."

"What kind of credentials?"

"Oh, printed papers. You know."

"Mr. Coyle," Kling asked, "when was the last time a man from Motor Vehicles came to inspect?"

"This was the first time," Coyle said.

"They've never sent an inspector down before?"

"Never."

Slowly, wearily, Meyer said, "What did this man look like, Mr. Coyle?"

"He was a tall blond guy wearing a hearing aid," Coyle answered.

Fats Donner was a mountainous stool pigeon with a penchant for warm climates and the complexion of an Irish virgin. The complexion, in fact, overreached the boundaries of common definition to extend to every part of Donner's body; he was white all over, so sickly pale that sometimes Willis suspected him of being a junkie. Willis couldn't have cared less. On any given Sunday, a conscientious cop could collar seventy-nine junkies in a half-hour, seventy-eight of whom would be holding narcotics in some quantity. It was hard to come by a good informer, though, and Donner was one of the best around, *when* he was around. The difficulty with Donner was that he was likely to be found in Vegas or Miami Beach or Puerto Rico during the winter months, lying in the shade with his Buddha-like form protected against even a possible reflection of the sun's rays, quivering with delight as the sweat poured from his body.

Willis was surprised to find him in the city during the coldest March on record. He was not surprised to find him in a room that was suffocatingly hot, with three electric heaters adding their output to the two banging radiators. In the midst of this thermal onslaught, Donner sat in overcoat and gloves, wedged into a stuffed armchair. He was wearing two pairs of woolen socks, and his feet were propped up on the radiator. There was a girl in the room with him. She was perhaps fifteen years old, and she was wearing a flowered bra and bikini panties over which she had put on a silk wrapper. The wrapper was unbelted. The girl's near-naked body showed whenever she moved, but she seemed not to mind the presence of a strange man. She barely glanced at Willis when he came in, and then went about the room straightening up, never looking at either of the men as they whispered together near the window streaming wintry sunlight.

"Who's the girl?" Willis asked.

"My daughter," Donner said, and grinned.

He was not a nice man, Fats Donner, but he was a good stoolie, and criminal detection sometimes made strange bedfellows. It was Willis' guess that the girl was hooking for Donner, a respectable stoolie sometimes being in need of additional income which he can realize, for example, by picking up a little girl straight from Ohio and teaching her what it's all about and then putting her on the street, there are more things in heaven and earth, Horatio. Willis was not interested in Donner's possible drug habit, nor was Willis interested in hanging a prostitution rap on the girl, nor in busting Donner as a "male person living on the proceeds of prostitution," Section 1148 of the Penal Law. Willis was interested in taking off his coat and hat and finding out whether or not Donner could give him a line on a man named Dom.

"Dom who?" Donner asked.

"That's all we've got."

"How many Doms you suppose are in this city?" Donner asked. He turned to the girl, who was puttering around rearranging food in the refrigerator, and said, "Mercy, how many Doms you suppose are in this city?"

"I don't know," Mercy replied without looking at him.

"How many Doms you know personally?" Donner asked her.

"I don't know any Doms," the girl said. She had a tiny voice, tinged with an unmistakable Southern accent. Scratch Ohio, Willis thought, substitute Arkansas or Tennessee.

"She don't know any Doms," Donner said, and chuckled.

"How about you, Fats? You know any?"

"That's all you're giving me?" Donner asked. "Man, you're really generous."

"He lost a lot of money on the championship fight two weeks ago."

"Everybody I *know* lost a lot of money on the championship fight two weeks ago."

"He's broke right now. He's trying to promote some scratch," Willis said.

"Dom, huh?"

"Yeah."

"From this part of the city?"

"A friend of his lives in Riverhead," Willis said.

"What's the friend's name?"

"La Bresca. Tony La Bresca."

"What about *him?*"

"No record."

"You think this Dom done time?"

"I've got no idea. He seems to have tipped to a caper that's coming off."

"Is that what you're interested in? The caper?"

"Yes. According to him, the buzz is all over town."

"There's always some buzz or other that's all over town," Donner said. "What the hell are you doing there, Mercy?"

"Just fixing things," Mercy said.

"Get the hell away from there, you make me nervous."

"I was just fixing the things in the fridge," Mercy said.

"I hate that Southern accent," Donner said. "Don't you hate Southern accents?" he asked Willis.

"I don't mind them," Willis said.

"Can't even understand her half the time. Sounds as if she's got shit in her mouth."

The girl closed the refrigerator door and went to the closet. She opened the door and began moving around empty hangers.

"Now what're you doing?" Donner asked.

"Just straightening things," she said.

"You want me to kick you out in the street bare-assed?" Donner asked.

"No," she said softly.

"Then cut it out."

"All right."

"Anyway, it's time you got dressed."

"All right."

"Go on, go get dressed. What time is it?" he asked Willis.

"Almost noon," Willis said.

"Sure, go get dressed," Donner said.

"All right," the girl said, and went into the other room.

"Damn little bitch," Donner said, "hardly worth keeping around."

"I thought she was your daughter," Willis said.

"Oh, is that what you thought?" Donner asked, and again he grinned.

Willis restrained a sudden impulse. He sighed and said, "So what do you think?"

"I don't think nothing yet, man. Zero so far."

"Well, you want some time on it?"

"How much of a sweat are you in?"

"We need whatever we can get as soon as we can get it."

"What's the caper sound like?"

"Maybe extortion."

"Dom, huh?"

"Dom," Willis repeated.

"That'd be for Dominick, right?"

"Yes."

"Well, let me listen around, who knows?"

The girl came out of the other room. She was wearing a miniskirt and white mesh stockings, a low-cut purple blouse. There was a smear of bright red lipstick on her mouth, green eyeshadow on her eyelids.

"You going down now?" Donner asked.

"Yes," she answered.

"Put on your coat."

"All right," she said.

"And take your bag."

"I will."

"Don't come back empty, baby," Donner said.

"I won't," she said, and moved toward the door.

"I'm going too," Willis said.

"I'll give you a buzz."

"Okay, but try to move fast, will you?" Willis said.

"It's I hate to go out when it's so fucking cold," Donner answered.

The girl was on the hallway steps, below Willis, walking down without any sense of haste, buttoning her coat, slinging her bag over her shoulder. Willis caught up with her and said, "Where are you from, Mercy?"

"Ask Fats," she answered.

"I'm asking *you.*"

"You fuzz?"

"That's right."

"Georgia," she said.

"When'd you get up here?"

"Two months ago."

"How old are you?"

"Sixteen."

"What the hell are you doing with a man like Fats Donner?" Willis asked.

"I don't know," she said. She would not look into his face. She kept her head bent as they went down the steps to the street. As Willis opened the door leading outside, a blast of frigid air rushed into the hallway.

"Why don't you get out?" he said.

The girl looked up at him.

"Where would I go?" she asked, and then left him on the stoop,

walking up the street with a practiced swing, the bag dangling from
her shoulder, her high heels clicking along the pavement.

At two o'clock that afternoon, the seventeen-year-old girl who
had been in the convertible that crashed the river barrier died without
gaining consciousness.

The Buena Vista Hospital record read simply: Death secondary
to head injury.

9

THE SQUADROOM PHONE began jangling early Monday morning.

The first call was from a reporter on the city's austere morning daily. He asked to speak to whoever was in charge of the squad and, when told that Lieutenant Byrnes was not in at the moment, asked to speak to whoever was in command.

"This is Detective 2nd/Grade Meyer Meyer," he was told. "I suppose I'm in command at the moment."

"Detective Meyer," the reporter said, "this is Carlyle Butterford, I wanted to check out a possible story."

At first, Meyer thought the call was a put-on, nobody had a name like Carlyle Butterford. Then he remembered that *everybody* on this particular morning newspaper had names like Preston Fingerlaver, or Clyde Masterfield, or Aylmer Coopermere. "Yes, Mr. Butterford," he said, "what can I do for you?"

"We received a telephone call early this morning . . ."

"From whom, sir?"

"An anonymous caller," Butterford said.

"Yes?"

"Yes, and he suggested that we contact the 87th Precinct regarding certain extortion calls and notes that were received before the deaths of Parks Commissioner Cowper and Deputy Mayor Scanlon."

There was a long silence on the line.

"Detective Meyer, is there any truth to this allegation?"

"I suggest that you call the Public Relations Officer of the Police Department," Meyer said, "his name is Detective Glenn, and he's downtown at Headquarters. The number there is Center 6-0800."

"Would he have any knowledge of these alleged extortion calls and notes?" Butterford asked.

"I guess you'd have to ask him," Meyer said.

"Do *you* have any knowledge of these alleged . . . ?"

"As I told you," Meyer said, "the lieutenant is out at the moment, and he's the one who generally supplies information to the press."

"But would *you,* personally, have any information . . . ?"

"I have information on a great many things," Meyer said. "Homicides, muggings, burglaries, robberies, rapes, extortion attempts, all sorts of things. But, as I'm sure you know, detectives are public servants and it has been the department's policy to discourage us from seeking personal aggrandizement. If you wish to talk to the lieutenant, I suggest you call back at around ten o'clock. He should be in by then."

"Come on," Butterford said, "give me a break."

"I'm sorry, pal, I can't help you."

"I'm a working stiff, just like you."

"So's the lieutenant," Meyer said, and hung up.

The second call came at nine-thirty. Sergeant Murchison, at the switchboard, took the call and immediately put it through to Meyer.

"This is Cliff Savage," the voice said. "Remember me?"

"Only too well," Meyer said. "What do you want, Savage?"

"Carella around?"

"Nope."

"Where is he?"

"Out," Meyer said.

"I wanted to talk to him."

"He doesn't want to talk to you," Meyer said. "You almost got his wife killed once with your goddamn yellow journalism. You want my advice, keep out of his sight."

"I guess I'll have to talk to you, then," Savage said.

"I'm not too fond of you myself, if you want the truth."

"Well, thank you," Savage said, "but that's not the truth I'm after."

"What *are* you after?"

"I got a phone call this morning from a man who refused to identify himself. He gave me a very interesting piece of information." Savage paused. "Know anything about it?"

Meyer's heart was pounding, but he very calmly said, "I'm not a mind reader, Savage."

"I thought you might know something about it."

"Savage, I've given you the courtesy of five minutes of valuable time already. Now if you've got something to say . . ."

"Okay, okay. The man I spoke to said the 87th Precinct had received several threatening telephone calls preceding the death of

Parks Commissioner Cowper, and three extortion notes preceding the death of Deputy Mayor Scanlon. Know anything about it?"

"Telephone company'd probably be able to help you on any phone calls you want to check, and I guess the Documents Section of the Public Library . . ."

"Come on, Meyer, don't stall me."

"We're not permitted to give information to reporters," Meyer said. "You know that."

"How much?" Savage asked.

"Huh?"

"How much do you want, Meyer?"

"How much can you afford?" Meyer asked.

"How does a hundred bucks sound?"

"Not so good."

"How about two hundred?"

"I get more than that just for protecting our friendly neighborhood pusher."

"Three hundred is my top offer," Savage said.

"Would you mind repeating the offer for the benefit of the tape recorder?" Meyer said. "I want to have evidence when I charge you with attempting to bribe a police officer."

"I was merely offering you a loan," Savage said.

"Neither a borrower nor a lender be," Meyer said, and hung up.

This was not good. This was, in fact, bad. He was about to dial the lieutenant's home number, hoping to catch him before he left for the office, when the telephone on his desk rang again.

"87th Squad," he said, "Detective Meyer."

The caller was from one of the two afternoon papers. He repeated essentially what Meyer had already heard from his two previous callers, and then asked if Meyer knew anything about it. Meyer, loath to lie lest the story eventually broke and tangentially mentioned that there had been a police credibility gap, suggested that the man try the lieutenant later on in the day. When he hung up, he looked at the clock and decided to wait for the next call before trying to contact the lieutenant. Fortunately, there were now only four daily newspapers in the city, the leaders of the various newspaper guilds and unions having decided that the best way to ensure higher wages and lifetime employment was to make demands that would kill off the newspapers one by one, leaving behind only scattered goose feathers and broken golden egg shells. Meyer did not have to wait long. The representative of the fourth newspaper called within five minutes. He had a bright chirpy voice and an ingratiating style. He got nothing from Meyer, and he finally hung up in cheerful rage.

It was now five minutes to ten, too late to catch Byrnes at home.

While he waited for the lieutenant to arrive, Meyer doodled a picture of a man in a fedora shooting a Colt .45 automatic. The man looked very much like Meyer, except that he possessed a full head of hair. Meyer had once possessed a full head of hair. He tried to remember when. It was probably when he was ten years old. He was smiling painfully over his own joke when Byrnes came into the squadroom. The lieutenant looked dyspeptic this morning. Meyer surmised that he missed the painters. Everyone on the squad missed the painters. They had added humanity to the joint, and richness, a spirit of gregarious joy, a certain *je ne sais quoi*.

"We got trouble," Meyer said, but before he could relate the trouble to the lieutenant, the phone rang again. Meyer lifted the receiver, identified himself, and then looked at Byrnes.

"It's the Chief of Detectives," he said, and Byrnes sighed and went into his office to take the call privately.

Thirty-three telepone calls were exchanged that morning as police and city government officials kept the wires hot between their own offices and Lieutenant Byrnes', trying to decide what to do about this latest revolting development. The one thing they did not need on this case was publicity that would make them all appear foolish. And yet, if there really *had* been a leak about the extortion attempts, it seemed likely that the full story might come to light at any moment, in which case it might be best to level with the papers *before* they broke the news. At the same time, the anonymous caller might only have been speculating, without any real evidence to back up his claim of extortion, in which case a premature release to the newspapers would only serve to breach a danger that was not truly threatening. What to do, oh, what to do?

The telephones rang, and the possibilities multiplied. Heads swam and tempers flared. The mayor, James Martin Vale himself, postponed a walking trip from City Hall to Grover Park and personally called Lieutenant Byrnes to ask his opinion on "the peril of the situation." Lieutenant Byrnes passed the buck to the Chief of Detectives who in turn passed it back to Captain Frick of the 87th, who referred JMV's secretary to the police commissioner, who for reasons unknown said he must first consult with the traffic commissioner, who in turn referred the police commissioner to the

Bridge Authority who somehow got on to the city comptroller, who in turn called JMV himself to ask what this was all about.

At the end of two hours of dodging and wrangling, it was decided to take the bull by the horns and release transcripts of the telephone conversations, as well as photocopies of the three notes, to all four city newspapers. The city's liberal blue-headline newspaper (which was that week running an exposé on the growth of the numbers racket as evidenced by the prevalence of nickel and dime betters in kindergarten classes) was the first paper to break the story, running photos of the three notes side by side on its front page. The city's other afternoon newspaper, recently renamed the *Pierce-Arrow-Universal-International-Bugle-Chronicle-Clarion* or something, was next to feature the notes on its front page, together with transcripts of the calls in 24-point Cheltenham Bold.

That night, the early editions of the two morning newspapers carried the story as well. This meant that a combined total of four million readers now knew all about the extortion threats.

The next move was anybody's.

Anthony La Bresca and his pool hall buddy, Peter Vincent Calucci (alias Calooch, Cooch, or Kook) met in a burlesque house on a side street off The Stem at seven o'clock that Monday night.

La Bresca had been tailed from his place of employment, a demolition site in the city's downtown financial district, by three detectives using the ABC method of surveillance. Mindful of the earlier unsuccessful attempts to keep track of him, nobody was taking chances anymore—the ABC method was surefire and foolproof.

Detective Bob O'Brien was "A," following La Bresca while Detective Andy Parker, who was "B," walked behind O'Brien and kept him constantly in view. Detective Carl Kapek was "C," and he moved parallel with La Bresca, on the opposite side of the street. This meant that if La Bresca suddenly went into a coffee shop or ducked around the corner, Kapek could instantly swap places with O'Brien, taking the lead "A" position while O'Brien caught up, crossed the street, and maneuvered into the "C" position. It also meant that the men could use camouflaging tactics at their own discretion, changing positions so that the combination became BCA or CBA or CAB or whatever they chose, a scheme that guaranteed La Bresca would not recognize any one man following him over an extended period of time.

Wherever he went, La Bresca was effectively contained. Even in parts of the city where the crowds were unusually thick, there was no danger of losing him. Kapek would merely cross over onto La Bresca's side of the street and begin walking some fifteen feet *ahead* of him, so that the pattern read C, La Bresca, A, and B. In police jargon, they were "sticking like a dirty shirt," and they did their job well and unobtrusively, despite the cold weather and despite the fact that La Bresca seemed to be a serendipitous type who led them on a jolly excursion halfway across the city, apparently trying to kill time before his seven-o'clock meeting with Calucci.

The two men took seats in the tenth row of the theater. The show was in progress, two baggy-pants comics relating a traffic accident one of them had had with a car driven by a voluptuous blonde.

"You mean she crashed right into your tail pipe?" one of the comics asked.

"Hit me with her headlights," the second one said.

"Hit your tail pipe with her headlights?" the first one asked.

"Almost broke it off for me," the second one said.

Kapek, taking a seat across the aisle from Calucci and La Bresca, was suddenly reminded of the squadroom painters and realized how sorely he missed their presence. O'Brien had moved into the row behind the pair, and was sitting directly back of them now. Andy Parker was in the same row, two seats to the left of Calucci.

"Any trouble getting here?" Calucci whispered.

"No," La Bresca whispered back.

"What's with Dom?"

"He wants in."

"I thought he just wanted a couple of bills."

"That was last week."

"What's he want now?"

"A three-way split."

"Tell him to go screw," Calucci said.

"No. He's hip to the whole thing."

"How'd he find out?"

"I don't know. But he's hip, that's for sure."

There was a blast from the trumpet section of the four-piece band in the pit. The overhead leikos came up purple, and a brilliant follow spot hit the curtain stage left. The reed section followed the heraldic trumpet with a saxophone obbligato designed to evoke memory or desire or both. A gloved hand snaked its way around the curtain. "And now," a voice said over the loudspeaker system while one-half of the rhythm section started a snare drum roll, "and *now,* for the first time in America, direct from Brest, which is where the little lady comes from . . . exhibiting her titillating terpsichoreal skills for your pleasure, we are happy to present Miss . . . Freida Panzer!"

A leg appeared from behind the curtain.

It floated disembodied on the air. A black high-heeled pump pointed, wiggled, a calf muscle tightened, the knee bent, and then the toe pointed again. There was more of the leg visible now, the black nylon stocking shimmered in the glow of the lights, ribbed at the top where a vulnerable white thigh lay exposed, black garter biting into the flesh, fetishists all over the theater thrilled to the sight, not to mention a few detectives who weren't fetishists at all. Freida Panzer undulated onto the stage bathed in the glow of the overhead purple leikos, wearing a long purple gown slit up each leg to the waist, the black stockings and taut black garters revealed each time she took another long-legged step across the stage.

"Look at them legs," Calucci whispered.

"Yeah," La Bresca said.

O'Brien sitting behind them, looked at the legs. They were extraordinary legs.

"I hate to cut anybody else in on this," Calucci whispered.

"Me, neither," La Bresca said, "but what else can we do? He'll run screaming to the cops if we don't play ball."

"Is that what he said?"

"Not in so many words. He just hinted."

"Yeah, the son of a bitch."

"So what do you think?" La Bresca asked.

"Man, there's big money involved here," Calucci said.

"You think I don't know?"

"Why cut him in after we done all the planning?"

"What else can we do?"

"We can wash him," Calucci whispered.

The girl was taking off her clothes.

The four-piece ensemble in the orchestra pit rose to heights of musical expression, a heavy bass drum beat accentuating each solid bump as purple clothing fell like aster petals, a triple-tongued trumpet winding up with each pelvic grind, a saxophone wail climbing the girl's flanks in accompaniment with her sliding hands, a steady piano beat banging out the rhythm of each long-legged stride, each tassel-twirling, fixed-grin, sexy-eyed, contrived, and calculated erotic move. "She's got some tits," Calucci whispered, and La Bresca whispered back, "Yeah."

The men fell silent.

The music rose in earsplitting crescendo. The bass drum beat was more insistent now, the trumpet shrieked higher and higher, a C above high C reached for and missed, the saxophone trilled impatiently, the piano pounded in the upper register, a tinny insistent honkytonk rhythm, cymbals clashed, the trumpet reached for the screech note again, and again missed. The lights were swirling now, the stage was inundated in color and sound. There was the stink of perspiration and lust in the theater as the girl ground out her coded message in a cipher broken long ago on too many similar stages, pounded out her promises of ecstasy and sin. Come and get it, baby, Come and get it, Come and come and come and come.

The stage went black.

In the darkness, Calucci whispered, "What do you think?"

One of the baggy pants comics came on again to do a bit in a doctor's office accompanied by a pert little blonde with enormous breasts who explained that she thought she was stagnant because she hadn't fenestrated in two months.

"I hate the idea of knocking somebody off," La Bresca whispered.

"If it's necessary, it's necessary."

"Still."

"There's lots of money involved here, don't forget it."

"Yeah, but at the same time, there's enough to split three ways, ain't there?" La Bresca said.

"Why should we split it three ways when we can split it down the middle?"

"Because Dom'll spill the whole works if we don't cut him in. Look, what's the sense going over this a hundred times? We *got* to cut him in."

"I want to think about it."

"You ain't got that much time to think about it. We're set for the fifteenth. Dom wants to know right away."

"Okay, so tell him he's in. Then we'll decide whether he's in or out. And I mean *really* out, the little son of a bitch."

"And now, ladies and gentlemen," the loudspeaker voice said, "it gives us great pleasure to present the rage of San Francisco, a young lady who thrilled the residents of that city by the Golden Gate, a young lady whose exotic dancing caused the pious officials of Hong Kong to see Red . . . it is with bursting pride that we turn our stage over to Miss . . . *Anna . . . May . . . Zong!*"

The house lights dimmed. The band struck up a sinuous version of "Limehouse Blues." A swish cymbal echoed on the air, and a sloe-eyed girl wearing mandarin garb came into the follow spot with mincing steps, hands together in an attitude of prayer, head bent.

"I dig these Chinks," Calucci said.

"You guys want to stop talking?" a bald-headed man in the row ahead said. "I can't see the girls with all that gabbing behind me."

"Fuck off, Baldy," La Bresca said.

But both men fell silent. O'Brien leaned forward in his seat. Parker bent sideways over the armrest. There was nothing further to hear. Kapek, across the aisle, could not have heard anything anyway, so he merely watched the Chinese girl as she took off her clothes.

At the end of the act, La Bresca and Calucci rose quietly from their seats and went out of the theater. They split up outside. Parker followed Calucci to his house, and Kapek followed La Bresca to his. O'Brien went back to the squadroom to type up a report.

The detectives did not get together again until eleven o'clock that night, by which time La Bresca and Calucci were both hopefully asleep. They met in a diner some five blocks from the squadroom. Over coffee and crullers, they all agreed that the only thing they'd learned from their eavesdropping was the date of the job La Bresca and Calucci were planning: March the fifteenth. They also agreed that Freida Panzer had much larger breasts than Anna May Zong.

In the living room of a luxurious apartment on Harborside Oval, overlooking the river, a good three miles from where Detectives O'Brien, Parker, and Kapek were speculating on the comparative dimensions of the two strippers, the deaf man sat on a sofa facing sliding glass doors, and happily sipped at a glass of scotch and soda. The drapes were open, and the view of warm and glowing lights strung on the bridge's cables, the distant muted reds and ambers blinking on the distant shore gave the night a deceptively spring-time appearance; the thermometer on the terrace outside read ten degrees above zero.

Two bottles of expensive scotch, one already dead, were on the coffee table before the sofa upholstered in rich black leather. On the wall opposite the sofa, there hung an original Rouault, only a gouache to be sure, but nonetheless quite valuable. A grand piano turned its wide curve into the room, and a petite brunette, wearing a miniskirt and a white crocheted blouse, sat at the piano playing "Heart and Soul" over and over again.

The girl was perhaps twenty-three years old, with a nose that had been recently bobbed, large brown eyes, long black hair that fell to a point halfway between her waist and her shoulder blades. She was wearing false eyelashes. They fluttered whenever she hit a sour note, which was often. The deaf man seemed not to mind the discord that rose from the piano. Perhaps he really *was* deaf, or perhaps he had consumed enough scotch to have dimmed his perception. The two other men in the room didn't seem to mind the cacophony either. One of them even tried singing along with the girl's treacherous rendition—until she hit another sour note and began again from the top.

"I can't seem to get it," she said, pouting.

"You'll get it, honey," the deaf man said. "Just keep at it."

One of the men was short and slender, with the dust-colored complexion of an Indian. He wore narrow black tapered trousers and a white shirt over which was an open black vest. He was sitting at a drop-leaf desk, typing. The other man was tall and burly, with blue eyes, red hair, and a red mustache. There were freckles spattered over his cheeks and his forehead, and his voice, as he began singing along with the girl again, was deep and resonant. He was wearing tight jeans and a blue turtleneck sweater.

As the girl continued to play "Heart and Soul," a feeling of lassitude spread through the deaf man. Sitting on the couch, watching the second phase of his scheme as it became a reality, he mused again on the beauty of the plan, and then glanced at the girl, and then smiled when she hit the same sour note (an E flat where it should have been a natural E) and then looked again to where Ahmad was typing.

"The beauty of this phase," he said aloud, "is that none of them will believe us."

"They will believe," Ahmad offered, and smiled thinly.

"Yes, but not at this phase."

"No, only later," Ahmad said, and sipped at his scotch, and glanced at the girl's thighs, and went back to his typing.

"How much is this mailing going to cost us?" the other man asked.

"Well, Buck," the deaf man said, "we're sending out a hundred pieces of first-class mail at five cents postage per envelope, so that comes to a grand total of five dollars—if my arithmetic is correct."

"Your arithmetic is *always* correct," Ahmad said, and smiled.

"This is the damn part I can't get," the girl said, and struck the same note over and over again, as though trying to pound it into her memory.

"Keep at it, Rochelle," the deaf man said. "You'll get it."

Buck lifted his glass, discovered it was empty, and went to the coffee table to refill it, moving with the economy of an athlete, back ramrod stiff, hands dangling loosely at his sides, as though he were going back for the huddle after having executed a successful line plunge.

"Here, let me help you," the deaf man said.

"Not too heavy," Buck said.

The deaf man poured a liberal shot into Buck's extended glass. "Drink," he said. "You deserve it."

"Well, I don't want to get crocked."

"Why not? You're among friends," the deaf man said, and smiled.

He was feeling particularly appreciative of Buck's talent tonight, because without it this phase of the scheme would never have become a reality. Oh yes, a primitive bomb *could* have been assembled and hastily wired to the ignition switch, but such sloppiness, such dependency on chance, had never appealed to the deaf man. The seriousness with which Buck had approached the problem had been truly heart-warming. His development of a compact package (the inverter had weighed a mere twenty-two pounds and measured only ten by ten by five) that could be easily transported and wired in a relatively short period of time, his specific demand for an inverter with a regulated sine-wave output (costing a bit more, yes $64.95, but a negligible output in terms of the hoped-for financial realization), his insistence on a briefing session to explain the proper handling of the dynamite and the electric blasting cap, all were admirable, admirable. He was a good man, Buck, a demolition expert who had worked on countless legitimate blasting jobs, a background essential to the deaf man's plan; in this state, you were not allowed to buy explosives without a permit and insurance, both of which Buck possessed. The deaf man was very pleased indeed to have him in his employ.

Ahmad, too, was indispensable. He had been working as a draftsman at Metropolitan Power & Light, earning $150 a week in the Bureau of Maps and Records, when the deaf man first contacted him. He had readily appreciated the huge rewards to be reaped from the scheme, and had enthusiastically supplied all of the information so necessary to its final phase. In addition, he was a meticulous little man who had insisted that all of these letters be typed on high-quality bond paper, with each of the hundred men receiving an original rather than a carbon or a photocopy, a touch designed to allay any suspicion that the letter was a practical joke. The deaf man knew that the difference between success and failure very often depended on such small details, and he smiled at Ahmad in appreciation now, and sipped a little more of his scotch, and said, "How many have you typed so far?"

"Fifty-two."

"We'll be toiling long into the night, I'm afraid."

"When are we going to mail these?"

"I had hoped by Wednesday."

"I will finish them long before then," Ahmad promised.

"Will you really be working here all night?" Rochelle asked, pouting again.

"You can go to bed if you like, dear," the deaf man said.

"What good's bed without you?" Rochelle said, and Buck and Ahmad exchanged glances.

"Go on, I'll join you later."

"I'm not sleepy."

"Then have a drink, and play us another song."

"I don't know any other songs."

"Read a book then," the deaf man suggested.

Rochelle looked at him blankly.

"Or go into the den and watch some television."

"There's nothing on but old movies."

"Some of those old films are very instructive," the deaf man said.

"Some of them are very crappy, too," Rochelle replied.

The deaf man smiled. "Do you feel like licking a hundred envelopes?" he asked.

"No, I don't feel like licking envelopes," she answered.

"I didn't think so," the deaf man said.

"So what should I do?" Rochelle asked.

"Go get into your nightgown, darling," the deaf man said.

"Mmm?" she said, and looked at him archly.

"Mmm," he replied.

"Okay," she said, and rose from the piano bench. "Well, good night, fellas," she said.

"Good night," Buck said.

"Good night, miss," Ahmad said.

Rochelle looked at the deaf man again, and then went into the other room.

"Empty-headed little bitch," he said.

"I think she's dangerous to have around," Buck said.

"On the contrary," the deaf man said, "she soothes the nerves and eases the daily pressures. Besides, she thinks we're respectable businessmen promoting some sort of hare-brained scheme. She hasn't the vaguest notion of what we're up to."

"Sometimes *I* don't have the vaguest notion either," Buck said, and pulled a face.

"It's really very simple," the deaf man said. "We're making a direct-mail appeal, a tried-and-true method of solicitation pioneered by businessmen all over this bountiful nation. *Our* mailing, of course, is a limited one. We're only sending out a hundred letters. But it's my hope that we'll get a highly favorable response."

"And what if we don't?"

"Well, Buck, let's assume the worst. Let's assume we get a one-percent return, which is the generally expected return on a direct-mail piece. Our entire outlay thus far has been $86.95 for a lever-action carbine; $3.75 for a box of cartridges; $64.95 for your inverter; $7.00 for the electric clock; $9.60 for a dozen sticks of dynamite at eighty cents a stick; sixty cents for the blasting cap; $10.00 for the stationery; and $5.00 for the postage. If my addition is correct . . ." (He paused here to smile at Ahmad.) ". . . that comes to $187.85. Our future expenses—for the volt-ohm meter, the pressure-sensitive letters, the uniform, and so on—should also be negligible. Now, if we get only a one-percent return on our mailing, if only *one* person out of the hundred comes through, we'll *still* be reaping a large profit on our initial investment."

"Five thousand dollars seems like pretty small change for two murders," Buck said.

"Three murders," the deaf man corrected.

"Even better," Buck said, and pulled a face.

"I assure you I'm expecting much more than a one-percent return. On Friday night, we execute—if you'll pardon the pun—the final phase of our plan. By Saturday morning, there'll be no disbelievers."

"How many of them do you think'll come through?"

"Most of them. If not all of them."

"And what about the fuzz?"

"What about them? They *still* don't know who we are, and they'll never find out."

"I hope you're right."

"I *know* I'm right."

"I worry about fuzz," Buck said. "I can't help it. I've been conditioned to worry about them."

"There's nothing to worry about. Don't you realize *why* they're called fuzz?"

"No. Why?"

"Because they're fuzzy and fussy and antiquated and incompetent. Their investigatory technique is established and routine, designed for effectiveness in an age that no longer exists. The police in this city are like wind-up toys with keys sticking out of their backs, capable of performing only in terms of their own limited design, tiny mechanical men clattering along the sidewalk stiff-legged, scurrying about in aimless circles. But put an obstacle in their path, a brick wall or an orange crate, and they unwind helplessly in the same spot, arms and legs thrashing but taking them nowhere." The deaf man grinned. "I, my friend, am the brick wall."

"Or the orange crate," Buck said.

"No," Ahmad said intensely. "He is the brick wall."

10

THE FIRST BREAK in the case came at ten o'clock the next morning, when Fats Donner called the squadroom.

Until that time, there were still perhaps two thousand imponderables to whatever La Bresca and Calucci were planning. But aside from such minor considerations at *where* the job would take place, or at exactly what *time* on March fifteenth, there were several unknown identities to contend with as well, such as Dom (who so far had no last name; and the long-haired blond girl who had given La Bresca a lift last Friday night. It was the police supposition that if either of these two people could be located, the nature of the impending job might be wrung from one or the other of them. Whether or not the job was in any way connected with the recent murders would then become a matter for further speculation, as would the possibility that La Bresca was in some way involved with the deaf man. There were a lot of questions to be asked if only they could find somebody to ask them to.

Donner was put through immediately.

"I think I got your Dom," he said to Willis.

"Good," Willis said. "What's his last name?"

"Di Fillippi. Dominick Di Fillippi. Lives in Riverhead near the old coliseum, you know the neighborhood?"

"Yeah. What've you got on him?"

"He's with The Coaxial Cable."

"Yeah?" Willis said.

"Yeah."

"Well, what's that?" Willis said.

"What's *what?*"

"What's it supposed to *mean?*"

"What's *what* supposed to mean?"

"What you just said. Is it some kind of code or something?"

"Is what some kind of code?" Donner asked.

"The Coaxial Cable."

"No, it's a group."

"A group of *what?*"

"A group. Musicians," Donner said.

"A band, you mean?"

"That's right, only today they call them groups."

"Well, what's the coaxial cable got to do with it?"

"That's the name of the group. The Coaxial Cable."

"You're putting me on," Willis said.

"No, that's the name, I mean it."

"What does Di Fillippi play?"

"Rhythm guitar."

"Where do I find him?"

"His address is 365 North Anderson."

"That's in Riverhead?"

"Yeah."

"How do you know he's our man?"

"Well, it seems he's a big bullshit artist, you know?" Donner said. "He's been going around the past few weeks saying he dropped a huge bundle on the championship fight, made it sound like two, three G's. It turns out all he lost was fifty bucks, that's some big bundle, huh?"

"Yeah, go ahead."

"But he's also been saying recently that he knows about a big caper coming off."

"Who'd he say this to?"

"Well, one of the guys in the group is a big hophead from back even before it got stylish. That's how I got my lead onto Di Fillippi. And the guy said they were busting some joints together maybe three, four days ago, and Di Fillippi came on about this big caper he knew about."

"Did he say what the caper was?"

"No."

"And they were smoking pot?"

"Yeah, busting a few joints, you know, social."

"Maybe Di Fillippi was out of his skull."

"He probably was. What's that got to do with it?"

"He might have dreamt up the whole thing."

"I don't think so."

"Did he mention La Bresca at all?"

"Nope."

"Did he say when the job would be coming off?"

"Nope."

"Well, it's not much, Fats."

"It's worth half a century, don't you think?"

"It's worth ten bucks," Willis said.

"Hey, come on, man, I had to do some real hustling to get this for you."

"Which reminds me," Willis said.

"Huh?"

"Get rid of your playmate."

"Huh?"

"The girl. Next time I see you, I want her out of there."

"Why?"

"Because I thought it over, and I don't like the idea."

"I kicked her out twice already," Donner said. "She always comes back."

"Then maybe you ought to use this ten bucks to buy her a ticket back to Georgia."

"Sure. Maybe I ought to contribute another ten besides to the Salvation Army," Donner said.

"Just get her out of there," Willis said.

"When'd you get so righteous?" Donner asked.

"Just this minute."

"I thought you were a businessman."

"I am. Here's my deal. Let the girl go, and I forget whatever else I know about you, and whatever I might learn in the future."

"Nobody learns nothing about me," Donner said. "I'm The Shadow."

"No," Willis said. "Only Lamont Cranston is The Shadow."

"You serious about this?"

"I want the girl out of there. If she's still around next time I see you, I throw the book."

"And lose a valuable man."

"Maybe," Willis said. "In which case, we'll have to manage without you somehow."

"Sometimes I wonder why I bother helping you guys at all," Donner said.

"I'll *tell* you why sometime, if you have a minute," Willis said.

"Never mind."

"Will you get the girl out of there?"

"Yeah, yeah. You're going to send me fifty, right?"

"I said ten."

"Make it twenty."

"For the birdseed you just gave me?"

"It's a lead, ain't it?"

"That's all it is."

"So? A lead is worth at least twenty-five."

"I'll send you fifteen," Willis said, and hung up.

The phone rang again almost the instant he replaced it on the cradle. He lifted the receiver and said, "87th, Willis speaking."

"Hal, this is Artie over at the school."

"Yep."

"I've been waiting for Murchison to put me through. I think I've got something."

"Shoot."

"La Bresca talked to his mother on the phone about five minutes ago."

"In English or Italian?"

"English. He told her he was expecting a call from Dom Di Fillippi. That could be our man, no?"

"Yeah, it looks like he is," Willis said.

"He told his mother to say he'd meet Di Fillippi on his lunch hour at the corner of Cathedral and Seventh."

"Has Di Fillippi called yet?"

"Not yet. This was just five minutes ago, Hal."

"Right. What time did he say they'd meet?"

"Twelve-thirty."

"Twelve-thirty, corner of Cathedral and Seventh."

"Right," Brown said.

"We'll have somebody there."

"I'll call you back," Brown said. "I've got another customer."

In five minutes, Brown rang the squadroom again. "That was Di Fillippi," he said. "Mrs. La Bresca gave him the message. Looks like pay dirt at last, huh?"

"Maybe," Willis said.

From where Meyer and Kling sat in the Chrysler sedan parked on Cathedral Street, they could clearly see Tony La Bresca waiting on the corner near the bus stop sign. The clock on top of the Catholic church dominating the intersection read twelve-twenty. La Bresca was early and apparently impatient. He paced the pavement anxiously, lighting three cigarettes in succession, looking up at the church clock every few minutes, checking the time against his own wrist watch.

"This has got to be it," Kling said.

"The payoff of the burley joint summit meeting," Meyer said.

"Right. La Bresca's going to tell old Dom he's in for a three-way split. Then Calooch'll decide whether or not they're going to dump him in the river."

"Six-to-five old Dom gets the cement block."

"I'm not a gambling man," Kling said.

The church clock began tolling the half-hour. The chimes rang out over the intersection. Some of the lunch hour pedestrians glanced up at the bell tower. Most of them hurried past with their heads ducked against the cold.

"Old Dom seems to be late," Meyer said.

"Look at old Tony," Kling said. "He's about ready to take a fit."

"Yeah," Meyer said, and chuckled. The car heater was on, and he was snug and cozy and drowsy. He did not envy La Bresca standing outside on the windy corner.

"What's the plan?" Kling said.

"As soon as the meeting's over, we move in on old Dom."

"We ought to pick up *both* of them," Kling said.

"Tell me what'll stick."

"We heard La Bresca planning a job, didn't we? That's Conspiracy to Commit, Section 580."

"Big deal. I'd rather find out what he's up to and then catch him in the act."

"If he's in with the deaf man, he's *already* committed two crimes," Kling said. "And very big ones at that."

"If he's in with the deaf man."

"You think he is?"

"No."

"I'm not sure," Kling said.

"Maybe old Dom'll be able to tell us."

"If he shows."

"What time is it?"

"Twenty to," Kling said.

They kept watching La Bresca. He was pacing more nervously now, slapping his gloved hands against his sides to ward off the cold. He was wearing the same beige car coat he had worn the day he'd picked up the lunch pail in the park, the same green muffler wrapped around his throat, the same thick-soled workman's shoes.

"Look," Meyer said suddenly.

"What is it?"

"Across the street. Pulling up to the curb."

"Huh?"

"It's the blond girl, Bert. In the same black Buick!"

"How'd *she* get into the act?"

Meyer started the car. La Bresca had spotted the Buick and was walking toward it rapidly. From where they sat, the detectives could see the girl toss her long blond hair and then lean over to open the front door for him. La Bresca got into the car. In a moment, it gunned away from the curb.

"What do we do now?" Kling asked.

"We follow."

"What about Dom?"

"Maybe the girl's taking La Bresca to see him."

"And maybe not."

"What can we lose?" Meyer asked.

"We can lose Dom," Kling said.

"Just thank God they're not walking," Meyer said, and pulled the Chrysler out into traffic.

This was the oldest part of the city. The streets were narrow, the buildings crowded the sidewalks and gutters, pedestrians crossed at random, ignoring the lights, ducking around moving vehicles with practiced ease, nonchalant to possible danger.

"Like to give them all tickets for jaywalking," Meyer mumbled.

"Don't lose that Buick," Kling cautioned.

"You think I'm new in this business, Sonny?"

"You lost that same car only last week," Kling said.

"I was on *foot* last week."

"They're making a left turn," Kling said.

"I see them."

The Buick had indeed made a left turn, coming out onto the wide tree-lined esplanade bordering the River Dix. The river was icebound shore to shore, a phenomenon that had happened only twice before in the city's history. Devoid of its usual busy harbor traffic, it stretched toward Calm's Point like a flat Kansas plain, a thick cover of snow uniformly hiding the ice below. The naked trees along the esplanade bent in the strong wind that raced across the river. Even the heavy Buick seemed struggling to move through the gusts, its nose swerving every now and again as the blonde fought the wheel. At last, she pulled the car to the curb and killed the engine. The esplanade was silent except for the roaring of the wind. Newspapers flapped into the air like giant headless birds. An empty wicker-wire trash barrel came rolling down the center of the street.

A block behind the parked Buick, Meyer and Kling sat and looked through the windshield of the unmarked police sedan. The wind howled around the automobile, drowning out the calls that came from the radio. Kling turned up the volume.

"What now?" he asked.

"We wait," Meyer said.

"Do we pick up the girl when they're finished talking?" Kling asked.

"Yep."

"You think she'll know anything?"

"I hope so. She must be in on it, don't you think?"

"I don't know. Calucci was talking about splitting the take up the middle. If there're three people in it already . . ."

"Well, then maybe she's old Dom's girl."

"Substituting for him, you mean?"

"Sure. Maybe old Dom suspects they're going to dump him. So he sends his girl to the meeting while he's safe and sound somewhere, strumming his old rhythm guitar."

"That's possible," Kling said.

"Sure, it's possible," Meyer said.

"But then, *anything's* possible."

"That's a very mature observation," Meyer said.

"Look," Kling said. "La Bresca's getting out of the car."

"Short meeting," Meyer said. "Let's hit the girl."

As La Bresca went up the street in the opposite direction, Meyer and Kling stepped out of the parked Chrysler. The wind almost knocked them off their feet. They ducked their heads against it and began running, not wanting the girl to start the car and take off before they reached her, hoping to prevent a prolonged automobile chase through the city. Up ahead, Meyer heard the Buick's engine spring to life.

"Let's *go!*" he shouted to Kling, and they sprinted the last five yards to the car, Meyer fanning out into the gutter, Kling pulling open the door on the curb side.

The blonde sitting behind the wheel was wearing slacks and a short gray coat. She turned to look at Kling as he pulled open the door, and Kling was surprised to discover that she wasn't wearing makeup and that her features were rather heavy and gross. As he blinked at her in amazement, he further learned that she was sporting what looked like a three-day-old beard stubble on her chin and on her cheeks.

The door on the driver's side snapped open.

Meyer took one surprised look at the "girl" behind the wheel and then immediately said, "Mr. Dominick Di Fillippi, I presume?"

Dominick Di Fillippi was very proud of his long blond hair. In the comparative privacy of the squadroom, he combed it often, and explained to the detectives that guys belonging to a group had to have an image, you dig? Like all the guys in his group, they all looked different, you dig? Like the drummer wore these Ben Franklin eyeglasses, and the lead guitar player combed his chair down in bangs over his eyes, and the organist wore red shirts and red socks, you dig, all the guys had a different image. The long blond hair wasn't exactly his own idea, there were lots of guys in other groups who had long hair, which is why he was growing the beard to go with it. His beard was a sort of reddish-blond, he explained, he figured it would look real tough once it grew in, give him his own distinct image, you dig?

"Like what's the beef," he asked, "what am I doing inside a police station?"

"You're a musician, huh?" Meyer asked.

"You got it, man."

"That's what you do for a living, huh?"

"Well, like we only recently formed the group."

"How recently?"

"Three months."

"Play any jobs yet?"

"Yeah. Sure."

"When?"

"Well, we had like auditions."

"Have you ever actually been *paid* for playing anywhere?"

"Well, no, man, not yet. Not actually. I mean, man, even The Beatles had to start *someplace,* you know."

"Yeah."

"Like, man, they were playing these crumby little cellar joints in Liverpool, man, they were getting maybe a farthing a night."

"What the hell do you know about farthings?"

"Like it's a saying."

"Okay, Dom, let's get away from the music business for a little while, okay? Let's talk about *other* kinds of business, okay?"

"Yeah, let's talk about why I'm in here, okay?"

"You'd better read him the law," Kling said.

"Yeah," Meyer said, and went through the Miranda-Escobedo bit.

Di Fillippi listened intently. When Meyer was finished, he nodded his blond locks and said, "I can get a lawyer if I want one, huh?"

"Yes."

"I want one," Di Fillippi said.

"Have you got anyone special in mind, or do you want us to get one for you?"

"I got somebody in mind," Di Fillippi said.

While the detectives back at the squadroom fuzzily and fussily waited for Di Fillippi's lawyer to arrive, Steve Carella, now ambulatory, decided to go down to the fourth floor to visit Patrolman Genero.

Genero was sitting up in bed, his wounded leg bandaged and rapidly healing. He seemed surprised to see Carella.

"Hey," he said, "this is a real honor, I mean it. I'm really grateful to you for coming down here like this."

"How's it going, Genero?" Carella asked.

"Oh, so-so. It still hurts. I never thought getting shot could hurt. In the movies, you see these guys get shot all the time, and they just fall down, but you never get the impression it hurts."

"It hurts, all right," Carella said, and smiled. He sat on the edge of Genero's bed. "I see you've got a television in here," he said.

"Yeah, it's the guy's over in the next bed." Genero's voice fell to a whisper. "He never watches it. He's pretty sick, I think. He's either sleeping all the time or else moaning. I don't think he's going to make it, I'll tell you the truth."

"What's wrong with him?"

"I don't know. He just sleeps and moans. The nurses are in here day and night, giving him things, sticking him with needles, it's a regular railroad station, I'm telling you."

"Well, that's not so bad," Carella said.

"What do you mean?"

"Nurses coming in and out."

"Oh no, that's *great?*" Genero said. "Some of them are pretty good-looking."

"How'd this happen?" Carella asked, and nodded toward Genero's leg.

"Oh, you don't know, huh?" Genero said.

"I only heard you were shot."

"Yeah," Genero said, and hesitated. "We were chasing this suspect, you see. So as he went past me, I pulled my revolver to fire a warning shot," Genero hesitated again. "That was when I got it."

"Tough break," Carella said.

"Well, you got to expect things like that, I suppose. If you expect to make police work your life's work, you got to expect things like that in your work," Genero said.

"I suppose so."

"Well, sure, look what happened to you," Genero said.

"Mmm," Carella said.

"Of course, you're a detective," Genero said.

"Mmm," Carella said.

"Which is sort of understandable."

"What do you mean?"

"Well, you expect detectives to get in trouble more than ordinary patrolmen, don't you? I mean, the ordinary patrolman, the run-of-the-mill patrolman who doesn't expect to make police work his life's work, well, you don't *expect* him to risk his life trying to apprehend a suspect, do you?"

"Well," Carella said, and smiled.

"Do you?" Genero persisted.

"Everybody starts out as a patrolman," Carella said gently.

"Oh, sure. It's just you think of a patrolman as a guy directing traffic or helping kids cross the street or taking information when there's been an accident, things like that, you know? You never figure he's going to risk his life, the run-of-the-mill patrolman, anyway."

"Lots of patrolmen get killed in the line of duty," Carella said.

"Oh, sure, I'm sure. I'm just saying you don't *expect* it to happen."

"To your*self,* you mean."

"Yeah."

The room was silent

"It sure hurts," Genero said. "I hope they let me out of here soon, though. I'm anxious to get back to duty."

"Well, don't rush it," Carella said.

"When are *you* getting out?"

"Tomorrow, I think."

"You feel okay?"

"Oh yeah, I feel fine."

"Broke your ribs, huh?"

"Yeah, three of them."

"Your nose, too."

"Yeah."

"That's rough," Genero said. "But, of course, you're a detective."

"Mmm," Carella said.

"I was up the squadroom the other day," Genero said, "filling in for the guys when they came here to visit you. This was before the shooting. Before I got it."

"How'd you like that madhouse up there?" Carella said, and smiled.

"Oh, I handled it okay, I guess," Genero said. "Of course, there's a lot to learn, but I suppose that comes with actual practice."

"Oh, sure," Carella said.

"I had a long talk with Sam Grossman . . ."

"Nice fellow, Sam."

". . . yeah, at the lab. We went over those suspect notes together. Nice fellow, Sam," Genero said.

"Yeah."

"And then some kid came in with another one of those notes, and I held him there till the guys got back. I guess I handled it okay."

"I'm sure you did," Carella said.

"Well, you've got to be conscientious about it if you expect to make it your life's work," Genero said.

"Oh, sure," Carella said. He rose, winced slightly as he planted his weight, and then said, "Well, I just wanted to see how you were getting along."

"I'm fine, thanks. I appreciate your coming down."

"Oh, well," Carella said, and smiled, and started for the door.

"When you get back," Genero said, "give my regards, huh?" Carella looked at him curiously. "To all the guys," Genero said. "Cotton, and Hal, and Meyer and Bert. All of us who were on the plant together."

"Oh, sure."

"And thanks again for coming down . . ."

"Don't mention it."

". . . Steve," Genero ventured as Carella went out.

Di Fillippi's lawyer was a man named Irving Baum.

He arrived at the squadroom somewhat out of breath and the first thing he asked was whether the detectives had advised his client of his rights. When assured that Di Fillippi had been constitutionally protected, he nodded briefly, took off his brown Homburg and heavy brown overcoat, placed both neatly across Meyer's desk, and then asked the detectives what it was all about. He was a pleasant-looking man, Baum, with white hair and mustache, sympathetic brown eyes, and an encouraging manner of nodding when anyone spoke, short little nods that seemed to be signs of agreement. Meyer quickly told him that it was not the police intention to book Di Fillippi for anything, but merely to solicit information from him. Baum could see no reason why his client should not co-operate to the fullest extent. He nodded to Di Fillippi and then said, "Go ahead, Dominick, answer their questions."

"Okay, Mr. Baum," Di Fillippi said.

"Can we get your full name and address?" Meyer said.

"Dominick Americo Di Fillippi, 365 North Anderson Street, Riverhead."

"Occupation."

"I already told you. I'm a musician."

"I beg your pardon," Baum said. "Were you questioning him *before* I arrived?"

"Steady, counselor," Meyer said. "All we asked him was what he did for a living."

"Well," Baum said, and tilted his head to one side as though considering whether there had been a miscarriage of justice. "Well," he said, "go on, please."

"Age?" Meyer asked.

"Twenty-eight."

"Single? Married?"

"Single."

"Who's your nearest living relative?"

"I beg your pardon," Baum said, "but if you merely intend to solicit information, why do you need these statistics?"

"Mr. Baum," Willis said, "you're a lawyer, and you're here with him, so stop worrying. He hasn't said anything that'll send him to jail. Not yet."

"This is routine, counselor," Meyer said. "I think you're aware of that."

"All right, all right, go on," Baum said.

"Nearest living relative?" Meyer repeated.

"My father. Angelo Di Filippi."

"What's he do?"

"He's a stonemason."

"Hard to find good stonemasons today," Meyer said.

"Yeah."

"Dom," Willis said, "what's your connection with Tony La Bresca?"

"He's a friend of mine."

"Why'd you meet with him today?"

"Just friendly."

"It was a very short meeting," Willis said.

"Yeah, I guess it was."

"Do you always go all the way downtown just to talk to someone for five minutes?"

"Well, he's a friend of mine."

"What'd you talk about?"

"Uh music," Di Fillippi said.

"What about music?"

"Well uh he's got a cousin who's gonna get married soon, so he wanted to know about our group."

"What'd you tell him?"

"I told him we were available."

"When's this wedding coming off?"

"The uh sometime in June."

"When in June?"

"I forget the exact date."

"Then how do you know you'll be available?"

"Well, we ain't got no jobs for June, so I know we'll be available."

"Are you the group's business manager?"

"No."

"Then why'd La Bresca come to you?"

"Because we're friends, and he heard about the group."

"So that's what you talked about. His cousin's wedding."

"Yes, that's right."

"How much did you tell him it would cost?"

"I said uh it uh seventy dollars."

"How many musicians are there in the group?"

"Five."

"How much is that a man?" Meyer asked.

"It's uh seventy uh divided by five."

"Which is how much?"

"That's uh well five into seven is one and carry the two, five into twenty is uh four, so that comes to fourteen dollars a man."

"But you didn't know that when you asked for the seventy, did you?"

"Yes, sure I knew it."

"Then why'd you have to do the division just now?"

"Just to check it, that's all."

"So you told La Bresca you'd be available, and you told him it would cost seventy dollars, and then what?"

"He said he'd ask his cousin, and he got out of the car."

"That was the extent of your conversation with him?"

"That was the extent of it, yes."

"Couldn't you have discussed this on the telephone?"

"Sure, I guess so."

"Then why didn't you?"

"Well, I like to see Tony every now and then, he's a good friend of mine."

"So you drove all the way downtown to see him."

"That's right."

"How much did you lose on that championship fight?"

"Oh, not much."

"How much?"

"Ten bucks or so. How do *you* know about that?"

"Wasn't it more like fifty?"

"Well, maybe, I don't remember. How do you know this?" He turned to Baum. "How do they know this?" he asked the lawyer.

"How do you know this?" Baum asked.

"Well, counselor, if it's all right with you," Meyer said, *"we'll* ask the questions, unless you find something objectionable."

"No, I think everything's been proper so far, but I *would* like to know where you're going."

"I think that'll become clear," Meyer said.

"Well, Detective Meyer, I think I'd like to know right *now* what this is all about, or I shall feel compelled to advise my client to remain silent."

Meyer took a deep breath. Willis shrugged in resignation.

"We feel your client possesses knowledge of an impending crime," Meyer said.

"What crime?"

"Well, if you'll permit us to question him . . ."

"No, not until you answer me," Baum said.

"Mr. Baum," Willis said, "we can book him for Compounding, Section 570 of the Penal Law, or we can book him for . . ."

"Just a moment, young man," Baum said. "Would you mind explaining that?"

"Yes, sir, we have reason to believe that your client has been promised money or other property to conceal a crime. Now that's either a felony or a misdemeanor, sir, depending on what the crime is he's agreed to conceal. I think you know that, sir."

"And what's this crime he's agreed to conceal?"

"We might also be able to book him for Conspiracy, Section 580, if he's actually *involved* in this planned crime."

"Do you have definite knowledge that a crime is to take place?" Baum asked.

"We have reasonable knowledge, sir, yes, sir."

"You realize, do you not, that no agreement amounts to a conspiracy unless some act *beside* such agreement is done to effect the object thereof?"

"Look, Mr. Baum," Meyer said, "this isn't a court of law, so let's not argue the case right here and now, okay? We're not going to book your client for anything provided he co-operates a little and answers . . ."

"I hope I didn't detect a threat in that statement," Baum said.

"Oh, for Christ's sake," Meyer said, "we know that a man named Anthony La Bresca and another man named Peter Calucci are planning to commit a crime, misdemeanor or felony we don't know which, on March fifteenth. We also have very good reason to believe that your client here knows *exactly* what they're up to and has demanded money from them to keep such knowledge or information from reaching the police. Now, Mr. Baum, we don't want to pull in La Bresca and Calucci for conspiracy because (a) it wouldn't stick without the 'act' you were talking about, and (b) we might end up with only a misdemeanor, depending on what they've cooked up. As I'm sure you know, if they've planned the crime of murder, kidnaping, robbery One, selling narcotics, arson or extortion, and if they've committed some act other than their agreement to pull the job, each of them is guilty of a felony. And as I'm sure you also know, some very big officials in this city were recently murdered, and the possibility exists that La Bresca and Calucci are somehow involved and that this crime they've planned may have to do with extortion or murder, or both, which would automatically make the conspiracy a felony. As you can see, therefore, we're not after your client *per se,* we're merely trying to prevent a crime. So can we cut all the legal bullshit and get a little co-operation from you, and especially from him?"

"It seems to me he's been co-operating splendidly," Baum said.

"It seems to me he's been lying splendidly," Meyer said.

"Considering what's involved here . . ." Baum started.

"Mr. Baum, could we please . . . ?"

". . . I think you had better charge Mr. Di Fillippi with whatever it is you have in mind. We'll let the courts settle the matter of his guilt or innocence."

"While two hoods pull off their job, right?"

"I'm not interested in the entrapment of two hoodlums," Baum said. "I'm advising my client to say nothing further, in accordance with the rights granted to him under . . ."

"Thanks a lot, Mr. Baum."

"Are you going to book him, or not?"

"We're going to book him," Meyer said.

"For what?"

"Compounding a crime, Section 570 of the Penal Law."

"Very well, I suggest you do that with reasonable dispatch," Baum said. "It seems to me he's been held in custody an extremely long time as it is. I know you're aware . . ."

"Mr. Baum, we're aware of it inside out and backwards. Take him down, Hal. Charge him as specified."

"Hey, wait a minute," Di Fillippi said.

"I suggest that you go with them," Baum said. "Don't worry about a thing. Before you're even arraigned, I'll have contacted a bail bondsman. You'll be back on the street . . ."

"Hey, wait one goddamn minute," Di Fillippi said. "What if those two guys go ahead with . . . ?"

"Dominick, I advise you to remain silent."

"Yeah? What can I get for this 'compounding,' whatever the hell it is?"

"Depends on what they do," Meyer said.

"Dominick . . ."

"If they commit a crime punishable by death or by life imprisonment you can get five years. If they commit . . ."

"What about a holdup?" Di Fillippi asked.

"Dominick, as your attorney, I must again strongly advise you . . ."

"What about a holdup?" Di Fillippi said again.

"Is that what they've planned?" Meyer said.

"You didn't answer me."

"If they commit a robbery, and you take money from them to conceal the crime, you can get three years in prison."

"Mmm," Di Fillippi said.

"Will you answer some questions for us?"

"Will you let me go if I do?"

"Dominick, you don't have to . . ."

"Do *you* want to go to prison for three years?" Di Fillippi asked.

"They have no case, they're . . ."

"No? Then how do they know the job's coming off on March fifteenth? Where'd they get *that?* Some little birdie whisper it in their ear?"

"We've leveled with you, Dominick," Willis said, "and believe me, we wouldn't have brought any of this out in the open if we didn't have plenty to go on. Now you can either help us or we can book you and take you down for arraignment and you'll have an arrest record following you for the rest of your life. What do you want to do?"

"That's coercion!" Baum shouted.

"It may be coercion, but it's also fact," Willis said.

"I'll tell you everything I know," Di Fillippi said.

He knew a lot, and he told it all.

He told them that the holdup was set for eight o'clock on Friday night, and that the victim was to be the owner of a tailor shop on Culver Avenue. The reason the hit had been scheduled for that particular night and time was that the tailor, a man named John Mario Vicenzo, usually packed up his week's earnings then and took them home with him in a small metal box, which box his wife Laura carried to the Fiduciary Trust early Saturday morning. The Fiduciary Trust, as it happened, was the only bank in the neighborhood that was open till noon on Saturday, bank employees being among those who did not like to work on weekends.

John Mario Vicenzo (or John the Tailor as he was known to the people along Culver Avenue) was a man in his early seventies, an easy mark. The take would be enormous, Di Fillippi explained, with more than enough for everyone concerned even if split three ways. The plan was to go into the shop at ten minutes to eight, just before John the Tailor drew the blinds on the plate glass window fronting the street. La Bresca was to perform that task instead, and then he was to lock the front door while Calucci forced John the Tailor at gun point into the back room, where he would tie him and leave him bound and helpless on the floor near the pressing machine. They would then empty the cash register of the money that had been piling up there all week long, and take off. John the Tailor would be left dead or alive depending on how co-operative he was.

Di Fillippi explained that he'd overheard all this one night in the pizzeria on South Third, La Bresca and Calucci sitting in a booth behind him and not realizing they were whispering a little too loud. At first he'd been annoyed by the idea of two Italians knocking over a place owned by another Italian, but then he figured What the hell, it was none of his business; the one thing he'd never done in his life was rat on anybody. But that was before the fight, and the bet that had left him broke. Desperate for a little cash, he remembered what he'd heard them discussing and figured he'd try to cut himself in. He didn't think there'd be too much static from them because the take, after all, was a huge one, and he figured they'd be willing to share it.

"Just how much money is involved here?" Willis asked.

"Oh, man," Di Fillippi said, rolling his eyes, "there's at least four hundred bucks involved here, maybe even more."

11

A LOT OF THINGS happened on Wednesday.

It was discovered on Wednesday, for example, that somebody had stolen the following items from the squadroom:

A typewriter.

Six ballpoint pens.

An electric fan.

A thermos jug.

A can of pipe tobacco, and

Four bars of soap.

Nobody could figure out who had done it.

Not even Steve Carella, who had been released from the hospital and who was very delicately walking around with his ribs taped, could figure out who had done it. Some of the squadroom wits suggested that Carella, being an invalid and all, should be assigned to the Great Squadroom Mystery, but Lieutenant Byrnes decided it would be better to assign him to the tailor shop stakeout instead, together with Hal Willis. At twelve noon that Wednesday, the pair headed crosstown to John the Tailor's shop.

But before then a lot of other things happened, it was certainly a busy Wednesday.

At 8:00 A.M., for example, a patrolman walking his beat called in to report that he had found a stiff in a doorway and that it looked to him as if the guy had been burned to death. Which meant that the two fire bugs had struck again sometime during the night, and that something was going to have to be done about them pretty soon before they doused every bum in the city with gasoline. Kling, who took the call, advised the patrolman to stay with the body until he could get a meat wagon over, and the patrolman complained that the doorway and the entire street stank to high heaven and Kling told him that was tough, he should take the complaint to Captain Frick.

At 9:15 A.M., Sadie the Nut came up to tell Willis about the rapist who had tried to steal her virginity the night before. Sadie the Nut was seventy-eight years old, a wrinkled toothless crone who had been protecting her virginity for close to fourscore years now, and who unfailingly reported to the squadroom every Wednesday morning, either in person or by phone, that a man had broken into her tenement flat the night before and tried to tear off her nightgown and rape her. The first time she'd reported this attempted crime some four years back, the police had believed her, figuring they had another Boston Strangler on their hands, only this time right in their own back yard. They immediately initiated an investigation, going so far as to plant Detective Andy Parker in the old lady's apartment. But the following Wednesday morning, Sadie came to the squadroom again to report a second rape attempt —even though Parker had spent an uneventful Tuesday night alert and awake in her kitchen. The squadroom comedians speculated that perhaps Parker himself was the rape artist, a premise Parker found somewhat less than amusing. They all realized by then, of course, that Sadie was a nut, and that they could expect frequent visits or calls from her. They did not realize that the visits or calls would come like clockwork every Wednesday morning, nor that Sadie's fantasy was as fixed and as unvaried as the squadroom itself. Her rapist was always a tall swarthy man who somewhat resembled Rudolph Valentino. He was always wearing a black cape over a tuxedo, white dress shirt, black bow tie, black satin dancing slippers. His pants had buttons on the fly. Five buttons. He always unbuttoned his fly slowly and teasingly, warning Sadie not to scream, he not going to hurt her, he was (in Sadie's own words) "only going to rapage her." Sadie invariably waited until he had unbuttoned each of the five buttons and taken out his "thing" before she screamed. The rapist would then flee from the apartment, leaping onto the fire escape like Douglas Fairbanks, and swinging down into the back yard.

Her story this Wednesday was the same story she had been telling every Wednesday for the past four years. Willis took down the information and promised they would do everything in their power to bring this insane womanizer to justice. Sadie the Nut left the squadroom pleased and excited, doubtless anticipating next week's nocturnal visit.

At a quarter to ten that morning, a woman came in to report

that her husband was missing. The woman was perhaps thirty-five years old, an attractive brunette wearing a green overcoat that matched her Irish eyes. Her face was spanking pink from the cold outside, and she exuded health and vitality even though she seemed quite upset by her husband's disappearance. Upon questioning her, though, Meyer learned that the missing man wasn't her husband at all, he was really the husband of her very best friend who lived in the apartment next door to her on Ainsley Avenue. And upon further questioning, the green-eyed lady explained to Meyer that she and her very best friend's husband had been having "a relationship" (as she put it) for three years and four months, with never a harsh word between them, they were that fond of each other. But last night, when the green-eyed lady's best friend went to play Bingo at the church, the green-eyed lady and the husband had had a violent argument because he had wanted to "do it" (as she again put it) right there in his own apartment on the living-room couch with his four children asleep in the other room, and she had refused, feeling it would not be decent, and he had put on his hat and coat and gone out into the cold. He had not yet returned, and whereas the green-eyed lady's best friend figured he was out having himself a toot, the husband apparently being something of a drinking man, the green-eyed lady missed him sorely and truly believed he had vanished just to spite her, had she known he would do something like that she certainly would have let him have his way, you know how men are.

Yes, Meyer said.

So whereas the wife felt it would not be necessary to report him missing and thereby drag policemen into the situation, the green-eyed lady feared he might do something desperate, having been denied her favors, and was therefore asking the law's assistance in locating him and returning him to the bosom of his family and loved ones, you know how men are.

Yes, Meyer said again.

So he took down the information, wondering when it was that he'd last attempted to lay Sarah on the living-room couch with his own children asleep in their respective rooms, and realized that he had *never* tried to lay Sarah on the living-room couch. He decided that he would try to do it tonight when he got home, and then he assured the green-eyed lady that they would do everything in their power to locate her best friend's husband, but that probably there was nothing to worry about, he had probably gone to spend the night with a friend.

Yes, that's *just* what I'm worried about, the green-eyed lady said.

Oh, Meyer said.

When the green-eyed lady left, Meyer filed the information away for future use, not wanting to bug the Bureau of Missing Persons prematurely. He was beginning to type up a report on a burglary when Detective Andy Parker came into the squadroom with Lewis the Pickpocket. Parker was laughing uncontrollably, but Lewis did not seem too terribly amused. He was a tall slender man with a bluish cast to his jowls, small sharp penetrating blue eyes, thinning sandy-colored hair. He was wearing a beige trench coat and brown leather gloves, and he carried an umbrella in the crook of his arm and scowled at everyone in the squadroom as Parker continued laughing uproariously.

"Look who *I* got!" Parker said, and burst into a choking, gasping fit.

"What's so special?" Meyer said. "Hello, Lewis, how's business?"

Lewis scowled at Meyer. Meyer shrugged.

"Best pickpocket in the precinct!" Parker howled. "Guess what happened?"

"What happened?" Carella asked.

"I'm standing at the counter in Jerry's, you know? The luncheonette?"

"Yeah?"

"Yeah, with my back to the door, you know? So guess what?"

"What?"

"I feel somebody's hand in my pocket, fishing around for my wallet. So I grab the hand by the wrist, and I whip around with my gun in my other hand, and guess who it is?"

"Who is it?"

"It's Lewis!" Parker said, and began laughing again. "The best pickpocket in the precinct, he chooses a *detective* for a mark!"

"I made a mistake," Lewis said, and scowled.

"Oh, man, you made a *big* mistake!" Parker bellowed.

"You had your back to me," Lewis said.

"Lewis, my friend, you are going to prison," Parker said gleefully, and then said, "Come on down, we're going to book you before you try to pick Meyer's pocket there."

"I don't think it's funny," Lewis said, and followed Parker out of the squadroom, still scowling.

"*I* think it's pretty funny," Meyer said.

A man appeared at the slatted rail divider just then, and asked in hesitant English whether any of the policemen spoke Italian.

Carella said that he did, and invited the man to sit at his desk. The man thanked him in Italian and took off his hat, and perched it on his knees when he sat, and then began telling Carella his story. It seemed that somebody was putting garbage in his car.

"Rifiuti?" Carella asked.

"Sì, rifiuti," the man said.

For the past week now, the man went on, someone had been opening his car at night and dumping garbage all over the front seat. All sorts of garbage. Empty tin cans and dinner leftovers and apple cores and coffee grounds, everything. All over the front seat of the car.

"Perchè non lo chiude a chiave?" Carella asked.

Well, the man explained, he *did* lock his car every night, but it didn't do any good. Because the way the garbage was left in it the first time was that *quello porco* broke the side vent and opened the door that way in order to do his dirty work. So it didn't matter if he continued to lock the car, the befouler continued to open the door by sticking his hand in through the broken flap window, and then he dumped all his garbage on the front seat, the car was beginning to stink very badly.

Well, Carella said, do you know of anyone who might want to put garbage on your front seat?

No, I do not know of anyone who would do such a filthy thing, the man said.

Is there anyone who has a grudge against you? Carella asked.

No, I am loved and respected everywhere in the world, the man said.

Well, Carella said, we'll send a man over to check it out.

"Per piacere," the man said, and put on his hat, and shook hands with Carella, and left the squadroom.

The time was 10:33 A.M.

At 10:35 A.M., Meyer called Raoul Chabrier down at the district attorney's office, spent a delightful three minutes chatting with Bernice, and was finally put through to Chabrier himself.

"Hello, Rollie," Meyer said, "what'd you find out?"

"About what?" Chabrier said.

"About the book I called to . . ."

"Oh."

"You forgot," Meyer said flatly.

"Listen," Chabrier said, "have *you* ever tried handling two cases at the same time?"

"Never in my life," Meyer said.

"Well, it isn't easy, believe me. I'm reading law on one of them, and trying to get a brief ready on the other. You expect me to worry about some goddamn novel at the same time?"

"Well . . ." Meyer said.

"I know, I know, I know," Chabrier said, "I promised."

"Well . . ."

"I'll get to it. I promise you again, Meyer. I'm a man who never breaks his word. Never. I promised you, and now I'm promising you again. What was the title of the book?"

"Meyer Meyer," Meyer said.

"Of course, *Meyer Meyer,* I'll look into it immediately. I'll get back to you, I promise. Bernice," he shouted, "make a note to get back to Meyer!"

"When?" Meyer said.

That was at 10:39.

At five minutes to eleven, a tall blond man wearing a hearing aid and carrying a cardboard carton walked into the Hale Street Post Office downtown. He went directly to the counter, hefted the carton onto it, and shoved it across to the mail clerk. There were a hundred sealed and stamped envelopes in the carton.

"These all going to the city?" the clerk asked.

"Yes," the deaf man replied.

"First class?"

"Yes."

"All got stamps?"

"Every one of them."

"Right," the clerk said, and turned the carton over, dumping the envelopes onto the long table behind him. The deaf man waited. At eleven A.M., the mail clerk began running the envelopes through the cancellation machine.

The deaf man went back to the apartment, where Rochelle met him at the door.

"Did you mail off your crap?" she asked.

"I mailed it," the deaf man said, and grinned.

John the Tailor wasn't having any of it.

"I no wanna cops in my shop," he said flatly and unequivocally and in somewhat fractured English.

Carella patiently explained, in English, that the police had definite knowledge of a planned holdup to take place on Friday night at eight o'clock but that it was the lieutenant's idea to plant two men in the rear of the shop starting tonight in case the thieves changed their minds and decided to strike earlier. He assured John the Tailor that they would unobtrusively take up positions behind the hanging curtain that divided the front of the shop from the rear, out of his way, quiet as mice, and would move into action only if and when the thieves struck.

"Lei è pazzo!" John the Tailor said in Italian, meaning he thought Carella was crazy. Whereupon Carella switched to speaking Italian, which he had learned as a boy and which he didn't get much chance to practice these days except when he was dealing with people like the man who had come in to complain about the garbage in his car, or people like John the Tailor, who was suddenly very impressed with the fact that Carella, like himself, was Italian.

John the Tailor had once written a letter to a very popular television show, complaining that too many of the Italians on that show were crooks. He had seventy-four people in his immediate family, all of them living here in the United States, in this city, for most of their lives, and none of them were criminals, all of them were honest, hard-working people. So why should the television make it seem that all Italians were thieves? He had received a letter written by some programming assistant, explaining that not all the criminals on the show were Italians, some of them were Jews and Irish, too. This had not mollified John the Tailor, since he was quite intelligent and capable of understanding the basic difference between the two statements *Not all Italians are criminals and Not all criminals are Italians*. So it was very pleasant to have an Italian cop in his shop, even if it meant having to put up with strangers in the back behind the curtain. John the Tailor did not like strangers, even if they were Italian cops. Besides, the other stranger, the short one, definitely was *not* Italian, God knew what *he* was!

The tailor shop did a very thriving business, though Carella doubted it brought in anything near four hundred dollars a week, which was apparently La Bresca's and Calucci's estimate of the take. He wondered why either of the two men would be willing to risk a minimum of ten and a maximum of thirty years in prison, the penalty for first-degree robbery, when all they could hope to gain for their efforts was four hundred dollars. Even granting them the minimum sentence, and assuming they'd be out on parole in three-and-a-half, that came to about a hundred and fifteen dollars a year, meager wages for *any* occupation.

He would never understand the criminal mind.

He could not, for example, understand the deaf man at all.

There seemed to be something absolutely lunatic about the enormous risk he had taken, a gamble pitting fifty thousand dollars against possible life imprisonment. Now surely a man of his intelligence and capabilities must have known that the city wasn't going to reach into its treasury and plunk down fifty thousand dollars solely because someone threatened murder. The odds against such a payoff were staggering, and any shrewd manipulator of odds would have realized this. The deaf man, then, had not *expected* to be paid, he had *wanted* to kill the deputy mayor, as he had earlier killed the parks commissioner. But why? Whatever else the deaf man happened to be, Carella did not figure him for a thrill killer. No, he was a hardheaded businessman taking a calculated risk. And businessmen don't take risks unless there's at least some hope of a payoff. The deaf man had asked for five grand at first, and been refused, and committed murder. He had next asked for fifty grand, knowing full well he'd be refused again, and had again committed murder. He had then advised the newspapers of his unsuccessful extortion attempts, and had since remained silent.

So where was the payoff?

It was coming, baby, of that Carella was sure.

In the meantime, he sat in the back of John the Tailor's shop and wondered how much a good pressing machine operator earned.

12

Mr. Carl Wahler
1121 Marshall Avenue
Isola

Dear Mr. Wahler:

<u>If you treat this letter as a joke, you will die.</u>
These are the facts. Read them carefully. They can
save your life.
1) Parks Commissioner Cowper ignored a warning and
   was killed.
2) Deputy Mayor Scanlon ignored a warning and was
   killed.
3) JMV is next. He will be killed this Friday night.

<u>What does all this have to do with you?</u>
1) This is <u>your</u> warning. It is your <u>only</u> warning.
   There will be no further warnings. Remember that.
2) You are to withdraw five thousand dollars in small,
   unmarked bills from your account.
3) You will be contacted by telephone sometime within
   the next week. The man you speak to will tell you
   how and when and where the money is to be delivered.
4) If you fail to meet this demand, you too will be
   killed. <u>Without warning</u>.

<u>Do not entertain false hopes!</u>

The police could not save Cowper or Scanlon, although
sufficiently forewarned. They will not be able to save
JMV, either. What chance will <u>you</u> have unless you pay?
What chance will you have when we strike <u>without warning</u>?

Get the money. You will hear from us again. Soon.

The letters were delivered to a hundred homes on Thursday.
The deaf man was very cheerful that morning. He went whistling
about his apartment, contemplating his scheme again and again,
savoring its more refined aspects, relishing the thought that one

hundred very wealthy individuals would suddenly be struck with panic come Saturday morning.

By five o'clock tonight, he could reasonably assume that most of the men receiving his letter would have read it and formed at least some tentative opinion about it. He fully expected some of them to glance cursorily at it, crumple it into a ball, and immediately throw it into the garbage. He also expected a handful, the paranoid fringe, to call the police at once, or perhaps even visit their local precinct, letter in hand, indignantly demanding protection. *That* part of his plan was particularly beautiful, he felt. The mayor was being warned, yes, but oh so indirectly. He would learn about the threat on his life only because some frightened citizens would notify the police.

And tomorrow night, forewarned, the mayor would nonetheless die.

Six months ago when the deaf man had begun the preliminary work on his scheme, several rather interesting pieces of information had come to light. To begin with, he had learned that anyone desiring to know the exact location of the city's underground water pipes need only apply to the Department of Water Supply in Room 1720 of the Municipal Building, where the maps were available for public scrutiny. Similarly, maps of the city's underground sewer system were obtainable at the Department of Public Works in the main office of that same building. The deaf man, unfortunately, was not interested in either water pipes or sewers. He was interested in electricity. And he quickly learned that detailed maps of the underground power lines were *not,* for obvious reasons, open to the public for inspection. Those maps were kept in the Maps and Records Bureau of the Metropolitan Light & Power Company, worked on by an office staffed largely by draftsmen. Ahmad had been one of those draftsmen.

The first map he delivered to the deaf man was titled "60 Cycle Network Area Designations and Boundaries Lower Isola," and it showed the locations of all the area substations in that section of the city. The area that specifically interested the deaf man was the one labeled "Cameron Flats." The mayor's house was on the corner of South Meridian and Vanderhof, in Cameron Flats. The substation serving South Meridian and Vanderhof was marked with a cross in a circle, and was designated "No. 3 South Meridian." Into this substation ran high-voltage supply cables (They're called "feeders," Ahmad said) from a switching station elsewhere on the transmission system. It would be necessary to destroy those supply cables if the mayor's house was to be thrown into darkness on the night of his murder.

The second map Ahmad delivered was titled "System Ties" and was a detailed enlargement of the feeder systems supplying any given substation. The substation on the first map had been labeled "No. 3 South Meridian." By locating this on the more detailed map, the deaf man was able to identify the number designation of the feeder: 65CA3. Which brought him to the third pilfered map, simply and modestly titled "65CA3," and subtitled "Location South Meridian Substation." This was a rather long, narrow diagram of the route the feeder traveled below the city's streets, with numbers indicating the manholes that provided access to the cables. 65CA3 passed through eleven manholes on its meandering underground travels from the switching station to the substation. The deaf man chose a manhole approximately a half-mile from the mayor's house and wrote down its number: M3860-120'SSC-CENT.

The last map, the crucial one, was titled "Composite Feeder Plate" and it pinpointed the manhole exactly. M3860 was located on Faxon Drive, a hundred and twenty feet south of the southern curb of Harris, in the center of the street—hence the 120'SSC-CENT. The high-voltage cables passing through that concrete manhole were five feet below the surface of the street protected by a three-hundred pound manhole cover.

Tomorrow night, Ahmad, Buck, and the deaf man would lift that cover, and one of Buck's bombs would effectively take care of the cables.

And then . . .

Ahhh, then . . .

The really beautiful part was still ahead, and the deaf man smiled as he contemplated it.

He could visualize the mayor's house at 10 P.M. tomorrow night, surrounded by policemen and detectives on special assignment, all there to protect the honorable JMV from harm. He could see himself driving a black sedan directly to the curb in front of the darkened brick structure, a police flashlight picking out the gold lettering on the front door, Metropolitan Light & Power Company (pressure-sensitive letters expertly applied by Ahmad to both front doors of the car, cost eight cents per letter at Studio Art Supply, total expenditure $4.80). He could see the car doors opening. Three men step out of it. Two of them are wearing workmen's coveralls (Sears, Roebuck, $6.95 a pair). The third is wearing the uniform of a police sergeant, complete with a citation ribbon pinned over the shield on the left breast (Theatrical Arts Rentals, $10.00 per day, plus a $75.00 deposit) and the yellow sleeve patch of the Police Department's Emergency Service ($1.25 at the Civic Equipment Company, across the street from Headquarters).

"Who's there?" the policeman on duty asks. His flashlight scans the trio. Buck, in the sergeant's uniform, steps forward.

"It's all right," Buck says. "I'm Sergeant Pierce, Emergency Service. These men are from the electric company. They're trying to locate that power break."

"Okay, Sergeant," the cop answers.

"Everything quiet in there?" Buck asks.

"So far, Sarge."

"Better check out their equipment," Buck says. "I don't want any static on this later."

"Good idea," the cop says. He swings his flashlight around. Ahmad opens the tool box. There is nothing in it but electricians tools: a test light, a six-foot rule, a brace, four screwdrivers, a Stillson wrench, a compass saw, a hacksaw, a hammer, a fuse puller, wire skinners, wire cutters, gas pliers, Allen wrenches, friction tape, rubber tape . . . "Okay," the cop says, and turns to the deaf man. "What's that you're carrying?"

"A volt-ohm meter," the deaf man answers.

"Want to open it for me?"

"Sure," the deaf man says.

The testing equipment is nothing more than a black leather case perhaps twelve inches long by eight inches wide by five inches deep. When the deaf man unclasps and raises the lid, the flashlight illuminates an instrument panel set into the lower half of the case, level with the rim. Two large dials dominate the panel, one marked "Volt-Ohm Meter," the other marked "Ammeter." There are three knobs spaced below the dials. Factory-stamped lettering indicates their use: the two end knobs are marked "Adjuster," and the one in the middle is marked "Function." Running vertically down the left-hand side of the panel are a series of jacks respectively marked 600V, 300V, 150V, 75V, 30V, and Common. Flanking the dials on the right-hand side of the plate there are similiar jacks marked 60 Amps, 30 Amps, 15 Amps, 7.5 Amps, 3 Amps, and Common. Another jack and a small bulb are below the second adjuster knob, and they are collectively marked "Leakage Indicator." In bold factory-stamped lettering across the length of the tester are the words "Industrial Analyzer."

"Okay," the cop says, "you can close it."

The deaf man snaps the lid of the case shut, fastens the clasp again.

"I'll take them inside," Buck says.

"Right, Sarge," the cop says, and the trio goes up the walk to the house, where they are stopped by a detective at the front door.

"Sergeant Pierce, Emergency Service," Buck says. "These men are from the electric company, here to check that power failure."

"Right," the detective says.

"I'll stick with them," Buck says, "but I don't want no other responsibility."

"What do you mean?"

"Well, if the mayor trips and breaks his ankle while they're on the premises, I don't want no static from my captain."

"We'll keep the mayor far away from you," the detective says, and smiles.

"Okay, where you guys want to start?" Buck asks. "The basement?"

They go into the house. There are battery-powered lights set up, but for the most part the house is dim, the figures moving through it are uncertainly defined. The three men start in the basement, going through the motions of checking out circuits. They go through every room of the house, never once seeing the mayor in the course of their inspection. In the master bedroom, the deaf man shoves the testing equipment under the huge double bed, ostensibly searching for a leak at the electrical outlet. When he walks out of the room, he is no longer carrying anything. The "Industrial Analyzer" is on the floor under the mayor's bed.

That analyzer, with its factory-sleek assortment of dials, knobs, jacks, and electrical terminology is real—but nonetheless fake. There *is* no testing equipment behind those meters, the interior of the box has been stripped bare. Hidden below the instrument panel, set to go off at 2 A.M., there is only another of Buck's bombs.

Tomorrow night, the mayor would die.

And on Saturday morning, the uncommitted would commit. They would open their newspapers and read the headlines, and they would know the letter was for real, no opportunist could have accurately predicted the murder without having engineered it and executed it himself. They would take the letter from where they had casually put it, and they would read it once again, and they would fully comprehend its menace now, fully realize the absolute terror inherent in its words. When one was faced with the promise of unexpected death, was five thousand dollars really so much to invest? Not a man on that list of one hundred earned less than $200,000 a year. They had all been carefully researched, the original list of four hundred and twenty names being cut and revised and narrowed down to only those who seemed the most likely victims, those to whom losing five thousand dollars at a Las Vegas crap table meant nothing, those who were known to have invested in speculative stocks or incoming Broadway plays—those, in short, who would be willing to gamble five thousand dollars in hope of salvation.

They will pay us, the deaf man thought.

Oh, not all of them, certainly not all of them. But enough of them. Perhaps a few more murders are in order, perhaps some of those sleek fat cats on the list will have to be eliminated before the rest are convinced, but they *will* be convinced, and they *will* pay. After the murder tomorrow night, after that, when they know we're not fooling, they will pay.

The deaf man suddenly smiled.

There should be a very large crowd around City Hall starting perhaps right this minute, he thought.

It will be an interesting weekend.

"You hit the nail right on the head," Lieutenant Byrnes said to Steve Carella. "He's going for the mayor next."

"He'll never get away with it," Hawes said.

"He'd better *not* get away with it," Brynes said. "If he succeeds in knocking off the major, he'll be picking up cash like it's growing in the park. How many of these letters do you suppose he's mailed?"

"Well, let's try to figure it," Carella said. "First he warned the parks commissioner and demanded five thousand dollars. Next the deputy major, and a demand for fifty thousand. Now he tells us he'll kill the mayor this Friday night. So if the escalation carries through, he should be bucking for ten times fifty thousand, which is five hundred thousand. If we divide that by—"

"Forget it," Byrnes said.

"I'm only trying to figure out the mathematics."

"What's mathematics got to do with JMV getting killed?"

"I don't know," Carella said and shrugged. "But it seems to me if we can figure out the progression, we can also figure out what's *wrong* with the progression."

Byrnes stared at him.

"I'm trying to say it just isn't enough for this guy to knock off the mayor," Carella said.

"It isn't, huh? Knocking off the mayor seems like *more* than enough to me."

"Yeah, but not for somebody like the deaf man. He's too proud of his own cleverness." Carella looked at the letter again. "Who's this man Carl Wahler?" he asked.

"A dress manufacturer, lives downtown in Stewart City, 17th Precinct. He brought the letter in there this morning. Captain Bundy thought we'd want to see it. Because of our involvement with the previous murders."

"It seems to fit right in with the pattern, doesn't it?" Hawes said. "He announced the other murders, too."

"Yes, but there's something missing," Carella said.

"What?"

"The personal angle. He started this in the 87th, a little vendetta for fouling him up years ago, when he was planting bombs all over the goddamn city to divert attention from his bank job. So why's he taking it *out* of the 87th all at once? If he knocks off the mayor, nobody looks foolish but the special police assigned to his protection. *We're* off the hook, home free. And that's what I can't understand. That's what's wrong with the pattern."

"The pattern seems pretty clear to me," Byrnes said. "If he can get to JMV after advertising it, what chance will anybody have *without* warning? Look at how many times he says that in his letter. Without warning, without warning."

"It still bothers me," Carella said.

"It shouldn't," Byrnes said. "He's spelled it out in black and white. The man's a goddamn *fiend*."

The instant reaction of both Hawes and Carella was to laugh. You don't as a general rule hear cops referring to criminals as "fiends," even when they're child molesters and mass murderers. That's the sort of language reserved for judges or politicians. Nor did Byrnes usually express himself in such colorful expletives. But whereas both men felt a definite impulse to laugh out loud, one look at Byrnes' face stifled any such urge. The lieutenant was at his wit's end. He suddenly looked very old and very tired. He sighed heavily, and said, "How do we stop him, guys?" and he sounded for all the world like a freshman quarterback up against a varsity team with a three-hundred-pound line.

"We pray," Carella said.

Although James Martin Vale, the mayor himself, was a devout Episcopalian, he decided that afternoon that he'd best do a lot more than pray if his family was to stay together.

So he called a top-level meeting in his office at City Hall (a meeting to which Lieutenant Byrnes was not invited), and it was decided that every precaution would be taken starting right then to keep "the deaf man" (as the men of the 87th insisted on calling him) from carrying out his threat. JMV was a man with a charming manner and a ready wit, and he managed to convince everyone in the office that he was more concerned about the people of his city than he was about his own safety. "We've got to save my life only so that this man won't milk hard-earned dollars from the people of this great city," he said. "If he gets away with this, they'll allow themselves to be extorted. That's why I want protection."

"Your Honor," the district attorney said, "if I may suggest, I think we should extend protection beyond the Friday night deadline. I think if this man succeeds in killing you anytime in the near future, the people of this city'll think he's made good his threat."

"Yes, I think you're right," JMV said.

"Your Honor," the city comptroller said, "I'd like to suggest that you cancel all personal appearances at least through April."

"Well, I don't think I should go into complete seclusion, do you?" JMV asked, mindful of the fact that this was an election year.

"Or at least *curtail* your personal appearances," the comptroller said, remembering that indeed this was an election year, and remembering, too, that he was on the same ticket as His Honor the Mayor JMV.

"What do you think, Slim?" JMV asked the police commissioner.

The police commissioner, a man who was six feet four inches tall and weighed two hundred and twenty-five pounds, shifted his buttocks in the padded leather chair opposite His Honor's desk, and said, "I'll cover you with cops like fleas," a not particularly delicate simile, but one which made its point nonetheless.

"You can count on however many men you need from my squad," the district attorney said, mindful that two of his most trusted detectives had been blown to that big Police Academy in the sky only days before.

"I would like to suggest," the city's medical examiner said, "that you undergo a complete physical examination as soon as this meeting is concluded."

"Why?" JMV asked.

"Because the possibility exists, Your Honor, that you've already been poisoned."

"Well," JMV said, "that sounds a bit farfetched."

"Your Honor," the medical examiner said, "an accumulation of small doses of poison administered over a period of time can result in death. Since we're dealing with a man who has obviously evolved a long-term plan . . ."

"Yes, of course," JMV said, "I'll submit to examination as soon as you wish. Maybe you can clear up my cold at the same time," he said charmingly, and grinned charmingly.

"Your Honor," the president of the city council said, "I suggest we have each of the city's vehicles inspected thoroughly and at once. I am remembering, sir, the bomb placed in . . ."

"Yes, we'll have that done at once," the district attorney said hastily.

"Your Honor," the mayor's press secretary said, "I'd like to suggest that we suppress all news announcements concerning your whereabouts, your speaking engagements, and so on, until this thing blows over."

"Yes, that's a good idea," JMV said, "but of course I won't be venturing too far from home in any case, will I, Stan?" he said, and grinned charmingly at the district attorney.

"No, sir, I'd advise your becoming a homebody for the next month or so," the district attorney said.

"Of course, there may be a bomb in this office right this minute," the police commissioner said tactlessly, causing everyone to fall suddenly silent. Into the silence, came the loud ticking of the wall clock, which was a little unnerving.

"Well," JMV said charmingly, "perhaps we ought to have the premises searched, as well as my home. If we're to do this right, we'll have to take every precaution."

"Yes, sir," the district attorney said.

"And, of course, we'll have to do everything in our power meanwhile to locate this man, this deaf man."

"Yes, sir, we're doing everything in our power right now," the police commissioner said.

"Which is what?" JMV asked, charmingly.

"He's got to make a mistake," the police commissioner said.

"And if he doesn't?"

"He's *got* to."

"But in the meantime," JMV asked, "do you have any leads?"

"Police work," the commissioner said, "is a combination of many seemingly unconnected facets that suddenly jell," and frowned, suspecting that his metaphor hadn't quite come off. "There are a great many accidents involved in police work, and we consider these accidents a definite contributing factor in the apprehension of criminals. We will, for example, arrest a man on a burglary charge, oh, six or seven months from now, and discover in questioning him that he committed a homicide during the commission of another crime, oh, four or five months ago."

"Well," JMV said charmingly, "I hope we're not going to have to wait six or seven months for our man to make a mistake while committing another crime."

"I didn't mean to sound so pessimistic," the commissioner said. "I was merely trying to explain, Your Honor, that a lot of police work dovetails past and present and future. I have every confidence that we'll apprehend this man within a reasonable length of time."

"Hopefully before he kills me," JMV said, and grinned charmingly. "Well," he said, "if there's nothing further to discuss, perhaps we can set all these precautionary measures into motion. I'll be happy to see your doctor, Herb, whenever you want to send him in."

"Meanwhile, I'll get in touch with the Bomb Squad," the police commissioner said, rising.

"Yes, that's probably the first thing to do," JMV said, rising. "Gentlemen, thank you for your time and your valuable suggestions. I'm sure everything will work out fine."

"You'll have men here in the next two or three minutes," the district attorney promised.

"Thank you, Stan," the mayor said, "I certainly appreciate your concern."

The men filed out of the mayor's office, each of them assuring him once again that he would be amply protected. The mayor thanked each of them charmingly and individually, and then sat in the big padded leather chair behind his desk and stared at the ticking wall clock.

Outside, it was beginning to snow.

The snow was very light at first.

It drifted from the sky lazily and uncertainly, dusting the streets and the sidewalks with a thin fluffy powder. By eight P.M. that night, when Patrolman Richard Genero was discharged from Buena Vista Hospital, the snow was beginning to fall a bit more heavily, but it presented no major traffic problems as yet, especially if—like Genero's father—one had snow tires on his automobile. Their ride home was noisy but uneventful. Genero's mother kept urging her son to talk to the captain, and Genero's father kept telling her to shut up.

Genero himself felt healthy and strong and was anxious to get back to work, even though he'd learned he would start his tour of duty on the four-to-midnight tomorrow. He had also learned, however, that Captain Frick, in consideration for his recent wound, was not asking him to walk a beat for the next week or so. Instead, he would be riding shotgun in one of the RMP cars. Genero considered this a promotion.

Of sorts.

The snow continued to fall.

13

The city was a regular tundra, you never saw so much snow in your life unless you happened to have been born and raised in Alaska, and then probably not. There was snow on everthing. There was snow on roofs and walls and sidewalks and streets and garbage cans and automobiles and flowerpots, and even on people. Boy, what a snowfall. It was worse than the Blizzard of '88, people who didn't remember the Blizzard of '88 were saying. His Honor the Mayor JMV, as if he didn't have enough headaches, had to arrange with the Sanitation Department for the hiring of 1200 additional temporary employees to shovel and load and dump the snow into the River Dix, a job estimated to cost five hundred and eight thousand four hundred dollars and to consume the better part of a full week—if it didn't snow again.

The men began working as soon as the snow stopped. It did not stop until three-thirty P.M., fifteen minutes before Genero began riding the RMP car, an hour and a half before Willis and Carella took their posts in the rear of the tailor shop. The city had figured on working their snow people in three continuous shifts, but they hadn't figured on the numbing cold that followed the storm and lowered the rate of efficiency, a biting frigid wave that had come down from Canada or someplace. Actually, nobody cared *where* it had come from, they merely wished it would continue going, preferably out to sea, or down to Bermuda, or even all the way to Florida; do it to *Julia,* everyone was thinking.

There was no doing it to Julia that day.

The cold gripped the city and froze it solid. Emergency snow regulations had gone into effect at noon, and by four P.M. the city seemed deserted. Most large business offices were closed, with traffic stalled to a standstill and buses running only infrequently. Alternate-side-of-the-street parking had been suspended, but stranded auto-mobiles blocked intersections, humped with snow like igloos on an arctic plain. The temporary snowmen fought the cold and the drifted snow, huddled around coal fires built in empty gasoline drums, and then manned their shovels again while waiting dump trucks idled, ex-haust pipes throwing giant white plumes into the bitter dusk. The lamppost lights came on at five P.M., casting isolated amber circles on the dead white landscape. A fierce relentless wind howled across avenue and street as the leaden sky turned dark and darker and black.

Sitting cozy and warm in the back room of John the Tailor's shop, playing checkers with Hal Willis (and losing seven games in a row since it turned out that Willis had belonged to the checkers club in high school, an elite group calling itself *The Red and The Black*), Carella wondered how he would get home after La Bresca and Calucci hit the shop.

He was beginning to doubt that they would hit at all. If there was one thing he did not understand, of course, it was the criminal mind, but he was willing to venture a guess that no self-respecting crook would brave the snow and the cold outside on a night like this. It would be different if the job involved a factor that might change in a day or so, like say ten million dollars of gold bullion to be delivered at a precise moment on a specific day, making it necessary to com-bine pinpoint timing with insane daring, but no such variable was in-volved in this penny-ante stickup. The men had cased the shop and learned that John the Tailor carried his week's earnings home in a metal box every Friday night after closing. He had doubtless been performing this same chore every Friday night for the past seven thousand years, and would continue to do it without variation for the next thousand. So, if not *this* Friday night, what are you doing *next* Friday, John? Or, better yet, why not wait until May, when the trees are budding and the birds are singing, and a man can pull off a little felony without the attendant danger of frostbite?

But assuming they did hit tonight, Carella thought as he watched Willis double-jump two of his kings, assuming they *did* hit, and as-suming he and Willis behaved as expected, made the capture, and then called in for a squad car with chains, how would he get home to his wife and children after La Bresca and Calucci were booked and put away for the night? His own car had snow tires, but not chains, and he doubted if the best snow tires made would mean a damn on that glacier out there. A possibility, of course, was that Captain

Frick would allow one of the RMPs to drive him home to Riverhead, but using city property for transporting city employees was a practice heavily frowned upon, especially in these days of strife when deaf people were running around killing city officials.

"King me," Willis said.

Carella snorted and kinged him. He looked at his watch. It was seven-twenty. If La Bresca and Calucci hit as expected, there was little more than a half-hour to go.

In Pete Calucci's rented room on North Sixteenth, he and La Bresca armed themselves. John the Tailor was seventy years old, a slight stooped man with graying hair and failing eyes, but they were not taking any chances with him that night. Calucci's gun was a Colt Government Model .45, weighing thirty-nine ounces and having a firing capacity of seven, plus one in the chamber. La Bresca was carrying a Walther P-38, which he had bought from a fence on Dream Street, with eight slugs in the magazine and another in the chamber. Both guns were automatics. The Walther was classified as a medium-power pistol whereas the Colt, of course, was a heavy gun with greater power. Each was quite capable of leaving John the Tailor enormously dead if he gave them any trouble. Neither man owned a holster. Calucci put his pistol into the right-hand pocket of his heavy overcoat. La Bresca tucked his into the waistband of his trousers.

They had agreed between them that they would not use the guns unless John the Tailor began yelling. It was their plan to reach the shop by ten minutes to eight, surprise the old man, leave him bound and gagged in the back room, and then return to Calucci's place. The shop was only five minutes away, but because of the heavy snow, and because neither man owned an automobile, they set out at seven twenty-five.

They both looked very menacing, and they both felt quite powerful with their big guns. It was a shame nobody was around to see how menacing and powerful they looked and felt.

In the warm snug comfort of the radio motor patrol car, Patrolman Richard Genero studied the bleak and windswept streets outside, listening to the clink of the chains on the rear wheel tires, hearing the two-way short wave radio spewing its incessant dialogue. The man driving the RMP was a hair bag named Phillips, who had been complaining constantly from the moment they'd begun their shifts at three forty-five P.M. It was now seven-thirty, and Phillips was still complaining, telling Genero he'd done a Dan O'Leary this whole past week, not a minute's breather, man had to be crazy to become a cop, while to his right the radio continued its oblivious spiel, Car Twenty-one, Signal thirteen, This is Twenty-one, Wilco, Car Twenty-eight, signal . . .

"This reminds me of Christmas," Genero said.

"Yeah, some Christmas," Phillips said. "I *worked* on Christmas day, you know that?"

"I meant, everything white."

"Yeah, everything white," Phillips said. "Who needs it?"

Genero folded his arms across his chest and tucked his gloved hands into his armpits. Phillips kept talking. The radio buzzed and crackled. The skid chains clinked like sleigh bells.

Genero felt drowsy.

Something was bothering the deaf man.

No, it was not the heavy snow which had undoubtedly covered manhole number M3860, a hundred and twenty feet south of the southern curb of Harris, in the center of Faxon Drive, no, it was not that. He had prepared for the eventuality of inclement weather, and there were snow shovels in the trunk of the black sedan idling at the curb downstairs. The snow would merely entail some digging to get at the manhole, and he was allowing himself an extra hour for the task, no, it was not the snow, it was definitely not the snow.

"What is it?" Buck whispered. He was wearing his rented police sergeant's uniform, and he felt strange and nervous inside the blue garment.

"I don't know," Ahmad answered. "Look at the way he's pacing."

The deaf man was indeed pacing. Wearing electrician's coveralls, he walked back and forth past the desk in one corner of the room, not quite muttering, but certainly wagging his head like an old man contemplating the sorry state of the world. Buck, perhaps emboldened by the bravery citation on his chest, finally approached him and said, "What's bothering you?"

"The 87th," the deaf man replied at once.

"What?"

"The 87th, the 87th," he repeated impatiently. "What difference will it make if we kill the mayor? Don't you see?"

"No."

"They get away clean," the deaf man said. "We kill JMV, and *who* suffers, will you tell me that?"

"Who?" Buck asked.

"Not the 87th, that's for sure."

"Look," Buck said gently, "we'd better get started. We've got to dig down to that manhole, we've got to . . ."

"So JMV dies, so what?" the deaf man asked. "Is money everything in life? Where's the pleasure?"

Buck looked at him.

"Where's the *pleasure?"* the deaf man repeated. "If JMV—" He suddenly stopped, his eyes widening. "JMV," he said again, his voice a whisper. "JMV" he shouted excitedly, and went to the desk, and opened the middle drawer, and pulled out the Isola telephone directory. Quickly, he flipped to the rear section of the book.

"What's he doing?" Ahmad whispered.

"I don't know," Buck whispered back.

"Look at this!" the deaf man shouted. "There must be hundreds of them, *thousands* of them!"

"Thousands of what?" Buck asked.

The deaf man did not reply. Hunched over the directory, he kept turning pages, studying them, turning more pages. "Here we are," he mumbled, "no, that's no good . . . let's see . . . here's another one . . . no, no . . . just a second . . . ahhh, good . . . no, that's all the way downtown . . . let's see, let's see . . . here . . . no . . ." mumbling to himself as he continued to turn pages, and finally shouting "Culver Avenue, *that's* it, that'll do it!" He picked up a pencil, hastily scribbled onto the desk pad, tore the page loose, and stuffed it into the pocket of his coveralls. "Let's go!" he said.

"You ready?" Buck asked.

"I'm ready," the deaf man said, and picked up the volt-ohm meter. "We promised to get JMV, didn't we?" he asked.

"We sure did."

"Okay," he said, grinning. "We're going to get *two* JMV's—and one of them's in the 87th Precinct!"

Exuberantly, he led them out of the apartment.

The two young men had been prowling the streets since dinnertime. They had eaten in a delicatessen off Ainsley and then had stopped to buy a half-gallon of gasoline in the service station on the corner of Ainsley and Fifth. The taller of the two young men, the one carrying the open can of gasoline, was cold. He kept telling the shorter one how cold he was. The shorter one said *everybody* was cold on a night like this, what the hell did he expect on a night like this?

The taller one said he wanted to go home. He said they wouldn't find nobody out on a night like this, anyway, so what was the use walking around like this in the cold? His feet were freezing, he said. His hands were cold too. Why don't *you* carry this fuckin' gas a while? he said.

The shorter one told him to shut up.

The shorter one said this was a perfect night for what they had to do because they could probably find maybe two guys curled up together in the same hallway, didn't that make sense?

The taller one said he wished *he* was curled up in a hallway someplace.

They stood on the street corner arguing for a few minutes, each of them yelling in turn, and finally the taller one agreed to give it another ten minutes, but that was all. The shorter one said Let's try it for another half-hour, we bound to hit pay dirt, and the taller one said No, ten minutes and that's it, and the shorter one said You fuckin' idiot, I'm telling you this is a good night for it, and the taller one saw what was in his eyes, and became afraid again and said Okay, okay, but only a half-hour, I mean it, Jimmy, I'm really cold, really.

You look like you're about to start crying, Jimmy said.

I'm cold, the other one said, that's all.

Well, come on, Jimmy said, we'll find somebody and make a nice fire, huh? A nice warm fire.

The two young men grinned at each other.

Then they turned the corner and walked up the street toward Culver Avenue as Car Seventeen, bearing Phillips and Genero clinked by on its chained tires sounding like sleigh bells.

It was difficult to tell who was more surprised, the cops or the robbers.

The police commissioner had told His Honor the Mayor JMV that "a lot of police work dovetails past and present and future," but it was fairly safe to assume he had nothing too terribly philosophical in mind. That is, he probably wasn't speculating on the difference between illusion and reality, or the overlap of the dream state and the workaday world. That is, he probably wasn't explaining time continua or warps, or parallel universes, or coexisting systems. He was merely trying to say that there are a lot of accidents involved in police work, and that too many cases would never get solved if it weren't for those very accidents. He was trying to tell His Honor the Mayor JMV that sometimes cops get lucky.

Carella and Willis got very lucky on that night of March fifteenth at exactly ten minutes to eight.

They were watching the front of the shop because Dominick Di Fillippi (who had never ratted on anybody in his life) had told them the plan was to go into the shop at ten minutes to eight, just before John the Tailor drew the blinds on the plate glass window fronting the street. La Bresca was to perform that task instead, Di Fillippi had further said, and then he was to lock the front door while Calucci forced John the Tailor at gun point into the back room. In Di Fillippi's ardent recital, there had been a lot of emphasis real or imagined, on the *front* of the shop. So everyone had merely assumed (as who wouldn't?) that La Bresca and Calucci would come in through the front door, open the door, ting-a-ling would go the bell, shove their guns into John the Tailor's face, and then go about their dirty business. It is doubtful that the police even *knew* there was a back door to the shop.

La Bresca and Calucci knew there was a back door.

They kicked that door in at precisely seven-fifty, right on schedule, kicked it in noisily and effectively, not caring whether or not they scared John the Tailor out of ten years' growth, knowing he would rush to the back of the shop to see what the hell was happening, knowing he would run directly into two very large pistols.

The first thing they saw was two guys playing checkers.

The first thing La Bresca said was, "Fuzz!"

He knew the short guy was fuzz because he had been questioned by him often enough. He didn't know who the other guy was, but he reasoned that if you saw *one* mouse you probably had fifty, and if you saw one *cop* you probably had a thousand, so that place was probably crawling with cops, they had stepped into a very sweet little trap here—and that was when the curtain shot back and the front door of the shop burst open.

It was also when all the overlapping confusion started, the past, present, and future jazz getting all mixed up so that it seemed for a tense ten seconds as if seven movies were being projected simultaneously on the same tiny screen. Even later, much later, Carella couldn't quite put all the pieces together; everything happened too fast and too luckily, and he and Willis had very little to do with any of it.

The first obvious fact that crackled up Carella's spine and into his head was that he and Willis had been caught cold. Even as he rose from his chair, knocking it over backwards, even as he shouted, "Hal, behind you!" and reached for his revolver, he knew they'd been caught cold, they were staring into the open muzzles of two high caliber guns and they would be shot dead on the spot. He heard one of the men shout, "Fuzz!" and then he saw both guns come up level at the same time, and too many last thoughts crowded into his head in the tick of a second. Willis whirled, knocking checkerboard and checkers to the floor, drawing his gun, and suddenly John the Tailor threw back the curtain separating the rear of the shop from the front, and the front door of the shop burst open in the same instant.

John the Tailor later said he had run back to see what the noise was, throwing the curtain between the two rooms, and then whirling to see what Carella only later saw, three men standing in the front doorway of his shop, all of them holding pistols.

This was what La Bresca and Calucci must have seen as well, looking through the now open curtain directly to the front door. And whereas they must have instantly known they had caught the back-room cops cold, they now recognized the threat of the three other cops standing in the front door, all of them with pistols in their fists and kill looks on their faces. The three men weren't cops, but La Bresca and Calucci didn't know that. The sergeant standing in the doorway shouted, "Fuzz!" meaning he thought La Bresca and Calucci were fuzz, but La Bresca and Calucci merely thought he was announcing his own arrival. So they began shooting. The three men in the door, facing what they too thought was a police trap, opened fire at the same time. John the Tailor threw himself to the floor. Carella and Willis, recognizing a good healthy crossfire when they saw one, tried to flatten themselves against the wall. In the flattening process, Willis slipped on one of the fallen checkers and went tumbling to the floor, bullets spraying over his head.

Carella's gun was in his hand now. He leveled it at the front door because he had taken a good look at one of the men standing there firing into the back room, and whereas the man was not wearing his hearing aid, he was tall and blond and Carella recognized him at once. He aimed carefully and deliberately. The gun bucked in his hand when he pulled off the shot. He saw the deaf man clutch for his shoulder and then half-stumble half-turn toward the open doorway. Someone screamed behind Carella, and he turned to see La Bresca falling over the pressing machine, spilling blood onto the white padding, and then four more shots exploded in the tiny shop and someone grunted, and there were more shots, Willis was up and firing, and then there was only smoke, heavy smoke that hung on the air in layers, the terrible nostril-burning stink of cordite, and the sound of John the Tailor on the floor, praying softly in Italian.

"Outside!" Carella shouted, and leaped the counter dividing the shop, slipping in a pool of blood near the sewing machine, but regaining his footing and running coatless into the snow.

There was no one in sight.

The cold was numbing.

It hit his naked gun hand immediately, seemed to wed flesh to steel.

A trail of blood ran from the shop door across the white snow stretching endlessly into the city.

Carella began following it.

The deaf man ran as fast as he could, but the pain in his shoulder was intolerable.

He could not understand what had happened.

Was it possible they had figured it out? But no, they couldn't have. And yet, they'd been there, waiting. How *could* they have known? How could they *possibly* have known when he *himself* hadn't known until fifteen minutes ago?

There had been at least twenty-five pages of "V" listings in the Isola directory, with about 500 names to a page, for a combined total of some 12,500 names. He had not counted the number of first names beginning with the letter "J," but there seemed to be at least twenty or thirty on every page, and he had actually gone through *eleven* names with the initials "JMV," the same initials as His Honor the Mayor James Martin Vale, before coming to the one on Culver Avenue.

How could they have known? How could they have pin-pointed the tailor shop of John Mario Vicenzo, the final twist of the knife, a JMV located within the very confines of the 87th? It's impossible, he thought. I left nothing to chance, it should have worked, I should have got them both, there were no wild cards in the deck, it should have worked.

There were *still* some wild cards in the deck.

"Look," Jimmy said.

The taller boy, the one carrying the gasoline can, lifted his head, squinted against the wind, and then ducked it immediately as a fiercer gust attacked his face. He had seen a tall blond man staggering off the pavement and into the center of the snowbound street.

"Drunk as a pig," Jimmy said beside him. "Let's get him, Baby."

The one called Baby nodded bleakly. Swiftly, they ran toward the corner. The wind was stronger there, it struck them with gale force as they turned onto the wide avenue. The vag was nowhere in sight.

"We lost him," Baby said. His teeth were chattering, and he wanted to go home.

"He's got to be in one of these hallways," Jimmy said. "Come on, Baby, it's fire time."

From where Genero sat in the RMP car, he could see the empty windswept avenue through a frost-free spot on the windshield, snow devils ascending with each fresh gust of wind, hanging signs clanging and flapping, an eerie graveyard sound rasping at the windows of the automobile. The avenue was deserted, the snow locked the street from sidewalk to sidewalk, lights burned behind apartment windows like warming fires in a primeval night.

"What's that?" he said suddenly.

"What's what?" Phillips asked.

"Up ahead. Those two guys."

"Huh?" Phillips said.

"They're trying doors," Genero said. "Pull over."

"Huh?"

"Pull over and cut your engine!"

He could hear them talking on the sidewalk outside, he could hear their voices coming closer and closer. He lay in the hallway with his shoulder oozing blood, knowing he had to climb those steps and get to the roof, get from this building to the next one, jump rooftops all night long if he had to, but first rest, just rest, just rest a little, rest before they opened the door and found him, how had they got to him so fast? Were there policemen all over this damn city?

There were too many things he did not understand.

He listened as the voices came closer, and then he saw the door-knob turning.

"Hold it right there!" Genero shouted.

The boys turned immediately.

"Fuzz!" Baby shouted, and dropped the gasoline can, and began running. Genero fired a warning shot over his head, and then be-latedly yelled, "Police! Stop or I'll shoot!" and then fired another warning shot. Up the street, where he had parked the RMP at the curb, Phillips was opening the door on the driver's side and un-holstering his revolver. Genero fired again, surprised when he saw the running boy drop to the snow. I *got* him! he thought, and then whirled to see the second boy running in the opposite direction, Holy Jesus, he thought, I'm busting up a *robbery* or something! "Halt!" he shouted. "Stop!" and fired into the air, and saw the boy rounding the corner, and immediately ran after him.

He chased Jimmy for three blocks in the snow, pushing through knee-deep drifts, slipping on icy patches, the wind a constant adversary, and finally caught up with him as he was scaling a back-alley fence.

"Hold it right there, Sonny," Genero said, "or I'll put one right up your ass."

Jimmy hesitated astride the fence, debating whether to swing his legs up and over it, or to get down before this trigger-happy bastard really carried out his threat.

Sighing, he dropped to the ground at Genero's feet.

"What seems to be the trouble, Officer?" he asked.

"*Trouble* is right," Genero said. "Get your hands up."

Phillips came puffing into the alley just then. He walked up to Genero like the hair bag he was, shoved him aside, and then pushed Jimmy against the fence while he frisked him. Genero was smart enough to make certain *his* handcuffs were the ones they put on the kid, though there was a moment there when it seemed like a touch-and-go race with Phillips.

By the time they got the kid back to the squad car, by the time they went up the street to ascertain that the other kid was still alive, though barely, by the time they located the hallway door the kids were about to open, by the time they opened that door themselves and flashed their lights into the foyer, all they saw was a puddle of blood on the floor.

The blood continued up the steps.

They followed the spatters to the top floor, directly to the open door of the roof. Genero stepped outside and threw the beam of his flash across the snow.

Bloodstains and footprints led in an erratic trail to the edge of the roof, and from there to the roof beyond, and from there to the rest of the city, or perhaps the rest of the world.

Two blocks away, they found Steve Carella wandering coatless in the snow like Dr. Zhivago or somebody.

14

THE CLEANUP in the tailor shop was a gruesome job.

La Bresca and Calucci were both dead. The big red-headed man named Buck was also dead. Ahmad was alive and breathing when they carted him off in the meat wagon, but he had taken two slugs in the chest from Calucci's .45, and another in the stomach from La Bresca's Walther. He was gushing blood, and spitting blood, and shivering and mumbling, and they doubted very much if he'd make it to the hospital alive.

Carella was shivering a little himself.

He stood near the radiator in the tailor shop, wrapped in his overcoat, his teeth chattering, and asked John the Tailor how much money there was in the metal box he was taking home.

"Due cento tre dollari," John the Tailor said.

Two hundred and three dollars.

Ahmad knew the deaf man's name.

"Orecchio," he said, and the nurse wiped blood from his lips. "Mort Orecchio."

"That's not his real name," Willis told him. "Do you know him by any other name?"

"Orecchio," Ahmad repeated. "Mort Orecchio."

"Is there anyone who *might* know his real name?"

"Orecchio," Ahmad repeated.

"Was there anyone else in this with you?"

"The girl," Ahmad said.

"What girl?"

"Rochelle," he said.

"Rochelle what?"

Ahmad shook his head.

"Where can we find her?"

"Three . . . three . . . eight . . . Ha . . . Ha . . . Ha . . ." he said, and died.

He had not died laughing.

He was trying to say 338 Harborside.

They found in Buck's pants pocket a letter addressed to him at 338 Harborside Oval. His full name was Andrew Buckley, and the letter was addressed to him c/o Mr. Mort Orecchio. Carella and Willis hit the apartment and found a pretty brunette girl in lounging pajamas, sitting at the piano playing "Heart and Soul." They waited while she got dressed and then took her to the squadroom, where they questioned her for a half-hour in the presence of a lawyer. The girl told them her name was Rochelle Newell and that she had known the deaf man for only a short time, two or three months. She insisted his name was Mort Orecchio.

"That's not his name," Carella said.

"Yes, that's his name."

"What'd *you* call him?"

"Mort," the girl said.

"What'd you call him in *bed?*" Willis asked suddenly, hoping to surprise her.

"Sweetie," the girl answered.

Jimmy could not stop giggling.

They had just told him that his friend Baby was dead, and yet he could not stop giggling.

"You know the kind of trouble you're in, son?" Meyer asked.

"No, what kind?" Jimmy said, and giggled.

"We're going to book you for homicide."

"It won't stick," Jimmy said, and giggled.

"It'll stick, son," Meyer said. "We got a dying confession from your pal, and it was taken in the presence of a lawyer, and we've got a cop outside who you tried to kill and who'll make a positive identification of both of you. It'll stick, believe me."

"Naw, it won't stick," Jimmy said, and kept giggling.

Meyer figured he was crazy.

Meyer figured Rollie Chabrier was crazy too.

He called at close to midnight.

"This is kind of late, isn't it?" Meyer said. "I was just about to head home."

"Well, I'm still working here at the goddamn office," Chabrier said. "You guys have it easy."

"Well, what is it?" Meyer said.

"About this book," Chabrier said.

"Yeah?"

"You want my advice?"

"Sure, I want your advice. Why do you think I contacted you?"

"My advice is forget it."

"That's some advice."

"Has Steve Carella ever had a book named after him?"

"No, but . . ."

"Has Bert Kling?"

"No."

"Or Cotton Hawes? Or Hal Willis? Or Arthur Brown? Or . . ."

"Look, Rollie . . ."

"You should be flattered," Chabrier said. "Even *I* have never had a book named after me."

"Yeah, but . . ."

"You know how many people go their entire lives and never have books named after them?"

"How many?"

"Millions! You should be flattered."

"I should?"

"Sure. Somebody named a book after you! You're famous!"

"I am?"

"Absolutely. From now to the very end of time, people will be able to go into libraries all over the world and see your name on a book, Meyer, think of it. On a *book*. Meyer Meyer," he said grandly, and Meyer could almost visualize him spreading his hands as though conjuring marquee lights. "God, Meyer, you should be thrilled to death."

"Yeah?" Meyer said.

"I envy you, Meyer. I truly and honestly envy you."

"Gee," Meyer said. "Thanks. Thanks a lot, Rollie. Really. Thanks a lot."

"Don't mention it," Chabrier said, and hung up.

Meyer went into the men's room to look at himself in the mirror.

Andy Parker brought the morning papers into the squadroom at 2:00 A.M.

"You want to read how smart we are?" he said, and dropped the papers on Kling's desk.

Kling glanced at the headlines.

"Sure," Parker said, "we busted the whole thing wide open. Nobody can lick *this* team, pal."

Kling nodded, preoccupied.

"Everybody can rest easy now," Parker said. "The papers tell all about the scheme, and how the ring is busted, and how none of those hundred marks have to worry anymore. And all because of the brilliant bulls of the 87th." He paused and then said, "I bet Genero gets a promotion out of this. His name's all over the paper."

Kling nodded and said nothing.

He was pondering the latest development in the Great Squadroom Mystery. The stolen electric fan, it seemed, had turned up in a hockshop downtown. There had been an apple green fingerprint on its base.

"Now who do you suppose . . ." he started, but Parker had already stretched out in the swivel chair behind his desk, with one of the newspapers over his face.

QUALITY PRINTING AND BINDING BY:
ORANGE GRAPHICS
P.O. BOX 791
ORANGE, VA 22960 U.S.A.